# The Final Testimony of
# Raphael Ignatius Phoenix

www.transworldbooks.co.uk

# The Final Testimony of Raphael Ignatius Phoenix

Paul Sussman

Doubleday

LONDON · TORONTO · SYDNEY · AUCKLAND · JOHANNESBURG

TRANSWORLD PUBLISHERS
61–63 Uxbridge Road, London W5 5SA
A Random House Group Company
www.transworldbooks.co.uk

First published in Great Britain
in 2014 by Doubleday
an imprint of Transworld Publishers

A CIP catalogue record for this book
is available from the British Library.

ISBN 9780857522184

Addresses for Random House Group Ltd companies outside the UK
can be found at: www.randomhouse.co.uk
The Random House Group Ltd Reg. No. 954009

The Random House Group Limited supports the Forest Stewardship Council®
(FSC®), the leading international forest-certification organisation.
Our books carrying the FSC label are printed on FSC®-certified paper. FSC is
the only forest-certification scheme supported by the leading environmental
organisations, including Greenpeace. Our paper procurement policy can
be found at www.randomhouse.co.uk/environment

Typeset in 11½/15pt Minion by
Falcon Oast Graphic Art Ltd, Exeter, Devon.
Printed and bound in Great Britain by
Clays Ltd, Bungay, Suffolk.

2 4 6 8 10 9 7 5 3 1

*For Ezra, Jude and Layla*

# FOREWORD

When Paul's agent suggested that we revisit an early manuscript that he had written prior to his published novels, my initial reaction was one of guilt: I was Paul's wife – and I should know more about this book.

Paul was writing *The Final Testimony of Raphael Ignatius Phoenix* when we first met. It was the mid-Nineties, he had just turned 30, and after a faltering career as an actor was starting to make a name for himself as a journalist and columnist. His writing was being published in magazines, broadsheets and on the radio, and lauded both for its intelligence and witty irreverence.

Like so many other up-and-coming writers, Paul also harboured ambitions of becoming a published novelist. Evenings and weekends would be spent writing, locked away in the tiny cupboard that he had converted into an office in his flat in Balham. He didn't talk much about the details of the book, and for the most part I didn't ask. I was too busy falling in love. And, besides, I had so much faith in this funny, clever man that I simply assumed I would read the finished book on publication.

But the much yearned for publication never happened – despite Paul's ambition, talent and enthusiasm for life, he was plagued by self-doubt. Privately, he worried that his writing wasn't good enough, and an early knock-back from a potential agent prompted the following entry in his journal: 'Everything I had dreamed of and hoped for has failed. I am a failure. It feels so horrible to say that. But it's true.'

Despite finding a new agent who did believe in the book, Paul continued to doubt his ability. I was offered the completed manuscript to read only once – hundreds of loose-leaf A4 sheets stacked in an enormous pile – but a week later Paul decided that I was reading it too slowly and took it away again before I could finish it.

The prospect of sending the book to publishing houses was almost too much for him to bear: 'It's on my mind all the time – that desperate, futile hope that someone will buy it. Not even buy it, just like it. It was better when I'd stuck it in the cupboard and forgotten about it – when I'd given up on it.'

In the end, that's what he did. He took the manuscript back from his agent and hid it away. But he didn't stop writing – he had another idea – an archaeological thriller set in the Egyptian desert, with a Muslim detective – Inspector Khalifa of the Luxor Police – as its central character. Gathering dust in a cupboard, *The Final Testimony of Raphael Ignatius Phoenix* became the book that he talked about coming back to once he had finished with Khalifa. Of course, he never finished with Khalifa – instead he enjoyed phenomenal success with a whole series of thrillers – selling across the globe in over 30 languages, and upwards of 3 million copies.

It wasn't until 15 years later that I finally read the unpublished manuscript in its entirety. But this time, there was no Paul to offer my thoughts to. Six months previously, he had suffered a totally unexpected and fatal brain haemorrhage. My world had fallen apart and, still reeling from the shock of losing him, my emotions were jumbled and raw. First, the guilt at not having read the manuscript before, and then the bitter-sweet agony of becoming immersed in his world again – but not being able to reach out and talk to him about it.

But in *The Final Testimony of Raphael Ignatius Phoenix* I found a very different world from the highly charged, fast pace of his thrillers. As the story of the book's maverick narrator unfolded, so too did an altogether more humorous, magical, sometimes dark and slightly surreal world. And, in it, Paul's voice was unmistakable: loud and clear, singing out to me – his offbeat humour, his eye for the most eccentric of details and his wonderfully vivid descriptions. Perhaps more than any of his other books, this is just so recognizably him.

When Paul's publishers, Transworld, agreed to publish, I was over the moon – just like Paul, this book was unique and funny yet also beautifully moving. Here was a chance for others to glimpse this side of him and enjoy a very different Paul Sussman novel.

The challenge of editing the manuscript – along with Simon Taylor, Paul's editor at Transworld, and his agent, Laura Susijn – was to stay true to Paul's voice. The process gave my grieving brain some respite. I was able to lose myself in his words – understand how he wove together his complex plots into a story that flowed effortlessly, and appreciate the depth of his characters. All the qualities so admired in his subsequent novels are very much in evidence here.

Ultimately, we changed very little. A loose end needed tying up, and there was some cutting back where Paul's fevered imagination had got carried away. As much as possible, I gleaned information from the journals that Paul kept throughout his adult life. They are a fascinating insight into his creative process and, of course – this being Paul – the self-doubt is there from the outset: 'I am terrified I shall become a man of first chapters – a writer who never gets beyond the opening ideas and paragraphs of a work.' But like the book he was writing – and so typical of him – there are life-affirming, even laugh-out-loud moments too: 'Today, at about 10 a.m., I finally finished my first draft . . . I'm pretty happy with the last chapter – it ends on the sort of upbeat I had always envisaged for the book. I didn't feel euphoric about my achievement . . . but I was contented and quite excited, and went into the bedroom to have a bit of a dance in front of the mirror.'

I will always be heartbroken that my funny, clever, kind man has gone, but I hope that, by publishing this book, another small part of him can be celebrated and enjoyed by others. In life, Paul had a wonderful way of lifting a room and leaving everybody around him feeling better about themselves. I hope that this book does the same.

Alicky Sussman, London, October 2013

# CHAPTER ONE

THIS IS GOING to be the longest suicide note in history. A titanic epitaph. A monstrous obituary. A real rolling spouting blue-whale bloody whopper of a confession. And since it's going to end with The Pill, I might as well start that way too.

Small and white and round, like a powdery tear, with no obvious defining features save a slight nick in its otherwise perfect circumference, The Pill was made by Emily's father, a pharmacist in turn-of-the-century London. It is not, admittedly, on the face of it, an object to particularly capture the imagination. Certainly not one to start as extraordinary a story as I shall forthwith be recounting. As with so many things in my long and convoluted life, however, there is more to The Pill than meets the eye. It is, you see, despite its bland and unassuming exterior, absolutely deadly, its constituent parts – one and a half grains of strychnine, one and half grains of arsenic, half a grain of salt of hydrocyanic acid and half of a grain of crushed ipecacuanha root – guaranteeing a swift, painless and permanent demise to any who might happen to swallow them. Which is exactly what I shall be doing in ten days' time, washed down with a glass of fine, blood-red claret (a Latour '66 perhaps? Or maybe a '70).

I have, to this day, no certain knowledge as to precisely when

11

The Pill was made, nor for what specific purpose. What I can tell you is that it was there the first time I ever visited Emily's home, resplendent on a small glass dish in the poisons cabinet in her father's pharmacy. And it was still there four years later, on 1st January 1910, the afternoon of my tenth birthday, when, aided, abetted and encouraged by Emily, I stole it. (Oh there are far worse crimes to follow!)

The day we purloined The Pill was, if memory serves me right, a Sunday. A fine, windy Sunday, with a smell of woodsmoke and roast-chestnuts in the air, and the clatter of hansom cabs on the London cobbles. It being my birthday I had been invited to Emily's home for the afternoon, where we had eaten a large celebratory tea of cream cakes and crumpets and then – on my instigation – set off around the house for an energetic game of hide-and-seek. Emily had had a nasty fever over Christmas, and was still feeling a little weak, so soon tired of traipsing up and down the stairs as I snuck between hiding places.

'Let's go downstairs to Father's shop,' she said, leaning on the bannister as she caught her breath. 'We're bound to find something interesting there.'

Her father's pharmacy occupied the ground floor of their house, and was closed for the day, it being New Year. Normally the shop was strictly off limits, but since its proprietor was out for the afternoon, and Emily's governess, Miss Wasply, had retired to her room to write letters to her eight sisters, there was no one to stop us having a nose around.

'If anyone finds us we'll say we heard a noise and came to investigate,' advised Emily. 'Just let me do the talking.'

We had, of course, been in the shop before, but always in the company of an adult. Alone, it took on an altogether more thrilling aspect; an Aladdin's cave of brightly coloured jars and bottles stacked on shelves from floor to ceiling, each with the name of its contents emblazoned on the front in tall gold lettering (Bermuda Arrowroot; Violet Powder; Chlorate of Potash; Extract of Henblane, etc.). Glass cabinets displayed the brand-name medicines of the day – Eno's Fruit Salts, Page Woodcock's Wind Pills, Jacob Townsend's American Sarsaparilla – whilst tall, swan-necked carboys glowed luminously and alluringly at either end of the long mahogany counter. A pair of mirrors on opposite walls reflected the shop between them into infinity.

'Don't break anything,' said Emily sternly. 'And don't put anything in your mouth, especially from the bottles with the ridged glass. They're dangerous.'

We pulled down a couple of jars from the more accessible shelves and sniffed their contents, and opened a tin of scented Russian bear's grease pomade, some of which I smeared on my hair. Then we crept into the workroom at the back of the shop and had a poke around amongst the mortars and scales and tincture presses and root cutters. Emily spent some time fiddling with a teat pipette. I found a large Büchner Funnel, through which I blew as though it were a bugle.

'Ssssh!' hissed my companion. 'Miss Wasply will hear us and we'll be in all sorts of trouble. Put it down and come back in the shop.'

We had a rummage through the labelled rosewood drawers lining the wall behind the counter, and spent some time playing with the till, standing on tiptoe and depressing its keys as though they were the notes of some large musical instrument. Then we sniffed a bottle of sal volatile, which made our eyes water, and sent us both into a fit of coughing.

'What did you get for your birthday?' inquired Emily when we had recovered from our sputterings.

'Some chocolate from Mrs Eggs,' I replied, 'and a special bible from Father.'

'What's special about it?'

'Well, you can pull out the New Testament and wear it as a sun hat. He invented it himself. Thinks it's going to make a lot of money. But then that's what he always thinks about his inventions.'

(More about my father later.)

We opened a cupboard behind the counter and pulled out a curious-looking, pump-like contraption, labelled 'Dr Eugisier's No. 2 Mechanical Reservoir Enema'.

'What do you think this is for?' I asked.

'Putting out fires, I think,' said Emily. 'Better put it back or you might break it.'

I did as she ordered, and wandered to the far end of the counter to examine a set of graduated glass dispensing measures.

'If you could have anything in the world for your birthday,' asked my companion suddenly, 'what would it be?'

There were, of course, many things in the world I would have liked at that particular moment, such as a pistol, or a sailing yacht, or a machine that would do all my schoolwork for me. A Rudge-Whitworth bicycle, of the type currently advertised in all the papers, would have been nice, as would a wireless, or a set of Siege of Mafeking toy soldiers. One thing, however, stood out head and shoulders above the rest – had, indeed, stood out head and shoulders since the day I'd first seen it four years previously – and I named it now.

'The Pill,' I replied, crossing to the poisons cabinet and pressing my nose against its thick glass front. 'That's what I'd have. That's definitely what I'd have. I wish I *could* have it.'

Emily looked at me in surprise and then, turning to the rosewood drawers behind her, opened one labelled 'Rhubarb Powder' and inserted her hand therein, removing it a moment later with a small brass key clutched between her fingers. This she wriggled into the lock of the poisons cabinet, turning it two full revolutions before easing open the door and removing the small glass dish on which The Pill sat. 'Do you want to touch it?' she asked, smiling, holding the dish towards me.

'Can I?'

'If you want. Be careful, though. Very careful.'

I held out my hand, and she tipped The Pill into my palm, where it sat like a dull white stigmata. I closed my hand about it, making a

14

cage of my fingers as though to hold in a dragonfly, or a moth.

'I never thought I'd get to touch it,' I said, awed. 'I thought I'd only ever be able to look.'

'Don't put it near your mouth,' urged Emily. 'It's very poisonous.'

'I do so wish I could have it,' I sighed. 'I don't think I've ever wanted anything so much in my life. It's so . . .'

'Pretty?'

'Not really that, more . . .'

'Magical?'

'Yes, that's it. Magical. It's like a magic thing. The start of great adventures. I do so wish I could have it.'

Emily stared at me, her head tilted to one side, a quizzical smile pulling at the edges of her mouth.

'Is that really what you'd choose? Of all the things you could have in the whole world you'd really have that pill?'

'Yes,' I replied. 'Definitely. I've always liked it, ever since the day I first came here. It makes me feel powerful just to hold it. Like I can do anything I want. Silly, I know.'

Emily raised her eyebrows – she had very fair eyebrows, and very thin ones, like snippets of golden string – and tugged at a golden forelock, apparently deep in thought. For a moment she was silent. Then, suddenly, she leant her head close to mine and whispered, in tones of utmost confidentiality:

'I have a plan.'

Even now, so many long and wicked years later, an old bent man tightrope-walking around the very cusp of life, I can still feel the excitement that rippled down my spine when Emily uttered those words.

'A plan?'

'Yes, a plan. To get you The Pill without Father knowing. Are you game?'

'Yes, yes!' I whispered. 'I'm game for anything! What are we going to do?'

'Follow me,' said Emily. 'And do exactly as I say.'

She held out her hand for The Pill, which, once I had passed it over, she replaced on its dish, sliding the latter back on to its shelf in the cabinet. She then led me upstairs to her bedroom, where, falling to her knees, she thrust her hands beneath her bed and pulled out a large tin of Farley's Mints.

'Are mints in the plan?' I asked, intrigued.

'Mints *are* the plan,' she replied. 'Look.'

She shook the tin twice, its contents rattling within, and then removed the lid. Inside were some two dozen sweets, small and white and round. I guessed her intentions immediately.

'They're just like The Pill!' I cried.

'Precisely,' she said. 'We're going to switch them. There's work to be done yet though.'

We took one of the mints and scampered downstairs again, hearts thudding at the audacity of our scheme. First we went into the kitchen, where we used a filleting knife to cut a small nick on the edge of the mint, like that on the side of The Pill itself. (What, I have often wondered, was the cause of this small chink in the casing of my death?) We then returned to the pharmacy, where, hands trembling with excitement, we swapped the real pill with the fake one, returning the latter to its shelf in the poisons cabinet and closing and locking the door behind it. Even up close it was impossible to tell the difference between the two.

'It works!' I hissed, barely able to contain my euphoria. 'They look exactly the same! We've done it! It's like Sherlock Holmes!'

Emily smiled, balancing the real pill in her hand. I reached out for it, but she stepped backwards and fixed me with a look of utmost seriousness (Emily had the most serious look of anyone I have ever known. It really did stop you in your tracks).

'Not yet,' she said. 'First you must tell me what you're going to do with it.'

'Do with it?'

'Yes. I have to make sure it's safe to give it to you. It's dangerous, you know.'

'I'm not really going to do anything with it,' I said. 'I just want to have it. To keep it. I like it.'

I was silent for a moment, before adding:

'I'm not going to use it to kill anyone, if that's what you think.'

'Do you promise?' she said.

'Of course I do. I'll never use it on anyone. It's quite safe with me.'

'Vow it,' she insisted.

'I do vow it, Emily. I vow it on my life. I vow it more than I've ever vowed anything before. Oh, let me have it now?'

She held me in her eyes for a moment – her big, burning, green eyes – and then passed The Pill across.

'And make sure you don't tell anyone what we've done,' she said. 'Or we could be in real trouble.'

I barely had time to clutch my prize before a clatter of feet on the stairs alerted us to the descent of the dreaded Miss Wasply. I glanced swiftly, triumphantly, at The Pill – my pill now – and then stuffed it into the pocket of my breeches, whereupon Emily's governess swept furiously into the shop.

'What on earth do you two children think you are doing in here?' she shrilled. 'You know full well that entry into your father's shop is forbidden!'

Emily opened her mouth to protest, but before she had the chance to proffer her excuses Miss Wasply had manoeuvred her considerable bulk across the shop floor and positioned herself behind the two of us; a hand placed firmly on each of our backs.

'You two should be outside, getting some fresh air,' she said, herding us purposefully towards the back door, 'not meddling and causing mischief where you are not wanted.'

'But my fever, Miss Wasply,' pleaded Emily, dragging her feet. 'I don't feel well. Can't we just go back to the nursery?'

Miss Wasply snorted and thrust coats and hats into our hands. 'It'll do you good!' she said and swung the back door open; an icy blast swept through the cloakroom. 'Hurry up now, you can have half an hour in the garden before it gets dark.'

With one final push, she propelled us outside into the frosty winter air and closed the door firmly behind her.

Emily sniffed despondently, shivering as she pulled her woollen hat down to cover her ears. To my shame, my thoughts were not primarily for the welfare of my dearest friend, and while I did momentarily offer an arm around her shoulders to fend off the bitter chill, my mind was elsewhere. Buoyed with the excitement of my recent acquisition, I raced to the end of the garden and started turning cartwheels.

'Keep moving, Emily! It's the only way to warm up!'

'Thank you,' she sighed, now perched on the garden bench and resigned to her fate. 'But I think I'll just watch.'

And so the afternoon continued. We did eventually return to the warmth of the house, and until last night, the affair was never again mentioned between us.

Which is, in a nutshell, how I got The Pill. My pill. The pill of death. And if I vowed never to use it on *anyone*, you will note *I* made no promises whatsoever with regard to using on my own self. Whatever other crimes I might have committed, I'd never dream of breaking my word.

I've now possessed The Pill for ninety years (or perhaps I should say, The Pill has now possessed me for ninety years). Sometimes I've kept it in my wallet, sometimes in a glittering gold locket around my neck, sometimes Sellotaped beneath my armpit, sometimes in a ring on my finger, but it's always been within reach. Always present. Death has never been further than a few inches from my outstretched hand. Aside from The Photo, it is by far and away my most treasured possession.

It's with me now, as I write this note. In the pocket of my cotton pyjamas. I dip in and tickle it, gently, reverentially, as a worshipper might an icon, a lepidopterist a rare butterfly wing. One and a half grains of strychnine, one and a half grains of arsenic, half a grain of salt of hydrocyanic acid and half a grain of crushed ipecacuanha root, and soon it'll be time to take it. 'Not long now, my old friend,' I whisper. 'Not long now. At last your moment is nigh.'

My name is Raphael Ignatius Phoenix and I am a hundred years old – or will be in ten days' time, in the early hours of 1st January 2000, when I kill myself. Observant readers will notice that my initials spell R. I. P. A most fitting coincidence, as you will shortly discover.

# CHAPTER TWO

I COMMITTED MY LAST and most recent murder 14 years ago. In 1985. It was at Nannybrook House, and her name was Bunshop. Mrs Ethel Bunshop, née Boocock. I can smell it even now: the acrid, nose-searing perfume of burning flesh. And hear it too. The whoosh and the scream and the crackle. Hideous old trout.

Her removal falls into that group of murders to which I can ascribe a very definite motive. In some instances I have killed on but the most flimsy of pretexts; in others done so without really meaning to kill at all.

With Ethel Bunshop née Boocock, however, I had a veritable sackful of valid inducements. Her nocturnal farts, for one thing. And those awful droopy knockers, and the way she said 'Sherry, Mr Phoenix?' as though offering me a sexual favour rather than a glass of tepid amontillado. She was in every respect a vile old bucket, and her immolation a source of deep and continued satisfaction to me.

That said, even with so many justifiable reasons for knocking her off, her death was in no way a premeditated one. I had not thought about it, or planned it, or prepared the ground beforehand. Rather, it was a sudden, intuitive, spur-of-the-moment type affair, an unavoidable rush of circumstance, and one that took the perpetrator (i.e. me) as much by surprise as the victim (i.e. old fruit bat).

Such has been the case with so many of my murders. Some I can justify to myself, some I can't, but all, with the possible exception of Miss Wasply, have come completely out of the blue, with little by way of intent on my part. I am not, so to speak, a thinking murderer. More an instinctive one. A natural-born killer, if you like. Yes, that's me. A natural-born killer.

It was Emily who got me into Nannybrook. Made all the arrangements, filled out the registration forms and paid my fees for the nine years I was there. Or at least I presume it was she who paid my fees. She never mentioned it, and I never asked. I can't think who else would have done it. I have no other friends.

God alone knows how she found me, a foul drunken vagrant slumped in a urine-sodden doorway in the middle of London. God alone knows how she ever finds me. But find me she did, and take me in her arms, and raise me up on to unsteady feet.

'Come on, Raphael,' she said. 'You can't live like this. You'd better come with me. I'll sort you out.'

And so we got in a black London cab, windows wound down because after five years on the tramp I stank abominably, and drove through the spring morning to Nannybrook House. And at Nannybrook they seemed to be expecting us, because I was met at the front door by a puffing, red-faced doctor, and taken upstairs, and bathed and shaved and examined and clothed and installed in a bright and airy room at the back of the house with a view over the flowery rose gardens beneath. And there I remained for nine years.

Nannybrook was a retirement home for the elderly. During the Fifties it enjoyed a certain celebrity when its warden pioneered a method of counteracting the ageing process by suspending residents upside down for an hour each day inside a specially adapted greenhouse. The Nannybrook Treatment, as it came to be known, made headlines around the world and sparked an international inversion craze amongst the over-seventies. Subsequent research, however, suggested that far from prolonging their lives, suspension of the

21

elderly merely exacerbated their varicose veins, and by the time I arrived the experiment had long since been abandoned. In the nine years I was there nothing half as interesting happened, except when the brakes failed on Mr Guttleib's wheelchair and he rolled out of the front gates into the path of an oncoming laundry van (shades of Lord Slaggsby there). Nannybrook was, above all else, a very sedate place to while away one's twilight years.

It occupied a large ramshackle Edwardian building at the top end of Putney Hill to which, over the years, various annexes and extensions and conservatories and wheelchair-access ramps had been added, so that, taken as a whole, it resembled something a dysfunctional child might have constructed out of Lego bricks. It had an enormous red front door, a weathervane that, even in the strongest winds, never pointed in any direction other than south, and was fenced off from the main road by a high stone wall with broken bottle shards cemented into the top, although whether the latter was to discourage vandals from getting in, or pensioners from getting out, I never discovered. The building was girded by a covered wooden veranda, and boasted extensive gardens to the rear, including a defunct orchard, several rose beds and a large vegetable patch wherein rheumatoid residents would cultivate curiously rheumatoid courgettes.

My room was on the second floor, at the back of the house. I had a bed, which was made for me every morning and which could, by the manipulation of various attached cranks and pulleys, be raised or lowered or tilted or swivelled depending on how one liked to sleep; also a desk, a lamp, an armchair and an en suite bathroom with special hand-grips beside the lavatory to stop me falling off when I was having a crap. I had my own phone, as did every Nannybrook resident, although I never used it because I had no one to call; whilst everywhere, all over the room like a pox, were strategically placed red electronic buttons which I could jab if I felt a coronary coming on. In nine years I never felt even the ghost of a coronary, but that didn't stop me jabbing the buttons anyway, just to annoy the staff.

There was also, in one corner of the room, built into the wall, a large, warm cupboard, and here I hid my most precious possessions: The Photo and The Pill. During my vagrant years I had kept the latter Sellotaped beneath my left armpit. With my arrival at Nannybrook, however, I was able to provide a more refined abode, wrapping it in a green silk handkerchief and secreting it each night in the cupboard behind a loose brick, removing it in the morning and transferring it to the pocket of whatever trousers I happened to be wearing that day. Needless to say, no one knew of its existence, and needless to say, I didn't tell anyone. The Nannybrook warden was bad enough about smoking. If he'd found out there were one and a half grains of strychnine, one and a half grains of arsenic, half a grain of salt of hydrocyanic acid and half a grain of crushed ipecacuanha root on the premises he'd have gone quite apoplectic. (Incidentally, this was not the same warden as had pioneered the Nannybrook Treatment back in the Fifties. He, by all accounts, had emigrated to South America to continue his research in a Bolivian prison.)

I was, I believe, one of some 50 people in residence, although it was difficult to put an exact figure on it because, what with old residents constantly dying, and new ones arriving to take their place, the population of Nannybrook was in a constant and bewildering state of flux. In one week alone, for instance, the entire house bridge team expired (a result, I suspect, of the pressures generated by their forthcoming grudge match against a home in Croydon). With such a high turnover any accurate census was impossible. There could have been as few as 30 residents, or as many as 70. I put the figure of 50 simply because that's how many turned out to cheer Eric Morecombe when he came to open the new physiotherapy room.

I was at the lower end of the Nannybrook age scale (76 when I arrived and 85 when I bumped off Mrs Bunshop). Most residents were well into their nineties, and several were over a hundred. One woman, the unfortunately named Mrs Yurin, celebrated her 106th birthday whilst I was there, although, somewhat to my amusement, she died in the middle of it. Just keeled over into her birthday cake whilst trying to blow out the candles. Her 88-year-old daughter, also a resident, was inconsolable, not least because she'd spent four days icing the bloody thing.

Although I wasn't the youngest person at Nannybrook – Mr Chudleigh was only 71 and, if the rumours were to be believed, Ms Clissold was a prematurely aged 26 – I certainly looked it. Indeed, judged on appearance alone I shouldn't have been there at all, for the wrinkles and cracks and droops and fissures so evident on the faces of my co-residents were markedly absent from my own long, pale-skinned visage.

After half a decade of living rough I did, of course, have a rather haggard look about me, and I certainly wasn't as sprightly as I had been in my youth. Given my age, however, I was in a most remarkable state of preservation. My back remained straight, my eyesight as good as ever and my muscles bouncy and active. Say what you like about murder, it certainly keeps you spry.

My fellow residents were, I suppose, a decent enough bunch, although there were few, if any, to whom I was close. Bernie Mtembe, Nannybrook's sole black resident, was always good for a game of backgammon; and when Mrs Goshen – she of the Australia-shaped birthmark splatted in the middle of her face – drank too much vermouth the results could be most amusing. Naturally I kept a good supply of vermouth concealed in my bedroom and regularly spiked her afternoon tea. She eventually fell down the stairs and broke her neck after her Margaret Thatcher-inspired pussy-bow blouse became entangled with the bannister, but as I hadn't done any spiking that day my conscience was clear.

I was, I think, quite popular, in a removed sort of way. People said good morning to me, and engaged me in faltering conversations, which I would reciprocate with as much interest as I could possibly muster. I always received several Valentines cards, most of them, I suspect, from an elderly woman with Alzheimer's; and was never forgotten at Christmas or on my birthday. On 1st January 1983 I was given a beautiful gold-plated fountain pen, inscribed 'R.I.P., from all at Nannybrook House'. There was a little tea party in my honour at which I made rather a witty speech and was arthritically applauded by all and sundry, bent and wrinkled hands slapping together like appreciative porpoises.

My only real friend at Nannybrook, however, if such he could be called, was Archie Bogosian, a small, pinch-faced leprechaun of a man who had, depending on what mood you caught him in and how much Guinness he had drunk, been a diamond smuggler, a big game hunter, an arms dealer, an astronaut, a mercenary, a racing driver and a bodyguard to the Shah of Iran.

'Let's cut the shit, Phoenix,' he'd whisper, leaning across to me as we sat downstairs in the day room. 'I've killed people and I don't mind admitting it.'

'Me too,' I'd sigh, patting his arm.

'Good, good,' he'd chuckle. 'We're professionals; not like these other fuckwits. We've lived, by God! Done things. People like us have to stick together. I remember during the war when I was air-dropped over Berlin . . . have I told you this one?'

'No,' I'd lie.

'Well, it was a midnight drop, very hush hush, direct orders from Churchill . . .'

And off he'd go on some wonderfully exotic tale of how he'd been sent to assassinate Hitler or perform some equally unlikely mission, for which he'd been awarded a veritable fruit salad of gallantry medals. I later found out from his sister that he had been unable to fight in the war because he had a spastic colon. He had done his bit for the voluntary fire service, and then spent the rest of his life working for a large company selling ladies' underwear in Swindon. It didn't matter. He had, if only in his mind, made of his life something fantastic, and I respected that. At least he didn't go on about gout and pension payments, which was the staple conversation of everyone else I lived with.

Thrown together by a shared sense of mischief, Archie and I became the Nannybrook pranksters, a task for which I was particularly well qualified, following my years with The World Freedom League.

We didn't do anything too outrageous; just dumped a small spanner in the works whenever the opportunity arose. We would, for instance, press the alarm bell in the lift, and then watch gleefully from round the corner as nurses came rushing with oxygen masks and flapping rubbery stethoscopes. Or pin small notes to the Residents' Notice Board with messages such as 'Bugger the Warden' and 'Want a blow-job? Contact Mrs Yurin Jnr in Rm 10' written on them. So intense became our note pinning, indeed, and so disgusting, that the entire board was eventually moved into the house office so it could be kept under constant surveillance, whereupon we took to graffiti-ing disgusting limericks on the walls of the downstairs lavatory.

Ultimately, however, our small revolutions caused little stir, for Nannybrook was essentially an easy-going place. There are, I have heard, retirement homes run along the lines of some Russian gulag, their residents herded back and forth like dangerous political malefactors, but Nannybrook, at least during my time there, was not one of these. Of course there was organization if you cared for it, and it was more than easy to spend one's entire twilight years in a tightly regulated round of communal calisthenics, cribbage competitions, Batik classes and trips to places of outstanding natural beauty. If none of that interested you, however – and it didn't interest me very much – one could simply do whatever one wished.

For myself, I didn't really do very much at all. I watched television – I was a particular fan of Mike Yarwood, and *The Two Ronnies* – and cultivated the odd, abortive crop of runner beans in the Nanny-brook garden. I spent a lot of time sitting out on the front veranda smoking cigarettes and staring at The Photo, did the odd crossword, and supplemented my meagre pension by regularly drubbing Bernie Mtembe at backgammon. ('You done me again, man!' he would wail. 'I gotta stop this bloody backgammon. You wiped me out!')

Most days, however, I would simply go out wandering, setting off early in the morning directly after breakfast, and returning late in the afternoon, tired and sweaty, just in time for tea. These excursions were not at all to the liking of the Nannybrook warden, who discouraged residents from venturing forth alone because so many of them tended to get lost or run over. Since I was clearly in full possession of all my faculties, however, there was little he could do, and I wandered on unchecked.

I went all over the place. To Wimbledon Common, or Richmond Park, or right the way up the King's Road, past the scene of Rick's murder, and so into the very heart of London, where I'd spend the day in the British Museum, or in St James's Park, or rowing about on the Serpentine. Sometimes I'd head over to Baker Street and stare at Emily's old home, now converted into offices, or go up to Regent's Park to gaze at the site of White Lodge, scene of my birth and first murder, now demolished and replaced with a gaggle of park amenities buildings. I never lingered, however. It made me unbearably melancholy to see my past so comprehensively obliterated.

Occasionally Archie Bogosian would accompany me on these jaunts, although he tired more easily than I and we tended to spend long periods in pubs and cafés, eating peanuts and supping Guinness while he got his breath back. Here he would regale me with intricate tales of his lifetime's adventures before suggesting a quick saunter up to Soho 'just to get the blood to the extremities'. We'd duly set off, Archie scampering ahead excitedly like a beagle on a scent, eventually ending up in the front row of some musty subterranean porno cinema on to whose mildewed screen would be projected scenes of quite breathtaking explicitness. We would watch for an hour or so, wide-eyed and open-mouthed, and then leave, Archie making a point of going up to the ticket booth and politely asking the woman therein whether they would be showing *The Sound of Music* the following week.

Aside from all that, there were two further pastimes in which I engaged during my years at Nannybrook.

The first was ballroom dancing. Every Friday afternoon, regular as clockwork, residents, or at least those of us who were still able to walk, would gather in the dining hall, where Mr Minghella, a dapper little androgyne with blue-rinsed hair and a red velvet waistcoat, would take us through a bewildering array of foxtrots, polkas, waltzes, rumbas, tangos, quadrilles and hip-juddering bossa novas, beating time against the panelled walls with an old snooker cue whilst deftly operating a monstrous gramophone which he brought down from his room each week specially.

There were always more women than men at these Friday-afternoon dance sessions, and many of the old ladies would thus have to dance together, clutching each other like star-crossed lovers. This delighted Archie Bogosian, who would waltz round the room whispering 'No kissing, you filthy old lesbos!' at any all-female pairings he happened to pass.

I didn't go every Friday, and politely declined to take part in the over-seventies competitions for which Mr Minghella was forever entering us, but it was, in its own way, thoroughly enjoyable. I would practise my steps alone in my room with a pillow, and, having suitably spiked her afternoon tea with vermouth, would generally get up a real head of steam with Mrs Goshen on the Mexican salsa. When Mrs Bunshop arrived, however, I stopped dancing, and never took it up again. The sight of her in the jazz disco session was, frankly, one of the most repugnant things I have ever seen in my entire life.

Finally, and what suicide note would be complete without such an admission, I had sex. Not with the residents, of course (what an abominable notion!), and not, perhaps, as much as I would have liked, but given my circumstances I think I did pretty damn well. Better, certainly, than I had any right to expect at my age.

My sex life has always been something of a cyclical affair, swinging from the strenuously active to the depressingly dormant and back again. When I was a film star, for instance, I had an awful lot of it; even more when I played in a rock band. At Cambridge I did OK, and whilst maybe not prolific, my years in Liverpool were by no means barren either. In the prison camp, on the other hand, I had none whatsoever, whilst the 24 years I spent at Tripally Hall were, with the exception of the local baker's wife, almost exclusively chaste. The insalubrious half-decade before my arrival at Nannybrook had been unmitigatedly sexless, and I now therefore felt I had a deal of catching up to do.

I started about a week after my arrival at Nannybrook with a large-breasted Irish nurse named Madeleine who wore a starched cotton uniform and had a small mole on her left cheek.

'You're very young-looking for your age, Mr Phoenix!' she said one evening, standing beside my bed with a cup of cocoa and three garibaldi biscuits on a plate. 'I could fancy you myself.'

'Do you?' I inquired, raising my eyebrows seductively. She blushed red as a sunset.

'Oh Mr Phoenix, what a question!'

'Because I fancy you,' I said.

'Mother of God, I work here!'

I said nothing.

'I work here!' she repeated.

Again, nothing.

'It's quite out of the question. You're 76.'

I ran my hand gently up her thigh and across her hip, and then leant over and turned out the light. By the time I got round to my cocoa it was quite cold.

After Madeleine, there was Pam, who worked in the kitchens, and Ms Crux the physiotherapist, and Cindy, who did the gardening, and a couple of other nurses, and even the warden's spinster sister. I had sex in my bedroom, and in their bedrooms, and in the backs of cars, and on Putney Heath, and even, once, in the downstairs lavatory, for which occasion I graffitied a special limerick:

> I hope the warden will treat with lenience
> This terrible act of disobedience,
> For where most people dump
> I'm having a hump
> Hooray for the great British convenience!

I enjoyed my sex – as I always do – and so, hopefully, did my partners. (The warden's spinster sister certainly seemed to have a good time, if her cries of 'Oh Christ, it's been so long!' were anything to go by.) I steered clear of any emotional attachment, however. Quite aside from the obvious impracticality of the thing, I had neither the desire nor the capacity to bestow anything beyond the most perfunctory of affections on those with whom I slept. When it comes to feelings, I've only ever had room for Emily.

And that, pretty much, sums up my life at Nannybrook. Walking, reading, backgammon, television, runner beans, dancing and sex. A little straight-laced by my standards, but then I was in my eighties, and I made up for it by doing for Mrs Bunshop. Not that anyone knew I'd done for her, of course. They all thought I was trying to save her. That's the funny thing about murder. It's so open to misinterpretation.

I had been at Nannybrook for eight years when Mrs Bunshop took up residence in the room beside mine, to the left as you looked at them from the corridor.

Archie Bogosian, with a certain prophetic foresight, had sniggeringly dubbed this room 'The Morgue', for more people had died in it than anywhere else in the house, six whilst I was there alone, two within a couple of weeks of each other. 'One for the morgue!' Archie would announce as each new occupant arrived. 'Break out the embalming fluid!'

So high, indeed, was the death count amongst my next-door neighbours, so regular and frequent their decease, that I began to wonder if perhaps mere proximity to me could kill people, without my even raising a finger. I mentioned the idea to Archie, who thereafter insisted I spend as much time as I could sending out my killer rays beside the Nannybrook warden. The latter remained resolutely and disappointingly alive, however, and my friend eventually put the whole thing down to the large metal floodlight bolted just beneath The Morgue's window.

'Too much electricity,' he explained. 'Pollutes the air. Worse than radiation.'

The Morgue had been empty for almost a month when Mrs Bunshop arrived, its previous occupant having died of a heart attack whilst practising yoga in his bathroom. I was sitting downstairs on the front veranda when she pulled up in a tiny yellow car, driven, I later discovered, by her son, Simon.

My first sighting of Mrs Bunshop produced an image, which, for me, was always to define her. Her son opened the passenger door and she swung herself out, skirt rucking up around her waist, legs open- ing violently in my direction. I looked up and caught her staring straight at me, right into my sapphire-blue eyes. She waved, winked, and made no effort whatsoever to close or lower her legs, remaining, indeed, spread-eagled in the car doorway for considerably longer than was strictly necessary to achieve egress from the vehicle.

'Cooey!' she screeched, nodding jovially at me.

'Jesus Christ,' I muttered.

Later that night I was lying on my bed, smoking a cigarette and scribbling limericks for the downstairs loo on a pad of paper, when there was a soft tap at my door.

Thinking that perhaps it was Archie come for a late-night chat, or Bernie Mtembe with the backgammon money he owed me, or perhaps a nurse with a cup of cocoa – wink wink! – I extinguished my cigarette, put on a dressing gown and threw open the door. And there was Mrs Bunshop.

'Surprise!' she bellowed, holding up two plastic cups and a bottle of Harveys Bristol Cream, singularly my least favourite drink ever. 'Getting-to-know-you time!'

'I'm just doing some writing,' I said, hoping she might take the hint and leave me alone. No such luck.

'Writing!' she cried, delighted. 'I knew you were an intellectual as soon as I saw you. Your eyes are full of wisdom. Are you a former professor?'

'No,' I replied. 'Nothing of the sort.'

'Oh well,' she chortled. 'You look like one. Like a genius. I'm your new neighbour.'

She was clad in a thick woollen dressing gown and high-heeled pink slippers. Her lips were smeared all over with a buttery layer of bright red lipstick and surmounted by a thick black moustache. She smelt of lavender perfume, with just the faintest tinge of formaldehyde, and carried beneath her left arm an ominously large red-leather photo album.

'I saw you through the window when I arrived,' she said, arching her false eyebrows in a most suggestive manner. 'You were staring at me as I got out of the car.'

I denied that I had been doing any such thing and endeavoured to manoeuvre her out of the door. She was having none of it, however, and, oblivious to my protests, barged into the room and poured me a huge cup of sweet sherry.

'Cheers,' she said, plonking herself on the end of the bed. 'Down the proverbial.'

I sighed, accepted the sherry and moved as far away from her as I possibly could.

'And have you settled in?' I asked by way of small talk.

'Oh yes,' she said. 'I'm perfectly comfortable. Although I would have preferred to stay at home. But he won't have me there, you see. Wanted me out so I won't see the Greek boys. He does it to them, you know.'

'He?'

'Simon, of course. My son. Makes out he's doing me a big favour bringing me here, but it's because he wants me out. So I won't see the Greeks. He's been bringing them back ever since Ted passed away. Ted wouldn't have stood for Greeks in the house. Ted wouldn't stand for any foreigners.'

'I see.'

'I watch them through the keyhole. Horrible. And we gave him such a good education. He once won the school egg and spoon race, you know.'

32

She downed her sherry and poured herself another.

'Drink up,' she said, indicating my as yet untouched glass. 'Don't hold back on my account. I'm Ethel, by the way. Ethel Bunshop, née Boocock.'

'Phoenix,' I said. 'Raphael Phoenix.'

She roared with laughter.

'Phoenix! Phoenix! What's that? A bird or something? A bird that catches fire.'

'In a manner of speaking.'

'I hope you won't be catching fire while I'm here.'

'I shall do my best to avoid it,' I answered.

'Seventy-four, and still got my own teeth,' she announced proudly. 'Simon won't at my age. Not the way he goes at it with those Greeks.'

She gulped at her sherry, draining the second glass and letting out a small burp.

'Noisy pipes you've got,' she said, wiping her mouth and trailing a blood-red smear of lipstick up to her ear. 'Mind, you're a handsome man, aren't you? Handsome and intelligent. I bet you're a one with the ladies. Secret liaisons late at night. Sweaty gropes in cramped cupboards. I see you have a cupboard over there.'

'I live quite a quiet life,' I assured her. 'Very quiet.'

'Married?'

'No, never.'

'Single! I do hope you're not going to ravish me.'

'Nothing could be further from my mind,' I said firmly.

'Oh.' She seemed rather disappointed, and lapsed into silence, tapping her feet on the floor and pouring herself another glass of sherry.

'I never thought it would end like this,' she sighed after a while. 'In a home. You never do, do you? You have such high hopes. Such dreams. But the dreams just fade.'

She sounded so despondent as she said this, and appeared so shrivelled and wretched, that I couldn't help but feel a twinge of

33

sympathy for the old moose. I took a sip of my sherry to try to appear friendly, and, forcing a reassuring smile across my face, told her that Nannybrook really wasn't that bad, and that I was sure everything would turn out OK. I obviously overdid it, for, rather than just perking up, as I had intended her to do, she leapt bodily from the bed, displaying in the process considerable elasticity for one her age, and threw her arms around me (she only came up to the level of my waist, leaving her rouge-lipped mouth pressed somewhere around my belly-button).

'Thank you!' she cried. 'Oh thank you. I've been so worried. But now I'm not any more. We'll get through it together.'

I tried to prise her off, but she was having none of it, clinging to me tenaciously like a koala to a tree trunk.

'Yes, yes,' she whispered. 'We'll get through it together. I think I'll have another sherry, and then we'll look at the photos. I'm only 58, you know.'

She stayed for three hours, finishing the Bristol Cream, smoking 18 of my cigarettes ('Just one more, to keep you company!') and guiding me with eviscerating slowness through the opening pages of the vast red leather album ('Nine aunts, you know, and all but one married to a vicar!'). Only when the grandfather clock on the landing struck one did she reluctantly shut the enormous tome and totter towards the door.

'You've kept me well past my bedtime – we'll have to finish this at a later date,' she cooed, her pudgy fingers stroking the spine of the album. 'You naughty boy.'

'Sorry,' I said curtly, opening the door and shepherding her out into the corridor. 'I can assure you it won't happen again.'

'I don't mind!' she trilled. 'It's good to talk. To' – and here she leaned towards me and grasped my hand – 'liaise. Goodnight, dear Mr Phoenix!'

She winked knowingly, and staggered off.

*

Over the ensuing weeks and months Ethel Bunshop née Boocock became the bane of my existence. I didn't think it possible that anyone could be quite that much of a nuisance. Could make my life quite that unpleasant. But she managed it. Oh boy did she manage it. Dreadful woman.

Every morning at 8 a.m., without fail, she would lurk in the corridor like some malevolent spirit, waiting to accompany me down to breakfast. I took to leaving my room earlier and earlier in the hope of avoiding her, but she always caught me. Once I crept out at 5.30 a.m. and she was still there, leaning against the panelled wall like a wrinkled courtesan.

'Do you sleep out here, Mrs Bunshop?' I asked angrily.

'I thought I heard a noise,' she explained. 'I came to investigate.'

'Well, there's nothing here, so you can go back to sleep.'

'Oh but I'm awake now. Perhaps I'll come downstairs with you.'

'I'm not going downstairs,' I lied.

'Well, where are you going?'

'Nowhere. Back into my room.'

'Then why did you come out?'

'I came out, Mrs Bunshop, so I could go back in again. So I could stand in the corridor and experience the inestimable pleasure of walking back across the threshold of my room and slamming the door behind me.' Which I duly did, with a crash and a growl.

'Have I said something wrong?' came a concerned voice from the other side of the door.

'No!' I shouted. 'Nothing at all.' And then went back to bed, falling into an uneasy slumber until I was woken at eight on the dot by a soft tapping on the door and a cry of 'Breakfast, Mr Phoenix. Jam and croissants, like lovers on the Champs Élysées!'

'Bollocks,' I muttered.

Nights were equally as bad, save that whereas in the mornings I dreaded coming out, last thing, I dreaded coming in. Again, she'd always be there, waiting, loitering, hovering like some horrible shrivelled wasp, ready to pounce with the next instalment from her photo album and bottle of disgusting sweet sherry.

'Well, fancy meeting you, Mr Phoenix,' she'd say as I reached the top of the stairs, all surprise and innocence, as if she hadn't been waiting for me at all and the whole thing was just some extra-ordinary coincidence. 'I was just doing some dusting, but now you're here we might as well have a glass of sherry. '

'No, thank you, Mrs Bunshop, I really am rather tired.'

'It'll help you sleep. It's Harveys, you know. Better than Mogadon.'

'I think not,' I'd say, edging towards my door, key at the ready. 'It's very kind, but I've been walking all day and feel like a nice long bath. So if you wouldn't mind . . .' All this whilst surreptitiously insinuating my key into the lock, opening the door and making ready to dash inside. But old bugger lips was quicker. God she was quick. I'd get halfway in and just be pushing the door shut when that fucking photo album would be jammed in the gap like an enormous leather doorstop.

'Frinton, every year,' she'd cry. 'Seaview hotel. Room five. Every year. Me, Mother, Father and Aunt Dotty. I know I've got the photos here somewhere.'

And that was it. I was trapped. Me on one side of the door, her on the other, and the photo album in between. Trapped in Frinton like a fly in a web.

I started going up to bed later and later, just as in the mornings I would be getting out of bed earlier and earlier. I would sit in the library long after lights out, eventually tiptoeing up to bed in the silence of the very early morning, holding my breath, measuring each step, hoping desperately that she would be asleep, that I might slip safely and deliciously beneath my duvet without a mention of Frinton or Aunt Dotty or Simon and his nocturnal activities with Levantine bodybuilders. But still she'd get me. Burst from her room with a cry of 'Mr Phoenix, might I just ask you . . .' and engage me in some tortuous conversation that left me drained and nauseous. She must have had ears like a bloody bat.

And even when I did finally get rid of her, did manage to prod her back into her room, still she would torment me. I would turn out the lights, curl exhausted in my bed clutching The Photo, breathe deep and start to relax. And then the noises would start.

Not big noises. Not bangings or clankings or screamings. Not the sort of noises about which you could put a letter in the house complaints box. No, these were silent noises. Furtive noises, like those made by rodents creeping around in a loft. I'd be drifting gratefully into sleep when I would hear a faint scratching on the other side of the wall. I would listen, it would stop, I would close my eyes again, and then scratch scratch scratch. I would get up, nerves jangling, and lay my ear against the wall. Silence. One minute. Two minutes. I'd go back to bed and then it would start again: scratch scratch scratch. And sometimes it would be a moaning sound, like someone having a bad dream, or a frightful porcine snoring, or an endlessly repeated series of sighs, or, on occasion, an ear-shatteringly loud fart, until I couldn't stand it any more and would fly from my bed and hammer furiously on the wall:

'Shut up, you abominable old haddock! Shut up, I say!'

The net result of which would be an interlude of blissful silence, and then a soft knock on the door.

'Are you in trouble, Mr Phoenix? Do you require medical attention?'

I started sleeping on Archie Bogosian's floor, or in a chair in the conservatory, or, on one hot night, out in the garden, head pillowed on a divot of turf. I even asked the warden if I could move to another part of the house but, as Sod's Law would have it, this was one of those rare periods when all the Nannybrook residents were in exceptional health and no one showed the least sign of dying and vacating their room.

For a while I took solace in sex.

'At least she can't stop me screwing,' I chuckled to myself one night, wandering upstairs after a tremulous moonlit assignation

37

amongst the mulchy fallen apples of the Nannybrook orchard. 'At least there's one thing she can't spoil, foul old toad.'

I spoke too soon, however, for two weeks later she discovered me having it off with Nurse Butcher in the back of the latter's Hillman Hunter.

'Excuse me!' she cried, tapping politely on a steamed-up side window. 'But are you lead-free?'

Thereafter I found myself quite unable to get an erection without suffering concomitant mental images of my appalling prune of a neighbour, and eventually I did myself a favour and stopped having erections altogether. My sex life withered like a flower in a desert.

My one release, it seemed, came in my daily rambles. She had a bad hip and, though on several occasions she tried, could not keep up with me. I would bolt my jam and croissant breakfast and charge down the drive with the old crone in hot pursuit. 'Mr Phoenix!' she would cry plaintively. 'Mr Phoenix! I have something urgent to discuss with you! Please wait a moment.' But I pretended not to hear and shot through the gates to freedom as she hobbled pathetically far behind. 'Please, Mr Phoenix. You're going too fast. My hips hurt!'

I'd hop on a No. 14 up to the centre of town and merge into the jostling crowds, delighting in the vast, noisy anonymity of it all. Delighting in the non-presence of Mrs Bunshop and her ubiquitous fucking bottle of Harveys Bristol Cream.

In time, however, even my expeditions became sullied with thoughts of her. I would be marching round the British Museum when suddenly I would be hit by the thought that at some point I would have to return home. Return to Nannybrook, where she would be waiting – hips, lips and all – like some nasty prowling spider.

'Bugger Bunshop,' I would groan, slumping on to a bench beneath the Elgin Marbles, my head in my hands. 'Bugger, bugger, bugger.'

I ceased rowing on the Serpentine because I kept imagining her lurking in the depths beneath like a malevolent squid, a thought that invariably caused me to drop my oars and nearly capsize in alarm. I stopped going to porno cinemas with Archie because of fears, admittedly irrational, that she might suddenly appear on the screen. I even began avoiding the site of White Lodge, my old home, after an old woman of Mrs Bunshop's height and build, her face hidden beneath a tartan headscarf, took to feeding the squirrels nearby. The mere thought of her was enough to darken the brightest day.

And yet for all that I never actually set out to kill the old ferret. I hated her, dreaded her, spent a disproportionate amount of time cursing her, yet I never specifically planned to set her alight. It just sort of happened. No one was more surprised than I when she erupted in flames. Except, of course, Mrs Bunshop. She was very surprised.

The day I murdered Mrs Bunshop, in the summer of 1985, was no different from any other day. I rose at 6.30 a.m. after a sleepless night and sneaked out into the corridor where, of course, she was loitering, like a nasty brooding phantom. I cursed her beneath my breath and, rather than wait for breakfast, set off immediately to catch the bus into town.

'Mr Phoenix!' she cried, pursuing me down the stairs. 'Dear Mr Phoenix, might I ask your advice on a matter of some urgency?'

'No, you can't,' I snapped, leaping down the steps two at a time. 'Leave me alone.'

'I know your game!' she trilled, hobbling arthritically in my wake. 'Playing hard to get, you naughty boy.'

'Mrs Bunshop,' I cried, turning at the bottom of the stairs, 'bugger off.'

Whereupon I hurried across the hallway, heaved open the enormous red front door, and charged off down the drive.

'You'll be back!' she cried as I went. 'You won't be able to help yourself!'

The rest of the day I spent sitting miserably on a bench beside the Thames, remaining there until dusk, when I took myself up to Leicester Square to watch a film. This didn't finish till past 11, and I then wandered around for another hour or so, mingling with the night-time crowds, before eventually catching a bus back to Putney. By the time I reached Nannybrook it was close on 1 a.m.

I let myself in, grabbed some garibaldi biscuits and a glass of milk from the kitchen, and then sneaked warily upstairs, senses at full alert for the inevitable Bunshop onslaught. I reached the first-floor landing without incident, however, and then the second-floor landing, and then my bedroom, and before I knew it I was inside with the door shut and not a sign of my egregious neighbour. For the first time in a year I was home and safe without a single whiff of Harveys Bristol Cream.

'Perhaps she's gone to sleep early,' I thought. 'Or maybe she's died. Oh God, let her have died!'

I secreted The Pill and The Photo in the corner cupboard and curled up on the bed, waiting for the nocturnal noises to begin. The sighs and scrapes and snores and burps. Nothing, however. Not a peep. All was silent. Ominously silent.

'There's something going on,' I muttered to myself. 'She's planning something. I can feel it. Hideous old yak.'

I lay for perhaps half an hour or so, chain-smoking, waiting nervously for whatever scheme it was that Mrs Bunshop was hatching to make itself known. When, after thirty minutes, however, all was still silent, I got up, put on a dressing gown and eased open my bedroom door.

All was quiet, save for a distant rumble of snoring from old Mrs Hibbert four doors down.

'Hello?' I whispered, peering out into the shadows.

No reply.

'Hello?'

Silence.

I leaned out into the musty corridor and looked to right and left. All was still.

'Perhaps she *has* died,' I thought, hardly daring to believe that something so fortuitous could have occurred with so little warning. 'Or been moved. Perhaps the nightmare's over!'

Emboldened, I said quite loudly, 'Ethel Bunshop, are you there?'

Still there was no reply, however, nor any sound whatsoever aside from Mrs Hibbert's snoring; and now, quite convinced that something *had* happened to her, I stepped right out into the corridor and made my way along to her room, the door of which I found, rather to my surprise, was slightly ajar. I pressed myself against the wall, heart thumping, and peered through the crack.

There was only a space of some six inches to look through, so I couldn't see very much. The room was illuminated by a pale, ghostly luminescence – from a television, I guessed, its sound turned down – by whose flickering light I was able to see the edge of her bed and a pair of furry, zip-up-the-front boots arranged against the further wall. All remained silent.

I stayed where I was for several minutes, and then, hardly daring to breathe, I pushed the door a little further open. I could now see the television screen, on which a black and white film appeared to be showing, and, lying open on the armchair next to it, as if abandoned in a hurry, the dreaded photo album.

'Mrs Bunshop?' I whispered. 'Mrs Bunshop?'

Again, no response, so I pushed the door wide open and stepped inside.

'Hello hello!' I said, raising my voice slightly, more confident now that – Glory be to God on high! – I was rid of the old goose.

Silence.

I quickened my pace, half expecting – positively hopeful even – that I would find her collapsed on the far side of the bed. But in my eagerness to confirm her demise, and in the darkened shadows of the room, I stumbled into the arm of the chair and knocked my shins hard against the sharp corner of the open photograph album. The bulky volume wobbled precariously on its perch for a couple of seconds and then crashed to the floor, ripping the leather-bound spine away from the pages of the book and scattering dog-eared black and white photographs all over the carpet.

Despite the many hours that Mrs Bunshop had pursued me with

it, I had never given the contents of her album much attention. While she wittered on about seaside holidays and her endless aunts, my mind had shut down. A constant stream of photographs had been relentlessly thrust under my nose but I remained steadfastly oblivious to the minutiae of her family tree. Now, as I bent down and hurriedly started to tidy the photographs back into the broken album I was suddenly struck with a heart-stopping twinge of recognition.

There she was. Staring up at me. In this particular photograph she was standing next to a chubby, five-year-old Ethel, who was grinning manically at the camera, clutching a lacy parasol. Despite only flickering light from the television and the fuzziness of the old photograph, her jutting chin and misshapen bulk were unmistakable. I slowly turned the photograph over. Scrawled in Ethel's childish writing on the back was confirmation of what I already knew: 'With Aunt Dotty, Frinton, Easter, 1907'.

A beloved Aunt Dotty she may well have been to Ethel Bunshop, but to me she will always be the abhorrent Miss Dorothy Wasply.

'I knew you wouldn't forsake me, Mr Phoenix,' said a voice suddenly, pitching me back to 1985. 'I knew you'd come back.'

Ethel Bunshop was, at that point, still very much alive. She was standing just to my left, in front of the open window, wearing a frilly nightgown, which glowed silver in the flickering television light. She smelt strongly of sherry and lavender water and was standing with her back to me, staring up at the stars.

'You couldn't help yourself,' she said seductively. 'Some urges are irresistible. Quite irresistible.'

I don't know whether it was the photograph that triggered it, or the suggestion of irresistible urges, but I was suddenly gripped by an overwhelming desire for action. Without quite knowing what I was doing I lurched forward, seized Mrs Bunshop's withered ankles and, like a gardener emptying a wheelbarrow full of compost, tipped her out of the open window. Just like that. No thought. No fuss. No preplanning. Just up and out. I had a brief glimpse of her creased thighs, and then she was gone. I didn't hear her hit the ground, but then it was 30 feet below.

'Bloody good riddance,' I huffed to myself. 'Now maybe I can get a proper night's sleep.'

I stood still for a moment, just back from the window, breathing deeply, both exhilarated and surprised and a mite concerned about my actions, and then leant out to get a better look at her crumpled corpse. At which point I saw a most amazing sight.

Some three feet below the level of the window, bolted to the outside, was a large floodlight. It was trained upon the flowerbeds below and switched on at nightfall to illuminate the roses and discourage 'undesirables' from prowling around the Nannybrook grounds. It was, according to Archie Bogosian, the reason so many people died in the room above. 'Too much electricity,' he explained. 'Pollutes the air. Worse than radiation.'

On this particular night, however, it appeared to have saved a life rather than taken one, for hanging upside down from the rust-fringed lamp-face, her nightgown snagged on one of its sharp corners, was Mrs Bunshop. Moths and other night-time insects fluttered around her face and, in a bizarre imitation of their movement, she flapped her arms as though trying to take off.

'You threw me out of the window, Mr Phoenix!' she squealed. 'I distinctly felt you throw me out of the window.'

I darted back into the room and looked wildly around. In the corner was her rubber-footed wooden walking stick. I rushed across, seized it and, flying back to the window, tried to poke the hideous old monster off her perch. Prod, prod, prod.

'Ugh!' she groaned. 'Ugh!'

For a moment I thought I had her, and she began to slip, but then, with alarming dexterity, like some circus acrobat, she managed to grasp hold of the stick with both hands and pull herself up, towards me.

'Die, trout!' I hissed, rattling the stick as hard as I could. But I was unable to shake her loose, and, with strength I didn't think possible in one her age, she groped her way from an almost upside-down position until she was virtually sitting astride the floodlight. Its rays shone upwards through her nightdress and set her glowing like a shrivelled Halloween pumpkin. A curiously acrid smell, as of burning hay, assaulted my nostrils.

'Oh Mr Phoenix!' she cried dramatically, now able to reach out and grab hold of each of my arms, locking them into a vice-like grip, 'will you murder me?'

'Too bloody right!' I replied. But bent double over the windowsill and with her clinging to me with the tenacity of a barnacle, I could actually do very little. Slowly, as she had done with the walking stick, she began to grapple upwards like a monkey until she was clutching me round the shoulders and her face was level with my own, whereupon, to my surprise, she headbutted me on the nose. I straightened, and there was a sound of shattering glass as Mrs Bunshop's feet smashed into the front of the floodlight. At the same time I noticed thick curlicues of smoke spiralling upwards from the hem of her nightdress where it lay across the floodlight.

'I always knew you were a bad seed!' she hissed.

She headbutted me again, harder than before, and I staggered backwards into her bedroom, dragging her inside with me, legs about my waist and arms about my neck. Smoke was now pouring from the bottom of her nightdress and, even as I banged against the wall, the material suddenly burst into flame, illuminating the room with infernal leaping shadows. Mrs Bunshop let out an ear-piercing scream, there was a faintly sweet smell as of simmering chicken, and then her entire nightgown erupted. Whoosh! Like a Roman candle. Flames were everywhere.

I tried to drop her, but she was having none of it.

'Like lovers on the Champs Élysées!' she cried, clutching me harder than ever, arms locked around my neck, legs around the small of my back. I bucked and writhed, but her grip was not to be broken. Flames burst into my face, my hair caught light, my dressing gown ignited, I screamed for all I was worth. The agony was beyond anything I can possibly describe. I whirled round the room, Mrs Bunshop still glued to my chest, smashing into the furniture, banging against the walls, enmeshed in searing flame and acrid sheets of smoke, until eventually I was overwhelmed and crashed to the floor.

Which is, apparently, how we were found. By old Mrs Hibbert, of all people, who smothered us with a duvet. Mrs Bunshop was dead. Charcoaled like an overdone corn on the cob. I was alive, but only just. I awoke briefly in the ambulance, but after that all is forgetfulness.

Whilst I was in hospital I received a visit from Emily.

Since the day, nine years previously, when she had scooped me up from my squalor and deposited me on the Nannybrook doorstep, I had seen neither hide nor hair of her. My residential fees had been paid – six-monthly, by postal order, no questions asked – and I received from somewhere a small allowance which, together with my pension and not insubstantial backgammon winnings, allowed me to live a more than comfortable existence. From Emily, herself, however, I had heard nothing.

And then, suddenly, she was there at my bedside, with a bunch of daffodils and an improbably large bunch of seedless South African grapes, which I couldn't eat because my face was all bandaged up. Typical Emily.

'Hello, Raphael,' she said, sitting down and taking my (bandaged) hand in hers. 'How are you feeling?'

'Hrmph,' I mumbled through my dressings. 'Hrmph.'

'Try not to talk, Raphael. The doctor says it's not good for you. You just lie there and I'll do all the chatting.'

'Hrmph,' I acknowledged, staring adoringly at her through my right eye, that being the one part of my anatomy my carers had seen fit not to bandage. 'Hrmph, hrmph, hrmph!'

My darling looked as young and fresh and vibrant as ever, her hair blonde and brilliant, her eyes a dazzling emerald. Which was strange because, like me, she was by then well into her eighties. Not the least curious of the many curious things about Emily is that for some reason she never seems to age. She has barely changed from the days I knew her when we were young. In her eighties she looked exactly the same as she did in her twenties, when in turn she looked exactly the same as she had done as a child. Old age – indeed any sort of age at all – appears to have completely bypassed her.

I can offer no proper explanation for this. More than once, indeed, the thought has crossed my mind that perhaps she *has* aged and I'm simply refusing to acknowledge the fact. That her youth is, so to speak, purely in the eye of the beholder. I don't think that's the case, however, and the way in which one of the young doctors kept staring at her when he came in to take my blood pressure – something he did eight times during her visit – seemed to confirm that I'm not the only person to recognize her exceptional, and exceptionally long-lived, pulchritude.

Whatever the truth, I lay there now gazing up at her beguiling pale-skinned face, its lips, as always, curved into a gentle smile, wishing to God my bandages were a little looser so I could sit up and embrace her.

'Hrumph, hrumph!' I mumbled, endeavouring to express how very pleased I was to see her, and how much I'd missed her these last nine years.

'Now, Raphael, you know you mustn't talk. Doctor's orders. Isn't that so?' This to the young doctor who'd just come in again with the blood-pressure apparatus.

'Quite right,' he stammered, pumping up my arm till it hurt. 'Quite right.'

She remained with me for about two hours, eating half the grapes and chattering away childishly about nothing of any great consequence. Not that I minded. It was good just to be with her after all these years. My relationship with Emily has always operated at a deeper level than language can express. Words for us are simply yachts sailing back and forth across an ocean of unimaginable profundity.

Mind you, she did come up with one interesting piece of information. Namely, that far from being suspected of murdering Mrs Bunshop, I was apparently being hailed as a hero for trying to save her. The police, it seems, had carried out an exhaustive investigation into the affair, and, as the police can always be relied upon to do in such circumstances, had drawn entirely the wrong conclusion. The coroner's final report stated that she had, for reasons best known to herself, climbed out of the window of her own accord and, whilst perching on the floodlight, caught fire. Death by misadventure. I hrumphed a long sigh of relief. Emily squeezed my hand.

Eventually, and all too soon, she stood to go. That's how it's always been with her. She appears suddenly from nowhere, like a daydream and, equally suddenly, disappears back into it again. You can never hold her for long.

'There is one thing,' she said, leaning over and stroking my bandaged forehead (bloody bandages!). 'I don't know if it's of any interest, but there's an old castle by the sea. It's been in the family for years. It's very remote, apparently. I've never been there myself, but if you want to go up and recuperate, you're more than welcome. Stay as long as you want. I've left all the details with the warden at Nannybrook. Goodbye, dear Raphael. My hero!'

Whereupon she kissed me on my mummified cheek and, with a farewell wave, disappeared from the room.

'Hrmph, hrmph, hrmph!' I gargled after her.

We didn't see each other for another 15 years.

There's not much left to say.

I remained in hospital for six months. Everyone expected me to be horribly disfigured by the fire, but when my bandages were removed I was, to general consternation, completely unscarred.

'Extraordinary,' muttered my doctors. 'Contrary to all natural laws. Extraordinary.'

I returned to Nannybrook, where my room had been kept for me, but things weren't the same. I felt restless. I wanted to move on. Even Archie Bogosian's stories had lost their sparkle.

I had been back for about a week when I remembered Emily's castle. I asked the warden about it, and he duly handed over a large manila envelope containing keys and details. It sounded just the ticket. I set off two days later.

And that was the beginning of the life I am about to end. I found the castle. I liked it. I moved in, with The Photo, a suitcase full of clothes, some odds and ends of furniture and, of course, The Pill. One and a half grains of strychnine, one and a half grains of arsenic, half a grain of salt of hydrocyanic acid . . . but then you know all that by now.

I thought I might get a moving-in card from Emily, but none came. Instead, after I had been at the castle a month, I received a letter from my old friend the Nannybrook warden.

Dear Mr Phoenix,
In view of your extraordinary and selfless bravery in attempting to save the life of the late, lamented Ethel Bunshop, née Boocock, it has been decided, by a unanimous vote of staff and residents, to rename the day room The Raphael Phoenix Room.
   We shall be holding a short opening ceremony, and would be most honoured if you would attend. The mayor will be there, as will Mrs Bunshop's son, and, of course, all the residents.
   I do hope you are well and look forward to hearing from you,

Yours sincerely,

Norman Stoppard, Warden

I declined the invitation. Acceptance would, in the circumstances, have been in extraordinarily bad taste. The Raphael Phoenix Room indeed. Outrageous. Quite outrageous!

# Chapter Three

AND SO I'M writing my note in Emily's castle. The castle at the end of the world, as I've christened it. And for good reason, for it sits on the very edge of a towering cliff, the land at its feet dropping 100 metres straight down into the churning sea. Far below, the waves crash furiously about incisors of jagged rock.

'Castle' is perhaps pushing it a bit. It certainly looks castle-shaped, and even boasts a few barred windows and a set of crenellated battlements. It is, however, not a real castle. No one has ever attacked it, nor, indeed, was anyone intended to. It was built in the middle of the last century as an astronomical observatory. The sky in this part of the world is, apparently, particularly rich in stars.

On top of my castle is a large metallic dome, protruding like a squashed head on an outsize body. This vast, weather-dulled semi-sphere once opened like a cleft fruit to reveal an enormous telescope, through which sundry experts would peer hopefully up at the night sky. The telescope and experts are long gone, but the dome remains. It's up there now, warming under the light of a climbing sun.

I have resided here, a hermit, for the past 15 years, ever since I left

Nannybrook. I have no phone, no radio, no television, no friends. I rarely venture more than a few yards from my own front door, and on the rare occasions when I do invariably have a panic attack and have to hurry back. I hear that great celebrations are planned for the turn of the millennium, but such things don't really interest me. I am wholly detached, perched on my promontory like a bird on the very edge of the sky.

My sole connection with reality, tethering me to the outside world like a knotted umbilical, is a narrow rutted drive that zigzags its way from my front door down to the local village, three miles southwards along the coast. Up this flinty track, once a week, in his mud-spattered Land Rover, comes Dr Bannen, with boxes of supplies, the odd bill and my pension money. It's not the sort of service doctors normally offer, but he seems happy enough to do it, and I don't complain. I have no other means of providing for myself. Churlish in my dotage, I have never once invited him in for a cup of tea. Not that he'd accept, of course. Dr Bannen thinks I'm mad.

I have worn badly these last 15 years. My limbs, supple and active right up till my mid-eighties, have slowed and stiffened, and my skin has succumbed to a barrage of wrinkles, leaving me looking like an over-ripe apple. My sapphire-blue eyes no longer see as well as they used to; and I have become distinctly stooped. I feel listless and slack, like a ship with a broken rudder. I walk very slowly, and cough a lot.

In my castle I have a bedroom on the first floor, to the right of the stairs, a bathroom, and, downstairs, directly beneath my bedroom, a perfectly adequate, if mouldy, kitchen. This is all I need or want. The rest of the building is empty, it's wood-floored rooms carpeted toe-deep in dust. For some reason, aside from a front one, the castle has no doors. Doorframes, yes, but nothing to fill them. Their absence makes the place appear even emptier than it actually is. For what it's worth, I append a floor plan of the building.

I don't really do very much any more. Not because I am old and infirm – which at 99 years and counting I am – but because I can't

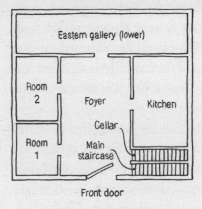

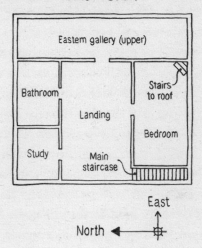

really think of anything I would especially wish to do. My existence is a void, bereft of ideas.

Each morning at five I struggle from my bed and shuffle downstairs to make myself a cup of tea. I nibble a bit of dry toast, light my first cigarette of the day, peer out of the window empty-headed and then make my slow way back upwards to the dome, stopping en route for a shit and a shave. I sleep in white cotton pyjamas and spend all day in them too. No wonder Dr Bannen gets nervous around me.

To reach the dome I climb a brief staircase, starting from a doorway in my bedroom, just to the left of my bed, and issuing after 13 steps (unlucky for some!) on to the flat concrete terrace of the castle roof, the latter hemmed in on all sides by chest-high battlements. To the west, in which direction my front door opens, purple hills roll away up to the horizon, climbing steadily to a rumour of mountains far beyond the edge of sight. To north and south a battered line of coast unfolds, its crumpled course disturbed by a series of promontories which cling to the land like so many severed limbs. Eastwards there is nothing but sea, dotted here and there with the occasional smear of a distant island. When the sea mist comes up about its feet the castle looks like it's floating in the air.

Crossing the roof north to south and east to west and bisecting each other at its centre are two sets of rails upon which sits, and presumably once moved, a circular iron turntable on wheels. On top of this is the dome, slumped like a large metallic jelly on a plate. The original idea, it seems, was that the turntable could be shunted back and forth and from side to side across the roof, and swivelled 360 degrees, hence giving astronomers the freedom to pursue their chosen stars across the heavens. Now, unfortunately, the wheels are rusted and the turntable unturnable, rather like my own atrophied joints, so that the dome rests like a stricken bug at the very centre of the crossed rails, gazing eternally eastwards to the sea and the rising sun.

It can, at least, still be opened. By turning a handle at its base its curved metal plates slide grudgingly aside to reveal a silent interior, from which, once upon a time, a giant telescope probed outwards into the cosmos. Now all that's there is my wickerwork chair, a small table, fag-ends, and a rather clever little mechanism I rigged up to allow me to open and close the structure from within. The latter would have made my father proud. Like all inventors, he adored gadgets.

The dome is where I have spent most of my time for the last 15 years. I ensconce myself there at dawn, propped in my wickerwork chair, a cigarette in my hand, legs crossed upon the arm of the winching mechanism, and then just sit, staring out across the ocean with not a thought in my head until suddenly, as though the day has been fast-forwarded by an unseen finger, I notice the first dusk stars twinkling far above me. Sometimes I gaze at The Photo, crumpled now almost beyond recognition, its subject dim and faded, and sometimes I caress The Pill. Usually, however, I just sit, still and silent, like a dried seed in a shrivelled pod. My blooming days, it seems, are well and truly over. Decay, decay. All is decay.

Or rather all *was* decay, before yesterday morning. Because yesterday morning I decided to kill myself, and suddenly my life was full of purpose.

It wasn't a hard decision to make. Strictly speaking, it wasn't even a decision at all. I neither argued nor debated nor agonized over the matter. I simply knew, instinctively, that the time was right. Death wasn't a choice. It was an inevitability. I felt very calm about the whole thing.

I rose painfully from my bed, dwelt for a moment upon the previous night's encounter with Emily, and then, with a shake of the head, descended to the kitchen. The weather was cold and frosty, and I shivered as I trudged down the stairs. Through the corner of the kitchen window I could see an icy yellow sun bubbling upwards into a cloudless December sky. I made myself a cup of tea and began ruminating on the practicalities of my decease.

That I'd kill myself with The Pill was obvious. What, after all, was the point of carrying it around with me for 90 years if, when I finally decided to top myself, I didn't use it? Slitting my wrists, hanging myself or leaping from the castle battlements were all out of the question. It was The Pill or nothing.

Other issues, however, remained to be decided. Where, for instance, would I do the deed? What location should I chose? Such considerations are important. It's like going on a train journey. If, say, you wish to travel to Manchester, you have to leave from the right station. Likewise, death. No point starting from the wrong place, or chances are you'll end up in the wrong place. And with suicide there's no return service.

I considered doing it in bed, but I am not a fundamentally slothful person and a corpse curled up under a duvet might have left quite the wrong impression. I thought about returning to London and imploding on the site of White Lodge, or outside Emily's old house on Baker Street, but neither option particularly appealed. At my age I didn't fancy a long journey, and anyway, the idea of bending double and expiring on a filthy London street seemed somehow so tawdry after a life as long and murderous as mine.

No, there was only really one place to do it, and that was in the dome. Sitting on my wickerwork chair, drinking wine and looking out into the void. I would settle back into the cupped palm of Fate and allow myself to be flung outwards into eternity. Perfect.

Where, but also when? Again, look on it in terms of a train journey. If you're travelling somewhere you need to know the time of the train you're on. Likewise, suicide. Knowledge of when you're leaving is imperative to the success of the expedition.

I wondered whether I should do it immediately. Finish my tea, trundle upstairs to the dome and start munching one and a half grains of strychnine, one and a half grains of arsenic, half a grain of salt of hydrocyanic acid and half a grain of crushed ipecacuanha root without further ado. No time like the present. Strike while the iron's hot, etc., etc.

But then I thought: No. Bollocks. I'm ten days from my hundredth birthday. What an extraordinary act of self-destruction to self-destruct ten days short of my full century. Ridiculous. Leave it till your birthday, I thought. One hundred years, and then an end. Much neater.

So it was decided. With The Pill, in the dome, on my hundredth birthday. Perfect. Absolutely perfect.

Which then left the question: what should I do for the last ten days of my life? It somehow didn't seem right, what with death so near, to just sit around twiddling my thumbs and staring into space. I needed something to occupy myself. A task. A mission.

And that's how I got the idea for my current endeavour. Why not, I thought, sparking up my first cigarette of the day, write a suicide note? Not a conventional suicide note, mind. Not one of those awful 'Goodbye, dear friends, I'm doing this because . . . and don't forget to feed the cat' sort of notes. No, this would be a quite different suicide note. Not even a proper suicide note at all. More a sort of suicide biography (Suicideography – could this be a new literary form I'm bequeathing?). A history. A self-portrait. A detailed chronicle of the life and crimes of Raphael Ignatius Phoenix, dead by a pill on the morning of his hundredth birthday. I would end my life by describing my life. Conjure myself from the past. Revisit and remake. It would be the greatest suicide note ever written.

'I shall carve myself a memorial in words!' I cried excitedly. 'It shall be my masterpiece.'

I got to work immediately.

Initially I thought I would write my note on paper, and duly set off on a hunt for the box of unused notebooks I had once noticed in a corner of one of the castle's rooms. As I searched, however, moving from room to room, up and down, tracking the notebooks, I was struck by the pristine whiteness of the castle's walls. The immaculate, virgin whiteness. I had never noticed how clean they were. Acres and acres of snowy white, smudged occasionally with a bloom of dampness or the shadow-marks where a picture had once hung, but on the whole as clean, crisp and dry as the untouched pages of an artist's pad. I ran my hand across them as I walked, delighting in their unalloyed smoothness. I stopped and gazed up at them, and along them, and across them and over them. Yards of white. Miles of it. Rooms and halls and staircases and landings. I was surrounded by white. Swamped by it. And I thought: 'Well, why not?'

And so I am writing my note on the walls of my home. I started in the foyer, directly to the left of the front door and to the right of the main stairway, filling the creamy whiteness with neat, three-foot-wide columns, ceiling to floor, ceiling to floor, ceiling to floor, one after another, like a row of identical skyscrapers. Before long I'd moved over to the right of the front door and then round the corner and into the first of my downstairs living rooms, the window of which commands an imposing view northwards up the coast. On and on and on I scribbled – my pen squeaking across the whitewashed plaster, my feet kicking up clouds of dust – until I'd filled that room, swung back into the foyer and thence into the next room along, a complete circuit of which I have now all but completed.

I'll keep moving towards the right, from wall to wall, room to room, until the whole ground floor's done. Then I'll write my way up the left-hand wall of the stairs to the first floor, continuing clockwise until eventually my pen leads me into my bedroom and so to a final full stop at the doorway to the roof stairs. The doorway to my death. It would have been nice to have filled every wall in the castle, but beyond that final door there will be nothing to say. The empty whiteness of the unwritten walls must speak for the empty whiteness of my oblivion.

According to my watch, I've now been at it solidly for well over 30 hours, it being now the afternoon of Wednesday, 22nd December. I don't feel at all tired. On the contrary, I'm brimful of energy and excitement. The whole thing looks fantastic. Like hieroglyphs on the tomb of a pharaoh. A great pharaoh.

Not that there haven't been problems, of course. There have. The height of the walls, for a start. On the ground floor they're over 15 feet from floor to ceiling, necessitating the use of a rickety old ladder to reach the upper levels. Even then, standing 6 foot four, as I do, I still have to stretch to get my pen to the very top. This makes my arm go numb, and the first 15 lines of each column, reading downwards from the ceiling, judder and sway as if written by a myopic drunkard. I did consider using only half the wall, leaving the more inaccessible top parts empty, but felt that to do so would be to leave parts of my life unsaid. It's the whole wall or nothing. I shall not, however, be covering the ceilings too. At a hundred you have to know your limitations. I'm not fucking Michelangelo, for Christ's sake.

Another difficulty concerned writing materials. What precisely does one use to write a suicide note on the walls of one's abode? There are, after all, hardly precedents for such a thing. And I don't want to go leaving my life looking messy. If I can't leave behind something neat and pleasing to the eye I might just as well forget the whole idea. One's death should, at the very least, be legible.

I started off with the gold-plated fountain pen given to me on my 83rd birthday by the residents of Nannybrook House. It soon became evident, however, that in order to write properly the pen needed to be held at a slight downward angle so the ink flowed to the tip, an angle that was damn near impossible to achieve when wobbling ten feet above the ground and writing with my arm up in the air at full stretch. I managed a couple of sentences but then had to climb down and rest for twenty minutes. I gave it another go, but exactly the same thing happened, and eventually I threw the pen away in disgust.

Next I turned to some sticks of red chalk, a goodly – if slightly damp – supply of which I found in a box in the kitchen cupboard. These, however, turned out to be far too slow and smudgy. Sentences unfolded at a snail's pace and dissolved into an incomprehensible blur as soon as I started the next line and inadvertently rubbed my wrist across what was written above. It furthermore took me two entire sticks to write one paragraph, on which basis I calculated I'd need about 10,000 of the damn things to finish the job. The chalk option was also abandoned early on.

I tried a pencil, but it kept breaking, and a ballpoint, but it wouldn't work on the plaster; and a stick of green crayon which disintegrated after half a paragraph; and even thought about painting my demise in doleful watercolours.

In the end, however, I settled for a felt-tip pen, two boxes of which I had purchased from Dr Bannen last year when I had it in mind to start a diary (abandoned after the first week, due to a total absence of subject matter). I have already used four of them – the walls of the castle appear to absorb ink like a sponge – but since there are 30 in each box, and provided I don't get too verbose, I should have more than enough to finish my task. I hope so. The thought of running out of ink is infinitely more upsetting than the prospect of killing myself.

Finally, and most frustratingly, I've had problems with light. (What do you expect after a life as dark and malevolent as mine?) The castle does, of course, have electricity, but half its light fittings are broken and those that do work throw off barely enough radiance by which to count the fingers of my own hand. My eyes, further-more, are not what they used to be, so that even in the middle of the day, working right beside a window, my words bend and sway in front of my face like seaweed in a strong current.

I have thus taken to wearing a large church candle strapped to my forehead with an old dishcloth. There is a plywood chest full of these candles down in the basement, stored there, according to Dr Bannen, when the local chapel was being renovated, and never re-claimed. They are big, thick, white things, rather like the erotic aids one finds gracing the windows of Soho sex emporiums, and provide more than adequate illumination for the job in hand. Molten wax drips down on to my face, forming brittle stalactites on the end of my nose. Taken with my white pyjamas, I look rather like a melting snowman.

And so here I am, felt-tip pen in hand, The Pill in my pocket, candle strapped to forehead, three quarters of the way down a pristine white expanse of wall.

I've barely started my note, and already it seems to have taken an unexpected turn, as though it were writing me rather than the other way around. Mrs Bunshop, you see, should, by rights, have appeared somewhere upstairs, near the end of the thing, her being my most recent victim. And what happens? She pops up slap bang at the start. Last murder first. Arse over tit. Cart before the horse. Madness. And totally contrary to my intentions.

What I had hoped, in my suicidal innocence, was to produce some-thing chronological. Not conventional, mind; but at least something forward-looking. A detailed A–Z of the crimes of Raphael Phoenix, starting with his youth and moving neatly onwards down the high-ways and byways of murderousness to his inevitable, spectacular, pill-popping end. Something coherent, goddammit.

Now, it seems, I am forced to do it all backwards. Z–A. Same in-formation, wrong direction. Last to first rather than vice versa, so that my end shall now be my beginning and my death coincide al-most precisely with the hour of my birth. Absolute bloody madness. But what can I do. My life, it seems, has taken over.

# Chapter Four

Continuing backwards, my penultimate victim, in 1976, was poor old Walter X. I'll never forget the way he shot up into the air with his eyes bulging and legs dangling like a pair of elongated Parma hams, and I'll never stop feeling slightly – although only very slightly – guilty about the whole thing. Unlike Mrs Bunshop, you see, I rather liked him, which just goes to prove what a broad church murder is. Friends are just as likely to fall victim to my homicidal urges as enemies. Let it never be said I'm a choosy killer.

I met Walter because of Emily. Well, because of a number of factors actually, although Emily was the deciding one. Had I not killed Keith, for instance, I probably wouldn't have been wandering the streets that chilly autumn night of 1971. And had I not been wandering the streets I would never have ended up in Trafalgar Square. And had I not ended up in Trafalgar Square I wouldn't have noticed Emily sitting on the plinth between the paws of the great brass lion. And – and this is the important point – had Emily been sitting on any other plinth, between the paws of any other brass lion, I would never have crossed paths with Walter, for that was *his* brass lion, the only one he trusted. A host of forces ushered me into destitution, with Emily the most irresistible of the lot.

*

I fell asleep on her shoulder, gazing up at the moon – 'God I feel rough,' I mumbled – and when I woke she was gone. In her place – Walter. Sitting precisely where she had sat, his chin cupped in his hands, peering soulfully upwards at the greying sky of dawn. He was extremely tall, extremely thin and clad in an array of loathsome mouldering rags, topped off with a battered bowler hat.

'You're on my lion,' he said.

'I beg your pardon,' I replied, sitting up and rubbing my eyes.

'You're on my lion. It's the only safe one, you see. The others have all got surveillance equipment inside them. Very dangerous.'

I wasn't sure what to say to this – my head still felt distinctly groggy from the excesses of the previous night – and so I said nothing at all. Instead I simply shrugged my shoulders and made ready to jump to the ground.

'Although that doesn't mean you have to go,' said my companion, motioning me to sit back down. 'In fact, you'd be a lot safer if you stayed. Just so long as you know it's *my* lion. Got any cake?'

'I'm afraid not,' I said, edging backwards slightly, for he smelt foul, and probably had fleas too.

'Shame. Haven't had cake for ages. They seem to have put an embargo on it.'

He shook his head disconsolately and, fishing in the pocket of his coat, withdrew a disintegrating cigarette end which he put between his lips, puffing on it forcefully, although the thing remained unlit.

'Who are They?' I asked, covering my nose with my hand.

'They?' He seemed surprised by my question. 'They're Them, of course.'

'Them?'

'That's right.' He looked surreptitiously around before jabbing his finger towards the sky. 'The ones up there. Watching us. Always watching us.'

'What, the police?'

He waved his hand dismissively.

'Oh, the police are part of it. And the politicians, and the doctors, and the milkmen. They're all *involved*. But they're just tools. It's Them you've got to watch out for. The string-pullers. The controllers. Nostradamus tried to warn us, but he's been suppressed. So have the Knights Templar, and the survivors of Atlantis. We've still got C. S. Lewis, thank God, but it won't be long before they get round to him too. They're taking over the world. That's why I joined the World Freedom League. To fight them. To the death if necessary.'

He was puffing heavily by the end of this homily, and, reaching into his pocket, withdrew a grubby tea-towel with which he dabbed at his forehead.

'Yes, yes, yes,' he sighed. 'We fight them where we can. It's not much, of course. A broken window here, a painted slogan there, some rotten fruit. But you have to make a stand.'

He sneezed violently, a long finger of mucous flipping out from his nose on to the front of his coat, where, to judge by the shiny, encrusted nature of the material, long fingers of mucous had been landing for many years now. He dabbed perfunctorily at it with his tea-towel.

'Naturally they know who I am,' he continued. 'They have eyes everywhere. Spies on every corner. Your life is in danger just sitting here beside me. I'm a marked man. But then' – and here he began to chuckle; a slow liquid gurgling in the back of his throat that set his body trembling and made his bowler hat shuffle back and forth across his shaggy head – 'I always manage to keep one step ahead. I'm smart, you see. Here, I've written a survival manual. I'm thinking of getting it published.'

He delved into an inside pocket of his coat, bringing out, along with a confetti spray of cigarette butts, crumbs, corks and used matches, a sheaf of muddled papers.

'Don't know any publishers, do you?'

'I'm afraid not,' I said, taking the proffered sheets.

'Shame. If I could publish this it might really help turn the tide. Go on, have a look.'

The papers he had handed me were blotched and crumpled to

the point of unintelligibility, but after staring at them for a while, and rearranging them, and spreading them flat on the surface of the plinth, it was possible to discern some vague order to the spidery scribbles thereon. They essentially comprised a list of numbered points, each elucidating a particular facet of how to survive under the rule of a malevolent superior power.

## How to Stay One Step Ahead

or

## Rules for Freedom Fighters

or

## The Handbook of the World Freedom League
by Walter X

1) Never watch television or films or plays, or listen to the radio. Never read papers or books, except C. S. Lewis. And only the ones about Narnia.
2) Always avoid eye-contact.
3) Look both ways before crossing the road.
4) Don't touch dairy products, especially milk.
5) Avoid people in uniforms. Particularly uniforms with boots.
6) Never stay in the same place for more than a night.
7) Don't cut your hair – reduces strength.
8) Don't take any prescribed medication.
9) Be alert for strange noises – especially knocking sounds, and hums.
10) Don't trust strangers.

'You appear to have broken rule ten,' I observed.
'Yes,' he admitted, taking back his papers and returning them to his pocket. 'It was a risk. But sometimes you have to take risks. Otherwise it would be so lonely.'

'Well,' I said, 'you can trust me.'

'Oh I know that. You've got blue eyes. You can always trust people with blue eyes. In fact, I'd better write that down. It could be important.'

He took out his papers once again and, retrieving a gnarled pencil from another pocket – his coat appeared to consist more of pockets than actual material – scribbled an addendum to rule ten to the effect, 'Don't trust strangers, unless they have blue eyes. Also, make sure they are real blue eyes and not glass ones.' Pleased with his endeavours, he let out a grunt of approval and leant back against the lion.

'Yes indeed,' he sniggered. 'They'll have a job catching me.'

By now the morning was creeping up on us. The hubbub of traffic was slowly increasing and a man with a wheelie-bin had arrived and begun sweeping up rubbish at the other end of the square. I wondered what had happened to Keith's body, and whether Marcie was still screaming, and if the forces of law and order were at that very moment fanning out across the capital in pursuit of a silver-haired, 71-year-old, mass-murdering ex-pop star in red sequinned trousers and cheesecloth shirt. I decided I'd better be moving on.

'Anyway,' I said, struggling to my feet and patting my pocket to ensure The Pill and The Photo were safe therein. 'Nice talking to you.'

My companion looked up at me mournfully, but said nothing.

'I'll be seeing you then. Best of luck. Don't let the bastards grind you down.'

I edged past him to the front of the plinth and leapt to the ground. I looked back once – he was still staring at me mournfully – and then set off across the road. Barely had I reached the other side, however, before I felt myself pushed – not roughly, but firmly – into the doorway of a shop. I smelt rather than saw that my assailant was Walter.

'What's going on!' I shouted, coughing at the wretched stench of the man.

'Ssssh!' he said, putting his finger to his lips. He leant outwards and looked to left and right to ensure we hadn't been seen, and then bowed his grimy head close to my own and whispered:

'I need soldiers.'

'Soldiers?'

'Yes,' he hissed. 'To carry on the struggle. You can only do so much on your own. Two together could do twice as much as one, which is double the damage. Do you see what I'm getting at? Join the cause! Fight for freedom! You and me. A team!'

'I'm very flattered,' I began, 'but right at the moment—'

'Wait!' he cried, leaning outwards and looking to left and right again. 'Don't answer yet. Think about it. Moments like this don't come often. Opportunities must be grasped. At least consider it.'

He prodded me even further into the doorway and turned his back, as though I were about to remove my clothes and he wished to afford me some privacy.

'It wasn't a coincidence you came to the lion today,' he said over his shoulder. 'It was fate. You were summoned. You can't ignore fate. It's even stronger than They are.'

That he was completely potty I had no doubt whatsoever. Probably not dangerously so, but potty nonetheless. To have had anything to do with him would, at any other time, and in any other set of circumstances, have been quite out of the question.

This, however, wasn't any other time, or any other set of circumstances. It was here and now, and I had just killed a man. So far as I knew I was, at that very moment, the object of an extensive police manhunt. Emily had gone. I had little money, and even less idea what to do or where to go. I needed to lay low for a while. I needed a way out. I needed – yes, a bit of fate. As Walter so percipiently said, opportunities have to be grasped. I pondered my options for a moment, and then, not without a certain reluctance, tapped him on the shoulder.

'OK,' I said. 'I'll join.'

He turned slowly, eyes wide.

'What?'

'I'll join. I'll come with you. For a while at least. It's not as if I've got anything better to do.'

Initially he wouldn't believe me, convinced I was playing some sort of joke, or trying to lure him into a trap. Only when I had repeated my offer several times, and reassured him of my good intentions, did he finally accept that I meant what I said. Tears pricked his eyes and, withdrawing his tea-towel, he dabbed tenderly at his irises before seizing my face in both hands and kissing me on the lips.

'And now,' he announced, 'we'd better get out of town. Before they get a fix on us. Although we should just have time for a bit of cake. Some always manage to get through the blockade. They don't have it all their own way!'

Whereupon he grabbed my arm and dragged me off down the street.

Which is how, contrary to all expectations and, indeed, all intentions, I joined the World Freedom League, remaining with that organization for five whole years until, again contrary to all expectations and, indeed, all intentions, I did for its founder member.

And although they were filthy years, and uncomfortable years, and footsore, flea-bitten, boozy, scabby, scavenging, disgusting years, they were also rather liberating ones too. I don't think I've ever felt quite as free as I did during my time with Walter. That's the thing about hitting rock bottom. You no longer worry about falling. As my companion himself put it, in one of his more pithy aphorisms:

'The finest daffodils always grow in shit.'


We left London that same day, my new associate having devoured an improbably large plate of shiny currant buns (purchased, I might add, at my own expense).

'Too many eyes,' he explained as we tramped out of town. 'Keep moving, keep low. That's how to stay ahead.'

We went, I believe, roughly north-west, spending our first night together underneath a bristly hedge somewhere in the foothills of the Chilterns. The next morning we rose early and set off again, as we did the morning after, and the morning after the morning after, and the morning after again. I think in the five years we were together we never stayed in the same place for more than a single night.

'Informers,' he muttered darkly when I once inquired whether we might not treat ourselves and spend two consecutive nights in a rather nice little barn we had discovered in Yorkshire. 'Informers everywhere. Stay too long and they find you out. Motion is survival.'

And so we kept moving, rolling ceaselessly and exhaustingly forward with barely a pause for breath.

We moved in a variety of manners during the course of those years. Usually it was by foot, pounding down lanes and through fields and up hills and across towns until our legs ached and our backs screamed and our feet were covered in blisters. Occasionally we would hitch, although it was rare for a car to stop for a pair of such disgusting-looking creatures as we were, and sometimes we would go by train, riding as far as we could until we were ejected at some back-end-of-beyond station for not having a ticket.

'Tickets are the currency of moral servitude!' Walter once informed a small, moustachioed train guard who had discovered us cowering in the carriage lavatory.

'Fuck off my train,' retorted the small, moustachioed train guard.

Other modes of transport included lorries, amongst whose cargo we would insinuate ourselves whilst the driver wasn't looking; small rowing boats, which we would untie from their moorings and splash around in for a couple of days before heading off once again cross country; and, on one memorable occasion, roller skates. We had 'liberated' these from a garden in Bracknell where the eagle-eyed Walter had spotted them languishing beneath a climbing frame, and thereafter skated merrily on our way for two whole weeks until one of my wheels went wonky and continued rolling became impossible.

Usually, however, it was by foot.

There seemed to be no great scheme to our movement, no particular route that we were following. For Walter, where we were going was always subsidiary to the actual going.

'Never think about destinations,' he advised me early on. 'If we don't know what we're doing, chances are no one else will. Ignorance is survival.'

'I thought motion was survival.'

'You're right!' he exclaimed. 'Perpetual ignorant motion, that's the recipe for staying alive. Don't think, just move.'

And so we moved without actually going anywhere, rather like flies zipping back and forth with no obvious thought or pattern to their zipping. In five years we covered the whole of mainland Britain, as well as enjoying a brief sojourn in Guernsey and an even briefer one on the Isle of Wight (from which we had to make a swift departure after Walter was discovered carving 'Bugger!' into a bowling green in Ventnor). Some places we only visited once, others we would come back to again and again. So far as I can recall, and this is one of the more vague periods of my life on account of the fact that I spent most of it pissed, we visited Liverpool five times, Edinburgh twice, Birmingham, Brighton, Eastbourne and Bude three times each and, for some inexplicable reason, Runcorn in Cheshire 17 times. The latter was a rather grim, red-brick town on the banks of the Mersey and had little to recommend such frequent attention other than the fact that its name made Walter laugh.

'Runcorn,' he chuckled throatily. 'Like something you get on your feet. "Oooh, Mum, I've got awful painsome Runcorns!" Ha, ha, ha! Thank God for places like that. They're like a slap in the face of modernism.'

We would sleep wherever we could find shelter. Sometimes, as I've already mentioned, this would be in barns or beneath hedges. On other occasions we bedded down in, variously, derelict houses, shop doorways, caves, packing crates, hayricks, bus shelters, sheds, greenhouses, abandoned cars and basically anywhere that would offer some measure of protection both from the elements and the legions of spies Walter was convinced were out to get us. In London, the one place we visited more than Runcorn, we frequented a rather bijou little tree house in Epping Forest, whilst I remember with some fondness a night spent curled in the pulpit of a church in Tunbridge Wells, although unfortunately we overslept the next morning and stood up to find ourselves in the middle of a wedding service.

'Three cheers for the bride!' cried Walter to the horrified congregation. 'Doesn't she look a peach!'

Working, of course, was out of the question during those years, since Walter considered any form of employment to be servitude and refused point-blank to submit to the 'noisome tyranny of wage-earning'. He likewise objected to the whole idea of state benefits, convinced they were a sort of financial honey-trap designed to attract and then enmesh dissidents such as ourselves, a conviction he backed up by pointing out that 'State Benefits' was merely an anagram of 'I Be A Fat Net'. We were thus forced to rely on other means to provide for our daily needs.

One of these was begging, although Walter steadfastly refused to consider it such, preferring instead to refer to it as 'fundraising' or 'the eliciting of donations towards the freeing of the oppressed masses'.

'We are not beggars,' he told me early in our acquaintance. 'Beggars want something for nothing. We, on the other hand, are offering a service. People give us money, we fight to set them free. It's a perfectly fair trade. Indeed, I would go so far as to say that we're cheap at the price.'

Whenever we came into a town we would duly scout around for a suitable street corner – 'It needs to be busy,' explained Walter, 'but not so busy that you get lost in the crowd' – and, having found one, would get down to business. A handwritten placard declaring 'Wounded in Action: Please Help', would be placed on the pavement, and my companion and I would then position ourselves to either side of it, me in such a way as to make it look as if I only had one leg, and Walter with his arms hidden inside his coat to give the impression they'd both been amputated. The public responded magnificently, especially when one of us managed to summon up a few tears, and the length and breadth of Britain the pennies came pouring in.

'It warms your heart to see such generosity,' Walter enthused after one particularly successful fundraising afternoon. 'The lamp of goodness burns bright in Doncaster.'

Anything we couldn't afford through fundraising we simply procured through what Walter, with another of his handy euphemisms, described as 'liberating' (i.e. theft).

I was introduced to 'liberating' on only my second day as a tramp. We were walking down a footpath, Walter ahead, me tagging along behind, when he suddenly turned and announced: 'You need new clothes.'

It was a fair point. Whilst red satin trousers and a cheesecloth shirt might have been suitable for my previous life, vagrancy required an altogether different uniform.

'You're probably right,' I replied. 'The problem is, I can't afford any new clothes. What little money I had was spent on currant buns.'

'"Afford" is a word I refuse to acknowledge,' chimed Walter, ignoring my barbed reference to tea-cakes. '"Afford" is an anachronism. There's no "afford" about it. We must do some liberating.'

The rest of the afternoon was duly spent lurking at the bottom of a variety of suburban gardens, sallying forth when the coast was clear to pilfer things from washing lines. In this way I accrued a pair of thick corduroy trousers, two pairs of socks, a polo-neck sweater and a rather nice silk tie which I was able to wear as a headband. In a musty potting shed we found a large grey overcoat and a pair of sturdy, if rather large, wellington boots and, with the unravelling mittens we discovered in a dustbin behind a fishmonger's shop, my outfit was complete.

'Now you look like something proper,' declared Walter, not without a hint of paternal pride. 'A warrior in the cause of freedom.'

The sole reminders of my past existence were The Photo, which I kept in an inside pocket of my new coat, and, of course, The Pill. The latter remained about my neck in its fake-gold locket for several weeks until the locket was pawned to raise funds for a bumper bag of Liquorice Allsorts, after which I secreted it beneath my armpit with a roll of liberated Sellotape.

As well as clothes and sticky tape, we also liberated, amongst other things, pork pies, Cornish pasties, sweets, biscuits, bottles of wine, pen-knives, loo rolls, cigarettes and even an entire mattress from a bedding showroom, although we were forced to abandon it the next day because it was too heavy for us to carry.

'Weighs us down,' said Walter ruefully as we dumped our prize over the edge of a quarry. 'In this life mobility is all.'

Liberating was, of course, illegal, although not, I would like to think, wholly immoral. Walter was very specific about this.

'We are not so much taking,' he opined, 'as exchanging. It's really a form of trade, the only difference being that our fellow traders don't have much say in the matter.'

To this end he insisted that, whenever we liberated something, we left something else in its place. The family who lost their corduroy trousers, socks and polo-neck sweater thus returned home to find themselves the proud possessors of three conkers and a half-eaten sandwich, whilst the wellington boots and overcoat we took from the mouldy potting shed were replaced with a live hedgehog and a bag of stones.

'I reckon that in many ways they come out of the deal better than we do,' opined Walter. 'Some of those stones could be really valuable.'

Although 'fundraising' and 'liberating' more than provided for most of our basic needs, tramping was still a tough, cold, uncomfortable life and would most probably have been an intolerable one too had it not been for one significant diversion – booze.

I have always been a drinker. During my half-decade with Walter, however, I became a real drinker. And by that I mean a *real* drinker. From day one I boozed deeply and indiscriminately, gulping down anything and everything I could lay my hands on. Wine and cider were my staples, but I was just as happy with beer, whisky, vodka, gin, schnapps, brandy, crème de menthe, avocat, cherry liqueur, Drambuie, Babycham and just about any alcoholic beverage you might care to mention, as well as several non-alcoholic ones such as lighter fuel, car de-icer, washing-up liquid and Baby Bio.

It was, of course, an extremely unhealthy way of going about things – car de-icer doesn't half give you a hangover – and once I parted from Walter I reformed my ways immediately. At the time, however, inebriation on that scale, and of that intensity, was quite essential to the lives we led. Without it we could never have stood the freezing winter nights spent sleeping in dank doorways and the backs of derelict cars. Nor put up with the fleas, and the worms, and the damp, and the insults, and the vile, hideous, all-pervasive stench of ourselves. And, of course, most importantly, The World Freedom League would not have been half so active had its duet of members not been so relentlessly and permanently sozzled. Next time you turn your nose up at a drunken vagrant, just remember – he might be fighting for your soul.

The origins of The World Freedom League are shrouded in mystery. Walter claimed it was at least 3,000 years old, and that he was merely the latest in a long line of members. When I pressed him on how he had been recruited, however, he became rather vague, and I suspect the organization was not quite as ancient as he would have had me believe.

Although he never actually said as much – and I certainly didn't confront him with my suspicions – I believe the League actually originated in the early Sixties, when Walter himself had first descended on to the streets.

My companion never said much about how or why or when he had become a vagrant, and I didn't push him, for the subject was clearly a source of some considerable pain. So far as I could glean from various hints and drunken asides, however, he originally hailed from Oxford, where he had owned a small antiquarian bookshop and enjoyed a perfectly normal, rather boring middle-class existence until his wife had suddenly upped sticks one day and run off with the milkman (hence, perhaps, his injunction to avoid dairy products, Rule Four of the 'How to Stay One Step Ahead' manual). After that things had fallen apart somewhat, and after a brief spell in a secure psychiatric unit – the origin, perhaps, of his conviction that some malevolent force is keeping a watchful eye on us – he had embarked on the way of life I've outlined above, The World Freedom League, I suspect, coming into being at much the same time.

Whatever its genesis and underlying motivations, the League was, by the time I joined, a firm and operational reality. Walter claimed it was an international organization, with agents as far afield as Siberia and Patagonia, although I personally saw no concrete evidence to support this assertion.

'Are you in contact with any other fighters, Walter?' I once asked.

'Let's just say there are channels,' he replied with a knowing wink. 'But at this stage the less you know the better.'

Since I never actually progressed beyond 'this stage' I can neither confirm nor deny reports of an active, pan-global revolutionary organization. Walter seemed to believe it existed, and that, frankly, was all that mattered.

The actual creed of the movement was a confusing rattlebag of not entirely complementary philosophies. Marxism, socialism, anarchism, communism, pacifism, Platonism, Sophism, Catharism, Buddhism, Sufism, obscurantism, reformism and Republicanism all got a look in, melded together with a healthy measure of paranoia, alcoholism and outright insanity. A typical rallying speech by Walter would go something along the lines of:

'The people must rise up and claim their rightful inheritance. With increased productivity and free hearing aids for all, we can break out of the abattoir of social debasement and pass through the eye of the needle to the 18 green and pleasant circles of paradise. Women's rights! That's the key! Liberate the woman, and you succour the child within,' etc., etc., etc.

What any of this signified intellectually I haven't the least idea, although it all seemed to make rather good sense after three bottles of crème de menthe and a half-pint of methylated spirits. What it signified practically was an endless succession of mini-assaults on anything that to Walter symbolized 'the tyranny of the ruling class'.

Our targets were legion. Post boxes, town halls, banks, expensive houses, moderately expensive houses, war memorials, statues, museums, libraries and churches all came in for our subversive attentions. Indeed, any structure whatsoever which didn't evince abject poverty and dilapidation – these being the province 'of the downtrodden masses' – was grist to our mill.

We never caused any really major damage; just enough, as Walter put it, 'to let them know they can't have it all their own way'. Thus we never planted any bombs, or started any fires, or in fact did anything to cause more than the most minor inconvenience. Considering the vehemence of Walter's denunciations of the ruling class, this revolutionary sheepishness always rather surprised me, but my mentor saw no incongruity in such gentle acts of sabotage.

'We are messengers, Raphael,' he explained. 'Not monsters.'

Our messages took a variety of forms. Sometimes it would be a brick through a window, sometimes a slogan graffitied on a wall – 'Free the people!' 'We are not slaves!' 'Fuck off, Edward Heath!' – sometimes a small heap of malodorous refuse pushed through a letterbox. If the manager of Barclays Bank in Halifax is still wondering how a pound of tripe found its way into the exhaust of his Morris Minor, I can now exclusively reveal that it was courtesy of The World Freedom League. Likewise, the gift-wrapped individual horse droppings secreted around the fur coat department of Harrods; the pornographic magazines in Canterbury Cathedral; the egg attack on Preston Town Hall; and the stink bomb in the reference section of Weston-super-Mare Municipal Library. All the work of The World Freedom League, and all accompanied by a small scribbled note declaring: 'WFL strikes again!'

Each attack would be minutely planned and carefully, if drunkenly, executed. We did at least one a day, sometimes two or three, and often attacked the same target more than once. Poor old Weston-super-Mare Municipal Library, hardly the most obvious symbol of social oppression, suffered three stink bombs, a urine-filled plastic bag and an unexplained spate of pig's livers in the gardening section, all in the space of a couple of months. I suspect such treatment was actually down to the fact that they once refused to lend Walter their copy of *The Lion, the Witch and the Wardrobe*, but I never said anything. Walter was very sensitive about his motives being questioned.

And so the years went by. We walked, we fundraised, we liberated, we battled the faceless forces of oppression. On and on, day after day, ceaselessly and without rest. And all the while as pissed as pissed can be.

Two years after entering The World Freedom League I discovered, quite by chance, that someone else had been arrested for Keith's murder, thus negating my original motive for joining the organization. I didn't leave, however. Quite the contrary – I remained with Walter for a further three whole years. Not because I particularly believed in what he stood for (I didn't even understand what he stood for, so belief never really entered the equation). Nor because I especially relished the lifestyle to which he'd introduced me. No, I stuck with Walter because deep down I derived an immense and inexplicable degree of satisfaction from watching the Weston-super-Mare Municipal Librarian emerge from her book stacks struggling beneath the weight of a bulging, urine-filled plastic shopping bag. I loved planting dog turds in sweet shops, and spraying graffiti on front doors, and cutting the brake-cables on vicars' bicycles. It appealed to my sense of mischief. It was fun.

But then, suddenly, one day, it stopped being fun. And poor old Walter paid for it with his life.

The beginning of the end came with the hot-air balloon. Walter spotted it first, as we emerged from a supermarket in Hammersmith where we'd been concealing some dead dormice amongst the frozen peas. It was 1976, springtime. Blossom was bursting on the trees and birds were cheeping amongst the blossom.

'Look at that,' cried my companion, pointing upwards into the pale morning sky. 'Just take a look at that, will you!'

'That' was an enormous hot-air balloon, which at that very moment was passing almost directly overhead, about 500 feet up. It was bright red, shaped like a light bulb, and beneath it was suspended a small, barely discernible basket from which sporadic tongues of flame leapt upwards towards the monstrous receptacle above. So far as I could ascertain it was drifting roughly north-east.

Walter was transfixed by the thing. He stopped dead in his tracks in the middle of a crowded pavement and stared upwards at it with a rapt expression on his face, oblivious to the obstacle he was presenting to passing pedestrians, who were forced to eddy to either side of him like water about a large, weed-covered rock. Occasionally his nose would twitch, and he would mutter something unintelligible, but for five whole minutes his eyes never left the enormous red balloon.

'Yes, by God, it's our duty!' he declared at last, his jaw fixed in a rictus of determination. 'We mustn't let it get away! We shan't let it get away!'

'What are you talking about?' I asked, swigging from a bottle of Greek whisky, one of three we'd liberated earlier that morning.

'The balloon!' announced my friend. 'We mustn't let it escape. We must catch it!'

'Catch the balloon?'

'Yes, yes! Run it to ground. Bring it to bay. Corner the beast.'

'Why, Walter? Why must we capture the balloon?'

'Because,' cried my friend dramatically, pointing up at the large red smudge above us, 'it's bad!'

'Bad?'

'Yes. Can't you see? It represents everything we've been struggling against. It's a symbol.'

'It's a balloon, Walter,' I sighed, taking another slug of whisky. 'Just a balloon.'

'Yes, true, a balloon on one level,' he huffed, pulling out his tea-towel and dabbing at his forehead. 'But a balloon whose significance far transcends its simple . . . balloonishness. Don't you see? It's their eye. Their eye in the sky. We must catch it, or they'll never stop looking at us. Come on! It's our duty!'

He grabbed my arm and tried to pull me down the street.

'I don't want to follow it, Walter. You go. I'll wait here.'

'I can't do this alone,' he hissed. 'I need you. It's too big.'

'I'm tired. My feet ache. For God's sake, Walter, it's just a fucking balloon.'

'Please,' implored my companion. 'It's what we've been working towards all these years. Everything up to now has just been a preparation. This is the big one. The climax. Trust me. We have to do this.'

'I don't see—'

'I need you!'

Tears were by this point welling in his eyes, and his hands were shaking. I had never seen him so worked up.

'Please,' he repeated. 'It's getting away. I beg you.'

He seized my hand.

'Please!'

'All right, all right. If it means so much to you, I'll come,' I said, relenting. 'Although I think you're making a lot of fuss about nothing.'

Walter embraced me, jamming my face into his foetid armpit.

'Freedom is many things,' he announced, 'but nothing isn't one of them. Now come on, or we'll lose sight of it. Follow that balloon!'

Which is what we did for the rest of that day, hobbling after it at a painful loping trot, stopping occasionally for a guzzle of Greek whisky, panting and sweating and coughing and choking, road after road, mile after mile, until eventually I passed into a sort of exhausted daze, moving forwards without really knowing what I was doing. And all the while Walter's frantic exhortation:

'Follow that balloon!'

We eventually caught up with it late in the evening, by which point we were both so drained we couldn't have gone any further even if we'd wanted to.

'Can't carry on,' I coughed. 'Got to rest!'

Even as I spoke, however, and as the light thickened and faded and a huge full moon bobbed up in the west, we emerged from a small coppice to discover the balloon descending gracefully 400 yards away into a field behind a high wire fence. We were somewhere on the outer edge of North London, although where, I had, and still have, no idea.

'Gotcha!' wheezed Walter triumphantly. 'The trap is sprung!'

We leaned against the fence and watched as our quarry came down in the field before us. Its two occupants threw ropes out to three men on the ground who scuttled around tethering the basket to a circle of thick iron stakes, into the centre of which the deflating balloon slowly sank. Once down it looked like a large, beached jellyfish, its sack slumped in a hopeless heap, its thin, sinuous tentacles radiating limply all around.

'I'm thirsty,' I moaned.

It was by this time all but dark, and somewhere away to our right a row of streetlights had come on. The five balloon keepers, now no more than a group of shadowy silhouettes, checked their charge, tugged separately on each rope to ensure it was secure, and then wandered off to the far side of the field, where they passed through a gate, locking the latter behind them and disappearing into the night. The moon was now well up, bathing the world in a pale and ghostly luminescence. It was very quiet.

'The hour of reckoning approaches,' intoned Walter. 'Destiny calls.'

'I'm shagged,' I muttered.

We remained where we were for perhaps half an hour, getting our breath back, swigging Greek whisky, and then, at Walter's urging, clambered unsteadily over the chain-link fence and scuttled forwards towards the deflated balloon. It was further away than it had looked, and by the time we finally reached it we were both red in the face and panting heavily. We crumpled to our knees and crawled under the silky, billowing canopy. My head was spinning, and I felt rather sick. I wasn't having fun.

'What now?' I coughed.

There was a loud, snorting sound as Walter blew his nose on the side of the balloon.

'Some graffiti, I think,' he said. 'Have you got the can?'

We always carried a can of spray-paint with us, and I withdrew it from my pocket.

'Excellent,' he sniggered, sending a billow of rancid whisky breath into my face. 'Come on. We need to stretch the balloon out so it's flat. Revolution!'

Wobbling to our feet, and with Walter whispering instructions, we each grabbed a handful of material and pulled in opposite directions as though stretching a sheet, repeating the process at intervals around the edge of the balloon until what had been a shapeless heap of crumpled nylon was transformed into a wide, flat, elliptical expanse of cloth, rippling slightly in the breeze.

'The can!' whispered Walter. 'Give me the can!'

I handed him the spray-paint, with which, bending double, he wrote 'UP YOUR ARSE' in huge letters on the side of the balloon. He stood back to admire his handiwork in the moonlight, and then, crouching down, added 'WFL STRIKES AGAIN' and 'DEATH TO MILKM—', the last word remaining unfinished because the paint ran out.

'That'll show 'em,' he chortled to himself. 'Bastards!'

'OK,' I said. 'We've done what we've come to do. Let's get out of here. Those men might come back.'

I took a few paces back towards the fence but then stopped, realizing Walter wasn't moving.

'What are you doing?' I hissed. 'Come on. Let's go.'

Walter, however, stayed where he was, staring at the balloon. He muttered something to himself and then, reaching into his pocket, pulled out a box of matches. More muttering.

'What are you saying?' I growled. 'I want to go.'

'It's not enough,' mumbled Walter. 'We need a bigger gesture.'

'What?'

'Just a bit of graffiti. It's not enough. This is a chance to make a giant statement.'

'What?'

'We must set it off.'

'What are you talking about Walter?'

'Yes,' he said, his voice rising in excitement. 'We must set it off. Fire her up and let her go. Reclaim the balloon for the people. What a gesture. We'll be household names, like Malcolm Muggeridge!'

He hurried across to the basket and, tipping it over on to its side, began fiddling with the gas tanks.

'I'll get the burner lit,' he said. 'You untie the ropes.'

'What are you saying, Walter!'

'Don't you see? That's why we were drawn here. We've got to inflate the balloon and send it up into the sky. It's all so clear.'

'You have to be joking!'

'No, no. It's our mission. Go and untie the ropes.'

'No way.'

'You have to. It's our duty.'

'I won't, Walter. This is too much!'

I turned and started to walk away, but he charged after me and, seizing me by the shoulder, spun me round. His eyes were burning, and there was a bubble of froth between his lips.

'Untie the damned ropes,' he snarled. 'Just go and untie them. This is important.'

It was the first time he had ever raised his voice to me, and I was unnerved by it.

'OK, OK,' I said. 'I'll do it. Keep calm.'

I stumbled off around the circle of iron stakes, removing the tethering ropes one by one whilst Walter got the burner lit. It hissed angrily, spitting a tongue of blue flame horizontally towards the base of the canopy.

'Christ,' I coughed, untying the last rope and hurrying across to the basket, 'Someone'll see us.'

'No time to worry about that now,' retorted Walter. 'Help me lift the balloon.'

Shaking my head, and fighting back an urge to vomit, I grabbed the lower end of the balloon and heaved it up into the air so that its opening yawned like a large red mouth. Walter, meanwhile, cranked the burners up to their highest setting before joining me at the base of the canopy, where we both stood silently, swathed in material, our arms above our heads, the monstrous balloon undulating beside us like some gargantuan, oversized colon.

'Go on, my darling,' urged Walter. 'Fill up! Fill up!'

For a long while it looked as if nothing was happening. Then, however, slowly, the canopy began to grow and swell, shuffling this way and that across the grass. It rose a few feet, fell, rose and fell again and then, with a great effort, its sides bulging, began to ascend directly upwards into the sky, gathering speed with every foot, dragging the basket up behind it. We backed away, ropes trailing all around us like creepers in a tropical forest.

'We've done it!' cried Walter, raising his arms in triumph, 'Our quest has been fulfilled. The balloon is . . . aaaaaargh!'

This final startled exclamation was a result of my having stepped forward, seized one of the dangling basket ropes and wrapped it several times around my companion's scrawny neck, tying it off with a swift knot and leaping aside as he shot up into the air, eyes bulging, legs kicking frantically. I did this because I was drunk, and because I was tired, and because I was angry at Walter for raising his voice at me. Above all, however, I did it because, standing there in the middle of that field, stinking, smelly, cold and worn out, it suddenly occurred to me that I was no longer happy being a tramp. The whole thing had stopped being fun and turned into a bit of a chore. I wanted out of The World Freedom League, and murdering its only other member seemed the most obvious way of making the point. It was an instinctive action, with little by way of malice aforethought. It just felt like the most appropriate thing to do.

As these thoughts spun dizzily around my head, the balloon, its canopy now fully swelled out, rose rapidly into the sky above me. I could just see Walter tugging at the knotted rope with his hands, swaying madly to and fro, legs flailing. One of his shoes fell off and hit me on the shoulder, whilst, as if to add to the indignity of his passing, his filthy trousers wiggled their way down around his ankles, revealing a pair of luminously pale white buttocks. I heard a strangled scream of 'Spy!', and then he was gone, floating into the face of the huge white moon, up and up and up, away across the rooftops of North London.

'Goodbye, Walter!' I called after him. 'It's been fun.'

I made my way slowly back into central London, polishing off the remaining bottle of liberated Greek whisky and collapsing, sometime around dawn, into an empty doorway halfway along the Strand.

Which is where Emily found me: sozzled, smelly, semi-conscious and swamped beneath five years' growth of hair and beard. Whether it was luck she happened to be passing at that moment, or whether there were deeper forces at work, I have no idea. I looked up and there she was, right in front of me, as young and radiant and beautiful as ever.

'Come on, Raphael,' she said gently. 'You can't live like this. You'd better come with me. I'll sort you out.'

And so she bundled me into the back of a black cab and we drove through the spring morning to Nannybrook House, windows wound down because I stank abominably. And at Nannybrook they seemed to be expecting us, because I was met at the front door by a puffing, red-faced doctor, and taken upstairs and bathed and shaved and examined and swaddled in new clothes, etc., etc., etc. And from that moment on I began as a whole new person.

*

81

One final incident to sign off those incident-packed years with Walter.

On the afternoon of the day I arrived at Nannybrook, as I sat in the dayroom, still acclimatizing to the warmth and cleanliness and comfort of the place, there was a great commotion out on Putney Hill. Fire engines whizzed past, and ambulances, and police cars, and overhead I heard several helicopters whirring. Residents crowded around the windows, thinking perhaps there'd been a car crash. Soon, however, word got out that a hot-air balloon with a naked man tethered underneath had come down slap-bang in the middle of Tibbet's Corner, and, much to the horror of the warden, everyone poured outside to investigate.

Only one person remained behind, and that was me. Not, I should stress, because I felt in any way ashamed about Walter's death. Far from it. Although it had only happened a few hours previously, the whole affair already seemed so distant I could barely connect with it at all. It was part of another world. Another life. I had moved on.

No, I stayed because it gave me the opportunity of moving some counters around in the game of backgammon I'd been playing with Bernie Mtembe. When he returned twenty minutes later it was to discover that a potentially winning position had somehow transformed itself into one that was quite beyond salvage. It was the first in a nine-year run of losses that was to make of Bernie's financial situation something rather less secure, and of mine something rather more, than either of us had ever expected.

'You got me, man!' he wailed. 'I gotta stop this backgammon. You wiped me out!'

# Chapter Five

Something rather disturbing happened earlier. Someone knocked on the door of the castle. There's a big brass knocker, greened with age, and someone banged it. Seven or eight times. Boom, boom, boom, the sound echoing through my home like a series of low, thumping groans. It gave me quite a shock, I can tell you.

No one ever comes up to see me in the castle, except Dr Bannen, but he only ever comes on Friday, and that's not till tomorrow. I know no one else in the neighbourhood – I know no one else any-where, for that matter – so I can't think who it would be. The whole thing's put me on edge. I want to be left in peace to get on with my death. But now someone's come knocking on the door. I feel like my silence has been raped.

I should, I suppose, have gone to see who it was. Told them to go away and leave me alone. I was so surprised by the sound, however, so troubled, so *offended*, that I simply couldn't move. I just stayed exactly where I was at the top of my ladder, pen poised midway through my life with Walter, whilst boom, boom, boom echoed all around me. It stopped eventually, but even when silence had been restored the effects of the knocking remained, like ripples in the surface of a pond, and it was almost half an hour before I could get back to work.

I'm feeling better about the whole incident now. I'm sure it was just a one-off – someone who'd got lost, perhaps, or a wandering Jehovah's Witness. Nothing to worry about. I do hope it doesn't happen again, though. It somehow sullies my enjoyment of my note. Muddies the aura. And things are going so well too.

It's now about 2 p.m, and, aside from the odd wine break and a couple of brief naps, I've been at it for well over 48 hours. I'm still not remotely tired. On the contrary: the longer I stay awake the more awake I feel. My back's a bit stiff, my throat a little sore and my eyes somewhat glazed, but apart from that I feel absolutely fine. More than fine. Wonderful. Reliving my past appears to have imbued my present with a wholly unexpected vigour. I swear that my limbs are loosening, and that my handwriting has speeded up.

I've now written myself into, and about halfway around, the long gallery that occupies the entire eastern side of the castle's ground floor. As you can see, it's an attractive room, high and spacious, with two huge windows peering eastwards across the ocean. Light floods inwards across the parqueted floor, and for a while this morning it was so bright I was able to blow out my candle and work by the light of nature. I've now relit it, however, because the sun's dropped west and everything's become rather shadowy. I can't stop sneezing for the dust.

It was on the threshold of the eastern gallery, at about 6 p.m. last night, just as I prepared to leave the front foyer, that I had something of a brainwave.

There had, up to that point, been little method in my note. I had simply charged ahead, my sole aim being to recount as much of my life as possible in the week or so left me before I swallowed my pill. I wasn't working to any great scheme. I just wanted to get it all down. At no point did I harbour what might be termed *grander* aspirations.

All that changed, however, with my arrival at the doorway of the eastern gallery, an event that coincided almost precisely with the start of my adventures with Walter. For several paragraphs the significance of this confluence of story and location quite escaped me. Only after I had written some nine feet of column on the gallery wall did the possibilities of the situation suddenly burst upon me, like a brilliant flash of light.

Why not, I thought, organize my note so that each murder corresponds to a specific room? Contain it within four walls, confine it to one area, like the galleries of a museum, each charting a particular period of history. That way, as well as being links in a longer chain, each murder could stand as an entity in its own right, part of a story, yet distinct from it. Just imagine! The Walter X Room. The Lord Slaggsby Gallery. The Keith Cream Salon. Places where you could not only read about a death but walk right into the middle of one. Feel it unfolding all about you, like a kaleidoscope of words and images.

'What a brilliant idea!' I yelled to myself, my voice ringing dully around the emptiness of my abode. 'I'm not just writing a suicide note. I'm creating something people can actually experience. A masterpiece of interior decoration!'

Thrilled by my brainwave, I threw aside my pen and hurried up to the dome to think it out properly, pouring myself a large glass of thick red wine to accompany my ruminations.

The obvious difficulty was that I've committed ten murders in my life but have only nine rooms in my castle, four on the ground floor, four, of exactly the same dimensions, above, and one cellar (see plan on north wall of foyer).

This was compounded by the fact that Mrs Bunshop, true to her nature as an annoying old hag, had taken up the best part of two rooms at the start of the note, leaving me only seven rooms in which to recount a further nine killings.

For a moment it looked as if my beautiful scheme wouldn't fit, like a jigsaw with too many pieces. Then, however, it occurred to me that the eastern gallery, and the corresponding room above it, were effectively the size of two rooms rolled into one, and could therefore contain two murders each. On that basis I would be able to shoe-horn the remaining deaths into the remaining rooms, my last murder (which was, of course, my first murder) taking place upstairs in my bedroom. This final death being a relatively short one, I would still have enough wall space left to explain what happened three nights ago with Emily, before concluding my note neatly at the doorway to the roof stairs. It would be a complicated business, and would require careful planning, but it was definitely within the realms of possibility. I whooped in delight, and poured myself another glass of wine to celebrate.

Here, then, is the scheme I have settled upon for my note. No longer a thoughtless, headlong rush into oblivion, but rather an assured procession of words and memories, leading me dignified towards the hour of my decease. In each room will be segment of my past; and between the rooms – in the foyer, and up the stairs, and around the first-floor landing, interspersing my misdeeds like white squares between black on a chessboard – shall be arranged the last days of my present. To keep the two absolutely separate might not be possible. Some murders, after all, are longer than others, and some rooms bigger, so that the past may well end up bursting its banks and flooding into the present, and the present, likewise, could leak annoyingly into a space that was meant to be past. In general, however, if I can create an impression, however flawed, of my past being on one side of a door and my present on another, then I shall have achieved all I want with my note.

'It will be the most splendid note ever!' I exclaimed excitedly, making my way back downstairs and setting to work again. 'The note to end all notes. The note that all future notes aspire to. I might even get in the papers!'

One adjustment that had to be made immediately was a reduction in the size of my writing. Up to that point it had been rather large, each letter the size of a ripe walnut, so that even from a distance, and with eyes as bad as mine, you could still clearly make out what had been written.

To have maintained that size of lettering, however, would have been to eat too quickly into the space I had available, to move along too hurriedly, not merely scuppering my one room/one murder idea, but exhausting the castle's entire supply of wall space before my story was half done.

I therefore decided to telescope my letters, reducing them from the size of walnuts to that of raisins. One can no longer read them from a distance, and the effort of concentration makes my eyes ache and my elbow and wrist cry out in disapproval, but at least I know I'll get it all in. A little further along I might increase the size again, if it's looking like I might come up short of my intended destination. To have space left would be as disappointing as to run out of it.

With my lettering reduced, and my intentions clarified, things really started to flow. My pen rushed across the wall like a skate across ice, the words racking up like line after line of marching ants. It was as if, imbued with a sudden sense of purpose, the note came alive beneath me. As though it were not a note at all, but rather some mythical creature galloping through my castle with little old me clinging desperately to its back. By dawn I had filled all the space between the door of the gallery and its northern wall, by late morning I had completed the northern wall itself and by early afternoon poor old Walter was descending towards Putney Hill attached to a giant balloon and the note had washed up against the first of the gallery's east-facing windows. Which is, pretty much, where I find myself now.

So far, then, things have been going well. I'm enjoying myself immensely, and thoroughly looking forward to dying. I keep bursting into song, anything from Wagnerian arias to Sixties pop hits, and every now and then shimmy backwards from the wall as if dancing, something I haven't done since old haddock-lips arrived at Nannybrook. The Pill sits contentedly in the breast pocket of my pyjamas, alongside The Photo. Every now and then, and rather to my embarrassment, I take them both out and hold them up so they can see what I've done so far. They are, of course, inanimate objects, but I like to think that, in their own way, they approve of my efforts to date.

It hasn't all been plain sailing, of course. Not by a long shot. The further I've got into the note, indeed, the more problems have arisen.

Bottoms, for instance. The bottoms of my columns, that is. I have already mentioned what a strain it is writing up near the ceiling, 15 feet above the ground. It is equally if not more exhausting, however, working at the other end of the wall, down near the floor. Here, in order to bring each column as close to the ground as possible, one is obliged to sink to one's knees and double up as though in prayer, hunching one's shoulders and bending one's arms as each successive line shunts you further and further downwards. By the time you finally hit the skirting board, about a foot from the floor, you're practically standing on your head, and every movement wafts an irritating billow of dust right into your face. Once again I have been tempted to narrow the parameters of the note, but once again have decided against it. The physical discomfort is easily outweighed by the extraordinary impression a wall covered floor to ceiling in teetering columns of writing makes. Without the backache my note wouldn't be half what it is.

Another obstacle has been doorways. The note, remember, is not being written along one continuous expanse of wall. It has corners to turn, and angles to negotiate. It is like a river, bending and twisting and squirming and writhing; and whilst its flow is always mono-directional – i.e. left to right – there are places where its progress is diverted or interrupted, just as with a river, with its rocks and sandbars and eddies and cataracts.

In most cases the confusion isn't too severe. At a right angle – between walls, for instance – it's fairly evident that the bottom of the column to the left of the angle corresponds to the top of the column to the right of it.

Doors, however, present more of a challenge. How, on reaching a doorway, is one to get the note round and into the room beyond without too much disruption to its flow? How is the reader, presuming there is a reader, to know that when the narrative breaks off near the floor on one side of the door it then reappears near the ceiling on the other?

To me it's obvious, but then I'm the author. A complete stranger might get horribly confused, and that won't do. I want my death to be a smooth and fluid progression, not a lurching, juddering struggle from one uncertainty to the next. I want its direction to be obvious and unavoidable, just as, in many ways, the direction of my own life has been obvious and unavoidable.

How, then, to clarify exactly where the note is going? One possibility was to write a belated preface to the whole thing, explaining exactly how it should be read. Something along the lines of 'Kindly remember that whenever this note reaches a door it continues in the room on the other side'. That, however, seemed rather heavy-handed, as did the idea of inscribing 'Please Go Through' or 'Enter!' or 'This Way If You Don't Mind' above every lintel.

In the end I settled for a somewhat simpler option, drawing a long arrowed line from the point where the note leaves off on one side of each door to the point where it reappears on the other. That way, like a fish on a hook, your attention is dragged inexorably from the bottom of one column around the corner and up to the start of the next. It looks a mite clumsy, like something you'd find in a child's drawing book, but at least it does the job. Better to have it clumsy and clear than neat and confused.

I don't want to go overboard about bottoms and doorways. They have presented difficulties, but by no means insurmountable ones. A greater, if less tangible concern, and one that has been causing me substantially more worry, has been memory.

I have always considered my memory to be, if not perfect, at least very nearly so. I have an extraordinary capacity for recalling my past, to the extent that tiny snatches of conversation, engaged in as many as ninety years ago, remain lodged in my mind like fish bones in a throat. Obviously I can't remember *everything* – to retain the entirety of one's history would be as burdensome as wandering around with a full set of *Encyclopaedia Brittanicas* strapped to your head – but most of it's still there, stored away in the distant recesses of my brain like books on the shelves of a library. All I have to do is to think to myself, 'Now, what happened at such and such a time?' and chances are the memory will be there. It might take a bit of looking to find it – if my mind's a library it's an exceedingly badly catalogued one – but I usually get there in the end. Not much has been lost these past hundred years.

Or at least that's what I thought. Now, however, doubts have begun to creep in. For instance, I initially had it in my head that Mrs Bunshop's name was in fact Mrs Burlap. I have absolutely no idea why, nor where the name Burlap came from, but I had already finished her story and moved on to a description of my castle when, like a thunderbolt from above, the truth suddenly burst upon me.

I was, to put it mildly, horrified. I'd murdered the bloody woman, after all. To forget the names of one's victims is the very worst form of impoliteness. Far worse than actually killing them. I had to spend a frantic half-hour going back over everything I'd written, scribbling out all mentions of Burlap and inserting the correct name.

At first I hoped this would just be a one-off, a momentary lapse, which is why I didn't mention it yesterday. Early in the eastern gallery, however, as I described my first meeting with Walter, I suddenly dropped my pen and cried in anguish:

'The Nannybrook warden's a man!'

For some inexplicable reason I'd recalled him as a woman, a rather malevolent female presence, prowling the midnight corridors with a bedpan, tweed skirt and large set of keys. Mistaking a name is one thing. Mistaking a gender, especially that of someone as conspicuously masculine as the full-bearded Norman Stoppard, was an error bordering on senility. Once again I was forced to stop what I was doing and hurry back across the walls, hunting down all references to 'she' and replacing them with a doubly underlined 'he'.

I have, I must confess, been profoundly unnerved by these

mistakes. It wouldn't have been so bad if I'd simply *forgotten* Mrs Bunshop's name, if where that name should have been there was merely a blank. It's not the actual loss of memory that worries me. Rather it is the fact that instead of losing memories I am unwittingly falsifying them. Burlap for Bunshop. Female for male. Minutely altering the tapestry of my past. Pulling out its threads and replacing them with ones of an altogether different colour. Damaging the picture.

This is most alarming. Memories, after all, impart our sense of self; the feeling that we have roots, a past, a journey preceding our present. To falsify that past, however unintentionally, is in a way to diminish ourselves. I don't want to be diminished. I want to be elevated. I want to die knowing where I've come from.

It's four hours later, about 6.30 p.m., and I feel a lot better. I think I got a bit hysterical back there. My handwriting certainly looks like that of a man on the verge of a breakdown, all scrawly and ragged, dipping up and down across the wall like the rails of a roller-coaster.

A visit to the roof, however, has done much to calm me. I watched the winter sun go down, and then sat in the dome for a while, chain-smoking and gazing out across the darkening ocean. It was very quiet, very peaceful, and I felt my concerns melting away. Two mistakes, after all, hardly merit a full-on existential crisis. Henceforth I shall just get on with it. I'll write it down as I think it happened, and if the truth is something completely different, well, so be it. What is truth, anyway? Were Archie or Walter any less real because they based their lives on fantasies? Of course not. It's what you believe that counts.

I believe my name is Raphael Ignatius Phoenix, that I am close on a hundred years old, that I have committed many murders, and that I have in my possession a small round pill that will kill in seconds. I believe I am homing in on my death, like a pigeon homes in on its loft after a long and exhausting flight, and that that death will take place in the dome early on the morning of 1st January 2000. I believe, above all, in me.

And if 'me' should turn out to be a mirage? Well, what can you do?

The alternative would be to ignore myself altogether, which is quite out of the question. The only thing worse than leaving a mistake-ridden account of my life would be to leave no account at all. I insist on posterity. I deserve to be known.

PS. I also have wings.

# Chapter Six

Next before Walter. (Question: Can one actually say 'next before', or does the use of 'next' presuppose a future occurrence rather than a past one? Sounds pedantic, I know, but these things are important. I shouldn't like my masterpiece to appear ungrammatical.) Anyway, right or wrong, next before Walter was Keith Cream, doyen of rock and, so far as I'm, aware, the only person I've ever killed accidentally.

I crossed paths with Keith in the February of 1969, shortly after the killing of Lord Slaggsby. Barely had the wheels of the latter's bathchair stopped turning before Emily had picked me up in her van and driven me south, depositing me a day later in the centre of London. I was clad, of all things, in a pair of candy-striped bell-bottoms and a tie-dyed shirt, and, as is generally the case after I've murdered someone, had not the least idea what to do with myself.

'Goodbye, Raphael,' cried my golden-haired darling as she dropped me off in Soho. 'You look fantastic!'

'Wait!' I shouted, banging on the side of her van. 'I don't know what to do! I'm almost 70, for Christ's sake!'

'You'll be OK. Have fun! Live a little!'

'How in God's name am I supposed to live? Money doesn't grow on trees, you know!'

'Do be careful, Raphael! You'll get run over. Goodbye! Goodbye!'

'Please, Emily! Where are you going?'

She shouted something, but it was lost in a blast of hooting from the cars behind. I grasped despairingly at her rusted bumper and then she was gone, swallowed up in a surge of traffic. Once again it looked like I was going to have to start my life from scratch.

'Bloody damn it,' I muttered, fingering The Pill in my pocket. 'Bloody damn damn it!'

Soho wasn't at all as I remembered it. The last time I'd been there was as a child over half a century ago when it had been a rather drab, nondescript confusion of narrow streets and small shops, peopled in the main by artisans and Italian immigrants.

The scene that now confronted me was rather different. Crowds of people bustled in all directions; music belched from the interiors of garishly lit cafés, and everywhere I looked there were strip clubs and sex cinemas and peep shows and porn shops. I'd never seen anything like it in my life.

I wandered around aimlessly for a while, staring up at the winking neon signs and taking in the unfamiliar clothes and sounds; and then, feeling decidedly disorientated, ducked into a pub and ordered a large whisky. Nothing like a large whisky to settle the nerves.

'Better make it a treble,' I told the barmaid.

She served me, and I looked around for somewhere to sit. Most of the tables were taken, but after a bit of casting back and forth I noticed a space in a smoky booth at the back of the pub and duly made my way over and sat down. To my right a young couple were kissing and fondling each other, whilst to my left sat a morose-looking man in dark glasses, supping a pint of bitter. He had a large moustache, bushy sideburns and a voluminous Afro hairdo, which, sitting as it did atop a livid green shirt, made him look rather like a dandelion. I wondered if I blew at him whether all his hair would fly away.

I'd been ensconced beside the latter for almost 15 minutes when, apropos of nothing, he suddenly spoke.

94

'Keith,' he said, his voice a blur of pained adenoids. Since he didn't actually look at me when he said it, it wasn't immediately obvious to whom he was addressing the words.

'I'm sorry,' I said. 'Were you speaking to me?'

Rather than answering he flipped out a hand in my direction.

'Keith Cream,' he elaborated, adjusting his sunglasses and sniffing. 'As in the music-industry Keith Cream.'

I shook the proffered hand.

'Pleased to meet you, Keith. I'm Raphael Phoenix.'

'That's cool, man. You are who you are.'

I agreed that certainly seemed to be the case.

'I run the Record Roundabout,' he continued. 'Down the King's Road. You probably know it.'

'I'm afraid I don't,' I confessed. 'I've been out of London for quite a while. I've only just arrived back.'

He nodded sympathetically and primped his Afro.

'That's cool, man. I don't judge people. Be as you are now, not what you were then. You dig The Turtles?'

'I can't say I know them,' I confessed.

''Cos I've got some bootlegs in today you can't get anywhere else in Europe. Mint quality.'

'Really.'

'I'm not saying *buy*. I'm just letting you know.'

'I see. Well, thank you.'

'That's cool, man. Cool.'

He slurped his beer, leaving a smudge of froth across the underside of his moustache.

'So what sort of music are you into?' he inquired after a moment's silence.

'Well,' I admitted, 'my tastes have been rather limited of late. It's been Wagner mainly.'

He thought for a moment.

'No,' he said, shaking his head. 'Don't know them. I've got something that might interest you, though. Big Brother and the Holding

Company, pre-Joplin, live in Seattle. It's a collector's piece.'

'That's really very kind of you, but I don't have anywhere to play it at the moment.'

'If you're looking for a cheap stereo I've got contacts. Nothing flashy, mind. Just a good deck, basic speakers. Twenty pounds.'

'I think not.'

'Ten pounds, and I'll throw in a couple of Richie Havens albums.'

'It's really not for me, but thank you anyway.'

'Cool, man. I'm not going to get pushy or anything. You just be as you are.'

We relapsed into silence and sipped our respective drinks.

'Although if you ever want anything by Moby Grape you know where to come.'

He finished his pint and, leaning forwards, fiddled in his back pocket, bringing out a crumpled cigarette packet.

'Smoke?' he said, offering me one.

'Thank you.'

'Been in music for years now,' he went on, striking a match. 'I'm what you might call an industry guru.'

I leaned forward to light my cigarette.

'I'll tell you someone I did rather like,' I said. 'Bing Crosby.'

Keith thought for a moment.

'I thought it was David Crosby?'

'No, definitely Bing.'

'As in Stills, Nash and Young?'

'I'm not sure. He smoked a pipe and made films with Bob Hope.'

'Yeh,' nodded Keith, 'probably the same guy. I've got all their albums back at the shop.'

I sipped my whisky and gazed around the pub.

'Everything seems to have changed so much,' I sighed. 'I grew up in London but now I hardly recognize the place. I've been away longer than I thought.'

'I know where you're coming from, man,' said Keith, nodding his Afro up and down. 'It's like that Dylan song.'

'Is it?'

'Yeh. "The Times They are a-Changin". It's, like, about times changing. You know, one day it's one thing, and the next it's something completely different.'

I told him it sounded very appropriate, and downed the remainder of my whisky.

'Another?' I asked, indicating his empty glass.

'Yeh, man, cool. And see if they've got any nuts, will you? I've suddenly got a real nut thing. Like, I've gotta have them or I'm gonna freak out and die.'

I squeezed my way to the bar and bought Keith's pint and peanuts, and another large whisky for myself. Several people had started dancing, including an extremely large woman in a short skirt, who almost knocked me over as I returned to our seat.

'So tell me,' said Keith once I'd sat down again, 'what're your plans now you're back in town?'

'I haven't the faintest idea,' I admitted, accepting another crumpled cigarette. 'I've got enough money to last a week at a pinch. Hopefully something will come up.'

He shoved a fistful of peanuts in his mouth and washed them down with a long gulp of bitter, smearing more froth across his already sticky moustache.

'I dig your style, man,' he said, wiping his mouth. 'Like, you're a real free spirit. Not like most oldies. You're cool.'

'Thank you,' I said.

'Take it from the guru.'

'I will.'

We raised our glasses and clinked them together.

'I'll tell you what, you don't want to come and see a band, do you? They're mates of mine. Very hip. We all share the flat above the record shop.'

'The Record Roundabout?'

'Yeh, man. You know it?'

'By reputation.'

'Nice one. So how about it?'

'Well, I'd like to, Keith, but I really ought to be finding myself a place to stay.'

'But that's just the point. We've got a spare room in the flat. Marvin's gone into rehab and we're looking for a new lodger. It all fits together, you know, like you coming into the pub now, at this time, looking for a place to stay.'

I sipped my drink and considered the proposition. Keith wasn't, admittedly, the sort of person I could ever imagine myself sharing accommodation with. Judging by what I'd seen of him so far the flat was sure to be noisy, disorganized and, if his taste in clothes was anything to go by, horribly decorated. On the other hand, there didn't appear to be any better options on the horizon and, as Emily had said, maybe it *was* time to start living a little. I therefore knocked back the remainder of my whisky and, not without a shiver of trepidation, accepted his offer.

'Cool, man,' he cried. 'Like, cool-out at the OK Corral. We'll have another couple here and then we'll go. The band's not on till midnight anyway. Single whisky, was it?'

'A treble actually.'

'Yeh, right. Cool. Life in the fast lane.' With which he heaved himself to his feet and wandered off to the bar, returning a minute later to borrow enough money to pay for the round. 'Bit short at the moment,' he admitted. 'Cash-flow problem with my agent in Nashville.'


The band Keith had mentioned were playing at a basement club on Windmill Street. It was a smoky, overcrowded affair, with a bar at one end, a stage at the other and a flag-stoned floor slippery with condensation and spilled drink. We arrived shortly before midnight, just as a group called The Magic Lizards were finishing their set.

'I'll go and tell the others we're here,' shouted my companion over the amplified cacophony. 'You get the drinks in.'

He pushed his way off into the crowd, his Afro bobbing up and down like a beach ball in choppy water, whilst I navigated a path to the bar, where I bought a pint for my new friend and two treble Scotches for myself. I'd barely had time to sip the first of these, however, before Keith was back. He seemed agitated, and was primping his Afro violently.

'We've got a serious situation, man!' he puffed, wiping mist from the lenses of his sunglasses. 'Like big-time serious. Dave's fucked off.'

'Dave?'

'Yeh. Keyboard player with the band. Just upped and fucked off. The group's buggered.'

'Can't you get someone else?'

'Not at this short notice. The others are in a right state. This mine?' He seized the pint and downed it in one.

'I used to play piano,' I said. 'Years ago. A Canadian guy taught me. Nice fellow.'

I only mentioned the fact to make conversation. Keith's reaction, however, was instantaneous.

'That's brilliant!' he cried, throwing aside his cigarette, grabbing my arm and propelling me in the direction of the stage. 'I knew you were in the business the moment I saw you. You've got that haggard, bluesy look about you.'

'No, no,' I protested, 'I didn't mean it like that. I used to play "Knees up, Mother Brown". I couldn't do the sort of stuff they play here.'

'Don't worry, man, it'll be cool. Hurry up, they're on in a few minutes.'

'I can't do it. It's impossible.'

'Nothing's impossible,' he cried, herding me onwards. 'Just look how well Rick Wakeman's done!'

Which is how, twenty minutes later, suitably fortified with several more whiskies, I found myself up on stage tinkling the ivories with what was later to become one of the seminal rock bands of the early Seventies. The crowd were going berserk, Keith was giving me the thumbs-up and I was thoroughly enjoying myself, especially when I looked down to see an extremely pretty girl gazing up at me and mouthing the words: 'I want you.'

'This is the life,' I thought.

The band of which I had become an impromptu member was a five-piece outfit. As well as myself, there was Linus on guitar and lead vocals; Otis on mandolin, sitar and occasional harpsichord; Libby on bass; and Big Baz, one of the fattest people I've ever met, on drums. They had, apparently, all met at art college, and been doing the rounds of the small-club circuit for almost three years now, with little notable success.

Linus was the driving force behind the band. He wrote the songs, sung them and fronted the group, with the rest of us positioned slightly behind him. An emaciated, spotty young man with straggling tendrils of beard and a thick Mancunian accent, he wore the same purple bell-bottoms for the entire time I knew him. I heard that in later years he developed rather a serious drug habit and became, especially during the recording of his nine-hour rock-opera *Hamlet, Prince of Moss Side*, almost impossible to work with. During our brief time together, however, I found him perfectly affable, although if you made a mistake musically he could get very upset.

'You fucked up the middle eight,' he screamed at me more than once during our two-year association. 'Don't ever fuck up the middle eight.'

My memories of our first gig together are somewhat confused on account of the fact that not only was I drunk, but I'd also smoked some cannabis for the first time in my life. I know that we kicked off with 'Love Typhoon', Linus shouting out the chords as we went (Em, C, Am, F, etc.), and did a storming, 15-minute version of 'Quintessence of Dust'. I definitely fucked up several middle eights, and played the whole of 'Song to Doris' in the wrong key (Gm as opposed to Dm), but on the whole I think I acquitted myself reasonably well. Indeed, considering I hadn't been near a piano for the best part of quarter of a century, and prior to that my only musical experience had been playing cockney standards in a German prisoner-of-war camp, my performance was nothing short of miraculous. My fellow musicians certainly thought so. When we finally wound up 'Tangerine Apocalypse' and left the stage they slapped me on the back and duly asked me to join the band.

'Your face fits, man,' said Linus, lighting up a monster of a joint and handing it to me in the backstage cupboard that passed for a dressing room. 'How about it? You wanna be in?'

I smiled, and took a deep puff on the joint.

'Oh yes,' I replied. 'I wanna be in. I definitely wanna be in.'

Indeed how could I possibly *not* wanna be in when the band was so obviously tailored towards a man of my malevolent proclivities. They were, you see, called The Executioners. If that's not a sign, I don't know what is.

These days, it seems, no one has heard of The Executioners. They've been consigned to the scrapheap of musical history and only rock aficionados or collectors of obscure records remember anything about them. Their songs do occasionally pop up on the radio, usually as questions in late-night trivia quiz shows, but aside from a certain kitsch nostalgic value, their contribution to the canon of popular music has been all but forgotten.

In their day, however, they were big. Very big, especially on the Continent, where their incomprehensible lyrics and extended instrumental solos elevated them to near-cult status. When I joined them, of course, they were some way off their prime – at that point, they didn't even have a record deal – but many of the songs that were later to become so popular were already in their repertoire. 'Love Typhoon', the first song I ever played with them, would later spend 31 weeks in the British charts, peaking at number eight, whilst 'Quintessence of Dust', 'Woman, Oh Woman', 'Peace Explosion' and 'Sexual Alchemist' were all destined for the hit parade of the early Seventies. 'Phantasmagoria Elixus No. 3', which I co-wrote with Linus, spent three years at Number One in Macedonia, and was later, apparently, used as a campaign theme tune by President Marcos of the Philippines.

All that, however, was in the future, as were the private jets, the white Rolls-Royces, the trashed hotel rooms and the sell-out concert tours of the world's major sporting stadiums. Whilst I was with the band we were a strictly small-time outfit, playing nothing bigger than clubs and pubs and church halls; and if we did do the occasional gig at a more prestigious venue it was always on a midweek night when there was no one there anyway. Freddie Mercury did once pinch my bottom and congratulate me on my keyboard solo in 'Fruit Surprise', and I remember The Doors standing us a round of drinks after they'd seen us at The Marquee, but on the whole we were no more, nor no less, successful than the thousand and one other small groups doing the rounds at the end of the Sixties.

'Do you think we'll ever make it big?' I once asked Linus.

'Well, we can't make it much smaller,' he replied.

We all lived together – myself, Linus, Keith, Otis, Libby and Baz – in a large, three-storey house on the King's Road, the ground floor of which was given over to Keith's music shop, The Record Roundabout. The latter was a small, dingy affair which, in the two years I knew it, was never once visited by anything that might reasonably be called a customer. People occasionally popped in to ask for directions, or collect for the Salvation Army, or escape from a sudden rainstorm, but they never stayed very long, and displayed not the least spark of interest in Jethro Tull or the latest themed triple album by Frank Zappa and The Mothers of Invention. All day Keith would sit behind his plywood counter, smoking pot and reading his *Record Mirror*, and all day more dust would settle on his sparse album racks and more grime accrue to the already grimy windows at the front of the shop. He did make a sale in early 1970, a bootleg recording of Pete Seeger and The Little Boxes, but by that point he was so stoned he undercharged for the tape and ended up losing out on the deal.

'It's a temporary slump,' he opined optimistically. 'Music's a fickle lady.'

If nothing much happened in the Record Roundabout, the same could not be said for the three floors above it. The flat in which we all lived, with its mouldy maroon carpets and disintegrating furniture, was the scene of a permanent party, and became, indeed, so renowned for its swinging 24-hour-a-day, anything-goes Bohemianism, that one merely had to mention 'The Flat' and anybody who was anybody knew precisely to which flat you were referring.

My bedroom was on the first floor, wedged between the kitchen and the living room. Linus and Baz were on the floor above, as were Otis and Libby, who were a couple and so shared a room. Keith lived in the attic, where he slept on a Lilo and, although he didn't know that we knew, kept a large stash of pornographic magazines secreted beneath the floorboards.

For reasons I never quite understood my room was always the room in which everyone chose to congregate. There was plenty of space elsewhere in the flat, and plenty of other rooms to choose from, but, as if by some irresistible magnetism, flatmates and visitors alike were constantly drawn to my particular bedroom where, once drawn, they would remain for hours and, in some cases, days at a stretch. It wasn't unusual for me to wake up to find myself sharing an eiderdown with five or six people I'd never met before, whilst on more than one occasion I ended up camping out on the living-room sofa because there was no longer any space left in my own bed. Even police raids, which occurred on a weekly basis, seemed to focus exclusively on my room, which was fortunate, because we always kept our drugs upstairs in the bathroom cabinet.

'What is it about my bedroom that makes everybody want to be in it?' I once asked Keith.

'I don't know, man,' he replied. 'It's just got this, like, karma. I reckon it might be on a ley line.'

After all those gloomy, silent years with Lord Slaggsby, this new, relentlessly communal lifestyle obviously took a bit of getting used to. I was particularly concerned that, with so many people about, especially so many stoned people, something untoward might happen to The Pill or The Photo (I could just see someone getting hold of The Pill, mistaking it for speed or something, and ending up having a rather more permanent trip than they'd intended). My killer tablet, therefore, I secured in a heavy gold locket about my neck, where I could keep an eye on it day and night, whilst The Photo I kept about me at all times in the pocket of my trousers.

Once the safety of my most precious possessions had been assured, however, and once I'd got used to the idea of co-habiting with what seemed, at times, like half the population of London, I found I was actually extremely happy in my new life. I enjoyed smoking dope, and dropping acid, and snorting cocaine and dancing all night. I liked being surrounded by young people, and listening to loud music, and wearing colourful clothes and letting my hair grow (Lord Slaggsby had insisted I keep it short). It was fun getting up at four in the afternoon, and eating baked beans out of the tin, and never doing the washing-up, and spending hours on end discussing the meaning of life with people who were so stoned they couldn't even remember their own names. Above all, I absolutely loved having all that sex.

Neither before nor since have I ever made love as often, as vigorously and with such wild abandon as I did during my brief sojourn with The Executioners. Those were crazy, carefree days. Anything went, nothing was taboo. I tried positions that made the Karma Sutra look like a Catholic training manual, and combinations that I wouldn't have dreamed possible had I not experienced them myself at first hand. Up to that point I'd been a strictly one-on-one type of lover. Now, however, I had three-in-a-bed sex, four-in-a-bed, five, six, so many I lost count and we had to spill out of the bed and on to the floor as well. I fucked Angie, and Carrie, and Anita, and Hermione, and Betty, and Mary, and Running Wolf (whose real name was Amanda but who was going through a Red Indian period at the time) and Sadie and Jan – and that was just in a single day. I had sex in parks, sex on trains, sex in swimming pools and, once, sex in Westminster Abbey. I even had a go at kissing with another man, although I didn't do it for long because he'd been drinking sweet sherry and I found the taste objectionable.

And I wasn't the only one to so indulge himself. Our King's Road flat seemed to be in the throes of a near-permanent orgy. Parties invariably culminated with everybody having sex with everybody else, and usually started that way too, whilst Otis and Libby seemed to do little else besides playing their instruments and bonking, often both at the same time. Even Baz got his end away, which, considering his elephantine girth and the multiple sweaty chins that spilled down over the neck of his soiled T-shirt, was a testament to the overwhelming sexual allure of playing in a band.

The one exception to this near-universal promiscuousness was poor old Keith. Although he talked about them at inordinate length, and never ceased to dole out advice as to what turned them on, Keith wasn't very good with women. He was, in fact, disastrous with them. At a time when everyone else was having sex, everywhere, all the time, Keith achieved the near impossible and remained celibate.

This wasn't, admittedly, for want of trying. Whenever we had a party or played a gig Keith went to enormous trouble to dress himself up and engage any attendant females in pithy conversation. Considering the number of parties we had, indeed, and the number of gigs we played, the law of averages alone should have assured him at least some small measure of success.

It was, however, not to be. Women rejected Keith in the same way as human bodies sometimes reject foreign organs (i.e. swiftly and violently). His dark sunglasses, blossoming sideburns, appalling fashion sense and dandelion Afro inspired a sort of instinctive vomit reflex in members of the opposite sex.

'Check out that bird over there, man,' he'd say, nodding towards some pouting lovely on the far side of the room. 'She's been giving me the eye all night. Probably recognizes me.'

'Do you think so?'

'Oh yeh. It's like that in music. Your face gets around. Stay here, man. I've got business in the love dimension.'

And off he'd trot, returning five minutes later with his sunglasses all skew-whiff, having been the recipient of a short, sharp slap around the face.

'Obviously looking for someone a little less successful,' he'd mutter. 'There's no accounting for taste.'

To his credit, Keith never let on that he was in the slightest bit perturbed by these setbacks. The way he talked, indeed, one would have thought he was the most highly sexed man in Britain. Not a day went by without him regaling us with tales of the previous night's frolics, this despite the fact we all knew the previous night he'd gone up to his Lilo early with a cup of Horlicks and a copy of *Record Mirror*.

Only once did the façade drop. We were lying, just the two of us, flat on our backs in the middle of Hyde Park, smoking dope, when he suddenly burst into tears.

'I'm a fucking failure, man,' he wailed. 'A big-time loser.'

'No, you're not,' I consoled.

'I fucking am, man. Compared to me, the worst loser in the world is like a fucking glowing success.'

'Come on, Keith. It's not that bad. Have another toke.'

'Everything I touch turns to shit. I've got failure written all over me.'

'No, you haven't, Keith.'

'Yes, I have!' he screamed, scrabbling to his feet. 'Look at me. Look at me and tell me I haven't got failure written all over me, from head to fucking foot.'

I looked, and was forced to concede there was some truth in what he said. I kept it to myself, however, and instead did my best to ring a more positive note.

'You look cool, Keith. Everyone thinks you look cool. You're our role model.'

'Yeh?' he sniffed.

'You're just ahead of your time, that's all. One day people will see you for the innovator you really are.'

'I guess you're right,' he said, wiping his eyes and puffing up his Afro. 'I guess pain's like the price you pay for being at the cutting edge. It's like that Hendrix song . . .'

Whereupon he launched into an extended homily on why The Jimi Hendrix Experience could never be the same now that bassist Noel Redding had quit to form Fat Mattress, by the end of which his earlier outburst had been quite forgotten.

'I tell you, man,' he droned. 'There's this bird who waits every day at the bus stop outside the shop, and I just know she's eyeing me up. It's the music connection. They can't resist it. I might just do her a favour and ask her out.'

The only thing I enjoyed doing more during that period than having sex, although only just, was making music. Surprising, perhaps, given that I'd never before displayed a particularly melodious bent. (Emily always used to tease me about my woeful inability to sing in tune.) During my two years with The Executioners, however, I discovered, to no one's surprise more than my own, that I actually wasn't that bad a musician. In fact, all things considered, I was rather a good one. It naturally took a few weeks to become fully conversant with the group's playlist; but once I'd found my feet, or rather my fingers, I got on splendidly.

None of our tunes was, admittedly, especially taxing – although the chorus of 'Vermicelli Minefield', all minor 7ths and sustained major 4ths, was a bit of a bugger – and once you'd got to grips with the basic melody there was plenty of room for improvisation and embellishment. Long instrumental solos were a hallmark of the band and, depending on where we were playing and how many drugs we'd done at the time, we could generally be relied upon to string out a reasonably simple tune into something resembling a Beethoven symphony. Our efforts were remarkably well-received, although things did sometimes get out of hand, such as the time at a club in Deptford when I unleashed an hour-long Hammond organ solo, by the end of which the entire audience had either left, fallen asleep or, in one unfortunate case, taken an overdose.

As well as playing keyboards I also supplied backing vocals on a number of tracks, proving particularly adept at the Shoo-be-doo-be-doo-wahs on 'Peace Explosion' and the Tra-na-na-na-nooos on 'Woman, Oh Woman'. I did the scream on 'Psychedelic Psychopath', read the Shakespeare soliloquy on 'Quintessence of Dust' and, most innovative of all, played the three-minute cowbell solo on 'Phantasmagoria Elixus No. 3'. There was some argument as to whether it should be me or Big Baz who did the latter, but seeing as it was I who had suggested the cowbell in the first place the honours eventually fell my way. When the song was subsequently released as a single in the mid-Seventies, long after I'd done for Keith and disappeared into another world, the cowbell was removed, in my opinion much to the detriment of the number as a whole.

We worked hard at our music, and days when we didn't rehearse (in my bedroom, naturally) for at least three hours were rare. Then, of course, we had gigs most nights, which involved loading all our equipment into the back of Otis's transit van, unloading it again at the other end, playing two or three sets, reloading the van, re-unloading it back at the King's Road, lugging everything upstairs into the flat (where it was stored in my bedroom), and then sitting down for a lengthy debrief on the night's performance ('You screwed up the fucking arpeggio on "Love Typhoon", Raph!' Linus would storm. 'It fucked the whole song!') If my hippy life was one of unabashed indulgence, it was also surprisingly hard work.

Not that we minded, however, for in the final analysis the hard work worked. The more we rehearsed and gigged the better we got, and the better we got the more fun we had. All bands, of course, have a high opinion of themselves, but in our case the confidence was not misplaced. We *were* good. Very good. And people eventually began to notice.

It didn't happen overnight. The band had been on the circuit for three years before I joined them, with little evident success, and my arrival heralded no immediate upturn in their fortunes. As the months went by, however, and 1969 slipped into 1970, and then 1970 into 1971, we gradually found ourselves getting offered bigger gigs, at better venues, for more money. We started doing tours around the country (and, once, to Luxembourg); began to get reviews in the music press; headlined on one of the side-stages at the Isle of Wight Festival (albeit the smallest one); and even supported Captain Beefheart when he played the Finsbury Astoria.

Shady-looking men in suits began approaching us and asking if we were looking for a manager (we turned them down). Linus got to do some session work for Marianne Faithfull, and I very nearly played on a Donovan album, although in the end he settled for someone else, which was a relief because I didn't much like his music. There was even talk that we might play at Woodstock, although it all came to nothing.

The band's reputation grew steadily throughout 1971 until, eventually, in the December of that year, to a great fanfare in the music papers, The Executioners were signed, for a record-breaking sum, to Decca, going on to release their first platinum-selling album, *Hymns to the Cosmic Walrus*, the following spring.

By that point, however, I was no longer with them, my place at piano being taken by one Dave Gittens, he being the very Dave whose original departure from the group had been the reason I joined them in the first place.

It was, you see, in the October of 1971, two months before the band's triumphal signing, that I murdered Keith, an event precipitating my departure into an altogether less glamorous life. Not, I should add, that I harbour any regrets. At 71 I was far too old for all that rock-stardom stuff.

Keith's murder was, I freely admit, a tragedy. Not so much because it happened, but rather because it did so at a time when, after years of relentless underachievement, things were finally beginning to look up for him.

The improvement in Keith's fortunes happened at much the same time as, and in large part because of, the improvement in the fortunes of The Executioners. He never actually acknowledged the connection, and we never made a thing of it, but the fact was that our success rubbed off on him, and the better things got for us, the better they did for Keith too.

It started with the bootlegs. Keith had, over the years, built up a sizeable collection of recordings of the band and, as our reputation grew, he began flogging copies of these to anyone who was interested. Word soon got around that if you wanted anything by The Executioners – and these, remember, were the days before the band had actually cut its first record – Keith Cream was the man to go to, and before long he was doing, if not a roaring trade, at least a steady one from behind his plywood counter in the Record Roundabout, paying the rest of us a nominal, and rather paltry, commission on each sale.

'What's important here, guys,' he'd explain, 'is not the financial angle, but what I'm doing for your image. I'm spreading the word. If you think of yourselves as Jesus, then I'm, like, your ten disciples.'

With more and more people coming into the Record Roundabout to buy bootlegs, Keith's other records began to sell too. Albums that had lain untouched for years, their sleeves yellowed with age, now, at last, started to find buyers. Richie Havens went, as did The Turtles, and Big Brother and The Holding Company, pre-Joplin, live in Seattle. He flogged all his Pete Seegers, and most of his Ramblin' Jack Elliotts, and had to order in more Grateful Dead. He even found a buyer for his entire Tiny Tim collection, which, as Keith himself admitted, 'was something I expected to do when, like, pigs began to fly'.

Girls stopped being quite so dismissive of Keith when he tried to chat them up at gigs, aware that he was a friend of the band. Music-industry executives no longer told him to fuck off when he sidled up at parties. He even got his photo in *Music Echo*, albeit with a caption announcing he was Aretha Franklin.

Most dramatic and life-changing of all, Keith found a girlfriend.

Marcie was, admittedly, not the most prepossessing of women. She wore thick bubble spectacles, sported even more chins than Baz, and was the only person I've ever met with legs hairier than Keith's. She was also extremely aggressive, tending to lash out violently with her fists and feet at anybody with whom she disagreed, which, so far as I could ascertain, was everybody.

None of that, however, seemed to matter to Keith, who was utterly devoted to Marcie. And she, in turn, was utterly devoted to him. So devoted were they, indeed, the one to the other, that they had little time for anyone else, so that from the moment they met – at one of our gigs in the Crawdaddy Club – communication between Keith and the rest of us dwindled to next to nothing. Which was just as well, because Marcie didn't like him talking to other people.

Such, pretty much, was the state of affairs that chilly October night of 1971.

Keith was out with Marcie for the evening, as he was most evenings now, and since for the first time in months we didn't have a gig, the rest of us were all crashed out in my room, listening to records and smoking dope. As well as the band, there were ten or eleven other people present, including a bald American poet who kept standing up and reciting his work, which was mostly about dying children and, probably on account of the dope, made us all laugh uproariously.

We'd been thinking of going out to a club, to which end I was wearing my hippest red sequinned trousers and cheesecloth shirt. As the evening wore on, however, and we got more and more stoned, the idea of moving became ever less appealing and was eventually abandoned altogether. Instead we just sprawled around the room, working our way through a large wedge of Moroccan hash and holding a long and at times heated discussion about whether the universe was simply a minute particle in the body of some superior being, which personally I didn't think it was.

Around midnight, by which point The American Poet had, thank

God, passed out in the living room, everyone decided to drop some acid. I, however, wasn't in the mood, and so whilst the others popped their tabs, I went upstairs to get some fresh air.

There was a large skylight in Keith's bedroom through which one could climb out on to the roof, and after downing a glass of water I duly clambered through this, ripping my lovely cheesecloth shirt on the way out. I was extremely stoned by this point, and when I saw the pumpkin at first thought I was having some sort of hallucination. It was only when I'd crawled over to it, and slapped it with my hand, and laid my cheek against its rindy orange skin, that I realized it was for real.

'A pumpkin,' I thought to myself. 'A pumpkin on the roof. Very strange.'

It was wedged in the angle between the slope of the roof and the brick parapet running along its foot. I presumed Keith had put it there, although for what purpose I had no idea. Probably something to do with Halloween, which was only a couple of weeks away. I staggered to my feet, swaying dangerously against the parapet, and, leaning down, tried to pick the giant vegetable up. It was extremely heavy, and it took all my strength to heave it up on to the top of the wall. So huge was its girth I could barely circle my arms around it.

'That is one motherfucker of a pumpkin,' I gasped to myself. 'Jesus.'

I rested for a moment to get my breath back, peering down at the cars passing along the King's Road 40 feet below, and then grasped the pumpkin once again, thinking it might be quite good fun to get it inside the flat and roll it down the stairs. As I was tensing to lift it, however, I was distracted by the sound of voices down below. It was Keith and Marcie, and they appeared to be arguing. Intrigued, I released my grip on the pumpkin and looked down.

'I'm not,' whined Keith. 'I respect you too much!'

'You are!' screamed Marcie. 'You are!'

'No, no, you got me all wrong.'

'Admit it!'

'There's nothing to . . . Ow! That hurts!'

'You're having an affair! I know you're having an affair!'

'No way, babe. Like, no fucking way. Please, not my hair!'

'Who is she? Tell me! Tell me or I'll rip your head off!'

There was a loud thud and, leaning dangerously far out, I saw, by the light of a nearby streetlamp, that Marcie had grabbed a handful of Keith's hair and was repeatedly banging his head against our front door. His sunglasses had fallen off, and he had his arms over his face to ward off her blows.

'It's you I dig!' he kept shouting. 'You're my girl!'

'Tell me!' screamed Marcie. 'It's Libby, isn't it! Oh God, I want to die!'

The banging continued for some while until, suddenly, in a manner no less violent than that she had recently been employing to berate her lover, Marcie seized his frightened face, pulled it towards her and jammed her mouth on his. Keith responded, throwing his arms about her ample waist and hugging her to him, Marcie treading on his sunglasses in the process. I could hear the slurp of their kisses, and Keith's muffled refrain of:

'I dig you too much to shag around, Marcie. I, like, dig you too much, babe.'

I watched them for some while, fascinated, as naturalists are by mating elephants or rare breeds of shrimp, wondering what it felt like to kiss Marcie, and whether she was as aggressive in bed as she was out of it; and then, rather repelled by the thought, turned my attention back to the pumpkin, hugging it to my chest, bending my knees and hoisting it off the parapet.

My intention was to swivel round, shuffle back to the skylight and drop the vast fruit through on to Keith's Lilo, which was on the floor directly beneath. Unfortunately, as I turned, I somehow lost my footing, crashing sideways against the slope of the roof and, in my desperation to break my fall, releasing the pumpkin, which thudded down on to the edge of the parapet. For a moment it wobbled back and forth as though undecided which way to fall. Then, however,

113

as though in slow motion, it rolled outwards into space and down, plummeting earthwards like a small orange comet. There was a hushed silence, and then what sounded like a loud squelch, followed closely by an ear-piecing scream.

I pushed myself upright, cursing, and peered over the edge, hoping the pumpkin hadn't hurt anyone. Unfortunately it had, for with a degree of accuracy I could never have achieved had I been aiming for it, my pumpkin had landed slap bang on top of Keith's head, the latter disappearing right inside the monstrous fruit as though into a large diving helmet. Amazingly, considering the weight of the thing and the speed at which it must have been travelling when it hit him, he was still on his feet, tottering to and fro across the pavement whilst Marcie, her face and clothes covered in freckles of pumpkin pith, screamed hysterically and tried to wrestle the rindy sphere off her lover's head. They continued thus for some seconds, swaying back and forth as though engaged in some bizarre dance, before Keith eventually slumped to his knees and, arms twitching manically, pitched face forward on to the pavement, dead, the pumpkin hitting the concrete with a resounding thud. Marcie's screams redoubled, and a crowd began to gather.

'Oh shit,' I mumbled. 'Oh shit.'

My immediate thought was to get out of the house for a bit and clear my head.

With a quick pat to ensure The Pill and The Photo were safe, therefore, I clambered back through the skylight, descended to our front door and slipped unnoticed out on to the street. Several police cars had by now arrived, and an ambulance. Marcie was still screaming loudly, and punching at a Chelsea pensioner who was trying to console her.

'Oh shit,' I mumbled, hurrying into the night. 'Oh shit!'

I didn't really know where I was going, and wandered aimlessly for an hour before eventually finding myself in Trafalgar Square. My head felt thick and woozy and, crossing to one of the fountains, I dunked it in the icy water, leaving it submerged for almost a minute before throwing it back and shaking a shower of droplets into the cold night air.

Which is when I noticed Emily, sitting between the paws of one of the ornamental bronze lions, her golden hair shining in the pale moonlight.

At first I could hardly believe it was her.

'Emily!' I cried, running over and standing at the foot of the plinth upon which she was seated. 'Emily, is that you!'

'Hello, Raphael.'

'Well, don't sound too surprised, will you!'

'I'm not surprised. I've been watching you since you came under Admiralty Arch. Come up and sit beside me.'

I struggled on to the plinth and stretched out at her side.

'It's unbelievable,' I said.

'What is?'

'Meeting like this, of course. It must be the biggest coincidence since . . . well, since the last time we met. I always seem to bump into you after I've . . .'

'What?'

I was going to say 'killed someone', but, of course, Emily knew nothing of my murders, and I thought it best to keep it that way.

'After you've what?' she repeated.

'Been thinking of you,' I said quickly. 'You always seem to pop up right after I've been thinking of you.'

'Perhaps you conjure me up, like a spirit,' she laughed. 'Perhaps I'm your magic genie.'

'You're my love, Emily,' I said, taking her hand. 'I love you. I miss you. I can't live without you.'

She put her arm around me and I snuggled down beside her.

'What rubbish you talk, Raphael. You've always talked rubbish. I don't know why I put up with you.'

'It's because you love me too.'

'Do I now!' she laughed.

'Marry me,' I said, closing my eyes. 'It's not too late. I'm only 71. And you don't look a day over 18.'

'Flatterer.'

'I'm serious.'

She tickled my nose.

'Not tonight, Raphael. But thanks, anyway.'

I pressed my head against her thigh.

'Where have you been these last couple of years?' I asked, breathing her in.

'Oh, here and there. Nowhere exciting. You seem to have been enjoying yourself.'

'Yes,' I sighed. 'I've had a lot of fun. I've been a pop-star, you know. I'm feeling a bit rough now though. God, I feel rough.'

She said nothing, just shifted a little closer. The sound of her breathing lulled me, and although I tried to stay awake, to make the most of the few moments we had together, it wasn't long before I'd drifted off. And then, when I awoke, she was gone. And in her place . . . Walter. Poor Walter, his chin cupped in his hands, peering soulfully upwards at the greying sky of dawn.

'You're on my lion,' he said.

Another day. Another victim. Another life. Off we go again.


A little story to end a story; another of those bizarre coincidences that pepper my life like rivets down the hull of an ocean liner.

Two years after the events described above I was lurking among the book stacks of Weston-super-Mare Municipal Library, looking for the best place to secrete a turd-filled paper bag, when I noticed an open book lying on a nearby table. Had it been any other book, or any other page, I would doubtless have ignored it. This particular one, however, caught my eye, prompting me to put the turd back in my pocket and go over and look. There was, you see, a photo of Marcie on it.

The book, a slim volume, was entitled *Lady Murderers of Our Time* and, in a chapter entitled 'The Black Widow of Rock' recounted the strange story of Marcie Goodfellow. The latter, I discovered (not entirely to my surprise), was a 'psychopath in the classic mould', who'd been in the habit of picking up unsuspecting men at rock concerts, wooing them and then bumping them off. She'd been doing this for several years, and might well have continued for several more had she not been foolhardy enough to commit her final murder in so eye-catching a manner (i.e. by slamming a pumpkin down on her victim's head) and in so public a place (i.e. the middle of a busy London street). At her subsequent trial she had pleaded guilty to six counts of murder, although she always maintained she was innocent of the death for which she'd actually been arrested, insisting the offending pumpkin had simply dropped out of the sky. No one believed her, however, and she was committed for an indefinite term of detention to a secure unit for the criminally insane.

I read all this both with interest and, also, with some considerable relief. Not just because it got me off the hook for Keith's death, but also because it unburdened me of any lingering feelings of guilt I might have harboured about the affair. He was going to be murdered anyway, I thought to myself. All I did was speed the process up a bit. Indeed by dropping the pumpkin I'd probably actually saved lives. God knows how many people the black widow of rock might have gone on to murder had she not been arrested that night. The whole thing made me feel quite good about myself, and I set off to plant my bag of dogshit with a carefree step and a big smile on my face.

# CHAPTER SEVEN

I DECIDED I HAD wings at about the age of four, although I'd suspected as much almost from the first moment I was capable of
thinking of such things.

Most children, of course, at some time or other, imagine themselves possessed of magical powers. In my case, however, it was more
than mere idle speculation. I *do* have wings. Or, at least, two small,
knotted humps at the top end of my back, to either side of my spine,
which I certainly know contain wings. Folded-up wings, ready to
burst out and flap at the appropriate moment.

I've possessed these humps since birth. Father once took me to see
a doctor about them, the latter pronouncing, with a lack of insight
typical of the medical profession, that they were, in fact, simply misshapen bones. I know better, however. I know they're wings.

They've never hurt, my wings, nor ached, nor, indeed, done very
much at all. They are simply there, folded up, waiting. I never talk
about them. Even Emily, who knows more about me than any other
person in the entire world, doesn't know about the wings. To look at
me, you wouldn't even think I had them. They're my special secret.

I still hope they might come out one day, although I suspect it's
now too late and after all these years they've probably shrivelled up
and withered. I never stop dreaming, though. It would be nice to fly,

if only for a moment. Life on the ground can be so dull and painful. I yearn to ascend to some greater contentment.

It's early afternoon on the fourth day of my note and I'm still feeling in tip-top condition. In even more tip-top condition than I did yesterday, when I in turn felt even more tip-top than the day before. As each hour passes I feel like I'm getting younger. I'm now scuttling up and down my ladder like a circus performer, and find that stretching upwards to reach the top of each wall, and crouching downwards to reach its bottom, no longer strains me as much as it did when I first started. Even my eyes are improving. This morning I was able to dispense with my candle for almost four hours. Things are becoming clearer.

I'm still hardly sleeping, although I have had a couple of half-hour snoozes up in the dome. It's almost as if, anticipating the eternal sleep into which I'll soon be pitching myself, my body is determined to make the most of what wakefulness it has remaining. I've never felt so alive. My eyelids are light as ether; my mind as sharp as a scalpel blade.

So far, my plan to coincide specific murders with specific spaces seems to be working pretty well. Walter's story slots neatly into the left-hand side of the eastern gallery, Keith's the right, with the door and windows acting as buffers between the two narratives. I've further emphasized the fact that they are two separate periods in my life by scoring a pair of thick lines across the dusty parquet flooring thus:

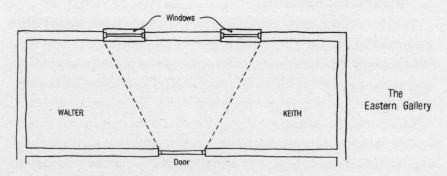

119

My account of the events of yesterday, meanwhile, fitted almost perfectly in the space between the two windows. It brings warmth to my heart to see note and architecture working in such close harmony.

Now, however, I have left the eastern gallery and, candle strapped to forehead, wax sploshing downwards across the bridge of my nose, am back in the gloom of the castle foyer.

There haven't, thank God, been any more memory crises like those of yesterday. A few slip-ups, yes – the chords to 'Love Typhoon' were, of course, Em C Am G, as opposed to Am F – but nothing too disastrous. Seven days from my hundredth birthday, I think I'm entitled to forget some things!

Indeed, as if to expiate its earlier misdemeanours, my brain has been throwing up not just those memories relevant to the task in hand, but ones I didn't even know I possessed in the first place.

For instance, way back by the gallery windows, just prior to my encounter with Keith Cream, you may recall my shouting to Emily: 'Money doesn't grow on trees, you know!' It was simply a turn of phrase, a chance remark. But then, as I wrote it, I suddenly remembered that as I child it had been my firm belief that money *did* grow on trees.

In the garden of White Lodge, you see, there was an old plum tree, whose branches in spring unleashed a snowstorm of blossoms across the lawn. My father told me this was a magic tree, and that as well as producing big, fat, purple plums, money also grew amongst its branches.

'No, it doesn't,' I would say.

'Oh yes, it does,' he'd chuckle. 'Look!' And he'd reach up into the leaves and bring down a bright ha'penny piece clutched between his fingers. It was a simple trick, of course, the ha'penny having been concealed in his hand before he raised it, but it never failed to convince me.

'More!' I'd cry. 'More!'

And he'd reach up again and pull down a succession of pennies and sixpences and shillings and farthings whilst I ran around trying to see precisely where he was picking them from. And he'd do the same thing with jelly babies and cigarette cards and marbles, until eventually I informed Mrs Eggs, our housekeeper, that there was no need for her to go to the shops any more because everything she might possibly need could simply be plucked from branches of the magic tree.

Some memories we know we possess, just as a librarian knows what books are kept in the library of which they are in charge. I know, for instance, that if I really thought about it I could dredge up a recollection of my first full day at Simsby's Banking and Financial, or of the night I lost my virginity, or the afternoons I played tennis with Charlie Chaplin. They might not be at the forefront of my mind, but I know these memories exist, somewhere, waiting to be called upon if need be. I remember that I have them.

There is, however, another class of memories, and those are the forgotten memories. The lost memories. The memories we had no idea we possessed in the first place, languishing deep within the repository of our minds like long-lost toys amidst the bric-a-brac of a dusty old attic.

The money tree is one such memory. Since the waning of my childhood it hasn't once entered my mind. It's been all but eradicated. I wouldn't have remembered it even if I'd wanted to.

And then, suddenly, there it was, popping up unbidden like a bubble in the middle of a millpond. Why it should appear now, at this time, with no warning, I have no idea. After all, I must have used the phrase 'Money doesn't grow on trees' dozens of times previously without it triggering that particular recollection. I feel like an actor who, having rehearsed a play a hundred times, suddenly finds it's sprouted an entirely new scene. My life, it would appear, is larger than I remember it.

This is all very exciting. It does, after all, turn the note into something of an adventure. Who knows what's waiting to happen in my past? Who knows what thrills are there to be discovered? Maybe there are daring escapades to be relived, exotic beauties to sleep with, distant places to visit. Maybe I once buried a large chest of treasure on some deserted beach, completely forgot about it, and am now on the point of miraculously recalling its whereabouts. The past, it would seem, is every bit as mysterious as the future, every bit as uncertain and pregnant with opportunity. I might only have seven days left in front of me, but behind there's a whole life waiting to be lived.

For the moment, however, I've no time for any more memory adventures, for the crunch of tyres on gravel and the tooting of a car horn alerts me to the arrival of Dr Bannen with the weekly provisions. I must remember to order a bottle of good claret to kill myself with. See you later.

Dr Bannen, as I have already mentioned, is the local quack. I believe his first name is John, although I'm not a hundred per cent sure and, frankly, don't really care. For 15 years I've only ever addressed him as Dr Bannen, and see no reason to get more familiar at this late stage in the proceedings.

A big, red-faced man, with broad shoulders, a slightly off-centre nose and hypnotically large eyebrows, Dr Bannen is not, it must be said, the ideal advert for the profession to which he belongs, suffering as he does from the most appalling infirmity of the lungs. Whether this is because he smokes too much, or has some sort of allergy, I can't say. He is, however, constantly wheezing, peppering every sentence with an unsavoury array of pants and gasps and puffs and coughs. Even at his least wheezy he still sounds like he's got a Brillo Pad lodged in his oesophagus, and the pleasure of receiving my weekly supplies is always tainted by the fear that he might suddenly keel over and suffocate in the middle of giving them to me. I've often wondered whether I should enrol myself on a first-aid course, just in case.

He's a perfectly friendly man, somewhere in his mid-fifties, married with three children and born and bred in the village, where he's now practised medicine for the best part of 30 years. He is, I gather, a leading light in the local rotary club, and numbers amongst his interests golf, the *Times* crossword puzzle and tropical fish. Aside from that, there's not really a great deal to say about him. He wouldn't, I suspect, write a particularly engrossing suicide note.

Dr Bannen is the only person on earth with whom I have any contact these days. In 15 years I've neither seen nor spoken to a single other soul. It was Dr Bannen who helped me move into the castle when I first arrived, and it's Dr Bannen who keeps me up to date with events in the outside world (or at least events in the village, which, so far as he's concerned, is the only part of the world that really matters). I suspect he thinks I'm batty, although he never actually says anything. I have noticed, however, that his wheezing tends to increase whenever I come close to him. I once brushed a greenfly from his shoulder and he coughed for upwards of two minutes.

Every Friday Dr Bannen's Land Rover comes clattering up the track from the village, bringing my supplies. I think he only intended this to be a temporary arrangement whilst I settled into the castle after first arriving, but it's somehow become a permanent fixture and I am now reliant upon him. I suspect he'd like to stop doing it, but he's too good a man to say so, and I'm too bad a one to give him the choice. He always comes at 3 p.m., never earlier, never later, and his visits have become the one fixed point in my otherwise timeless existence. Today, as always, he arrived on the dot, pulling up on the swathe of grass in front of the castle and tooting his horn to let me know he was there.

'Good afternoon, Dr Bannen!' I called, issuing from my abode and pulling the door to behind me. 'Cold weather we're having.'

'It certainly is,' he wheezed, clambering from the car, pulling open its rear doors and removing a box of goods. 'I reckon we could be in for some snow soon. On the doorstep OK?'

'Yes, yes. Absolutely fine. Just put it down anywhere.'

He struggled towards the door, looking at me out of the corner of his eyes, taking in my ink-stained white pyjamas, dusty feet and wax-encrusted face. He was clearly troubled by my appearance, and I could hear his wheezing getting thicker by the second. He didn't say anything, however. Like all medics, Dr Bannen plays his cards very close to his chest.

'We had the most beautiful sunrise this morning,' I said, endeavouring to put him at his ease (it is, I find, always the patient who has to calm the doctor rather than the other way around). 'And an amazing sunset last night too. Huge and red it was, like molten rock. It's as if nature's gearing up for the new millennium, don't you think? Putting on a firework display all of its own.'

He looked at me uncertainly, struggling to fathom my meaning. Dr Bannen, I fear, has never quite got to grips with the way my mind works.

'I read it was something to do with ozone,' he puffed. 'Too many armpit sprays or something. Damaging the atmosphere.'

'Well, if that's damage, let's have a bit more of it!' I laughed. 'Lots more of it. The more damage the better!'

He reached the door and deposited the box on the front step, before gasping his way back to the van and picking up another load.

'You're looking well, Mr Phoenix,' he remarked, steering the conversation back on to firmer ground. 'Extremely well.'

'Are you suggesting I didn't look well beforehand, Dr Bannen?' I teased.

'No, no, not at all. It's just that you seem . . . well, more sprightly. If I didn't know better, I'd say you were getting younger.'

'Is that so! Well, I'm pleased to hear it. Don't worry, I'll get the last one.'

I pulled the remaining box of supplies from the back of the car and carried it over to the door. Dr Bannen had already deposited his second box on the step and was recovering an errant tin of peaches that had dropped out en route.

'Doing anything for Christmas Day?' he asked, replacing the tin in its box.

'Oh, nothing really,' I replied. 'Just a quiet one, as usual. You?'

'We'll be down at Elsie's mother's,' he said. 'She's a bit gaga these days, so we don't like to leave her alone. It should be nice and peaceful, though her cats wreak havoc with my chest.'

Whereupon, as if to emphasize the point, he launched into an extended fit of coughing, his lungs emitting the most frightful hacks and gargles so that a pair of seagulls, sitting on the battlement above, took fright and, leaping into the air, flapped away up the coast at top speed. So bad did the fit become, and so uncontrollably did his body vibrate under its onslaught, that he was forced to lean forward and place both hands against the castle wall lest the violence of his coughing should knock him right off his feet. Bent double like that, his shoulders heaving up and down, he looked rather like Sisyphus toiling uphill with his giant rock.

'Are you all right?' I asked, concerned.

He nodded his head.

'It'll huh huh huh huh go away in a minute.'

'Should I slap you on the back?'

'No!' he spluttered, his wheezing redoubling at the prospect of physical contact. 'Just huh huh huh huh a minute.'

He continued juddering and snorting for some while, and I was beginning to wonder whether I shouldn't bundle him into his Land Rover and convey him down to civilization when, as suddenly as it had started, the fit came to an end. Aside from his face being a dark shade of magenta, and very sweaty, he appeared otherwise unaffected.

'Sorry about that,' he puffed. 'Now, where were we?'

He straightened his shirt, the collar of which had gone rather askew, and walked stiffly back to his vehicle, slamming shut its rear doors. He then took a notebook from his pocket and, with an old pencil, began ticking off my supplies.

'That's ten bottles of wine, five white, five red, 200 Embassy – you really should cut down your smoking, Mr Phoenix – two pints of milk, two loaves of bread, 3lbs of potatoes, a pound of cheese—'

A sudden, rapid, unexpected cough forced him to stop mid-sentence. He stood stock still, shoulders braced, eyes swivelling suspiciously to left and right, waiting for the inevitable onslaught that the cough appeared to herald. The latter thankfully failed to materialize, however, and after breathing very slowly and very carefully for a moment, he sighed with relief and continued with the list.

'. . . six eggs, two onions, five tins of curried mackerel fillets, two tins of peaches in syrup, two Battenberg cakes and a packet of garibaldi biscuits.'

'Perfect,' I said.

A broad smile broke across his face. Dr Bannen is one of those people for whom there are few greater pleasures in life than compiling long lists of things and then reading them out correctly in public. He looked as proud as a child who has just won an elocution prize at school.

Having confirmed that he'd delivered the correct groceries, Dr Bannen then handed over my pension money – he collects my cash weekly for me from the local post office – whereupon I handed most of it back to pay for the items he'd just listed.

'I'm thinking of buying myself a yacht,' I joked, indicating the paltry heap of change left in my hand.

Dr Bannen smiled awkwardly, as he always does when I make a joke, and then dived once more into the sanctuary of his pocket notebook, as if to seek safety therein from my uncertain humour,

'Now,' he said, leafing through its pages until he came to an empty one. 'What will you be wanting for next week?'

Given that next week I intended to kill myself, additional groceries weren't strictly necessary. I couldn't very well tell Dr Bannen that, however, or he'd have done something annoying like contact the social services, or send the local vicar up to talk me out of it. I therefore thought it best to simply carry on as normal, and duly ordered exactly the same supplies as I had the week before.

'There is just one thing,' I added. 'I need a bottle of good wine. Very good wine. Claret.'

'Having a celebration, are we?' he wheezed.

'You could put it like that.' I smiled. 'Yes, that's just what it is. A celebration.'

'Well, there's one of those specialist wine shops in town,' he went on, 'so I could get you something when I'm next in. Anything particular?'

There were, indeed, many particular wines I would have liked to kill myself with. A Margaux 1900, for instance. Or a Lafite 1920. How wonderful it would be, I mused, to settle down in my dome on the night of my death, pill in hand, stars blazing above me, and to ease my going with a glass or two of Haut-Brion 1919 or a Le Pin '66. The thought of it set my mouth watering, and sent a shiver of pleasure down my murderous old spine.

The chances of Dr Bannen finding such superlative wines at such short notice, however, even in a specialist wine shop, were not good, and even if he could I probably wouldn't be able to afford them. I therefore decided to lower my sights a little, and instead asked him to purchase any claret with a price tag of over £30.

'If you can find a Grand Puy Lacoste '78 or a Troplong Mondot '82, all the better,' I told him. 'Otherwise, whatever you can find.'

'You do know your wines, don't you!' exclaimed Dr Bannen as he scribbled these two names down in his notebook. 'For myself, I just like a nice glass of Blue Nun with a couple of ice cubes. Although those Bulgarian reds are very drinkable.'

'A little too sour for my liking,' I admitted.

'Well, each to his own, Mr Phoenix,' he said. 'Anyway, I need to be off. Elsie doesn't like to be left alone in the surgery for too long. Gives her the jitters.' (Dr Bannen always signs off with these particular words and, although he says them with great earnestness, I'm not entirely convinced they're true. From what he's told me of Mrs Bannen, she doesn't sound at all like the sort of person who'd get jittery and, although I'd never say as much, I suspect he's merely using her as an excuse to get away from me as quickly as possible.)

'Right you are, Dr Bannen,' I said, standing back as he clambered into his Land Rover and slammed shut the door. 'Be seeing you next week.'

He started the engine.

'Merry Christmas, Mr Phoenix!'

'And the same to you, Dr Bannen.'

He waved his hand and reversed round in front of the castle, pointing his vehicle downhill. Suddenly, however, he cut the engine and, leaning down beneath the passenger seat, pulled out a large bowl with a cloth over the top. He wound down his window and passed the bowl out.

'I'll forget my own head one of these days,' he panted. 'Elsie asked me to give this to you. She doesn't like the thought of you up here all on your own at Christmas. I said, "He's perfectly all right. He just likes a bit of privacy," but she insisted. It's a plum pudding.'

'Why, thank you, Dr Bannen,' I said, taking the proffered bowl. 'And please thank Mrs Bannen. That's a very kind thought. I shall enjoy eating it. I don't think I've had a Christmas pudding since . . . well, for a good few years now. Thank you. I'm touched.'

'Happy holiday!' he wheezed, restarting the engine, putting the car in gear and clattering off downhill in a swirl of dust, tooting his horn as he went. As always, I felt a certain relief that he had gone, leaving me once again to the luxury of my solitude. Also, however, a slight despondency. Sometimes I get just a little bit lonely in my aloneness.

I carried my plum pudding into the castle – it really did smell very good – and then one by one brought in the boxes of provisions, placing them side by side on the rickety old table in the kitchen. It was as I picked up the last of these that I had a curious feeling I was being watched. Why, I don't know, some sixth sense perhaps; but I had the distinct impression that someone, somewhere, was observing my movements. A slight shiver rippled down my spine.

Still holding the box, I screwed up my eyes and looked back and forth across the hills that rise behind the castle like the billows of a large green duvet, scanning them for anything out of the ordinary.

All seemed as empty and peaceful as ever, however, and, concluding I'd been imagining things, I was just turning to go back inside when something hit me in the buttock.

'Ow!' I yelled, spinning round. 'What the fuck—!'

On the ground at my feet lay a small, round, white pebble. It definitely hadn't been there a moment ago (I know all the ground within ten feet of the castle entrance like the back of my own hand) and was clearly the thing that just had hit me. I stooped, picked it up and then, casting my eyes rapidly over the undulating beds of bracken that come to within 20 feet of the castle door, I hurried back inside, slamming and locking the door behind me.

Someone had attacked me, and I had no idea who.

I'm now back at the foyer wall, writing down the left-hand side of the kitchen doorframe. I can't get that bloody stone out of my mind, nor the thought that it is in some way connected to that mysterious knocking on the door yesterday. I want these things to stop. Suicide, after all, should be about a diminution of irritants, not the introduction of new ones.

The sun is fast sinking westwards, and it's now very murky in my front vestibule. I've got the electric light on, and have a new candle strapped to my forehead, the latter's flickering flame sending smudged fists of shadow punching up and down the wall before me. My cheeks are hardening beneath a layer of wax; the squeak of my pen echoes about the empty interior of my home. I'm slowly getting back into my rhythm after the shock of the stone. My work is soothing me.

In about two lines' time I shall curl around the corner into the kitchen and get going on the murder of Lord Slaggsby. Before I do, however, I ought to say something I've been meaning to for a couple of days now. It is this: I ABSOLUTELY BLOODY LOVE MY NOTE!!!

# CHAPTER EIGHT

THE LONGEST I'VE ever gone without murdering anyone is 24 years, a period that began in 1945 after the deaths of the albino twins, and terminated, literally, in 1969, with the killing of Lord Slaggsby. So protracted was this era of peace and tranquillity and goodwill to all men, and so wholly uncharacteristic, that I seriously began to wonder if perhaps my murdering days were over. If I'd finally run out of steam.

Of course, it didn't work out like that. And I have to say, in retrospect, I'm glad it didn't (although Walter, Keith, His Lordship and Mrs Bunshop probably aren't). If I'd stopped murdering in 1945, after all, I wouldn't have left myself nearly enough material to fill all the walls of my castle. It's almost as if, subconsciously at least, I kept bumping people off simply so as to be able to write a good suicide note.

I had expected my journey home from Germany in April 1945 to be a tortuously slow one. The war, after all, was still raging, and all was turmoil and confusion. Thanks to Emily's official-looking document, however, I got back faster than I could possibly have hoped. I had merely to wave the thing and people literally fell over themselves to help me, so that barely three days after setting out from Bremen I found myself stepping off a troop ship on to Dover docks, the white cliffs towering above me, bright and welcoming in the morning sunlight. For me, at least, the war was over.

I spent six weeks in a comfortable, if rather sparse, military hospital, and was demobbed on 19th June 1945, jumping to the head of the queue, courtesy of Emily's document. In return for five years of my time, the War Office presented me with one three-piece suit (blue), two white shirts, a disgusting brown tie, a rail pass and precisely five pounds three shillings and sixpence cash. More important, despite the upheavals of the war years, I still had The Photo and, of course, The Pill. Hitler might have ravaged half the known world, but he wasn't getting his hands on *those*!

Once demobbed, I found myself temporary lodgings in a rather grotty boarding house on the outskirts of Hastings, settling down therein to decide my future. What I was going to do, I had no idea. I had no friends or relatives to turn to, no evident skills, and precious little money. Emily was somewhere in Germany and, after six years of war, England was in a shambles. As has been the case so many times in my life, I was at a complete dead end. And as has also been the case so many times in my life, something popped up, quite unexpectedly. An opportunity.

It popped up in a newspaper. *The Times*. I was sitting in the grotty lounge of my grotty lodging, sipping weak and grotty tea, when I spotted a small advert in the Domestic Situations Vacant column of that day's *Times*:

> **Wanted.** Manservant to foremost peer of the realm. Duties to include valeting, butlering, secretarial. Moral rectitude and utmost probity essential. Experience likewise. Must appreciate Wagner. Apply, with references to:
> Slaggsby of Tripally, Tripally Hall, Northumberland.

As adverts go, this one was, on the face of it, not that promising. After all, I had no experience whatsoever in the areas specified;

wouldn't know a piece of Wagner music if it dropped on my head from a hundred feet; and, as a mass murderer, could hardly be described as a man of rectitude and probity. What's more, I didn't have any references.

I was, nonetheless, for no obvious reason other than that I liked the idea of hobnobbing with the gentry, rather taken with the advert, and replied straight away. I got over the references problem by writing them myself, inventing, variously, an Italian count, a French Baron and a multi-millionaire American industrialist, all of whom claimed, in the most flattering terms imaginable, that I was without doubt the best manservant they'd ever had, bar none. I was rather pleased with my handiwork, and posted it off first class that afternoon. Three days later I had a reply, by telegram: *Come immediately stop Tripally station nearest stop Expect day after tomorrow stop Slaggsby end.*

And there it was. I set off the next morning, doing a dawn bunk from my grotty lodging and making my way slowly northwards by train into the rolling woody wilds of northern England. The journey took longer than I had expected, and it was not until the day after the day after tomorrow that I eventually disembarked at Tripally station and walked the two miles up to Tripally Hall, passing through its huge, rusted iron gates and so into another world, another life, another murder. I was 45 at the time, and had a moustache. A woman on the train told me I looked like Errol Flynn.

Tripally Hall, where I was to reside for the next quarter of a century, was a most impressive affair, standing in the midst of extensive woods and parklands, and commanding a spectacular view downwards to the distant rooftops of Tripally village, nestling in the valley below on the far side of a frothing, pebbly river. Say what you like about Lord Slaggsby's death, it at least occurred in nice surroundings.

The Hall itself was a two-storeyed structure of rather dour grey-brown sandstone, to either end of which, and at right angles to the main body of the building, had been added two wings in similarly coloured stone. Looked at from above, it would have resembled an elongated letter H, the original and oldest part of the house, forming the central horizontal. It had a large, iron-studded front door, mossy cylindrical towers at the end of each wing, and windows that seemed just a little too small for the walls in which they were set, giving an overall impression of a series of crossed eyes traversing the front and sides of the building. The whole thing exuded an air of defiant, slumberous inertia, as though the twentieth century had yet to percolate upwards past the rusted front gates.

'What on earth have I let myself in for?' I mused as I stood before the front door. 'It's like a bloody mausoleum.'

Whereupon, quite ignoring my own misgivings, I yanked the bell-pull and waited expectantly as it tinkled far off in the distant bowels of the building.

It was some five minutes before I heard footsteps approaching the door from the inside, by which point I had tugged the bell-pull twice more and walked right the way round the outside of the building. Finally, however, there was a clunk of bolts being drawn back and the slow creak of the door as it swung inwards to reveal a fierce-looking grey-haired lady with narrow eyes, serge stockings and a hare lip.

'I suppose you've come about the parsnips!' she hissed.

'I beg your pardon?'

'The parsnips.'

'What about the parsnips?'

'Don't play the ignorant with me! You know precisely what about the parsnips. They were shrivelled and sour!'

'Oh.'

'Rationing or no rationing, parsnips should be firm and sweet, and if you can't provide them like that we'll take our custom else-where. What do you have to say to that, eh?'

'Very little, I'm afraid, except that I'm the new butler.' I extended a hand.

'New butler?' she inquired suspiciously, ignoring my hand and staring me up and down.

'That's right. Raphael Phoenix. Lord Slaggsby sent me a telegram.'

She made no reply but continued to peer at me, her already narrow eyes getting even narrower so that in the shadows of the doorway she looked faintly oriental.

'You were expected yesterday,' she said eventually.

I apologized, and explained that I had had rather a difficult journey.

'We've won the war,' I joked, 'but still can't get the damned trains to run on time.'

She gave me a look of utmost distaste – the hairline scar on her upper lip appearing to throb somewhat, like a tiny luminous thread-worm – and then stood back and ushered me inside.

'And wipe your shoes,' she barked.

'Yes, ma'am.'

'Kindly keep your "ma'am"s to yourself!'

'I'm sorry. Might I inquire your name?'

'No you might not. If His Lordship wishes to tell you, that's up to him. For myself, I have no wish to discuss the subject with strangers. He's in his study. Follow me.'

She led me across a wide, lofty hallway and down a narrow corridor, at the far end of which stood a large suit of armour. There were closed doors to left and right, and pictures on the walls, although in the thick gloom I was unable to make out what they were of. One looked like a fox hunt, and another appeared to depict a woman having her head cut off.

'What a fascinating house!' I declared.

'Two hundred and fifty years old,' snapped my guide. 'Two hundred and fifty, and not a speck of dust in it. His Lordship insists on *standards*!' She placed heavy emphasis upon this last word, as though it denoted a concept of which I might well be unaware.

'So I can—'

'We keep ourselves to ourselves here at Tripally,' she went on, cutting me off mid-sentence. 'We don't like outsiders. They bring . . . ideas.'

And with that she bustled onwards towards the suit of armour with me trailing in her wake. We turned right, and then left, and then right again, went up some stairs, round a corner, down some more stairs, along a corridor, and then more rights and lefts, more stairs and corners and corridors until, eventually, after we had walked for what seemed like hours but was probably only a matter of minutes, we turned into a short, brightly lit corridor with windows down one side and a large oak door at the far end. I could hear music, loud music, coming from the room beyond, and noticed, by the view, that we were now at the back end of the left-hand wing of the house.

'Wait there!' ordered my hare-lipped guide, leaving me standing with my bag whilst she went forward and rapped forcefully on the oak doorway. There was a muffled cry of 'Come!' from within, followed by a blast of operatic wailing as she opened the door and stepped into the room.

'He's here!' announced the hare-lipped one.

'Who?' came a curt voice.

'Him,' she announced. 'Phoenix.'

'Phoenix? Phoenix? What are you talking about, woman?'

'Phoenix, Your Lordship. The new butler.'

'Butler? I thought I told him to be here yesterday.'

'So you did. Definitely yesterday.'

'So what's he doing here today?'

'He can answer that better than me, I'm sure. He's quite a talker.'

'Talker, eh! Well, let's hope he says the right thing, or we'll be sacking him before we even employ him. Chop, chop, get him in. Come on, come on! Where is he!'

The woman beckoned me into the room, and then, shooting me a look of murderous distaste, exited and closed the door behind her. The music – Wagner, I later discovered, although I didn't know it at the time – really was extremely loud. I began to wonder if I should have brought ear plugs.

Lord Rufus St John Arnold James Neville Maldon Slaggsby,

23rd Baron of Tripally – for he it was whose voice I had heard from the corridor – bore as close a resemblance to Adolf Hitler as it was possible to bear without actually being Adolf Hitler. Ensconced behind a large desk, upon which were arranged, with dazzling symmetrical neatness, various books, papers, items of stationery and, in one corner, an enormous gramophone with a crank handle and a speaker like a giant conch shell, he was, I guessed, in his late fifties, of small to medium height, with a curtain of dark hair sweeping down across the left side of his forehead. He had puffy bags beneath his eyes, a Teutonic pout to his chest and, atop his upper lip, a neatly clipped moustache. So striking was the similarity between him and the late Führer, indeed, so dazzling the likeness, that for a moment I genuinely wondered if the latter had somehow escaped from his Berlin bunker and sloped off to start a new life in the north of England. It was, frankly, as much as I could do not to click my heels together and give him a full-blown Nazi salute. From what I later came to know of him, he wouldn't have been altogether displeased with the gesture.

'You're late!' he snapped, peering at me across the top of his desk. 'Late!'

'I'm very sorry, sir—'

'Not "sir"! Your Lordship! We're not in America now, you know!'

For a moment I was unsure of his meaning until I recalled that, amongst my forged references had been one from multi-millionaire American industrialist Ulysses J. Bumbleberg.

'Dreadful people, Americans,' he went on, furrowing his brow and grimacing, as though he had eaten something distasteful. 'The sooner the war's over and they get back to their own country the better.'

'Yes, Your Lordship,' I mumbled.

'You met Crone?'

'Crone?'

'Crone, you fool! The housekeeper.'

'Ah yes, sir . . . Your Lordship. Mrs Crone. Charming lady.'

'Not Mrs Crone. Crone. Been with us thirty years now. She knows the form.'

I concurred that, from what I had seen of her, she certainly appeared to know her way about.

'Now what's all this lateness?' His Lordship continued, thrusting out his lower jaw. 'I wanted you yesterday. I won't stand for lateness. It's slack! Slack!'

'I can only apologize. It was the trains, you see. They kept getting cancelled.'

'Cancelled! Cancelled, you say. What's happening to this country? It's collapsing, that's what's happening to it. Mussolini. That's who we need in charge. No cancelled trains under Mussolini. And who do we get? Bloody Clement Attlee and the bleeding-hearts namby-pamby brigade. God have mercy on our souls!'

He slammed his fist down on the desk, sending a tremor through the room and causing the needle of the gramophone to jump, before launching into an extended tirade on the iniquities of the current government, his fulminations interspersed with a good deal more table thumping and a good many more 'God have mercy on our souls!' Eventually, however, he calmed down enough to turn his attention to a small pile of papers to his left. These, I noticed, were the false references I had sent him from Dover.

'Now,' he grumped, 'I am not at all impressed with these references. A recommendation from a foreigner is no recommendation at all. Indeed, when that foreigner happens to be [and here he crumpled up my carefully crafted forgeries and dropped them one by one into the wastepaper basket] an Itie, a Frog and a Yankee, then the recommendation becomes quite the opposite. It becomes a warning. These people have no standards. No standards, d'you hear! If staff weren't so hard to come by at present, I wouldn't have you within a hundred miles of Tripally. Not a hundred miles! Whoring yourself on foreign soil!'

I couldn't very well tell him that I had, in fact, been doing no such thing, and that the papers he had just scrunched up and binned were in fact forgeries. I therefore contented myself with a mumbled apology for past mistakes, and otherwise kept quiet.

'Yes, well,' he muttered, 'apologies are all very well, but you're at Tripally now, and at Tripally we expect standards. Do you know how old this house is?'

'Two hundred and fifty years, Your Lordship.'

'Two hundred and fifty years! And do you how long the Slaggsbys have been in England? Over two thousand years. I'm writing a monograph about it. *Slaggsby: A Very English Heritage.* Two thousand years, d'you hear! And that makes for high standards.'

'Standards I will do my utmost to maintain, Your Lordship.'

'Well,' he growled, 'let's hope your very utmost is enough! Now let's get down to the nitty-gritty. We run a tight ship here at Tripally. Crone does the cooking and the cleaning and the washing and the ordering of provisions. Those are her tasks and are not to be interfered with, do you understand?'

'Yes, Your Lordship.'

'The gardens, likewise, are the strict domain of Old Lummy. You will not touch anything in the grounds without his prior permission, particularly the lily pads. Lummy's very protective of his lily pads.'

'Yes, Your Lordship.'

'You will act as my valet and manservant, with all the duties concomitant thereto. In addition, you will attend me here in the study from nine to twelve of a morning and two to six of an afternoon to assist in the compiling of my monograph.'

'Yes, Your Lordship.'

'I expect absolute rectitude, probity and punctuality at all times. Anything less and you will be dismissed instantly, as you will be if caught consuming either cigarettes or alcohol anywhere within a ten-mile radius of the hall. Two thousand years of history makes for high standards, and I expect them to be kept.'

I nodded gravely.

'You will be paid twenty shillings a week, an excessive sum in my opinion, but then what can you expect with the bloody molly-coddling Bolsheviks in power, on top of which you are provided with board and lodging. You will have the last Sunday of each month as a free day, although I should point out that no Tripally manservant has ever yet seen fit to avail himself of the aforementioned privilege.'

'A tradition I shall doubtless continue, Your Lordship.'

'Very good. Very good. Possibly you won't be so bad after all. We'll have to see. Smotters was with the family for sixty-three years and gave absolute satisfaction throughout, even after they'd amputated his leg. You have a lot to live up to, Phoenix.'

'I shan't disappoint, Your Lordship.'

'I hope not. And for Christ's sake shave of that verminous moustache. You look like a damned Yankee dandy. Crone will show you to your room and provide you with suitable attire.'

Whereupon he reached beneath his desk and withdrew a large rubbery tube, to the end of which was attached a short brass funnel. It resembled those tubes down which the captains of transatlantic steamers were wont to shout orders to their engine rooms, and appeared to serve a similar purpose here, for, having blown vigorously into the funnel, and apparently attracted his housekeeper's attention thereby, Lord Slaggsby proceeded to issue a series of instructions concerning my room and clothing.

'And when you've done all that, come and fetch him and show him what's what. He'll be in the corridor.'

A distant, subterranean murmur of ascent wafted up the tube.

'Good type, Crone,' said Lord Slaggsby, shovelling his pipe back beneath the desk. 'Damn good egg. Knows the form. Now, give me a hand round to the gramophone so I can change the record. A bit of *Götterdämmerung*, I think. Bloody marvellous fellow, Wagner. Only good thing ever to have come out of Germany. Sometimes wonder if he was German at all. Far too much fibre for a damn Hun, if you ask me!'

He pushed himself backwards away from the desk and stared at me expectantly. Only then did I notice he was sitting in a wheelchair.

With the exception of each second Friday – of which more later – every day at Tripally Hall was exactly the same as every other day. Today was a precise replica of yesterday, and tomorrow a verbatim rerun of today. Nothing new ever happened; nothing unexpected ever occurred; the routine never varied. A single sequence of events was simply repeated over and over again throughout the 24 years I was there. Background details changed, of course – today might be rainy whereas yesterday was dry; tomorrow there might be roast lamb for dinner whereas today it was roast partridge – but the essence of the place remained immutable. Had probably remained immutable, indeed, for as long as the Slaggsbys had occupied their Hall, and most likely some considerable time before. At Tripally time went round in a loop, starting off from one point and returning to precisely the same point 24 hours later.

Each and every morning I would wake at 5.15 a.m. in my room in the eastern wing of the castle. It was a dingy room, devoid of all but the most essential furnishings, and, aside from a rubber communication tube that emerged like a large maggot from the wall at the head of my bed, quite without adornment.

Once awake I would lie for a few minutes gazing up at the ceiling before rising, washing and donning my uniform, an excruciatingly ill-fitting black satin affair with curlicues of faded gold braid down the front. Into the back pocket of this I would slip The Photo and into the front one The Pill, the latter wrapped in a small silk handkerchief. I would then brush my hair, turn down my bed and, at 6 a.m., make my way down to the kitchen, where Crone would be bustling about preparing the day's victuals.

'Morning, Crone,' I would say affably. 'Slept well, I hope?'

'How I sleep is none of your business,' she'd snap, her hare-lip throbbing angrily. 'Sit down and eat your breakfast.'

Whereupon she would slap a plate of greasy bacon and fried bread in front of me and get on with whatever it was she was doing at the time. I would eat my food in silence, peering out of the window at the bent figure of Old Lummy, who would, at that hour, be weeding in the herb garden, before at 6.30 a.m. retiring to the fireside to polish Lord Slaggsby's shoes for the day. This would occupy me until 6.50 a.m. when, with his footwear under one arm, his paper (*The Times*) under another, and a large breakfast tray in both hands, I would set off to His Lordship's apartments in the west wing of the house, arriving thereat on the dot of 7 a.m.

'Good morning, Your Lordship,' I would say, knocking and opening the door. 'I trust you had a good night.'

'No, Phoenix,' he would reply every morning, 'bloody tempestuous. Frightful attack of wind! Three rashers of bacon, I hope!'

I would help him up in bed, plump his pillows and put his tray on his lap, leaving him to eat his bacon and peruse his paper – 'Bloody upstart pickaninnies causing trouble on the subcontinent again!' – whilst I busied myself running his bath. This done, I would then stand mutely in a corner until 7.45 a.m., when I would lay aside his completed breakfast things, to be removed later by Crone, and carry him bodily into the bathroom for his morning ablutions.

'Ye gods, Phoenix, I've got the squitters again!'

'I'm very sorry to hear it, Your Lordship. A little milk of magnesia, perhaps?'

'Rubbish. Fresh air's what I need. Get those windows open.'

'It's raining, Your Lordship.'

'For God's sake, man, we're not in bloody pansy school now. Little bit of rain never did anyone any harm. Get 'em open! Get 'em open!'

From the bathroom, it was into the dressing room, where I would clothe, shave and brush my employer before lifting him into his wheelchair and setting off, at precisely 8.15 a.m., for his study (except for every second Friday, when, as I believe I have already mentioned, something quite different would happen).

When I say that His Lordship was confined to a wheelchair I am not being strictly accurate, for he was actually confined to seven of them (although not, of course, all at the same time). These seven chairs – large, creaking mahogany things, with wickerwork seats,

141

big rumbling wheels and built-in commodes – were positioned at various points around the house in a sort of relay system so that, for instance, rather than having to carry Lord Slaggsby down a flight of stairs and then climb all the way up back again for his chair, there was already one waiting at the bottom. In this manner, Tripally Hall, without doubt one of the most bendy, twisty, uppy-downy sort of places I have ever lived, was negotiated with a surprising degree of ease. True, there were several sharp corners to deal with, and a couple of extremely long, steep staircases up which one was obliged to trudge with Lord Slaggsby cradled baby-like in one's arms – how on earth old Smotters managed with only one leg is quite beyond me – but the whole thing actually worked out rather well.

'Napoleonic,' explained my employer. 'Modelled the whole thing on his battlefield dispatch system. Might have been a Frog but by God he knew how to organize things. Not like Attlee. The man's a walking disaster area.'

It took us 15 minutes and three wheelchairs to cover the distance between His Lordship's bedroom and his study, where we would arrive at 8.30 a.m. (it took two wheelchairs to get from his study to the library; two from the library to the dining room; four from the dining room to the bedroom; and five from his bedroom to the front door). Having arrived, I would install him behind his desk, wind up the gramophone – 'Damn it, Phoenix, let's have "The Ride of the Valkyries"! Set the day off with a bang, eh!' – and then return to the kitchen to fetch him a cup of tea and his mail, which he would, respectively, slurp and open until 9 a.m. when, on the dot, he would begin work on his monograph: *Slaggsby: A Very English Heritage.*

If Lord Slaggsby was to be believed, which I'm not entirely sure he was, his family had been involved in just about every event of any significance to have occurred in Britain since the last Ice Age.

'We're not just English,' he would inform me, 'we're *the* English. Do you see what I'm getting at, Phoenix? We're as much a part of the landscape as the River Thames. Our blood is pure. No Froggie or

Kraut in us, by God. We're untainted. Even the royals can't say that much!'

Slaggsbys, according to His Lordship's monograph, had been there since the beginning. They were there when Stonehenge was built, very possibly acting as architects of the latter, and were still there when the Romans arrived, giving 'that filthy little Itie Caesar a fucking good hiding' when he first arrived from Gaul. King Alfred's shield-bearer was a Slaggsby, and a Slaggsby, Gunthwine by name, stood beside King Harold when the latter was shot through the eye by a Norman arrow at Hastings. There was a Slaggsby with Thomas a Becket when he was murdered in Canterbury Cathedral; another with King Richard on the Third Crusade; another still with Robin Hood in Sherwood Forest; and no fewer than three of them sitting with King Arthur at his legendary Round Table. There were Slaggsbys at Crécy and Agincourt; Slaggsbys at Bannockburn and Culloden; Slaggsbys at Trafalgar and Waterloo; Slaggsbys at Inkerman and on the Somme; and, indeed, Slaggsbys at every major military engagement, either at home or abroad, in which Englishmen had ever been involved. One Slaggsby had been the lover of Queen Elizabeth I – 'Damn fine filly!' – another had assisted Wren in the construction of St Paul's Cathedral, and there was compelling evidence to suggest that William Shakespeare was, in fact, a Slaggsby. There was even one Slaggsby, a distant half-cousin named Alfonso, aboard the *Santa Maria* when Columbus discovered America. Aside from God, there was probably no single force in the universe which had, according to His Lordship, so affected the history of mankind as the family Slaggsby.

It was for the purposes of imparting this information to an ignorant public that my employer was compiling his monograph. All day, from nine o'clock in the morning to six o'clock at night, with a two-hour break in the middle for lunch and a nap, His Lordship would toil away at his opus; and all day, from nine in the morning to six at night, I would assist him with it, fetching books from the library, taking notes and cross-referencing, transcribing, proofreading, checking dates and facts and names and spellings, sharpening pencils, tidying the desk, cranking up the gramophone, fetching cups of tea and biscuits and basically doing everything short of writing the damn thing. Towards the end, indeed, I even started doing a bit of that too, when my employer became old and senile and unable to hold his pen properly.

Work on *Slaggsby: A Very English Heritage* continued uninterrupted until 6 p.m., when we would down pencils, turn off the gramophone and head off back up the wheelchair relay to His Lordship's room, where I would bath and dress him for his evening meal.

Even when rationing was still in place, which it was until the early Fifties, dinner at Tripally Hall was a sumptuous affair. Taken at 7 p.m. in the main dining room, it consisted of a minimum of five courses, cooked by Crone, served by me and eaten by His Lordship in complete silence and totally alone (although if memory serves me right he did have one guest sometime in the early Sixties). The whole thing never took less than two hours to complete, more if His Lordship fell asleep between courses, which he did increasingly as he got older, and it was not usually before 9 p.m. that the last plates would be cleared away and I would wheel my burping employer into the billiard room, where I would allow him to thrash me at balls for an hour.

'Ye gods, Phoenix, you're even worse than Smotters,' he would cry.

'Yes, Your Lordship.'

'Hit the bloody thing, man! Give it a whack, for Christ's sake. You're not a liberal!'

From the billiard room it was back up to the bedroom, at 10 p.m., where I would undress His Lordship and help him into bed. There would then be a deal of fuss over his pillows – 'Plump them up, damn it, man, plump them up! It's like sleeping on a bloody sandbag!' – before I eventually closed the curtains, turned out the lights and at 10.30 p.m. wished him a good night.

'I sincerely doubt it will be, Phoenix. And make sure Crone gives me three rashers of bacon in the morning.'

His Lordship safely tucked up, I would return to the kitchen for my own dinner, which would have been left in the oven by Crone. I would pop down to the wine cellar for a surreptitious swig or two – Lord Slaggsby had a formidable wine cellar, including almost 500 bottles of Château d'Yquem 1921, and as many of Margaux 1900 and Lafite 1920 – before sneaking a quick, illegal cigarette in the pantry garden. At 11.30 p.m. I would then retire to my own room and prepare for bed. Off would come my excruciatingly ill-fitting uniform, under the pillow would be slipped The Photo and The Pill, and beneath the covers would go I. By midnight I'd be fast asleep.

That, however, was not quite the end of my day, because every night, without fail, after a brief period of respite, I would be woken at precisely 2.30 a.m. by a whistling from the funnel-ended rubber tube beside my bedstead.

'Phoenix!' would come Lord Slaggsby's distant voice. 'Phoenix! I've got the gripes! Christ, I've blown up like a bloody bagpipe!'

'Yes, Your Lordship,' I would mumble sleepily. 'On my way.'

Whereupon I would get up, heave on my uniform, light a candle and traipse all the way over to his bedroom, arriving only to find that he'd gone back to sleep again. I put up with this pantomime every night for 23 of my 24 years at Tripally Hall before I eventually lost patience and, taking a ball of paper, stuffed it down the mouth of the communication tube so I could get an uninterrupted night's sleep.

And then at 5.15 a.m. I'd wake up and do the whole thing all over again.

Such was a day in my life at Tripally Hall. And since, as I've already explained, each day was precisely the same as every other day (except second Fridays), such was my *entire* life at Tripally Hall.

It was not, admittedly, the most scintillating of existences, and His Lordship could certainly be a handful when he put his mind to it, which he did most of the time. Crone, too, was a constant thorn in my side (the fact that I killed His Lordship rather than her is further proof, if further proof were needed, of just how illogical a thing murder is).

It wasn't all bad, however. I had an unparalleled selection of wines at my disposal in the Tripally cellar, and actually rather enjoyed working on His Lordship's monograph, deriving therefrom the same sense of satisfaction as I imagine a storyteller must derive from spinning a particularly long and colourful adventure yarn. There was even a bit of sex, believe it or not, albeit only sporadically, in Old Lummy's potting shed, with big-boobed Mrs Shine, the local baker's wife.

So it wasn't all bad. Not by any means. And if 24 years might seem a long time to those looking in from the outside, to those of us on the inside it went by in a flash. That's what happens when every day is exactly the same as every other day. You lose all sense of time passing. Working for Lord Slaggsby – always following the same routine, always doing the same thing – was akin to a form of transcendental meditation. I slipped into a sort of coma, emerging in February 1969 as though from a deep sleep. When Emily told me how long I'd been there I could barely believe it. I felt like Rip van Winkle. And my hair had gone completely white.

I have now, on three separate occasions, mentioned that something curious happened every second Friday at Tripally, and the time has now come to reveal just what that something curious was. To reveal my master's terrible secret. His skeleton in the closet. Lord Slaggsby, you see, was addicted to cream cakes.

Why this should have been a source of such humiliation to him I have no idea. A penchant for cream cakes, after all, hardly constitutes a crime. It is not treason, or pederasty, or incest, which are the sort of things aristocrats usually get upset about. For some reason, however, His Lordship was ashamed of his craving, as though it in some way represented a betrayal of all that he held most dear in life.

To his credit, he struggled manfully to control his addiction. He did not eat cream cakes every day. Nor even every week. He managed to last a whole fortnight between one bunfest and the next, during which time he would become increasingly irritable and twitchy, and play his Wagner increasingly loudly until, eventually, every second Thursday night, as I put him to bed, he would cry with an edge of despairing anguish to his voice:

'God bloody bugger it, Phoenix, it's too strong. I can't hold out any longer. If I don't have an éclair I'll go mad. We'll pop down to the village tomorrow. And not a word to Crone or Lummy, d'you hear? I won't have the name of Slaggsby sullied because I happen to be a filthy weak-willed blackguard.'

'You really are too hard on yourself, Your Lordship.'

'I ought to be flogged! Flogged through the streets. And then burnt!'

Thus it was that every second Friday morning, directly after breakfast, whilst Crone was off the estate visiting her sister, and Lummy working on the rose gardens at the back of the Hall, I would take Lord Slaggsby down the five-wheelchair relay from his bedroom to the front door, and thence down the steps on to the front drive.

'By Christ, this is risky, Phoenix!' His Lordship would mutter. 'We're skating on damned thin ice here. It only takes one person to spot us and the secret would be out. I'd be ruined! Ruined!'

'It's really not as bad as you think, Your Lordship.'

'Not as bad! It's worse! Now get a move on. And for God's sake put some oil on these wheels next time. They're squeaking fit to wake the dead!'

The simplest way to cover the three miles from Tripally Hall to the village below was to follow the driveway down to the front gates and then turn right on to the narrow country road that led up from the valley. To do so, however, might have risked bumping into someone, and since His Lordship was most particular about not being seen on his fortnightly foraging expeditions, we were forced to negotiate a rather more circuitous path. This involved crossing the front lawn – the heavy mahogany wheelchair leaving deep ruts in Old Lummy's neatly clipped grass – and then following a narrow path that wound down through the estate like a thin, coiled snake, the latter eventually emerging on to the village road just at the point where it began its final steep descent down to the river.

Beyond this point Lord Slaggsby refused to go – 'Can't risk being seen,' he would snap. 'Can't risk the shame!' – and I would therefore wheel him behind a large holly bush before continuing alone.

'Quick as you can,' he would hiss, peering excitedly through the foliage. 'And don't forget the strawberry pastry horns. Dear God, it gives me a turn just to think of them!'

I would duly descend the steep incline to the river, cross the old stone bridge and make my way up through the village to Shine's Bakery at the far end of the high street.

Here Mrs Shine – the same Mrs Shine with whom I enjoyed an occasional liaison amongst the compost bins and tomato plants of Old Lummy's potting shed – would be serving behind the counter, aided from the mid-Sixties onwards by a large-boned local girl called Sharon Maggot.

'Good morning, Mr Phoenix,' the baker's wife would coo, her titanic bosoms bulging over the top of her apron like flour-sacks dangling on a garden gate. 'Come for your *cream* cakes.'

'That's right, Mrs Shine,' I would reply innocently. 'And kindly make sure you include one of your pastry *horns*.'

'Now, Mr Phoenix, you know I always give you a *horn*.'

'Indeed you do, Mrs Shine.'

'And today I'm going to give you an extra *big one*.'

'I'm sure it'll be a real *mouthful*, Mrs Shine. I can barely wait to get my tongue into it.'

So the innuendo would fly – the large-boned Sharon Maggot completely oblivious to the double entendres zipping about all around her – until Mrs Shine had boxed up His Lordship's cakes, whereupon, with a nod and a wink, I'd leave the shop and set off back to my waiting employer.

'Damn you, Phoenix, where've you been?' he would cry as I approached. 'I've been sitting here like a bloody pig in a poke! Stop for a nap on the way, did you?'

'I'm sorry, Your Lordship. There was a queue in the shop.'

'To hell with queues. Give me those cakes. Any éclairs?'

And with that he would rip off the lid of the cardboard box and set to, devouring cake after cake in glutinous silence as I wheeled him slowly back up the snaking path to Tripally Hall. By the time we reached the front lawn his moustache would be covered in cream, his jacket with crumbs, the box would be empty and His Lordship's face a luminous shade of green.

'God have mercy on my soul, Phoenix,' he would cry, belching loudly. 'I'll burn in hell for this.'

'They are just cakes, Your Lordship.'

'No, Phoenix, they are not just cakes. They are weakness. Womanly weakness. Now get me back up to the study so I can get on with some work. And not a word of this, d'you hear. Not a word.'

'No, Your Lordship,' I assured him. 'Not a word. You can rely on me.'

Such was the curious ritual that was enacted every second Friday at Tripally Hall; and such, in large part, was the curious ritual that was enacted on that second Friday in February 1969 when I did for His Lordship, so bringing to an end 24 years in his service.

The day had started in its usual fashion with me wheeling my grumbling employer, now well into his eighties and slightly deaf, down the winding path to the point where the latter joined the road to the village. Here, in time-honoured fashion, I had left him behind the holly bush and continued alone, his exhortations not to forget the strawberry pastry horns ringing in my ears.

'And make sure they're creamy ones!' he'd hissed from amongst the branches. 'Last week they were dry as a dervish's backside!'

In Shine's Bakery I had been served, as always, by Mrs Shine, now slightly greying, although still the possessor of a spectacular pair of knockers, exchanging innuendos whilst big-boned Sharon Maggot had bustled around with trays of gingerbread men. Carrying my cakes under my arm, I had then set off back through the village, across the bridge and up the hill to His Lordship, just as I always did.

'Damn you, Phoenix, where've you been?' he bellowed as I approached. 'I've been sitting here like fucking Robinson Crusoe on his island! Fall down a mineshaft, did you?'

'I'm sorry for the delay, Your Lordship,' I replied patiently. 'I had to wait for the pastry horns.'

'You're a damned slacker, Phoenix. Now hand over those cakes. Any walnut whips?'

Which is the point at which, for no obvious reason, everything suddenly started to change. Why it should have happened then, on that particular second Friday, rather than the one before, or the one after, I really can't explain. There was nothing out of the ordinary about it. His Lordship was no more hectoring than usual, nor any ruder; nor was I in any worse a mood than I had been the previous fortnight, or the one before that. It was in all respects a second Friday just like every other second Friday for the past 24 years. For some reason, however, on this particular one I suddenly decided I'd had enough. After a quarter of a century I reached the end of my tether, and rather than handing over His Lordship's comestibles when he asked me to, as I usually did, I instead took a step backwards and kept hold of them.

'You can't have them,' I said.

'What's that!' he sputtered. 'Give me those cakes! Give them to me now!'

'No,' I said, as surprised as he was to hear myself say it.

'What!' he cried, leaning forward in his chair and cupping his hand about his ear. 'What did you say?'

'You can't have your cakes, Your Lordship,' I repeated, raising my voice.

'Can't have them! Why can't I have them?'

'Because I don't want to give them to you.'

'What are you talking about, you filthy seditious blighter? Hand them over now, I say! I want my pastries.'

I said nothing, just took another step backwards. After 24 years of unquestioning deference it felt rather good to goad him thus.

'What in the name of God's got into you, Phoenix? Have you taken leave of your senses? Smotters never took leave of his senses, and he only had one leg. Now give me those cakes or I'll have you birched to within an inch of your life!'

He seized the wheels of his chair and began to propel himself towards me. After a couple of feet, however, the wheels became bogged down in a patch of soggy grass and he juddered to a halt.

'Bloody damn thing!' he snapped, feebly banging the armrest with his fist. 'Bloody damn thing!'

I remained where I was, clutching the cakes, watching him as he rocked back and forth, his face becoming increasingly red. He looked, I thought, rather like a large jack-in-the-box.

'Do you want me to have a seizure, Phoenix?' he roared. 'Is that your idea, eh? I always knew you were a bloody Jew-boy pansy-man. Help me, damn it! Help me!'

I stayed where I was for a moment longer and then, laying aside the box of cakes, crossed to the chair, took hold of its handles and, with a heave, pushed it forwards on to the side of the road. Here I swung it round through 90 degrees so that it was facing downhill, and applied the brakes.

'That's more like it,' he puffed. 'Coming to your senses at last. Now hand me my cakes and we'll be on our way. Acting like a bloody Itie you were!'

I retrieved the pastries and walked round to the front of his chair, where I held them just out of reach of his outstretched hand.

'Well, come on then! Hand 'em over!'

He leaned right forward in his chair, fingers stretching, eyes fixed despairingly on the cardboard cake box.

'Dear God, if I don't have a creamy puff I think I'll die. Give me my damn cakes I say!'

'Do you really want them?' I asked.

'You know I bloody want them, you filthy arse-reaming Bolshevik scoundrel. Now I'll ask you one more time: give me my cakes, or you'll never work in this country again!'

'If His Lordship wants his cream cakes,' I said, smiling, 'then His Lordship shall have his cream cakes.'

Whereupon, rather enjoying my game, I slowly pulled off the ribbon with which the box was done up and opened the lid. Inside was arranged a mouth-watering selection of éclairs, cream slices, strawberry pastry horns, doughnuts, meringues and custard tarts.

'Oh God, I can smell them!' whimpered Lord Slaggsby. 'I can smell the cream!'

I selected the largest strawberry pastry horn I could find – as the name suggested, a horn-shaped pastry filled with cream and strawberries – and, leaning forward, screwed it on to His Lordship's nose. Really screwed it on, as hard as I could, twisting it back and forth and pushing it right up against his withered old cheeks, so that it remained in place even when I withdrew my hand, protruding from the middle of his face like a large rocket. Thick tongues of cream dripped downwards on to his coat.

For a moment my employer was lost for words – the only time, incidentally, I ever knew him to be so – before, with a great deal of rocking back and forth in his seat, and thumping of fists on the chair's armrests, neither of which activities, incidentally, served to dislodge the offending pastry horn, he screamed:

'I'm going to fucking horsewhip you, you dirty little queer—'

He got no further, however, for, picking out a particularly extravagant meringue, I worked the latter firmly into his mouth like a cork into a bottle.

'Urgggggh!' he sputtered, a spray of cream emitting from the corners of his lips. 'Urgggggh!'

I watched him as he blustered and spat, and then upended the box on to his head – one éclair dangling down on either side like a pair of earmuffs – before walking round to the back of the chair, knocking off the brakes and, with a heave, sending it flying off down the hill. It gathered speed as it went, despite His Lordship's frantic efforts to reapply the brakes, and by the time it reached the humpback bridge at the bottom must have been going at near enough 50mph. This itself was not necessarily enough to kill him. What was, however, was the tractor approaching from the far side of the river, into the front of which Lord Slaggsby and his wheelchair slammed with a sickening thud as they both met at the very apex of the bridge, His Lordship disappearing head-first into the tractor's radiator as though into the mouth of some large animal. I looked on for a moment as the tractor driver hurried round to the front of his steaming vehicle and tugged vainly at His Lordship's inert legs, and then stepped back from the road and crouched down behind the holly bush to consider my next move.

I was still crouching behind the holly bush considering my next move thirty minutes later when the camper van pulled up. It was a blue camper van, with a puttering exhaust and rusty bumpers, and initially I thought it might be a police vehicle. Police vehicles, however, don't generally have 'Peace' painted in large white letters down the side, and after a moment of panic I relaxed.

'They've probably just stopped to take in the view,' I mused. 'I'd better move further back into the trees, though. I don't want anyone to see me just at the moment.'

I duly came to my feet and, turning, began to creep further back into the woods. I had only gone a few yards, however, when I was brought up by the sound of a voice. A familiar voice.

'Is there anyone there?'

'No,' I thought. 'It can't be. Not here. Not now. It's just too outrageous.'

'Hello,' came the voice again. 'I seem to be lost. I'm looking for Tripally village.'

'Emily?' I cried, turning round and hurrying back to the road. 'Emily, is that you? Tell me it's you!'

'OK,' she laughed – for her it was, sitting in the van, as young and beautiful as ever, an enormous map spread on the dashboard before her – 'it *is* me!'

'I don't believe it,' I yelped. 'It can't be true. What are you doing here?'

'I told you. I'm trying to find Tripally village.'

'Why, for God's sake?'

'Because once I find Tripally village I'll know where I am on this map.'

She lifted the giant map and tried to fold it in half, but it refused to cooperate, buckling back and over her head, which it enveloped like a large bonnet. I leaned through the window and peeled it off her.

'The village is just down there,' I said, helping her bring her chart back under control, 'on the other side of the river.'

'Oh dear,' she sighed. 'I seem to have gone round in a big circle. Still, at least I know where I am now.'

She crumpled the map into a large ball and threw it over her shoulder.

'Well, get in then,' she said.

'What do you mean, "get in"?'

'I mean get in, of course. We're going to London. You can keep me company. And we'll have to do something about those clothes. You look ridiculous.'

And that was that. I got in the van, we drove down the hill and over the bridge into the village – 'Oh look!' said Emily. 'Someone's tractor seems to have broken down' – and then onwards towards the south. In the early afternoon we stopped off for a bite to eat and to exchange my butler's uniform for a pair of candy-striped bell-bottoms and a tie-dyed shirt – 'That's much better,' said Emily. 'You

154

look 20 years younger' – and then continued on our way. At about 9.30 that night we pulled into gaudy, neon-lit Soho. Which is, you will remember, where an entirely different murder begins.

'Goodbye, Raphael!' cried Emily, nosing her van out into the traffic. 'You look fantastic.'

'Bloody damn it!' I muttered, fiddling with The Pill in my pocket. 'Bloody damn damn it!'

Which is, pretty much, all I have to say about Lord Slaggsby. I still have a little space left in this particular room, however – the kitchen – and so I shall clarify two final points before closing.

I was, of course, suspected of having a hand in the death of His Lordship. Even the police aren't obtuse enough to miss the connection between a man who buys a box of cream cakes at 9.30 in the morning and the reappearance of the same cream cakes 15 minutes later smeared all over the face of a recently deceased peer of the realm. Whether they looked for me or not I have no idea. What I do know is that they never found me, for my new life as a rock star acted as an impenetrable disguise. A fact that was demonstrated some 18 months later when The Executioners played a gig at a club in Newcastle. It was a good gig, and the audience loved it, particularly one big blonde-haired girl who kept clambering up on stage and kissing me on the cheek. At the end of our set she came over and asked me for my autograph, clearly unaware that we had met a number of times before. She was, you see, Sharon Maggot, the big-boned girl who assisted behind the counter in Shine's Bakery. Needless to say, I made my autograph as illegible as possible. No point tempting fate.

And, secondly, Emily's official-looking document. The document that got me out of Germany and back to England, out of one life and into another. What happened to it? Well, I kept it on my bedside table for the best part of 23 years, kissing it before I went to sleep each night, running my hand across it as though it were a part of Emily herself, until one night in 1968 when, fed up with being woken by His Lordship for no reason whatsoever, I seized it in a fit of anger, scrunched it up into a ball and jammed it violently into the mouth of the rubber communication tube that hung at the head of my bed. Which is, for all I know, where it remains to this very day; yellowed, rotting, forgotten, a pale shadow of its former self. In its heyday, however, what a door-opener it was! Oh what a door-opener!

# CHAPTER NINE

OH MY GOD, I've dropped The Pill down the lavatory! I was lean-ing over and it just rolled out of the top pocket of my pyjamas into the bowl. It's gone! Gone for ever! Hit the water with a plop, fizzed like an aspirin, and dissolved into nothingness. It's been taken from me, like a minuscule white turd. After all these years. My Pill! My darling Pill!

Only joking. Sorry, I couldn't resist it. It's Christmas Day and I'm feeling more than usually playful. I really am in exceedingly high spirits. I can barely contain my euphoria. I've been dancing round the kitchen since daybreak, clapping my hands like a flamenco dancer and singing carols at the top of my voice. I've now done 'The Holly and the Ivy' twenty times, and 'God Rest Ye Merry Gentle-men' at least as many. I can't remember all the words so I'm just making them up as I go:

> God rest ye merry gentlemen,
> Let nothing you dismay,
> For Mrs Bunshop's dead and gone,
> Oh hip hip hip hooray!
> And so's Lord Slaggsby and Keith Cream,
> It's murders by the day!

Oh-oh tidings of people that I've killed
People that I've killed!
Oh-oh tidings of people that I've killed!

I really haven't the faintest idea where this sudden rush of seasonal cheer has come from. Had Dr Bannen not mentioned it yesterday I wouldn't even have remembered today was Christmas in the first place. It would have slipped past unnoticed, just as it has done ever since I have been in the castle. For 15 years I haven't pulled a single cracker, thought a single festive thought or hung a single sprig of mistletoe. Yuletide and all its paraphernalia have been packed away and forgotten, like a set of defunct fairy lights.

And yet now, just a few days from my suicide, with not a Christmas tree or slice of roast turkey in sight (when I was young we used to have roast goose at Christmas, cooked to perfection by dear old Mrs Eggs), I'm suddenly awash with festive cheer. I'm at a loss to explain it. It's almost as if I'm being hijacked by my emotions. As if they are forcing themselves upon me, irrespective of the circumstances, aware that unless they take the initiative now they might never have the chance to be experienced again.

'It's your last Christmas,' they seem to be saying, 'and, whether you want to or not, you're bloody well going to enjoy it.'

And so I am. I'm having a whale of a time. Hello: I feel another carol coming on.

Hark! the herald angels sing,
Glory to the newborn king, etc., etc.

Note-wise things are going marvellously well. Far better than I thought they would yesterday afternoon, after that damned stone hit me in the buttock. After that little incident I feared I might be too distracted to work. Too neurotic. Too full of suspicion about who was doing these things to me, and why.

Once I got going on the note, however, my worries receded. I lost myself in my story, holding up my narrative like a shield against the outside world, fighting it off, keeping it at bay.

All last night I wrote like a man possessed, my pen flying across the plaster like a bird skimming a snowy field (or, it being Christmas, perhaps I should say a sleigh rushing down an icy slope). The kitchen is now finished, as is all but a narrow strip of the front foyer, and I am currently writing my way downwards into the cellar, the door of which opens off the foyer to the left of the main stairs (see plan). It's very dark down here, even with the light on, and I have had to strap a second candle to my forehead to provide adequate illumination. I feel like Orpheus descending into the underworld.

Nothing of any great significance happened in the kitchen – a gloomy, south-facing room with a cracked enamel sink beneath its window, a sagging sideboard along one wall and a rusty oven and fridge at either end of the sideboard – nothing, I repeat, of any great significance, save that, early on, I decided to increase the size of my writing. This is because the kitchen is a large room, and had I kept my letters as they were (i.e. the size of raisins), Lord Slaggsby's demise would only have filled about a half of it, hence ruining my one room/one murder scheme. I therefore inflated them from raisins to hazelnuts and was able to achieve a perfect fit. The most perfect fit, indeed, of any murder to date, which would doubtless have pleased its victim, who was always a stickler for neatness.

My writing's now back to raisin proportions again, although further manipulation might prove necessary later, especially in the cellar, which is also quite a sizeable space. I like the idea of my note expanding and contracting as it goes. It reminds me of a beating heart.

Size of writing aside, the only other real problem has been with pipes. The kitchen has more than its fair share of these – God alone knows who did the castle's plumbing, but they made a right hash of it – and it's been quite a job picking a path over and under and through and around them. On the room's eastern wall, for example, there is a veritable spaghetti of the damn things – big pipes, small

159

pipes, plastic pipes, copper pipes, straight pipes, curly pipes – and I had somehow to steer my note cleanly amongst these without ruining its shape or flow. It was like playing an exceedingly complex game of hopscotch, each sentence having to be carefully slotted into the space available like a foot between the cracks in a pavement. I managed it in the end, but it took a lot of effort and concentration, and by the time I was finished I was drenched in sweat, as though I had been defusing a large bomb.

Even with the pipes, however – the big pipes, the small pipes, the plastic pipes, the copper pipes, etc. – I still managed to complete the kitchen in record time. I entered it around seven o'clock last night, and was out again by eight this morning, by far the quickest progress I have yet made. My past, it seems, is going faster and faster, hurtling through the castle like a runaway train. If I really push it I reckon I could fill a room in under ten hours.

For the moment, however, enough of all that. It's now about nine o'clock, and as clear and fresh a Christmas morning as you could possibly wish for. I'm feeling fit and cheerful and replete with energy, and have, after almost four days and nights of solid writing, decided to take the day off. I'm well on target to complete my note in the allotted time, and therefore intend to take some wine, cigarettes and Mrs Bannen's plum pudding up to the dome, slump in my red wickerwork chair and while away the hours getting drunk and gazing out across the still, green sea. I can think of no better way to spend my Christmas. Except, perhaps, with Emily. Emily, however, has gone, so I guess I'll just have to make do with the pudding.

Season's greetings, everyone!

I'm only a couple of inches further down the wall, but it's ten hours later. Later than the exclamation mark above, that is. It's 7 p.m., and I'm a bit pissed. I've drunk four bottles of wine, two each of red and white, and my writing is looking distinctly wonky. Personally, I blame it on the cellar stairs. Very uneven. Putting me off my balance.

I've had an excellent day. Very sedate, very peaceful, very relaxing. The perfect hundredth Christmas.

'Merry Christmas, Raphael!' I've been saying to myself.

'Why, thank you,' I've been replying. 'And a Merry Christmas to you too!'

As planned, I climbed up to the roof, carrying with me my pudding and drink and cigarettes. Despite the crispness of the air, it wasn't unbearably cold, and as soon as I arrived I winched the dome open as far as it would go, its curved plates creaking backwards like the cheeks of a fat, smiling man. I then sat down on my old wickerwork chair and poured myself a large glass of vino.

'Bottoms up!' I toasted. 'Down the proverbial.'

Mrs Bannen's plum pudding was emitting the most delightful aroma – a rich, fruity fragrance, tinged with a faint perfume of brandy – and, having downed another couple of glasses of wine and smoked a cigarette or two, I removed its muslin covering and poked my fingers greedily into the sticky, yielding dessert (no point worrying about manners a week before you kill yourself!). I gorged out a large chunk and, grunting with pleasure, pushed it into my mouth. The taste brought tears to my eyes.

'Oh Jesus, that's good,' I mumbled, spilling thick clumps of pudding on to my pyjama front. 'That is so, so good. I don't think I've ever tasted anything so good. Oh God!'

I levered out another squidgy handful, and another, and another, ladling them into my mouth until, eventually, after twenty minutes or so, the bowl was completely empty. I licked my fingers like a cat, burped, and fired up a post-prandial cigarette.

'To Mrs Bannen!' I toasted, downing another glass of red. 'A queen amongst doctors' wives!'

Having eaten my pudding, and with my stomach distended as though I were pregnant, I settled back in my chair, propped my feet on the dome's winching mechanism and gazed contentedly out to sea.

There are, directly eastwards from the castle, a small group of islands – vague blips on the unerringly straight line of the horizon – and it has often amused me to search for shapes in their blurry outline, in much the same way as some people search for shapes in the billowing, fluffy whiteness of the clouds. One, for instance, has always struck me as looking distinctly like a forehead poking up out of the water, with the top of a slightly cabbage ear on one side, whilst another is the spitting image of a ship, seen in profile, with a pointed prow and a squashed funnel in the middle. Today I noticed for the first time that the largest of the islands, to the far left of the chain, bore an uncanny resemblance to a bedpan. One of those disposable cardboard bedpans you get in old people's homes and asylums. The more I stared at it, the more real it became, until I was almost convinced I could get up and go and have a piss in it. I couldn't of course, and so did one over the castle battlements instead.

I drank more wine, smoked more cigarettes, had a snooze, fetched and ate one of the packets of garibaldi biscuits Dr Bannen had delivered yesterday (suicide doesn't half give you a sweet tooth), and then, although at what precise point in the day I'm not sure, started thinking about death.

It is a curious fact that I have been writing my suicide note for the best part of five days and in all that time haven't once contemplated the actuality of my decease. I've announced it, I've written about it, I've planned it and I've accepted it, but at no point have I given serious thought to what it might actually entail. I've been like a typist, busily transcribing a document without taking much notice of its actual contents.

'I'm going to die!' I gasped, as though someone had just informed me of the fact. 'I'm bloody well going to kill myself!'

The first thought that crossed my mind was whether or not it was going to be painful. Hopefully not. The main reason I've carried The Pill around for so long, after all, is on the assumption that if and when I do finally pop it, it'll do its job instantaneously. What, however, if it doesn't? What if it takes time, and if during that time it hurts? True, Emily told me it would kill within seconds, but that was almost a hundred years ago. Its potency might have faded. Diminished over the decades.

I became, I must confess, a little alarmed. Nobody, let's face it, sets out to kill themselves painfully. Perhaps, I thought, I shouldn't do it with The Pill after all. Or perhaps I should take The Pill and then immediately jump off the castle battlements, thereby ensuring that if it did give me a bad tummy I wouldn't have to endure it for too long before I was smashed to death on the rocks 300 feet below.

My fears, however, were only momentary. I trust my pill. Over the years we've built up quite a rapport, and I know for a fact it would never hurt me, any more than I would hurt it. Of course, I won't be certain until I swallow it, but I'm as convinced as one can be without proof that, when it comes to the crunch, The Pill will do its business swiftly, neatly and with a minimum of fuss.

'I've absolute faith in you, old boy,' I said, holding the tiny white disc up into the pale sunlight. 'We'll do it together, and we'll do it painlessly. Teamwork. That's what it's all about.'

'I quite agree,' said The Pill.

Having laid those worries to rest, I then turned my thoughts to what I'd look like after I'd died.

It's strange to think of oneself dead. Not an easy connection to make. Whenever we picture ourselves it's invariably in a living context: running through summer meadows, bonking attractive women, performing heroic deeds – an active, breathing, thinking, sensate being, full of flowing blood and tingling nerves and pulsating tissue. It's hard to conjure yourself as a carcass, devoid of those vital elements which, taken together, make you the person you are. It's like trying to paint a self-portrait of a complete stranger.

Ideally, I'd like to be an attractive corpse. A noble cadaver, sitting bolt upright in my red wickerwork chair, a peaceful expression on my face, my eyes, perhaps, still open; a picture of dignified decease. Something people can admire. Something that allows me to maintain a little self-respect.

Whether it'll work out like that, however, I've no idea. I might just

163

as easily fetch up slumped on the floor of the dome covered in vomit. Or with a bright-blue face. Or a snotty nose and a frothy mouth. I might be a ridiculous corpse. Or a disgusting one. I might even start to smell. (I remember seeing a corpse in France during the war, and it was a horrible-looking thing, with bulging eyes and a trickle of blood coming out of its mouth. Very unappetizing.)

Ultimately, however, I suppose it doesn't really matter what I end up looking like, any more than it matters what happens to a house once you've moved out of it. My body will be just an abandoned casing, no more and no less, something that was once a part of me but has now been sloughed off, like the skin of a snake. I do hope, however, that I don't shit myself, particularly in my white pyjamas. That would simply be too demeaning.

I wondered who would find my body – Dr Bannen, probably, the discovery no doubt precipitating a particularly intense bout of wheezing on his part – and what would happen to the castle, and all the various odds and ends within it. I wondered if I would be buried or cremated, and what sort of effect my suicide note would have on those who read it. I wondered, too, if I'd get a mention in the papers.

Above all, however, I wondered, as I'm sure do all those who are preparing to die, what exactly is waiting for me on the far side of death. If, indeed, there is a far side of death, and the whole thing isn't simply a vast, blank, all-consuming void. A sort of eternal full stop against which the essay of my life will run up like a train against a set of buffers.

Emily, for her part, believed, or at least she did when she explained the whole thing to me aged ten, that when you died you became, of all things, a breeze, blowing endlessly around the world, conscious yet intangible, an awareness without form or shape. Sometimes a group of breezes gathered together and formed themselves into a wind, whilst a hurricane was little more than a large and somewhat unruly convocation of the dead.

'It's wonderful,' she opined. 'You can go where you want, and do what you want. You can fly right up in the air, and knock old ladies' hats off. It's fun.'

Personally, I've never been entirely convinced by this, although I can't help wondering if there isn't *something* beyond that final moment. Not so much an after-life – I've never been a great one for heaven and hell – as a new life. A different life. Perhaps death will be just one full stop amongst many in an essay that runs on for ever. Perhaps I'll finish the chapter of this life and straightaway begin another. Perhaps we simply go on and on, disintegrating and re-forming, breaking up and coming together, across the aeons, ad infinitum.

I tried to picture what things might be like after death. If there *is* a continuance, for instance, will it be in this world – the world I know – or an entirely different one? Will I go up, down, forwards, backwards, sideways or in some completely other direction, one that physicists, or whoever it is who deals with these things, have yet to discover? Maybe I'll reappear in the past, or way, way in the future. Maybe I'll live exactly the same life again, or the same life but with subtle differences, or perhaps a completely different life, but one that has, at some point or other, intersected the one I'm soon about to end. Perhaps I'll come back as one of my own victims, as though time were a merry-go-round about which we revolve eternally, on each circuit riding a different character. Perhaps I'll return as Keith, or Walter, or even, God forbid, Mrs Bunshop. Perhaps, in eternity, we are everyone we have ever known.

I grappled with these and other such conceits for the remainder of the day, and before I knew it the sun was sinking behind the heads of the westward hills, the first stars were twinkling in the east and I was shivering with the evening cold.

'How time flies when you're killing yourself,' I chuckled.

I emptied my fourth bottle of wine and stepped from the dome on to the concrete surface of the roof. As I did so, however, I tripped and fell backwards on to the dome's winching mechanism, banging the upper part of my spine against the metal handle. Had I been sober, it would have been extremely painful. Fortunately, however, I wasn't, and simply got back on to my feet, laughing at my frailty, and headed downstairs to get on with the note.

'Merry Christmas, stars!' I called as I descended into my bedroom.

No one knocked on the door all day, or threw any stones.

I've wasted more time and space than I intended describing the events of this afternoon – if one can indeed call the processes of one's mind events – and am already well on my way along the first wall of the cellar. It's cold and damp down here, which, if nothing else, is helping to sober me up, and I have had to pull on a jumper over my pyjama top. My writing, thank heavens, is rather straighter than it was an hour ago.

I've got a funny feeling in my back, where I banged it on the roof. It's not a pain, or an ache, more a soft tingling, like gentle bolts of electricity radiating outwards from the upper part of my spine. It's covering the area of my wings, and I'm a bit worried I've damaged them. It's not an entirely unpleasant sensation, however, so I'm not too concerned. I suppose if you fall over at my age you have to expect some sort of after-effect.

Back problems or no back problems, however, I need to get on. Time's ticking away and I still have a brace of murders to commit. My candles are burning, my pen is scribbling and The Pill sits contentedly in the pocket of my pyjamas. My last ever Christmas, and it's all but finished. I feel a little sad. One more carol, I think, just for the road:

> Silent night,
> Holy night,
> All is clear,
> All is bright, etc.

And now onwards.

# CHAPTER TEN

I GOT INVOLVED IN the Second World War because of – who else? – Emily. Before I bumped into her that freezing late-January morning of 1940, shortly after the accident with the giant safe, I had no intention whatsoever of going into the army. On the contrary, I had every intention whatsoever of staying out of it.

Then, however, I saw her, golden-haired and perfect, scrabbling round on the pavement picking up her spilled shoeboxes, and, as always happens, my excitement got the better of me, so that before I knew what I was doing I was waving my call-up papers and making all sorts of rash promises about going off to fight for king and country.

'Oh Raphael,' she cried. 'You're so brave! I knew you'd do something like this. You must let me see you off.'

Of course, at that stage, neither of us knew that I would be doing very little in the way of actual fighting. My war was to be one of prolonged incarceration. Not the easy option, by any means – many around me were sent utterly doolally by the whole experience – but, all things considered, I think I coped with imprisonment remarkably well. I'm not sure Emily would agree, but that's getting ahead of myself. In the harsh winter chill that morning, she stood on the platform waving a monogrammed silk handkerchief as my train puffed out of Liverpool's Lime Street station, and appeared utterly enthralled.

'You're a hero, Raphael!'

'I'm an idiot,' I muttered, slumping back into my seat and wondering how on earth I got myself into these situations. 'A bloody idiot.'

'We're all going to die,' wailed a ginger-haired young conscript beside me. 'We're going to die! Die! Dieeeeeeee!'

I shan't waste time and wall space with too detailed an account of the early part of my army career. Suffice to say that after eight weeks' basic military training, and a further six weeks' instruction at an officer-training unit, I was duly posted to the 7th Battalion of the Green Howards with the exalted rank of Second Lieutenant.

I spent some two weeks at the Howards' headquarters in Yorkshire before, at the end of April 1940, my battalion was suddenly ordered to France. On arrival at Cherbourg I was promoted to First Lieutenant, for no obvious reason other than that at that particular time, in that particular place, first lieutenants appeared to be in rather short supply.

A further two weeks were spent building airfields in the freezing countryside up near Boulogne, before we were all stuck in trucks again and moved south-eastwards to Arras, where the 4th Battalion of the Green Howards were frantically holding positions along the River Scarpe. Casualties, apparently, had been heavy, particularly amongst the officers, which probably explains why I received another lightning promotion as soon as I arrived, to Captain this time. Given the circumstances, I was somewhat less than flattered by my additional pip.

Thus it was that a little less than four months after killing Mr Popplethwaite, and only four weeks after joining my regiment, I found myself sitting in a crumbling dugout beside the River Scarpe with a Bren gun, several very frightened soldiers and a bottle of excellent Chablis I'd been given by a local restaurateur. The Pill and

The Photo were buttoned up in the pocket of my battledress, whilst a nightingale was tweeting in a thicket away to the left, even though it was the middle of the night.

'When do you think they'll attack, sir?' asked one of my men.

'I have absolutely no idea, Jenkins,' I replied. 'I don't even know where they are, so keep your eyes peeled.'

'We're all going to die. Die! Dieee!' This from the young ginger-haired conscript I'd met on the train from Liverpool, who, by an extraordinary turn of fate, had fetched up not only in the same regiment as me, but in the very unit I was now commanding.

'No, we're not going to die, Lemon,' I told him firmly. 'Just keep down and keep quiet and keep looking. I'm going to have a shit.'

Whereupon I stood up and, taking my bottle of Chablis, clambered out of the dugout and scampered over to the thicket on our left, where I pulled down my trousers and squatted amongst the brambles. The nightingale continued tweeting for a moment above me, and then flew away with a chirrup of disgust.

'What I wouldn't give for a nice comfortable lavatory,' I groaned, 'with a proper seat and nice loo paper and a chain that . . . Jesus Christ Almighty.'

A huge explosion shook the ground, throwing me forward on to my face. There were screams, more explosions and the jarring rat-at-at of machine-gun fire. Momentary plumes of light illuminated the scene, giving way to an intense, inky blackness. I struggled to my feet, but, quite forgetting that my combat trousers were still around my ankles, pitched forward again, smashing my nose on an old tree stump.

'Bollocks,' I hissed.

I could vaguely make out people running to and fro. One came directly towards me, running at full tilt, before another explosion lifted him off his feet and deposited him on the ground about two feet from where I was sprawled. He lay very still with his head twisted at a curious angle, eyes bulging and blood seeping from the corner of his mouth. It was Jenkins, and he was dead.

Had I been a halfway decent officer, I would, at that moment, without hesitation, have pulled up my trousers, unbuckled my Webley .455 and charged forward to help my men. As it happened, however, I didn't move an inch. I buried my face in a tussock of grass, held my breath and prayed for the ground to swallow me up. Even when I heard Private Lemon's pathetic voice squealing, 'Sir! Sir! Help me, sir!' I still didn't move. I kept perfectly still, perfectly quiet, perfectly pathetic.

Which is how, twenty minutes later, I was found by the German soldiers: spread-eagled, face down, with my face buried in a mound of grass and my trousers around my ankles. There was a cackle of laughter, and I felt the muzzle of a rifle being wiggled between my buttocks. I was then hoisted to my feet, relieved of my bottle of Chablis and led away into captivity. I was a prisoner of war, and hadn't fired a single shot.

Although we didn't know it at the time, Offizierslager 18B, fondly known as The Bosch Butlin's, was situated about 30 miles west of Bremen. I was in the first batch of prisoners to arrive, and remained there for the duration of the war, until we were liberated in April 1945. As the title suggests, it was a prison camp solely for officers – 500 of them at full capacity, from Britain and the Commonwealth; no Americans: a fact which, if it didn't necessarily make for more comfortable living, at least allowed us the illusion of being prisoners of the highest class. No hoi polloi in our compound!

A square affair some 600 yards long by the same wide, 18B sat in low scrubland with hills away to the west and a large forest to the east. It was surrounded by an electrified wire fence on which birds would land and immediately burst into flames, as well as the five barrack blocks (A, B, C, D and E) in which prisoners were housed, two guard rooms, a camp office, the commandant's quarters, a punishment block, a kitchen block and a set of foetid washrooms. Seen from the air, it would have looked something like this:

## Aerial View of Offlag 18B

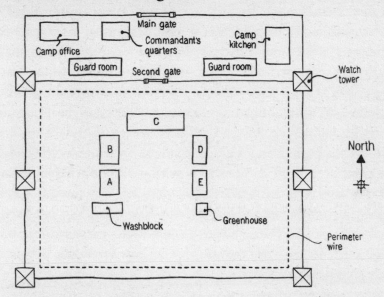

I was assigned to barrack room C, where I had the bottom half of a bunk-bed in the corner nearest the door. The top half was occupied by a large Welch Fusilier who snored and farted in his sleep. Snored and farted, indeed, louder than anyone I've ever known in my life, so that in five years of captivity I don't think I enjoyed a single decent night's kip.

'Is there no way you could move him, sir,' I asked Colonel Dishby. 'It really is intolerable.'

'I sympathize, Phoenix, I really do, but I'm afraid you're just going to have to pucker-up and knuckle down. We're in a bally pickle here, and we've all got to pull together. Chin up, nose to the grindstone, that's the way.'

'But, sir—'

'Now, now, Phoenix! Don't want Jerry to see us squabbling, do we? Grit your teeth, give it a bit of gumption and we'll be back in Blighty in no time.'

'Yes, sir.'

'That's the ticket! Now, how about a game of whist?'

Colonel Dishby was the senior ranking officer in our barracks, in the whole camp, indeed, and it was to him that we deferred on all matters concerning our daily life. A small, rotund man with a bristling moustache and a pronounced limp – 'Bally sniper got me in the knee. Damn poor show!' – he spoke a language entirely of his own devising: an arcane, bantering gobbledegook that owed less to the English vernacular than it did to the extraordinary workings of his own imagination. A trip to the lavatory block would thus be described as 'a lightning shimmy down to the old flush-wallahs' whilst a meeting with the camp commandant was termed 'a quick how's-your-father with Obersturmführer Pisspot.' Amazingly, despite the prosaic obtuseness of his sentences, we generally understood what he was getting at. Not so the Germans, who were convinced he was talking in some sort of secret code and took him off for frequent interrogations with sallow-faced SS cryptographers.

'Gave me the old once-over with the bally thingummy-do-daa,' he would declare cheerfully on his return. 'Silly blighters.'

The colonel was determined that prolonged captivity should in no way dampen our spirits.

'Got to keep morale up!' he opined. 'Don't want Jerry to think we're rum-baba. Plenty of bing and bong, that's the ticket!'

To this end he organized an endless round of activities to keep us busy. A typical day in Offlag 18B would begin with a bit of drill practice, followed by some gardening on the camp vegetable plot, then a game of cricket, some football, a gym session, more cricket, more football, more drill, some singing, a play rehearsal, a bit of barrack cleaning and all manner of other little diversions to while away the time and persuade us that, despite our enforced inactivity, there was, in fact, some overriding purpose to our existence.

There was but one area of camp life over which the colonel didn't exercise control, and that was escapes, these being the preserve of a haggard-looking major from the Black Watch called, appropriately, Major Burrows. The latter arrived some five months into my captivity and immediately assumed responsibility for all break-out attempts, although what actually qualified him for the job I never found out. Rumours abounded that in peacetime he was a circus escapologist.

Where Colonel Dishby spoke in a sort of prosaic bluster, Major Burrows was laconic to the point of muteness. He rarely spoke, and when he did employed the fewest words possible to convey his meaning, so that talking to him was uncannily similar to conversing with a telegram.

'Tunnel, Barrack D,' he would whisper. 'Start washroom, under sink. Four hundred yards to woods. Dig round clock. Complete four weeks. Begin tonight.'

Major Burrows loved tunnels. There was, for him, something peculiarly escape-like about them, as though the entire experience of breaking free was somehow enhanced by doing it down a long, muddy, underground shaft. I have no idea how many tunnels he initiated in the course of his sojourn at 18B, but it must have been a lot because by the final stages of our captivity, local roads were regularly subsiding into the excavations beneath them, and the overall volume of tunnels in the vicinity heavily outweighed that of soil.

Burrows' tunnels generally started in one of the barrack huts and headed eastwards towards the forest 400 yards beyond the camp perimeter, the soil in that direction being rather looser and less stony than it was at every other point of the compass. There were, of course, exceptions, such as the tunnel that started in the wash block and headed westwards, or the one that began in the mini-greenhouse on the camp vegetable plot and headed nobody knew quite where. In the main, however, we usually aimed for the forest. We would all pitch in, working in shifts, and using whatever delving implements we could find or make. Tunnels would be shored up with wood stripped from the walls, floors, rafters and beds of our barracks, whilst soil would be disposed of in our mattresses, beneath our huts, on our garden, or, as the years passed and more and more tunnels were built, in old shafts that were no longer of any use.

Major Burrows planned his tunnels to the minutest detail. He would draw graphs and maps and plans and charts. He would measure and calculate and ponder and determine. Nothing was left to chance; every possibility was considered. Which made it all the more surprising that they were, without exception, to prove such unmitigated failures. Some surfaced short of the mark and were spotted by vigilant guards; others made it to the woods but then, once there, couldn't find anywhere to exit because the trees were too thick. In 1943 we thought we'd cracked it with a tunnel from Barrack B, only to find, after four months of digging, that we'd somehow gone round in a circle and ended up beneath Barrack D.

'Sure it's not roots?' Major Burrows inquired of the captain who'd made this unfortunate discovery.

'No, sir,' he replied. 'It's my bed.'

If his subterranean endeavours bore little fruit, the major enjoyed more – although only slightly more – success with his schemes above ground. These were invariably colourful, hare-brained affairs, the entertainment value of which easily made up for the fact that they rarely came off. On one occasion, for instance, he tried to escape by clinging to the underside of the commandant's car – foiled because the car broke down before it reached the front gates – whilst on another he and four others almost got away disguised as members of a visiting Red Cross inspection team, the ruse only failing because one of the real team, who we had tied up and concealed beneath the floorboards of Barrack D, struggled free and raised the alarm. He had people pole-vaulting over the electrified perimeter fence, squirming under it and, in one memorable instance, endeavouring to fly above it in a home-made hot-air balloon, the latter scheme, like the balloon itself, singularly failing to get off the ground. Most spectacular of all, he once donned a wig made of mattress stuffing and, hips swaying provocatively, insinuated himself into a group of prostitutes as they left the compound after a night entertaining the camp guards. He would have made it, too, had one of the guards not taken a fancy to him and tried to kiss him on his way out, whereupon his true identity was discovered and he was consigned to the punishment block for two weeks on quarter-rations.

'If at first you don't succeed,' he had sighed laconically, 'try, try, try again.'

Like every other prisoner at Offlag 18B, I played my part in these escape attempts. I dug tunnels, I tied up unsuspecting Red Cross workers, I helped stitch the canopy of our hot-air balloon. In but one respect did I differ from the others: I had no desire whatsoever to escape.

Don't get me wrong, I wasn't happy at 18B. Neither, however, was I especially unhappy. On balance I would rather have been there than, say, getting blown up in North Africa or shot at on the beaches of Normandy. It might not have been much, but the camp offered a degree of security when everywhere else in the world appeared singularly insecure. For my fellow prisoners escape was a duty. For me the only duty was staying alive.

The problem was, of course, that everyone assumed you *did* want to escape, and I was therefore required to tread a thin line between, on the one hand, enthusiasm and, on the other, inertia. Like a negative image of Major Burrows, I became an expert at *not* getting out of the camp whilst all the while giving the impression that I actually wanted nothing more. I thus tunnelled and stitched and rioted with the best of them, yet when it came to my turn to enjoy the fruits of that tunnelling/stitching/ rioting, I became curiously indisposed. When it was my turn to pole-vault over the fence, for instance, I developed an inexplicable paralysis of the right leg, whilst the night before I was due to escape concealed inside a large packing crate I engineered a slight altercation with one of the guards, as a result of which I ended up consigned to the punishment block for a week.

'Damn hard cheese, old boy,' consoled Colonel Dishby. 'Must learn to control the old temper poo-poos.'

Most reprehensible of all, I alerted the Germans to the presence of certain tunnels when it began to look like those tunnels might actually reach their destinations. I enacted my treachery via small notes posted beneath the door of the camp office, suggesting, in pigeon German, that were the authorities to look beneath such and such a bunk in such and such a barrack they might well find something to their interest. There is no real excuse for such shabby behaviour, and I felt wretched doing it, but the desire to stay well and truly put was overwhelming. I could simply not take the risk, minuscule as it was, of one of Major Burrows' tunnels actually emerging where it was supposed to, for had it done so there would have been no excuse for not using it. Half a century after the event, I apologize unreservedly to those whose hopes I so cruelly dashed. For what it's worth, I feel far worse about my snitching than I do about murdering all those people.

And so the five years of captivity passed. I played cricket, I did drill, I worked on the camp vegetable garden, and I didn't escape. The Pill remained secreted in the inner pocket of the calfskin wallet in which I had kept it since the early Thirties, whilst The Photo I pinned to the wall beside my bunk. Aside from that, nothing else happened. Nothing whatsoever.

Except for one thing. I learnt how to play the piano. There was an old, out-of-tune upright in the corner of our barracks, and a captain in the Canadian Marines taught me how to use it, introducing me to keys and scales and chords, and taking me through a variety of simple tunes. I wasn't very good to start with, and it took me almost six months to learn 'Jingle Bells'. I gradually improved, however, and by the time we were liberated I'd become remarkably proficient, enlivening our camp concerts with extended, jazzy renditions of such popular favourites as 'I'll Remember You, My Darling', 'There'll Always be an England', 'Underneath the Arches' and 'I Leave My Heart in an English Garden'. At the time it was just a bit of fun, and I never suspected that, a quarter of a century later, I'd be doing it professionally, let alone as part of one of the seminal rock bands of the early Seventies. Which just goes to show how unexpected life can be.

*

The albino twins arrived at Offlag 18B in July 1944, and things immediately started to become more interesting.

I was playing cricket when they arrived, fielding at gully as the camp gates swung open and a covered truck drove through. It pulled up in front of the camp office and from the back two of the most extraordinary-looking creatures I have ever seen stepped down. Or rather one of the most extraordinary creatures, accompanied by his mirror image.

Clive and Matthew Brain, for such were their names, were identical twins. And identical they were in every sense of the word. They were absolutely indistinguishable; as like one another as it was possible to be without actually *being* one another. More than once over the ensuing months, indeed, I wondered if perhaps they were actually the same person and their apparent duality was simply a result of my having gone cross-eyed during my years of captivity.

They were precisely the same height and girth, walked in precisely the same manner and spoke in precisely the same voice. They were dressed in precisely the same uniform, that of RAF flight lieutenants, and, as I later discovered in the communal showers, were blessed with interchangeable, and extremely large, private parts. And as if all that wasn't enough, they were both albinos, with brilliant white hair, white parchment skin and piercing magenta eyes.

'Like a pair of mythical what-you-ma-call-its,' opined Colonel Dishby, who was so fascinated by the new arrivals that, for the first time in four years, he gave an incorrect umpiring decision (LBW when the ball was at least two feet outside the off stump).

Fate being what it is – i.e. inescapable – the Brain twins were assigned to my barrack. Not only that, but to the bunk immediately beside mine.

'I'm putting the what-you-ma-do-das in beside you, Phoenix,' announced the colonel. 'They're a bally odd couple, so keep an eye on 'em, there's a good man. Think they might be a bit, you know, how's your father.'

'Yes, sir.'

And keep an eye on 'em I did. Two eyes indeed. Had I had ten eyes I would have kept all of them on the twins, all of the time, for they were the sort of people you couldn't help but look at.

It wasn't just that they were of such strikingly similar appearance, but that they seemed to do and say and think the same things, as though possessed of a single will. They would, for instance, sleep in precisely the same position, turning over at the same time and, to general amusement, each cuddling an identical teddy bear in the crook of his left arm. They would finish each other's sentences, or both say the same thing at the same time. When the Lancaster Bomber in which they'd been flying – Clive as a navigator, Matthew as a bombadier – had been shot down, they had both, according to one of their colleagues, screamed at precisely the same pitch, and with precisely the same degree of terror. Even the normally unflappable Major Burrows was transfixed by them.

'Incredible,' he muttered, staring at the twins. 'Wonder what like digging tunnels.'

As was to be expected of a couple with so many shared characteristics, the Brain twins – or, as I came to know them, the albino twins – enjoyed a quite unrivalled depth of sibling attachment. They always hugged affectionately before clambering into their respective bunks for the night, laughed uproariously at each other's not especially amusing jokes, and were often to be seen holding hands, as if they were not merely identical but in fact Siamese twins, inseparably joined at the fingertips. On the football field more than one scoring opportunity was missed because, at the moment when he was about to kick the ball into an open goal, a player might happen to glance up, spot the albino twins arm in arm on the touchline, lose concentration as a result and hammer the ball twenty yards wide of the mark.

'Damned bad miss,' Colonel Dishby would cry before spotting the twins himself and running straight into a goalpost.

Most extraordinary of all, and most fascinating, the Brain brothers appeared to possess rudimentary powers of telepathy.

One evening, for example, they were working in one of Major Burrows's tunnels. Matthew emerged with a large sack of earth and was halfway across the barrack on his way to depositing it on the camp vegetable plot when he stopped dead and uttered a piercing cry.

'Clive!' he screamed. 'He's in trouble.'

He dropped his sack and rushed back to the tunnel where, it transpired, his brother and two other men had been buried by a roof collapse. There had been no noise, and there was no way he could possibly have known what had occurred a hundred yards away and ten feet underground. And yet know he did. It was uncanny.

'Gives me the chumbly-rumblies,' admitted the colonel. 'Like a pair of bally radars.'

It was shortly after the aforementioned incident that I found myself lying on my bunk talking to the twins, who were sitting side by side on Clive's bunk a few feet away.

'Can I ask you a rather personal question?' I asked.

'If you like,' they replied, glancing at one another and smiling.

'Well, I don't want to pry or anything, but have you ever had a disagreement?'

'A disagreement?'

'Yes. You seem so close in every respect, I was wondering if you'd ever argued, or held opposing views on a given subject? Has there ever been a time when you haven't liked each other?'

They gasped in surprise and linked hands as though to emphasize the indissolubility of their relationship.

'Never!' they cried with one voice. 'Never.'

Which is when I got the idea.


I didn't actually set out to kill the albino twins. At no point did it occur to me my actions might result in their deaths. Rather, I just wanted to experiment. See how far I could push them. To ascertain whether, in the light of their seeming inseparability, it might be possible to drive a wedge between the pair.

'It's just a bit of fun,' I assured myself. 'I'll get them to argue and then stop. I won't cause any lasting damage. Just one little argument, that's all. It'll help pass the time. Keep my spirits up.'

And indeed it did. From the moment I began plotting against the twins my spirits rocketed. I felt better than I had done in years.

I began my campaign by observing. For two whole months, from the middle of August 1944 to the middle of October, I did nothing but watch the Brains, surreptitiously gathering a wealth of data upon which to base my forthcoming activities.

I learnt, for instance, that each hid his toothbrush beneath his pillow and kept a photo of his family concealed beneath the mattress of his bed. Both, I found out, were highly partial to mint humbugs, hated insects (Clive having a particular aversion to spiders, Matthew to woodlice), collected stamps and received a fortnightly letter from their sister, Kitty. From camp medical records, copies of which I saw courtesy of a bribed guard, I discovered Clive had a chronic allergy to cheese, that broad beans brought Matthew out in a rash and that both suffered from a mild form of eczema, for which they were prescribed a soothing potassium cream. For two months I did nothing but probe and delve and nose and note, prying relentlessly into every aspect of the twins' lives until I knew them almost as well as they knew each other. Until I knew them almost as well as I knew myself.

And then it was time to begin.

From the outset I knew that patience was the order of the day. The Brains were devoted to each other, and that was not something that could be changed overnight. I needed to plant seeds, sow doubts, nurture antipathy. A poke here, a nudge there; nothing too obvious or dramatic.

To this end I planned my campaign in three stages. Firstly, I would target just one of the twins. To have hit them both at the same time might have been to engender a sense of shared victimhood which would only serve to throw them closer together. By tormenting one alone I would, hopefully, pry them apart a little, laying the foundations of doubt and uncertainty upon which I could build in Stage Two, when I intended to widen my operations to encompass both together. If things went according to plan, they would, by the end of this second stage, be like parched brushwood, ready to burst into flame at the least spark. That spark would come in Stage Three, which is when the teddy bears would come into play.

With this framework in mind, and with my intelligence gathered, I lay on my bunk one evening and flipped a coin. Heads for Matthew, tails for Clive. It came up tails. Clive it was. I embarked on Stage One.

I started with his family photo. One night, whilst everyone was asleep, I slid my hand carefully beneath the mattress of Clive's bottom bunk and removed the photo from its hiding place. In the intermittent illumination of the camp searchlights I was confronted by the assembled Brain family arranged around a table in a country garden. Had they not pointed themselves out to me on an earlier occasion I would never have guessed which twin was which. As it was, however, I knew that Clive was the one standing behind his mother and, glancing across to make sure the albinos were still safely asleep, duly took a pencil and scored a thick cross through his face before returning the photo to its hiding place beneath the mattress. I then curled up on my own bed and went to sleep.

The next morning all hell broke loose.

'Matthew!' cried the distraught owner of the defaced picture. 'Someone's ruined my photo!'

I peered surreptitiously from beneath my blanket to see Clive perched on the edge of his bunk, clutching his photo, a look of pained bewilderment on his face. Matthew sat beside him, arm around the shoulder of his trembling sibling.

'Who would so such a thing?' whimpered Clive. 'Who would be so cruel?'

'There, there,' consoled Matthew. 'There, there.' And then, raising his voice so the whole barrack could hear. 'It's probably just someone

181

who's jealous. Someone who can't bear the thought of other people being happy. Swine!'

'But why just *my* face?' inquired Clive. 'Why have they just crossed out my face? Look, they haven't drawn on yours.'

'I don't know,' replied Matthew, shaking his head. 'Unless . . .' And with that he leapt to his feet and pulled his own version of the photo from beneath the mattress of his top bunk.

'No,' he said, sounding rather disappointed, as though the pristine state of his photo denied him the opportunity of sharing in his brother's distress. 'They haven't touched mine. It's most peculiar. I think we should have a word with Colonel Dishby.'

This they did, and later that afternoon the entire barracks was subjected to a long lecture on the importance of the old camp-fire stuff (trust) and the need to respect one another's personal felicity plum-plums (possessions). I glanced over at the albino twins, standing hand in hand in a corner. They appeared more united than ever, and I began to wonder if perhaps I'd set myself an impossible task.

Not to be deterred, however, I next turned my attention to Clive's daffodil.

Each Brain had a daffodil which they kept in an old evaporated-milk tin on the window ledge opposite their bunks. Clive's was in the tin on the left, Matthew's on the right. They were extremely proud of their respective plants, and were forever watering, pruning, spraying and pampering them. Not surprisingly, each daffodil was exactly the same size, and flowered at exactly the same time.

'Damn pretty daffodils!' the colonel would expostulate. 'Pukka as anything I ever saw at Chelsea.'

'Thank you, sir,' the twins would return, puffing with pride.

I attacked the daffodils late one afternoon when everyone else was outside watching an inter-barracks bowls tournament. Sneaking back on the pretext of fetching my cigarettes, I swiftly removed Clive's daffodil from its tin and severed its stem from its bulb. The stem I then put back in the tin, whilst the bulb I replanted beside Matthew's daffodil. Outwardly the two flowers looked exactly as they had done before, and I went back outside with a sly smile on my face.

Nothing happened for a couple of days. Then, to my immense satisfaction, and the consternation of my victims, Clive's daffodil began to wilt whilst in Matthew's tin a new daffodil began to grow. Each morning thereafter they would wake up and rush over to their respective plants, Matthew to gaze in joy, Clive in despair.

'I can't understand it,' wailed the latter. 'My beautiful daffodil!'

'I'm so sorry, Clive,' consoled his brother.

'I just can't think what's happened to it,' said Clive, cupping the wilting stem in his hand. 'I just can't think what's happened.'

Eventually Clive's ailing daffodil gave up the ghost altogether and subsided into a sort of mushy pulp, whereupon he removed it from its pot and discovered the absence of its bulb. His face went even whiter than its normal white – a sort of transparent white, as though he possessed no colour at all – and his crimson eyes narrowed.

'The bulb's gone,' he said simply.

'Gone?' inquired Matthew

'Yes, gone. Someone's stolen the bulb. That's why it died.'

'Well, I can't think why someone would steal your bulb.'

'Neither can I. But I can guess where they've put it.'

'Where?'

'In your tin, of course. That's why you've got a new plant growing.'

'But that's growing from my bulb. It's a new stem.'

'I think not, Matthew. I think some unknown person has for some unknown reason taken my bulb and put it in your tin. Would you mind if I had a look?'

'Not at all.'

And so Clive had a dig around in Matthew's tin and, of course, discovered the pilfered bulb.

'I just can't understand it,' mumbled Matthew. 'It's so strange. It's so—'

'Sneaky,' whispered Clive, looking at the floor. 'Very, very sneaky.'

That afternoon we had another lecture from Colonel Dishby

about the rotten beastliness of persecuting a fellow prisoner when we ought to be directing such behaviour against our captors. Once again I glanced across at the albino twins. They appeared as united as ever. I noticed, however, that they were no longer holding hands. It might have been nothing. But then again . . .

Thereafter I stepped up operations. I stole Clive's toothbrush from beneath his pillow and slipped it beneath Matthew's pillow.

'Someone's taken my toothbrush!' yelled Clive the following morning.

'Hello!' said Matthew innocently. 'Here it is, under my pillow. I wonder how it got there.'

'So do I,' mumbled Clive. 'Gremlins, I suppose.'

I mixed a little salt into Clive's eczema cream, eliciting howls of agony when he applied it to the afflicted portions of his anatomy, and bribed one of the camp guards to hand over all letters addressed to him before they were delivered.

'They're just getting lost in the system,' said Matthew, after yet another post hand-out at which he'd received four letters and his brother none. 'Don't worry, Clive. Here, you can read mine. I've got one from Kitty.'

'I don't want to read yours. I want my own letters. My own letters, do you hear! This whole thing's driving me mad. Someone's got it in for me!'

Over the next two months I collected 22 envelopes addressed to Clive Brain. Then, just after Christmas, I slit a hole in the side of Matthew's mattress and, removing some of the stuffing, concealed the pilfered missives therein, where they were discovered three days later during a routine barracks search.

'What are these?' asked the guard, holding up the letters.

'I don't know,' stumbled Matthew in bewilderment. 'They seem to be—'

'Letters!' cried Clive. 'My letters! They're *my* letters, hidden in *your* mattress!'

'Clive,' said Matthew, shaking his head. 'Clive, believe me, I have no idea how they got there. You must believe me.'

'I don't know what to believe any more, Matthew,' snapped Clive. 'I need some fresh air. My head's going round and round.'

And with that he stormed out of the barracks, the first time either twin had been alone since they'd arrived at the camp. Stage One was complete, and things were looking good.

Early in the New Year of 1945 – shortly after my 45th birthday – I initiated Stage Two. Heretofore I had concentrated my efforts solely against Clive Brain. Now I brought Matthew into the picture too. The time had come to target both twins at once.

I began on the football pitch. The Brains loved football, and played as often as they could, always knocking in an average of two goals apiece per game.

'It's because we support each other,' they explained when I once commented on the remarkable synchronicity of their scoring patterns. 'We're a sort of team within a team.'

The twins always played on the wing, Clive to the right, Matthew to the left. I, on the other hand, always played in goal, my unusual height and agility making me ideally suited to the task, and it wasn't long before I realized the potentialities of my position for furthering my anti-twin endeavours. With flamboyant and ostentatiously showy efforts to keep them out, I began letting in goals by Clive. Shots that in normal circumstances I would have parried with ease I now allowed to dribble under me, or bounce over me, or creep into the corner of the goal just past the ends of my outstretched fingertips. Where previously he had made an average of two scores per game, Clive now found himself making ten or more. At the same time I redoubled my efforts to keep Matthew's shots *out* of the goal: leaping, jumping, diving and throwing myself about with near-suicidal abandon in order to block his every kick. Whilst his brother was basking in the glory of another double-figure tally, Matthew would cut a forlorn figure, trudging off the pitch with head bowed after yet another game in which he'd failed to put one on the back of the net.

185

'Well played, Clive!' he would say, slapping his brother on the back. 'Absolutely tremendous game.'

'Oh, it was nothing really.'

'Nothing! You scored eleven goals. I don't call that nothing.'

'It was luck, Matthew. Pure fluke.'

'It wasn't fluke, Clive. It was skill.'

'Not at all, Matthew. I'm no more skilful than you.'

'Yes, you are. You're a better footballer.'

'I'm really not, you know.'

'Yes you are, damn it. That's why you scored eleven goals and I didn't score any. And why yesterday you scored nine and I still didn't score any. And why the day before you scored 17 and I scored an own goal. You're a better footballer than me, Clive. Just accept it!'

And with that he stalked off to his bunk, where he curled up under the blanket and cuddled his teddy.

Whilst I was tormenting them on the football pitch, I was stepping up operations off it. I pilfered half of Matthew's stamp collection and secreted it at the bottom of Clive's kit bag, where it was discovered during another routine barracks search.

'I don't know how they got there,' protested Clive. 'I'm as bewildered as you were when they found my letters in your mattress.'

'Yes,' said Matthew pointedly, 'although I didn't steal your letters.'

I found a large dead spider in a corner of the lavatory block and put it on Clive's pillow, causing him to faint when he saw it; and did the same to Matthew with three dead woodlice, causing him to faint too. I concealed some mint humbugs in Clive's bed, creating the impression that he had a secret hoard of their favourite confectionery which he wasn't prepared to share with his snow-haired sibling; whilst a momentary distraction when they were playing chess allowed me to move Matthew's queen to a more advantageous position on the board, the implication being that he himself had surreptitiously moved it when his opponent's attention had been diverted.

Most insidiously of all, I played upon the twins' respective allergies. I hid some cheese inside Clive's mattress, causing him to suffer uncontrollable diarrhoea for a week, and scattered some broad beans – pilfered from the camp kitchen – around Matthew's pillow whilst he was asleep one night, as a result of which he turned bright orange.

'Someone's trying to kill me,' he groaned the following morning, fixing Clive with a hard stare. 'Someone who knows I'm allergic to broad beans.'

'Perhaps it was just an accident,' suggested Clive.

'How,' inquired Matthew, 'do eighteen broad beans suddenly appear by accident on my pillow? Tell me, how?'

'I have no idea, Matthew. None whatsoever. But if you're suggest-ing—'

'Yes?'

'If you're suggesting I had anything to do with it—'

'Well, you are the only one who knows I'm allergic to them.'

'This is preposterous. You're the only one who knows I'm allergic to cheese, but I don't go accusing you of trying to murder me.'

'I'm not accusing you, Clive. I'm just saying—'

'What? What are you saying?'

'I'm just saying that it's damned strange. Oh, let's just forget it. Let's just forget the whole thing.'

And so it went on. A poke here, a nudge there; a little bit of push, a little bit of shove; a succession of small provocations which had, by the end of March 1945, brought the twins, if not into open conflict, at least to the very brink of it. They never actually spoke a cross word to each other; they were invariably polite and seemed, outwardly at least, as close as ever. Beneath the surface, however, fires were raging. You could see it in their eyes. Previously a dull, drab red, these now flashed furious scarlet whenever they were in close proximity. I had brought them to the edge. Now all I had to do was push them over. Time for Stage Three. Time for the teddy bears.

As I mentioned, each Brain had a teddy bear. Clive's was called Beppo, Matthew's Flumdy. They loved their teddy bears almost as much as they loved each other, and, again as I mentioned, always slept with them tucked snugly in the crook of their left arm.

They had, apparently, had their teddy bears since they were children, and took them everywhere. When they'd flown bombing missions over Germany, Beppo and Flumdy had gone with them – each bear sporting a rather becoming pair of flying goggles – and when they were shot down and forced to bail out, the first thing each seized was his beloved cuddly toy.

So close was the bond between each twin and his teddy it was hardly surprising that, when they began to lose faith in each other, they turned to their stuffed companions for solace. When, for instance, Clive scored ten goals during a game of football and Matthew none, the latter immediately returned to his bunk and sought comfort in his bear. When Clive was suffering from dreadful cheese-induced diarrhoea, he always took Beppo to the lavatory with him, hugging the bear whilst all manner of frightful liquids gushed from his pained posterior.

The dependence of Clive and Matthew on Beppo and Flumdy increased in direct proportion to the decrease in their trust for one another, until eventually they were spending more time with their bears than with their sibling. I waited for the moment when it seemed they couldn't possibly become more dependent on the teddies, whereupon I unleashed Stage Three of my campaign. I stole the bears.

I stole both at the same time, during the night, when the twins were fast asleep, easing them gently from the crooks of their arms and concealing them in the barracks lavatory, beneath a loose floor-board.

The following morning I, and just about everyone else in the camp, was woken by the most ear-splitting of double-screams.

'Beppo! Flumdy! No!'

I peered from my bunk to see the Brain brothers frantically scrabbling beneath their blankets in a forlorn search for their stolen cuddlies. They emptied their kit-bags, they tore open their pillows, they threw aside their mattresses and, finally, having convinced themselves their bears were gone, they sat down and wept. Even Colonel Dishby was at a loss as to what to do.

'Looks like they've gone a bit ging-gang-gooly,' he sighed, tugging at his moustache. 'Dashed odd couple. I mean, I don't approve of theft, but I can hardly go to Obersturmführer Pisspot and say we're missing a couple of bears. We'd be a laughing stock.'

The twins cried for an entire day, before subsiding into a dejected silence. They spoke neither to each other nor to anyone else. Occasionally one of them would leap to his feet and rush around the barracks, peering under beds and behind lockers, but otherwise they remained as inert and deflated as a pair of punctured inner tubes.

I let them stew for about a week, and then began sending them bits of their teddies. One afternoon they returned from a stint of tunnel digging only for Matthew to find one of Flumdy's eyes sitting on his pillow. He said nothing, just picked up the eye, clenched it in his fist and stared very hard at his brother. Two days later Clive woke to discover some of Beppo's stuffing sticking out of his shoe. Again, he made no comment. Just turned the stuffing over in his fingers and gazed at his brother, eyes blazing. Clive opened his Red Cross parcel to find Beppo's paw therein. Matthew found Flumdy's foot hanging from the girder of one of Major Burrows's escape shafts. Clive was sitting on the lavatory when Beppo's ear came flying over the door. Matthew was drying himself after a shower when Flumdy's other foot fell from his towel. On each occasion they uttered not a sound. They merely picked up whatever part of their teddy they happened to have found, grimaced, and stared at their sibling with ever more murderous intensity.

Of course, had they thought about it, the twins would have realized the kidnapper could not possibly be one of them. Had Clive stolen Matthew's bear, for instance, or vice versa, he would have noticed in so doing that his own bear had gone. Logic alone dictated that there had to be a third party at work.

Fortunately, however, the Brains were, by that point, quite beyond rational thought. They had, over the months, developed such a degree of mutual distrust, and worked themselves up to such a level of uncontrolled paranoia, that had I walked over and hit one in the face he would most likely have persuaded himself that his brother was somehow responsible for the action.

'As dry as tinder,' I sniggered to myself, enjoying the whole experiment more and more with each passing day. 'All it needs now is a small spark. Just a small spark, and they'll be arguing like there's no tomorrow.

The spark came one evening in mid-April when each twin found a note beneath his pillow.

Clive's note read as follows: 'Go to the camp greenhouse at 2 a.m. tonight and look under the upturned flowerpot. You might find something of interest. Tell no one, or Beppo dies.'

Matthew's note, on the other hand, said: 'Go to the camp washroom at two o'clock tonight and look beneath the second basin to the left. You might find something of interest. Tell no one, or Flumdy dies.'

Each twin read his note, reread it, bit his fingernails and then, very slowly, very carefully, leaned out from his bunk and looked – in Clive's case up, in Matthew's down – at his brother. Their eyes met and locked. Not a word was spoken, not a flicker of recognition passed across their faces. They stared at each other for upwards of a minute before nodding gravely, as if to acknowledge that they knew exactly what the other was up to, and then withdrawing into their bunks.

At around five minutes to two the next morning Clive Brain sneaked silently out of the barracks. At around four minutes to two Matthew Brain did exactly the same. The entire camp was, by that point, fast asleep. Only the guards manning the searchlights and patrolling the electrified perimeter fence were still awake. Otherwise, the compound was still as a graveyard.

In order to appreciate fully what happened next I would refer you to the map of the camp as shown two walls back. As you will see, to reach the destination specified on his note, Clive had to turn left outside our hut and, keeping low to the ground and dodging the sweeping arcs of the camp searchlights, scuttle past Barracks D and E and so to the greenhouse beyond. To reach *his* destination, on the other hand, Matthew had to turn *right* outside our hut and, also keeping low to the ground and dodging the sweeping arcs of the camp searchlights, scuttle past Barracks A and B and so to the wash-block situated at the end of the latter.

Once inside the greenhouse, Clive, as instructed, looked beneath the large upturned flowerpot, where, rather to his surprise, he discovered not Beppo, as he had supposed, but his brother's bear Flumdy, the latter looking distinctly out of sorts following the removal of his ear, feet and one eye. Matthew, meanwhile, foraging beneath the second basin on the left of the camp washblock, was equally surprised to discover not Flumdy, as anticipated, but *his* brother's bear, Beppo, the latter looking equally forlorn minus one paw, one eye, one ear, and most of his stuffing.

Precisely what looks crossed their faces as they made their respective discoveries I have no idea. Perhaps they rubbed their high pale foreheads in bewilderment, or shook their heads from side to side, or muttered to themselves. Perhaps, on the other hand, they displayed not the least sign of emotion at all. Any suggestion on my part would be pure conjecture. Only when they emerged clutching their twin's bear, each at precisely the same moment, and began to make their way carefully back to the barrack the way they had come, was I able to see precisely what was going on, for I had taken up a grandstand position at the window by the hut door, thereby affording myself a perfect view of the scene.

Clive saw Matthew first. He was creeping past the front of D Hut, holding the remains of Flumdy, when he happened to glance to his left. Even in the darkness of the April night the figure scampering past the barrack opposite was unmistakeable. His pale skin and luminous hair stuck out like white paper on black card. What's more, he appeared to be holding something in his hand. Something distinctly teddy-like.

Clive stopped dead. As he did so, alerted by heaven's knows what inner sense, Matthew did the same. Shrinking into the shadows, he turned slowly to his right and fixed his eyes on his snow-haired sibling 100 feet away. A searchlight beam passed just in front of his feet, at exactly the same moment as another beam passed just before the feet of Clive. The whole scene was like a mirror image, with Clive and the barrack behind him simply a reflection of Matthew and the barrack behind *him*. They stood thus, staring at each other, without moving, for I do not know how long. Then, at precisely the same moment, as though their actions were part of a choreographed dance, each walked purposely forward towards the centre of the area between the barrack blocks. Searchlight beams wheeled above and around them, but somehow failed to pick them out.

They came to a halt, face to face, almost toe to toe. A searchlight flashed just to their left, another just to their right and, in their momentary illumination I caught the expression on the twins' parchment-white, red-eyed faces. It was more than I could possibly have hoped for: total, utter, complete and unconcealed hatred. I don't believe I have ever before, or since, seen two people look at each other with such absolute mutual loathing. I'd done it! I felt an overwhelming sense of achievement.

What happened next, however, came as a complete surprise. I had assumed that, having confronted each other, the twins would merely exchange bitter words, snatch back their respective bears and stalk back to the barracks in high dudgeon. What I had not expected, however, was that, having stood in the centre of the compound for several minutes staring at each other venomously, they would, without a word of warning, without, indeed, any sound whatsoever, suddenly drop their teddies and launch themselves at each other's throats.

That, however, was precisely what they did. Acting in perfect unison, each threw aside his respective bear and flung his hands around the neck of his brother, feet scrabbling on the ground as each struggled to remain upright. Clive appeared to have a slightly better grip, and he shook his arms furiously, making Matthew's head bounce back and forth as though it were made of straw. This went on for some while, and, from the bulging of his eyes, it looked as if Matthew was about to pass out when, suddenly, the latter brought his right knee smartly upwards into his brother's groin, causing the latter to lose his grip and collapse to his knees. Matthew then raised his arm and smashed his clenched fist down on to Clive's head, pitching him face forward into the dirt.

They remained still for a moment, panting, before Matthew lifted his foot ready to kick his once beloved sibling in the face. Clive, however, was wise to the move, rolling aside at the last minute, grabbing his brother's heel and twisting him round on to the ground, where he booted him in the face with his own foot. There was a crunching sound and, as a searchlight beam flew overhead, I saw blood streaming from Matthew's nose.

They floundered about on the floor for a while, still in complete silence, rolling over and over each other so that I was unable to make out which was which. Then one of them – Clive, I presumed, since his nose was unbloodied – struggled to his feet and set off at a run towards the southern perimeter fence, with his brother in hot pursuit. There was a cry from one of the watchtowers, and the beams from two searchlights rushed together to illuminate the twins. A siren went off, and there was a brief burst of gunfire.

'What the dickens is going on?' came a voice beside me. It was Colonel Dishby, who, like the rest of the barracks, had been woken by the commotion outside.

'It's the twins, sir.'

'What are they doing? Not escaping, are they? Burrows didn't say diddly-squat about a break-out tonight.'

'It looks like they're fighting, sir.'

'Fighting! Fighting! Not in this camp they're not! Come with me.'

And with that he charged out of the hut and limped off after the twins. I went with him, as did most of the other members of our barracks.

'Hold your fire!' cried the colonel to the guards. 'Holden Sie deine fire!'

The twins were by this point almost up to the southern perimeter. As he approached the fence, intending to do heaven knows what once he got there, Clive was tackled from behind by his broken-nosed brother, both men once again tumbling to the ground, where they rolled around scratching and pummelling each other. The searchlights were now trained full on them, forming a pool of light in which they punched and struggled like a pair of circus clowns. From the left a guard came running, shouting something in German, and another from the right. Colonel Dishby waved his arms and cried 'Shooten Sie nicht!'

Oblivious to the cries of the guards, Matthew somehow broke free of Clive's grip, clambered to his feet and launched a vicious kick into his brother's ribs. Even from fifty feet away we could hear the crack of bone. Clive scrabbled backwards on the ground, propelling himself with his feet, breaking through the warning wire that was staked out 10 feet from the fence and continuing until his head was just a yard or so away from the latter's electric bars. The guards stopped, shouted again, and then, raising their rifles into the air, fired a shot over the combatants' heads.

The brothers, however, ignored the sound. With an ear-piercing scream of '*Thief!*', Matthew ran at the prostrate Clive and tried to stamp on his neck. The latter, however, somehow managed to avoid the blow and, squirming to one side, gripped his attacker's foot and, with a grunt, pitched him face forwards on to the electrified wires of the fence. There were no sparks, no flashes, no explosions; just a very loud buzzing sound as Matthew bucked and jerked, head snapping back and forth, arms and legs flapping, before he eventually came to rest in a kneeling position, propped against the fence as though in prayer. His face had turned black; smoke was emitting from his ears and, in a sudden, dramatic encore to his demise, his hair burst into flame.

'Shocking,' muttered Colonel Dishby. 'Absolutely damned shocking.'

Clive, in the meanwhile, whilst his brother smoked and trembled behind him, had clambered to his feet and was standing facing us, breathing heavily and nursing his ribs.

'Don't you see?' he cried. 'He stole Beppo. Don't you understand? Matthew stole my Beppo!'

He turned a little to the side and reached out his hand towards one of the camp guards. It was, presumably, a gesture of submission, but the guard misinterpreted the action and, thinking Clive was threatening him, lifted his rifle to his shoulder and shot him plum between his shimmering red eyes. He stood perfectly still for a moment, a trickle of blood running down his nose, and then fell backwards to the ground, dead. In the ensuing silence, Colonel Dishby was heard to mutter:

'Totally damned pasha-washa the pair of 'em. Knew it from the moment they arrived. Totally damned pasha-washa!'

We stood watching as the guards removed the twins' bodies – momentarily switching off the electric fence so as to retrieve Matthew's charred remains – and then as a group wandered slowly back across the compound. As we passed the point where the twins had first confronted each other, the colonel pointed at something lying on the ground.

'What on earth's that, Phoenix?' he inquired.

'It looks like teddy bears, sir.'

'Teddy bears! Well pick 'em up quick. Can't have the Jerries thinking we've gone softie. And better organize a cribbage competition for tomorrow night. Take the men's minds off things. Put the word around, there's a good man.'

And with that we stuffed our hands in our pockets and returned to bed.

*

As it happened, Colonel Dishby's cribbage competition never materialized, for the following day we were liberated.

For some months now, despite an almost total news embargo, we had known that things weren't going well for the Germans. New prisoners had informed us of the D-Day landings the previous June, and the removal of the more experienced camp guards, to be replaced by old men and teenage boys, suggested an ever more urgent need for fighting troops on the German front line. Over the past two weeks all the files from the camp office had been loaded into trucks and driven away, and a number of Allied planes had been spotted flying overhead. The sound of shelling could be heard far away in the south and west.

The morning after the albino twins died we woke to discover our captors had fled. We wandered from our huts and broke into a spontaneous round of applause. Then we played cricket for the rest of the day until, late in the afternoon, an advanced unit of the Durham Light Infantry arrived in front of the camp gates. Colonel Dishby took the salute of the officer in charge, we let out three cheers, and that was that. We were free.

Or rather, that was almost that, because amidst the euphoria of liberation there came a surprise that even I had not expected. I was sitting on the guardroom steps, gazing at The Pill and thinking of all the extraordinary times we'd been through together, when an ambulance drove in through the gates and pulled up just in front of me. It was driven by a large man wearing a Red Cross armband. I, however, had eyes only for the nurse sitting beside him. I would have recognized her anywhere. She looked more beautiful than ever.

'Emily!' I cried, rushing over and taking her in my arms. 'Emily! Can it really be you?'

'I hope so, Raphael!' she laughed. 'Because if it's not you're hugging a total stranger!'

'What are you doing here?'

'I'm a nurse, you silly. Can't you see by the uniform?'

'Of course I can see you're a nurse. I'm not blind. It's just amazing that you should happen to be nursing right here, right now. Just in time to meet me.'

'I suppose it is,' she conceded. 'I hadn't really thought about it.'

'How can you be so calm, Emily? It's a miracle! God, it's good to see you.' I hugged her again, and kissed her cheek, and then promptly burst into tears.

'I'm so happy,' I cried. 'I'm so happy to see you.'

Emily dabbed at my eyes with the sleeve of her uniform.

'And I'm happy to see you, Raphael. Now come on, stop crying and help me unload my things from the van. I've got some chocolate if you'd like it.'

And so I helped Emily unload her van and set up a makeshift hospital in the old camp office. Soon, however, more nurses arrived in another truck and I was no longer needed, so I took three of the chocolate bars Emily had mentioned and wandered out of the camp gates and across to the edge of the forest – the forest that had for so long foiled Major Burrows and his tunnel-digging operations. I sat down under a tree and ate my chocolate, whistling to myself and worrying that, now I was free, perhaps I might be sent back to active duty. I must have fallen asleep, because when I woke it was dark, and cold, and Emily was sitting beside me.

'I've got something for you, Raphael,' she said, handing me an official-looking document.

'What is it?'

'A pass.'

'A pass?'

'Yes. It will get you home quicker. Otherwise it might take you weeks. It's chaos everywhere.'

I scrutinized the document in the light of a match.

'How on earth did you get hold of something like this?' I inquired incredulously. 'It's signed by Montgomery.'

'Oh, it wasn't that difficult. I've got a few contacts. I thought it might come in useful. You leave tonight.'

'Tonight!'

'Yes, in about ten minutes. There's a truck going back down the line. You'd better get your things.'

'But I don't want to go. I want to stay here with you. I haven't seen you for five years. I've got so much to tell you.'

Emily sighed. 'Oh Raphael, you need to get away from here as soon as possible. You've been through so much.'

She placed her hand lightly on my forehead and tilted her head to one side, her pale forehead crinkling into a frown. 'You seem a little . . . disturbed.'

'I'm absolutely fine, Emily! I want to talk now! I want to make the most of you.'

'Don't be troublesome, Raphael,' she murmured softly, and then stood up, smoothing down the folds of her nurse's pinafore. 'It's all arranged. Now go and get your things. I've got work to do.'

'But Emily—'

'No arguing,' she said, putting her finger to my lips. 'We'll catch up with each other again. Don't we always? Now come on, I've got sick people to attend to.'

And so, with a resigned sigh, I trudged back to the compound and collected my things from the hut. I didn't have very much, just The Photo, which I unpinned from the wall beside my bed, The Pill, a few odds and ends of clothing, and the sheet music to 'Run, Rabbit, Run', which had been written out for me by the captain in the Canadian Marines who'd taught me to play the piano. These I shovelled into an old kit-bag before bidding farewell to my fellow inmates and clambering into the back of a large, rumbling Bedford truck.

'Chip, chip, Phoenix,' called Colonel Dishby as I pulled away through the gates. 'We gave it some gumption, eh!'

'Goodbye, Raphael!' called Emily, waving a stethoscope. 'Goodbye. I'll see you soon.'

'Soon', as it transpired, was actually 24 years. Few people have quite the same capacity for understatement as dear, darling Emily.

*

Which is how I killed the albino twins. Within a week I was back in England, and within two months was ensconced in an entirely new life in the service of Lord Slaggsby.

I shall end this particular room with a brief word about Private Lemon, the fatalistic ginger-head whom I had met on the train from Liverpool the day I joined the army. I had presumed him killed with the rest of my unit in our dugout on the banks of the River Scarpe, the night I was captured.

'Sir! Sir! Help me, sir!' he had cried, before his voice was lost in a barrage of gunfire.

Unbeknown to me, however, he had somehow managed to escape the German onslaught, scampering away into the night and eventually joining those other troops evacuated from the beaches of Dunkirk. Over the next four years he was to fight in North Africa, Italy, the Far East and Europe, winning a kaleidoscope of gallantry medals before eventually being shot saving a colleague's life during the airdrop on Arnhem, an action for which he was awarded a posthumous Victoria Cross. There is a plaque to his memory on the wall of the church in the village where he grew up. It is a small village, in the far north of England. You might, perhaps, have heard of it. It is, you see, called Tripally.

# CHAPTER ELEVEN

MY BACK STILL feels funny. I must have banged it harder than I thought yesterday evening. It doesn't actually hurt – it just tingles, as though there were lots of ants running around beneath the skin. For some reason I can't shake the thought that my body's full of maggots. Spending an entire night down in the cellar probably didn't do it much good either. The atmosphere's very damp down there. Unhealthy. Like a dungeon.

Now, however, I'm out of the cellar and on my way up the left-hand wall of the castle stairway. Beneath me, a rippling sea of words and letters fills the downstairs rooms and foyer as though they've been flooded. It looks, though I say it myself, absolutely bloody spectacular.

I'm still getting by on next to no sleep, and my body, too, is feeling younger by the hour. In the middle of the night I removed my candles because, even in the murk of the cellar, with only a flickering 40 watt bulb for illumination, I suddenly discovered I could see perfectly well without them. It's as if, in recording the events of my life, I'm somehow transferring the years from my own person on to the walls of my home. Unburdening myself. I really am feeling remarkably vigorous.

And a good thing, too, because the cellar, with its damp, stale air and legions of creepy-crawlies, has proved by far the most difficult writing space I've yet encountered. In places, the note's progress was brought almost to a standstill, and whilst I'm still well on course to get it all done before I top myself, I experienced for the first time a sense of frustration and disillusionment with the whole thing.

'What the hell are you doing this for?' I thought. 'Why are you punishing yourself like this?'

The main problem, amongst many, was that the cellar walls aren't flat. Whereas all the other rooms in the castle have been neatly plastered and painted, the cellar was, by all appearances, hewn out of the solid rock, like a catacomb. Its whitewashed walls, as a result, bulge and ripple and twist, making them hellishly difficult to write over. In addition, they are also, in places, extremely damp, with pearl-sized beads of moisture oozing from the rock like a chalky sweat. My felt-tip pen was useless in such conditions, its ink refusing to adhere where there was the least hint of wet, so that rather than filling the entire wall I had to scurry from dry patch to dry patch, as though negotiating my way across a particularly treacherous bog. Where I had initially assumed I would have to increase the size of my writing, I was in fact, with so much wall space unusable, forced do quite the opposite, reducing the size of my letters so as to fit them all in, cramming them together like shipwrecked sailors into overloaded life rafts. Even then I still didn't have quite enough space to say everything I wanted to, and having filled every available inch of the cellar walls and written my way back up to the foyer, I was forced to conclude the albino twins episode on the lower reaches of the castle stairway. Bang goes my dream of confining each murder to a single room.

And as if all that weren't enough, there were a hundred and one other little nuisances to contend with, such as trying to balance my ladder on the uneven cellar floor and the century's worth of bric-a-brac I had to move around so as to give myself enough room to write in, and the earwigs that kept dropping off the ceiling on to my head (I detest earwigs), and the mouldy atmosphere, and the cold, and the fact that every couple of hours or so the light bulb would, for no reason at all, suddenly flicker off, leaving me cursing and shivering in pitch-darkness for a few moments before, equally suddenly, coming back on again.

Finally, I seem to have used more than double my ration of pens in the cellar (ten, as opposed to the four it normally takes to describe each murder). Given that I had 60 pens to start with – two boxes of 30 each – and have only used 26, I've still got plenty left, but I can't help feeling annoyed. I don't like the idea of my surroundings getting the better of me.

I started work in the cellar at around seven o'clock last night, and only finally emerged at 5 p.m. this evening. Twenty-two hours, by far the longest it's taken me to describe any murder. I feel somehow soiled by the delay. And to think that yesterday I reckoned I could complete a room in under ten hours!

Now, however, thank God, I'm out, and the cellar is history. If it had a door I would shut and lock it. Since all the castle's interior doors have, for some reason, been removed, however, I shall just have to imagine it has a door, and that the latter is firmly closed. I never intend to go down there again. Ever. Dreadful place. Damned earwigs!

The castle stairway, however, where I'm writing now, provides an altogether more cheerful working environment. It's warm and airy and light, with pale sunbeams streaming through the windows and, if it's a bit of a bugger balancing my ladder on the narrow stairs, I have, at least, been able to get my note back up to speed. I have now written my way up to the midway landing and turned the corner towards the first floor, which I should reach in a couple of columns' time. Fingers crossed that henceforth things continue smoothly.

My one slight worry is how I'm going to fill the wall space between here and the first room on the upper floor (the study, as I call it, although why, I've no idea, since in 15 years I've barely set foot in it, let alone done any studying there). If I wasn't doing my utmost to keep murders within rooms, of course, it wouldn't really matter. I could start the next one right here and now. As it is, however, and despite the disaster of the cellar, I'm still determined to keep as closely as possible to my scheme for the note. As a result, Mr Popplethwaite can't appear for some time yet, leaving me a considerable stretch of whiteness in which to twiddle my literary thumbs. Perhaps I could tell a few jokes, or write some poetry, or even do some drawings. It might be nice to enliven my death with a few illustrations.

First, however, I think I shall pop up to the dome for a glass of wine and a quick snooze. After all that boasting about how young and vigorous I feel I've suddenly come over rather tired. All that hassle in the cellar has clearly worn me down. I need to go up top and recharge. Perhaps I'll have some curried mackerel fillets too. And a bit of Battenberg cake. See you in a while.

I've just had a rather disturbing experience. Two rather disturbing experiences, actually. The first of which was the dream.

I'd gone up to the dome with my wine and mackerel fillets and cake, but was so overcome with exhaustion that barely had I plonked myself down on my wickerwork chair than I fell into a deep slumber, head thrown back, arms dangling at my sides, my food and drink forgotten beside me. And as I slept I had a most curious and up-setting vision.

I was standing in a long, carpeted corridor, with doors off it to either side. There was a faint, rather noisome smell of urine and boiled cabbage, and from behind the doors came a sort of sucking, squelching sound, as though the rooms beyond were full of maggots and slugs and other damp, sticky, slimy creatures. I felt sick and scared and disorientated, and cowered against the wall. Then, however, a voice behind me said: 'Are you all right, Mr Phoenix?' and when I turned I saw it was Mrs Bunshop, except for some reason she was bald, and the skin on her scalp was all brown and shrivelled and shiny, like the scum on the surface of a cold cup of tea.

'Are you all right, Mr Phoenix?' she repeated.

'Yes,' I said, although my voice felt thick and muffled, as though I had cotton wool in my mouth. 'Yes, thank you. Quite all right.'

'You look pale. Perhaps you should sit down.'

'No,' I mumbled. And then with greater vehemence: 'No!'

I started off down the corridor away from her. I tried to run, but I couldn't get my legs to move properly and only went forward at a shuffle.

'Shall I get the nurse, Mr Phoenix?'

'No!' I said. 'No! Leave me alone.'

I continued down the corridor, past the doors with the sucking, squelching sounds behind them, Mrs Bunshop following in my wake, urine and cabbage in the air, until eventually I turned a corner and found myself in a large open area with bright windows down one side and row of armchairs lined up in front of the bright windows. There were people sitting in the armchairs, some of them familiar. Lord Slaggsby was there, and Walter, and the albino twins, and several other of my victims.

'Hello, Mr Phoenix,' they said. 'How are you feeling today?'

'Stop it!' I said. 'Stop it. You're dead.'

By this point Mrs Bunshop had come up beside me.

'I think you should call the nurse,' she said.

'I don't need the nurse,' I said, my voice rising. 'I don't need the fucking nurse.'

'Get the nurse,' said Mrs Bunshop.

'I don't fucking need the nurse. Fuck the nurse.' By now I was screaming. 'Stop this! Stop it! You're dead! You're all dead! This is some sort of fucking dream! I've killed you all! This is a nightmare!'

I felt hands taking my arms. I struggled, hitting out feebly, but more hands took me round the waist and the legs and the neck. There were hands everywhere and I couldn't move and I couldn't breathe and everywhere stank of piss and boiled cabbage and this horrible slurping sucking squelching sound, and there were faces all around, and I started to cry and call out for Emily.

'I want Emily!' I whimpered. 'I want Emily.'

'Now, now, Mr Phoenix,' said a voice. 'Now, now.'

And that's when I woke up, my pyjamas drenched in sweat, even though it was quite cold up on the roof.

'Christ,' I mumbled. 'Christ.'

I fumbled for my cigarettes, lit one and took a deep drag, shaken. My hands were trembling, and although it was a clear moonlit night there were still deep inky shadows in the corners of the roof which seemed to me full of menace. I swigged from my bottle of wine.

'Christ,' I repeated. 'Jesus Christ.'

Never before have my victims appeared in my dreams. I have committed the most appalling crimes, yet always slept untroubled. Now, however, a whole group of them had popped up, unbidden, to torment me in my slumber. I was being harassed by ghouls. Terrorized by stiffs. And I didn't like it. Dreams, after all, can't be regulated. Not like memory, where you have a degree of control over the images in your head. In dreams, the images have the upper hand. You're at their mercy. They can do what they want to you. Exact their revenge. I shuddered, envisaging a succession of visitations over the final few days of my life, each more disturbing than the last, culminating in something truly gut-wrenching like a sex scene with Mrs Bunshop, or a sodomy tableau with the Brain brothers, their giant albino dream dicks pounding into my aged backside whilst I dream-screamed for mercy. I extinguished my cigarette half smoked and immediately lit up another one.

'God help me,' I muttered. 'I'm going mad.'

I smoked and drank and muttered for almost two hours, telling myself over and over again it was just a dream and nothing to worry about whilst all the while making damned sure I didn't go back to sleep in case Mrs Bunshop and the others were waiting back there to hijack my slumber. Eventually, after I'd emptied the bottle and raised a small hillock of fag butts at my feet, I managed to calm myself to the point where I'd actually started to see the amusing side. Then, however, the knocking started.

After the peace and quiet of yesterday, I'd assumed, hoped, that whoever it was who had been banging on my door and throwing stones at me – if, indeed, it was one and the same person – had decided to abandon their tricks and leave me alone. Now, however, the knocker was crashing against the front door like a hammer on an anvil, the whole castle shivering at the force of the blows. Boom! Boom! Boom! I could feel the vibrations purring up through my feet.

I sat still for a moment, frozen, and then jumped from the dome, ran to the westward battlements – damn nearly tripping over one of the dome rails in my hurry to get there – and looked down into the shadows beneath. It was too dark to make out anything clearly, but I could definitely see a vague figure standing below on the door-step, arm raised to the knocker, swinging it furiously up and down against the woodwork. Boom! Boom! Boom!

'What do you want?' I cried. 'Who are you?'

The knocking stopped abruptly and the figure stood still.

'I can see you,' I shouted. 'I can see exactly where you are! Why are you knocking on my door? And throwing stones at me? I'm an old man!'

The figure did nothing, just stayed exactly where he (or she) was, hidden in the shadows. We remained thus for what seemed like several minutes, silent, my enemy not daring to move lest I should see him, me not daring to move lest in averting my gaze I gave him a chance to escape. The stalemate was only broken when the moon passed behind a small cloud and, in the brief moment of deeper darkness that followed, the person beneath gave one more loud bang on the door and scampered off into the night.

'Leave me alone!' I screamed after him, my voice echoing over hills like the cry of a madman. 'Leave me alone to die, why can't you!'

There was only silence, however. I can't be certain, but I think my tormentor might be a child.

So that's what's been happening this evening. And very upsetting it's all been too. I feel raw and exposed, like a tortoise that's been ripped out of its shell. I need to get back into my note. I need to hide in the forest of words.

The one good thing to come out of it all is that it's furnished me with sufficient material to fill the remaining space between the top of the stairwell and the doorway to the study. You may recall that earlier I was agonizing over what to do with these walls. Now, thanks to the disturbing events of the last couple of hours, it's no longer a problem. I have arrived at my destination with words to spare, and am at this very moment writing down the left-hand side of the doorframe that at one point I thought I'd never reach. My writing is, admittedly, the largest it's yet been (each letter the size of a ripe plum), and the gaps between the lines somewhat wider than usual (about an inch as opposed to a centimetre). I have, nonetheless, got where I need to be, and it now only remains to draw an arrow from the bottom of this column round the door and up into the room beyond, and then I can get started on my next murder.

Which, after another glass of wine and a fag, is precisely what I intend to do.

# Chapter Twelve

MY LAST VICTIM prior to the outbreak of the Second World War, and the second of the three employers I've murdered (Luther being the first, Lord Slaggsby the third), was Mr M. Popplethwaite, manager of the high-street bank at which I worked throughout the Thirties.

My entry into the world of high-street banking, and subsequent murder of one of its most respected citizens, would most likely never have happened had I not become separated from Emily as we disembarked from the *Scythia*. I had gone down the gangplank ahead of her, legs rather wobbly after nine days pitching about on the Atlantic, intending to meet her on the quayside. As more and more people came off the ship, however, and more and more people pressed forward to meet them, I found myself irresistibly sucked away from the waterfront and backwards into the multitude. I thought I caught a glimpse of her disembarking, gold hair gleaming in the mellow autumn light, but she didn't hear my shouts and by the time I'd pushed my way to the front of the crowd once more she was gone.

'Emily!' I cried. 'Emily! Where are you?'

There was no reply, however, and after a fruitless hour of searching I was forced to admit defeat. Emily had disappeared once again and, not for the first time in my life, I was left entirely to my own devices. I had The Photo, 15 dollars cash and, of course, The Pill, the latter set into the face of a rather ostentatious gold ring which I'd purchased at the height of my Hollywood extravagances. These, together with a faded carpet bag and the clothes I was standing up in, comprised the sum total of my worldly possessions. It was 1931 (August) and I was on the dock fronts of Liverpool. I heaved a deep sigh. Back to the old drawing board.

My immediate concern – before I started worrying about accommodation, or work, or when I was next to see Emily – was to get a stiff whisky. And since to get a stiff whisky I needed money, and since, having been in America for the last 12 years, all my money was in dollars, and since dollars were useless now I was back in England, I decided my first task should be to exchange my American currency for some good old English pounds sterling. To this end I therefore inquired of a cloth-capped docker where I might find the nearest bank, and was duly directed by the latter up towards the centre of town.

It took me almost an hour of searching to track down the bank, and when I did finally run it to ground it was almost certainly not the one to which the docker had directed me in the first place. It sat plum in the middle of a broad thoroughfare of tall, soot-darkened sandstone buildings, hemmed in on one side by a large hotel and on the other by the head offices of a transatlantic shipping company.

There was little about Simsby's of Castle Street ('Excellence and Security since 1781!') to suggest that it was actually a bank, and I most probably wouldn't have noticed the fact had I not happened to stop right in front of it to take my bearings. It had an unobtrusive, four-storey façade peppered with unobtrusive windows. An unobtrusive sign announced the institution's name and pedigree as unobtrusively as possible, whilst unobtrusive-looking people went in and out in a manner that could best be described as . . . unobtrusive. Everything about the place spoke of modesty, diffidence, reserve and sobriety, a fact that doubtless assured its customers of the absolute security of their finances, since no company of so evidently conservative a character would be likely to do anything outlandish, risky, rakish or charismatic with its clients' investments. In only one respect did Simsby's display a hint of idiosyncracy – it had a large revolving front door; the first such door, apparently, to be installed on commercial premises anywhere in Britain.

I duly passed through the latter, the revolving plates of glass creaking as I pushed them, and found myself in a large vestibule with a highly polished wooden floor and row of tills on the far side. To my right a wooden stairway led upwards to a first-floor landing, whilst to my left was arranged a series of wooden tables at which customers could sit whilst filling out the complex documentation of which modern banking appeared increasingly to consist. Above my head was suspended a gently rotating fan, large as an aeroplane propeller, whilst along the walls were hung sepia-tinged photographs of various ocean liners, the owners of which, I later discovered, were amongst the bank's most important customers. The place smelt, if such a smell exists, of complete financial security.

It was by now just short of midday, and there was a considerable press of people waiting to be served. Since my legs were aching somewhat, and noticing a couple of comfortable-looking chairs placed against the wall just to the right of the stairway, I decided to rest for a moment before joining one of the queues before the tills. Barely had I plonked myself down, however, when a door beside me flew open and a young, rather dejected-looking man in an oversized, double-breasted suit walked out past me and exited the bank.

'Next!' came a loud voice from beyond the door.

I looked around the vestibule, but no one seemed to have noticed the command and, thinking that maybe this was an opportunity to jump the queue and transact my business that bit quicker, I got to my feet and walked into the room from which the young man had just emerged. The door had the largest, shiniest brass handle I have ever seen, and carried the inscription 'M. Popplethwaite, Manager' upon it in tall gold lettering.

'Close the door and sit down then,' commanded Mr M. Popplethwaite – for such I took him to be – a brilliantined, near-spherical figure wedged behind a tennis-court-sized desk at the far end of the room. He had plump, roseate cheeks, a waxed moustache and a chin that segued into his chest with no evident join between the two. He wore a dark suit, a bow tie and had small round spectacles behind which his eyes darted to and fro like goldfish in a bowl. Behind him was a large bookcase in which were arranged rows of bound copies of the *Bankers' Journal* and *Lloyds Weekly Shipping Index*.

'Sit down, young man,' he repeated, indicating a chair before his desk. 'Come, come, let's not dawdle. Dawdling wastes time, time is money and money's what makes the world go around. Speed and organization, that's what we like at Simsby's. We've been speedy and organized since 1781, and will continue to be so as long as I have anything to do with it. Sit down, I say.'

So brisk and assertive was his manner; so utterly confident, that, having told me to sit down, I would not fail to do otherwise, that I felt compelled to obey and, almost without realizing what I was doing, I crossed the room and installed myself on the straight-backed wooden chair he had indicated with his chubby finger.

'Now,' he said, examining a sheaf of papers on his desk, 'I see you've applied for the post of trainee assistant till clerk, second class.'

'No,' I corrected. 'I've come to change some money.'

He twitched, as though he had just received a minor electric shock, and a look of surprise bordering on consternation washed across his face. He adjusted his spectacles and referred once again to the papers in front of him.

'Trainee assistant till clerk, second class,' he repeated, as though I had perhaps misheard him the first time and that by saying the phrase again he could thereby persuade me of its applicability to my own person.

'I'm afraid not,' I responded. 'I just want to exchange some dollars for pounds sterling.'

He was silent for a moment, and then, suddenly, craftily, shouted, 'Assistant till clerk, second class, trainee!' hoping, it would seem, to trick me into answering in the affirmative.

'No,' I repeated firmly. 'Not assistant till clerk, second class. Not assistant till clerk any class. I simply wish to exchange some money. Fifteen dollars and eight cents, to be precise. And a few nickels, but I suspect you don't do those.'

He shook his head from side to side, blinked, fiddled with his bow tie and then, with a swiftness of movement quite at odds with his rotund physique, shot off across the room to a filing cabinet in the far corner. I was quite dazzled by the speed and smoothness of his passage, and it was a moment before I realized he had not even stood up but was in fact propelling himself upon his chair, to the legs of which were affixed small castors. The latter hissed across the floor with a sound similar to that made by skates on ice.

From the filing cabinet he withdrew more sheaves of paper before spinning back to his desk again.

'It says here that you've come for an interview with regards to the position of trainee assistant till clerk, second class,' he announced triumphantly, waving a sheet of paper in the air. 'It's perfectly clear. 12 a.m. appointment – assistant till clerk, class two, trainee. You can see for yourself. It's all been arranged, noted, confirmed and double checked.'

'I can only repeat,' I replied, 'that I am not, nor have I ever been, desirous of working as an assistant till clerk in a bank. It is, I am sure, a most rewarding occupation, but not one I would wish to undertake at this present juncture in my life.'

'So,' he said slowly, deliberately, as if trying to convince himself of a fact quite beyond human comprehension, 'you're not applying for the post.'

'No,' I said. 'There must be some mistake.'

This provoked another convulsion, more violent than the one

previously. The ends of his waxed moustache appeared to curl up and down of their own volition and, delving into his jacket pocket, he removed a small bottle of pills, two of which he popped into his mouth. He then seized the side of his desk and propelled himself around it as though riding on a waltzer, coming to a halt directly in front of me.

'We do not,' he growled, 'make mistakes at Simsby's of Castle Street. "Mistake" is not a word we know or use within this institution. We number amongst our clients three lords, two admirals, eighteen knights of the realm and some of the most important industrialists of our time. We have five times been voted best bank in the North of England' – he gestured to a row of framed certificates on the wall to his left – 'and were recently awarded the Lloyds Bank badge of merit' – another gesture to another certificate, this one hanging beside the window. 'We are renowned far and wide for the extraordinary soundness of our financial advice, and in three weeks' time I shall be lunching with none other than the Governor of the Bank of England himself. We have awesome responsibilities, and in the discharging of those responsibilities – three lords, two admirals and eighteen knights of the realm, don't forget – we DO NOT MAKE MISTAKES!'

He removed his glasses and polished them vigorously with his handkerchief before grabbing his desk and spinning himself back to its far side. He re-examined the papers lying before him, scribbled some notes on a blotter, re-re-examined the papers, squinted, and then, laying his hands calmly upon the surface of the desk, said:

'So, you've applied for the post of trainee assistant till clerk, second class.'

What do you do when destiny makes so obvious a show of opening His door and ushering you through? Do you ignore Him, insisting that one, and only one, person will decide your future and that's you? Or do you submit? Accept the inevitable, bow to the signs and do what Fate tells you. Do you struggle, or do you lie down? In my case, I am sorry to say, it has invariably and unavoidably been the latter. Always has been, always will be, never could be any different.

That's why I'm going to kill myself. It was pre-ordained in my initials. There's no escaping pre-ordination.

'Yes,' I sighed wearily, rubbing The Pill against my cheek with one hand and with the other replacing the dollar notes I had intended to change in my trouser pocket. 'Yes. I've come to be a trainee assistant till clerk, second class.'

'Good,' said Mr Popplethwaite, clapping his hands. 'Very good and proper. Now, your name, please . . .'

'Raphael Ignatius Phoenix, late of Tropical Drive, Los Angeles . . .'

Which is how, to no one's surprise more than my own, I found myself working as a trainee assistant till clerk (second class) in Simsby's Banking and Financial of Castle Street, Liverpool. What happened to the person whose interview I so unwittingly purloined I have no idea, but I applied myself assiduously to my duties, and within a year was considered sufficiently versed in the cabala of till clerkdom to lose the trainee bit of my title and assume the post of Assistant Till Clerk, Second Class.

This, however, was simply the beginning of my meteoric rise through the ranks of the banking world. Within two years of stepping off the *Scythia* I was no longer an assistant but a fully fledged Till Clerk, Second Class, and then a fully fledged Assistant Till Clerk, First Class and then – honour of honours – a fully fledged Till Clerk, First Class, with assistants and trainees and second-classers beneath me, at my beck and call.

I remained in this position for almost three years, until January 1938, when to general consternation and over the head of Mr Froops, who had been widely expected to assume the post, I was promoted to the giddy heights of Temporary Deputy Assistant Under-Manager, Bullion Division, which is where I remained until I murdered Mr Popplethwaite two years later.

The position Temporary Deputy Assistant Under-Manager, Bullion Division, brought with it certain perks which, whilst not in themselves particularly impressive, nonetheless seemed so within the introverted perkless world of high-street banking. I was, for instance, allowed to wear a bow tie, which, after seven years in a normal black one, came as a sartorial boon of immeasurable value. I was also permitted to sport a handkerchief in my jacket pocket, and wear a bowler hat. To the people I passed each day on the street I must have appeared normal to the point of drabness. Compared with my fellow Simby's workers, however, I looked positively rakish, and took considerable pride in the admiring looks I received from the company secretaries when I arrived for work each morning.

Best of all, as Temporary Deputy Assistant Under-Manager, Bullion Division, I had my own office. It was not a large office – more of a glorified cupboard really – but it had my name on the door, and a key with which I could lock it and, most significantly, was on the first floor of the bank, directly above Mr Popplethwaite's room.

To be promoted from the ground floor to the first (or second or third or fourth) floor of Simsby's was an honour to which every employee aspired. Small-minded it might have been, but to be able to enter the bank of a morning and ascend the stairway to the rarefied heights above imparted a sense of achievement and self-importance that quite turned one's head. Those on the ground floor gazed upwards at those on higher levels with much the same awed reverence as humans gazed upwards at the blessed of heaven; and, like the blessed of heaven, we gazed downwards at those beneath us with a sense of benevolent pity, bolstered by the knowledge that our lives were so much better than theirs were, or indeed ever could be. We were financial superbeings, incremental demi-gods, and if Mr Popplethwaite chose to have his office at the foot of the stairs it was simply because he had the power and supreme self-confidence to do so, much as Jesus had the power to come to earth and make his dwelling amongst the poor.

'As Mrs Popplethwaite will tell you,' our manager would frequently declare, twitching slightly at the mention of his wife's name, 'I am a simple man of simple tastes. In banking, modesty is all.'

Within my small office – which was, I repeat, on the first floor of the bank – I had a small desk with a small chair, a small filing cabinet and, on a small pedestal beside the small filing cabinet, an extremely small potted plant. Everything within my office was small, and indeed needed to be, for had it not been there would have been insufficient space to accommodate the room's main feature – a large free-standing safe located against the right-hand wall.

'Large' is perhaps to understate the case somewhat. The safe with which I shared a room was not so much a large safe as an enormous one. It was a vast safe, a gigantic safe, the biggest safe I have ever seen or, I suspect, am ever likely to see, constructed of solid, four-inch-thick Sheffield steel, eight feet high, four wide and four and a half deep, and covered from top to bottom with a bewildering assortment of dials, wheels, levers, cranks, handles, knobs and keyholes. God alone knows how it had got up on to the first floor, and God alone knows how it managed to stay there, for it must have weighed at least five tons and was supported by but the flimsiest of floorboards. For the two years I cohabited with it, indeed, I lived in constant fear that it might suddenly disappear before my eyes, crashing downwards with a whoosh into Mr Popplethwaite's office below as its weight eventually got the better of its surroundings. Fortunately, it never did so, until the very end that is, but that didn't stop me moving around the room with extreme caution, tiptoeing from place to place and ensuring I never made any sudden movements lest by so doing I should disturb the safe's precarious stability.

'Good to see you sweating, Mr Phoenix!' Mr Popplethwaite would enthuse. 'Sweat signifies respect, and respect for money, particularly bullion, is the very crux of banking.'

As Temporary Deputy Assistant Under-Manager, Bullion Division, it was my responsibility to look after this gigantic safe. My only responsibility, indeed, for aside from making the odd phone call and filling out an occasional form, I did nothing else in the two years I occupied the post.

Each morning I would arrive in my tiny office at 8 a.m. and, having hung up my coat and bowler hat, would duly set to work with a feather duster about the safe's top and sides. I would then oil its hinges and lubricate its dials. I would polish its handles and blow into its keyholes and buff up its cranks and burnish its levers. I would ensure that the large brass wheels on its door could be rotated without impediment, and that the Simsby's of Castle Street plaque just above those wheels was scoured to an eye-aching degree of brilliance. In warm weather I was expected to keep the safe cool (by fanning it), and in cool weather to keep it warm (by massaging it), and in all weathers to be on the lookout for any signs of rust, the appearance of which I dreaded in much the same way as some people dread the idea of contracting a virulent skin contagion.

Most important of all, I would, each day at 4 p.m., actually open the safe. This was a complex procedure, and one I could not undertake singlehandedly, since it took five keys to get the door open, and I only possessed one of them, the other four being held by, respectively, the Assistant Under-Manager of the Bullion Division, the Under-Manager, the Manager and Mr Popplethwaite himself. Also required was the presence of a small, wizened man called Jones the Safe, the latter apparently the only person alive in possession of the full combination thereto, and that of Mr Cree and Mr Blain, the twin heads of in-house security. With these eight people all in position, and with Mr Popplethwaite shouting out instructions ('Insert keys!', 'Turn keys!', 'Dial combination!', etc.), the safe door would be slowly and dramatically heaved open to reveal, languishing on a black velvet cushion at the very back of the vault, a single, rather small, silver ingot.

This ingot was the only thing in the Simsby's bullion safe. It was, so far as I could ascertain, the only thing that had ever been in the Simsby's bullion safe, and, despite persistent rumours that we were about to take delivery of a sizeable shipment of South African gold, remained the only thing in the Simsby's bullion safe for the whole time I was there. We would look at it briefly, Mr Popplethwaite mumbling, 'Ah, the blessed allure of precious metals!' and then get to work closing the safe again. Once it was shut, the others would all return to their respective offices and I would type up a general memo to the effect that staff could sleep easily at night in the knowledge that all was well with the Simsby's bullion. Then I would take a duster and set to work wiping away my colleagues' fingerprints.

'It's not the amount of bullion that counts,' explained Mr Popplethwaite when I once asked him whether such an enormous safe was really needed for such a small amount of silver, 'but rather the fact that there *is* bullion. And where there is bullion, there must be security. Without that, Mr Phoenix, we are lost. Quite lost.'

And who was I to argue? When it came to money and how to look after it, no one in the world knew more than Mr M. Popplethwaite of Simsby's of Castle Street.

Caring for the Simsby's bullion safe was an exacting business, and my life beyond the bank during those years was a quiet and unassuming one.

I took a room in a rather quaint Georgian house on Mount Pleasant and, having returned from work each evening and eaten my dinner, would thereafter spend the rest of the evening in an armchair in front of the wireless listening to Arthur Askey and Jack Warner.

My landlady was a Mrs Gristle, rather like her chops, who had taken lodgers since her husband, Alf, was blown up on the Somme in 1916. She was a large woman, with dishevelled red hair and an unnaturally pendulous lower lip, and was a strong candidate for the title of 'World's Most Devoted Liverpudlian'.

Mrs Gristle revered Liverpool in much the same way as Mr Popplethwaite revered money. There was nothing about the city that she didn't know, and no aspect of its history about which she couldn't discourse at extraordinary length. She had a veritable library's worth of books and pamphlets about the place, as well as what she proudly claimed to be the world's largest collection of Merseyside postcards. She seemed to know everybody within a ten-mile radius of the centre, and was probably the only person in footballing history to support both Liverpool and Everton at the same time.

'How can I choose between them,' she exclaimed, 'when they both come from the same place?'

Almost the first thing Mrs Gristle said to me, before I had even agreed to take the room, was: 'This is a fine city, my lad, and I'll throttle anyone who says different. Throttle them with my bare hands, I will!'

I informed her that from what little I had seen it was indeed a most pleasant place to live, a comment which endeared me to her no end and moved her to knock a whole shilling off the price of my rent. Thereafter, no conversation, however brief, could pass without her delivering in the midst of it a brief encomium to the city of her birth.

'We've got steak and kidney pudding tonight, Mr Phoenix,' she would say, 'and did you know that over 3 million tons of shipping passes through this city every year? Then spotted dick to follow.'

There was but one thing that interested Mrs Gristle more than Liverpool, or rather three things, and those were her daughters. Clara, Angeline and Poppeta Gristle shared a room on the top floor of the house and were, despite having inherited their mother's pendulous lower lip and dishevelled hair, all in their own way rather pretty. They had long legs and flashing emerald eyes and were the subject of constant attention from the local male population, whom they would tease and torment to the point of distraction.

I had been under Mrs Gristle's roof for less than a week when I first had sex with Clara. She was at that point 21, and one of the most athletic young women I had ever met. We continued having sex at least four times a week for the next three years – usually in my bedroom, occasionally in a shrubbery in a local park – when, to everyone's surprise, she ran off with a sailor, whereupon I transferred my attentions to Angeline. The latter was by that point herself 21 and, if not quite as pneumatic as her elder sister, certainly no less satisfying. We bonked on and off until 1937, when she decided to marry a shipyard rivetter, necessitating the withdrawal of my affections from her and their bestowal instead upon Popetta, the youngest and most coquettish of the sisters. With Popetta I enjoyed a further three years of illicit nocturnal tumbling before she too decided to tie the knot – with, to her mother's horror, a Greek Jewish saxophonist – leaving me sexless for the first time in nine years. I was rather disappointed by her departure, although in the long run it didn't matter, since it was only three days after she left that I did for Mr Popplethwaite and disappeared into the Second World War.

Mrs Gristle, of course, had no idea I was knocking off her daughters. Had she done so, it would have sent her quite over the edge, for they already caused her enough worry without the added distress of knowing they were sleeping with her lodger.

'They're quite wild, Mr Phoenix,' she would wail, ladling cabbage on to my plate. 'Quite wild. Lord alone knows what they get up to when my back's turned. If my Alf was here, he'd put them right, but Alf got blown up on the Somme so I have to do my best alone. Alone, Mr Phoenix. I'm all alone. More greens? Frankly, it'll be a blessed relief when they're all married. I do worry so.'

'I'm sure everything will turn out just fine,' I assured her. 'They really seem very pleasant girls. I'm sure they wouldn't do anything rash.'

'Oh Mr Phoenix, you do put my mind at rest! You're right, I'm sure. They *are* wild, but at least' – and here she leaned close to my ear and dropped her voice to a whisper – 'at least they are unblemished. Oh dear, Mr Phoenix, has something gone down the wrong way? Here, let me pat your back. Did you know Liverpool's had a royal charter since the reign of King John?'

Aside from making love to the Miss Gristles and listening to the wireless, the only other social life I enjoyed was an occasional visit to the cinema – as a simple, thr'penny punter, of course; my matinee-idol days were long gone – and a Friday-night trip to the pub with Bentham of Bonds.

As his name implied, Bentham worked in the Simsby's Bonds Department. An averagely built man with extremely bad skin, his first name was Isembard, but he never used it, preferring to be addressed simply as Bentham.

Bentham was what you might call my best friend of the period. He was, indeed, what you might call my only friend of the period, since, the Gristle girls apart, he was the only person with whom I enjoyed anything that might fairly be termed regular social intercourse. Not that our friendship was a particularly close one. We neither confided in each other nor bought each other drinks, nor even particularly liked each other. Looking back on it, indeed, I am at a loss to explain why I bothered to spend any time with him at all, since he was without doubt one of the most inane people I have ever met.

Spend time with him, however, I did – four hours of it, every Friday evening, when at 6 p.m., having completed our day's business, we would meet beside the revolving front door of the bank and walk together to the Empire in Hanover Street.

'Go Dutch, shall we?' Bentham would inquire as we pushed our way to the bar.

'Fine by me,' I would reply.

We would purchase our drinks separately – a half of stout for Bentham, a large Scotch for me – and ensconce ourselves in a corner seat.

'A good week?' my companion would inquire.

'Passable,' I would reply. 'And yourself?'

'Passable,' he would respond. 'Very passable. And how goes it in Bullion?'

'Fine, fine. Nothing untoward. The bank's silver is as safe as ever.'

'Good, good!'

'Although I did find a dead fly in the safe on Tuesday.'

'Gosh.'

'And Bonds?'

'Same as ever. Nothing out of the ordinary. They're thinking of printing them on a new type of paper.'

'Good heavens!'

'Although nothing's been decided as yet.'

221

'I see.'

'Bus fares are going up again, you know.'

'Really?'

'Yes. It's going to cost me tuppence extra to get to work.'

'Dear oh dear!'

And so it went on, a slow back and forth of inanities until the clock struck 10 p.m., by which point I would be on my fifth double and Bentham on his sixth half of stout.

'Good heavens above,' my companion would exclaim. 'Is that the time! I really must be going or I'll miss my bus.'

'Well, if you do, at least you'll save yourself the fare!'

'Ha ha ha! I like that. Miss the bus but save the fare. I'll have to tell my mum that. She likes a laugh. Good night.'

As he stood in front of me buttoning his raincoat – which he invariably wore, whatever the weather – I always had the urge to lean forward and squeeze his penis very hard through the material of his trousers, just to see how he reacted. I resisted the temptation, however, instead accompanying him on to the street, where we each went our separate ways, he back to the house he shared with his mother in Knowsley, me back to Mrs Gristle for a cup of tea and a chat about her daughters.

'Driving me mad, they are, Mr Phoenix! Mad as a hatter. I feel you're the only one who understands.'

'There there, Mrs Gristle. It'll all turn out right in the end. They're good girls, of that I'm sure.'


Which is, in a nutshell, how I spent my nine years in Liverpool. They were admittedly unspectacular years, and in many senses rather dull ones, but after the whirlwind of my life in America it was actually quite pleasant to slip back into quiet and anonymous mediocrity. I certainly never found myself wishing things were any different.

The Photo I kept snug in the inside pocket of my jacket, removing it every now and then for a wistful look at its cracked and fading image. The Pill, meanwhile, I extracted from the gold ring in which

I had kept it during my Hollywood days – pawning the latter to raise money for my first month's rent – and consigned to an inner pocket of an old calfskin wallet which I purchased at a Sunday flea-market. From Emily I heard not a word.

And so things might have continued – steadily, dully, anonymously – had the Germans not taken it upon themselves to invade Poland in 1939, thus precipitating the outbreak of the Second World War. Amongst the many crimes that can be laid at the doorstep of the Third Reich, not the least was the scuppering of my brilliant banking career.

Like most people in Britain, I'd listened to Prime Minister Chamberlain's radio broadcast announcing that we were now at war with Germany and, like most people in Britain, I had, over the subsequent weeks, gradually adjusted myself to the exigencies of the situation. I had, for instance, helped Mrs Gristle take all her pots and pans to a local collection point so that they could be melted down and made into armaments, and joined in enthusiastically with the construction of large, baize-covered frames to black out the windows of the bank. One thing that never occurred to me, however, was that I might actually be expected to do something ridiculous, such as fight.

The awful truth only hit me one morning in early December of that year when I received a letter from the conscriptions department of the War Office requesting my attendance at a medical fitness test. I immediately wrote back informing them that, since only those aged between 18 and 28 were at that time being called up, and since I was currently just shy of my 40th birthday, there must have been some mistake. I heard nothing for a fortnight, and then received another letter exactly the same as the one before, and from exactly the same department. You have to give it to the Civil Service: they're certainly persistent.

Suspecting I might have more success face to face, I decided to attend the fitness test and argue my case in person. I duly presented myself at a nondescript building on the outskirts of Liverpool one bitterly cold late-December morning, queuing for half an hour with several hundred others before eventually finding myself in front of a puce-faced man in a white coat sitting at a trestle table.

'Name?' he snapped.

'Phoenix,' I replied. 'But there seems to have been some mistake—'

'How do you spell that?'

'P.H.O.E.N.I.X., but you see, I'm 39. I'm too old to be here. There's obviously some confusion—'

'Initials.'

'R.I. I was in America for some time, you see, which might be why your records are—'

'Address?'

'117 Mount Pleasant, Liverpool. Look, I shouldn't be here. I'm 40 in a couple of days.'

'Take this form and go behind that screen. Next!'

Behind the screen was another man in a white coat, who shoved a wooden spatula in my mouth and made me say 'Ahhh!' I tried to tell him there had been a mistake, but had barely begun when I was dispatched to another part of the room to have my reflexes tested, and then another to have my chest examined, and another to have my testicles squeezed, and so on, and so on. In the end I had to do the whole bloody medical from start to finish, and suffer the indignity of being told I was one of the healthiest people they had ever seen, before I finally managed to collar a senior official and make my grievance known.

'Thirty-nine, you say, sir?'

'That's right. Almost 40.'

'Well, I must say, you're in extraordinarily good shape for your age.'

'That's not the point. I shouldn't be here. I'm outside the age group.'

'That would certainly seem to be the case. I can't think what's happened. Most unusual. We're not examining anyone over 28 at the moment.'

'Well, there you go. I'm entirely the wrong age.'

'So it would seem.'

'And you'll do something about it?'

'Oh yes. Up to 28 and no older. That's the order. There's been a slip-up somewhere. We'll put it right, don't you worry.'

'Thank you!' I said, relieved. 'I don't mind saying I've been rather worried about it. Not that I don't want to fight, of course. I'd just rather do it alongside people of my own age.'

'I quite understand. We'll get it sorted out. Trust me.'

Which, foolishly, I did. Foolishly because, four weeks later, in the freezing late January of 1940, by which point I had convinced myself that December's error had now been fully rectified, I received my enlistment notice. It took the form of a rectangle of grey-green card bearing my name, address, registration number (LHZ 35720) and an instruction to present myself to No. 6 Training Regiment, Catterick Camp, Yorkshire (nearest railway station Richmond.) And as if that wasn't enough, I was expected to do it that very day. Whoever was screwing up at the War Office wasn't doing it by half-measures.

I stared at the damned thing in horror, and then – having no intention whatsoever of acting upon it – stuffed it into my jacket pocket alongside The Pill and The Photo and stomped off to work. Which is where, just an hour or so later, I killed my Mr Popplethwaite. Bad day all round.


There were two separate, and quite distinct, factors involved in Mr Popplethwaite's murder. One was the Simsby's bullion safe, of which more in a moment. The second was a large wheel which dropped, quite unexpectedly, through the roof of the bank as we all went about our morning business.

The wheel, all 500lbs of it, rubber and metal, belonged to a Blenheim bomber, one of a number of such planes engaged in low-level training exercises up and down the Mersey River. Each day a number of these would take off from an airfield just to the north of Liverpool, drone south across the city, fly up and down the river for a while, and then drone away back north again, their business complete.

On the morning of Mr Popplethwaite's murder, the very same morning I received my enlistment notice, at about 9 a.m., as I was getting down to dusting the bullion safe, one of these planes was experiencing difficulties with its undercarriage, which refused to close as it was supposed to after take-off. The pilot wrestled manfully with his undercarriage controls, but was unable to rectify the problem and, directly above the centre of Liverpool, at a height of about 9,000 feet, radioed Control to say he was returning to base. Even as he spoke, however, there was a loud wrenching sound and one of his wheels dropped off the underside of the plane.

Precisely why the wheel fell off was never properly established – theories aired at the subsequent inquiry included metal fatigue, sabotage and a fundamental flaw in the design of the Blenheim. Fall off it did, however, dropping from the plane's belly like a large rubber birdshit and plummeting earthwards straight towards the roof of Simsby's of Castle Street.

I had, I recall, just finished oiling one of the bullion safe's combination dials, and was tiptoeing across the room to water my house plant, when I heard a loud crash somewhere in the building above me. Several loud crashes, in fact, each getting closer until, with an ear-splitting roar, an enormous round object burst through the ceiling and smashed through the floor directly in front of me, its passage throwing up a lung-choking billow of dust and plaster and knocking me backwards off my feet.

For several moments I was too stunned to do anything and merely lay, flat on my back, covered in biscuits of rubble, coughing violently and mumbling, 'What the hell!' over and over again. Eventually, however, I pulled myself together and, rubbing dust from my eyes, knocking lumps of plaster from my shoulders and checking to make sure I didn't have any broken bones, struggled to my knees and took stock of the situation.

The wheel appeared to have hit the building at a slight diagonal, punching its way like a large fist through whatever floors and ceilings happened to be in its path, so that from where I was kneeling it was possible to gaze upwards through a succession of gaping, jagged-edged holes to a large patch of blue morning sky high above.

'Bloody hell!' I muttered. 'Bloody hell.'

Having noted the state of affairs overhead, I duly turned my attention to that around and below me. The middle of my room, where only a few minutes ago my desk had been standing – where only a few minutes ago *I* had been standing – now consisted of a wide, gaping crevasse, the sides of which were formed of teeth-like shards of splintered wood. Looking into this chasm, I could, despite the dust, clearly make out Mr Popplethwaite's room beneath, in the corner of which the wheel had eventually come to rest, lying on its side like some enormous snail.

'The bloody Germans are dropping wheels on us!' I cried. 'Bastards!'

So fascinated was I by the sight of the wheel, and so outraged by the thought that the Germans had dropped it, that it was some while before I noticed, almost directly beneath me, covered in dust like a heavily floured suet dumpling, the recumbent figure of Mr Popplethwaite. He was slumped on his castor-footed chair with his head thrown backwards, one of his spectacle lenses shattered. A small chunk of plaster sat plum in the middle of his forehead like a third eye, whilst in his left hand he was holding his pill bottle, the contents of which had spilled out all over the floor. His bow tie was all skew-whiff.

'Are you all right, Mr Popplethwaite?' I called, uncertain whether he was alive or dead. 'Are you injured?'

He made no reply.

'Mr Popplethwaite! Can you move?'

Still no reply. I fumbled in my pocket and found an old pencil rubber, which I dropped through the hole. It landed on his nose, and caused him to judder somewhat.

'Burghhhhh,' he mumbled. 'Burghhhh.'

'What is it, Mr Popplethwaite? Are you trying to say something?'

'Burghhhh!' he repeated, lips trembling, chest heaving up and down. 'Booooooo!'

'Blood?' I offered. 'Are you bleeding, Mr Popplethwaite? Should I get bandages?'

He shook his head wearily from side to side.

"Boo . . . Boo!'

'I can't understand what you're saying, Mr Popplethwaite. I think you might be delirious.'

Again he shook his head, this time more violently than before, and, clutching the arm of his chair and taking a long, deep breath, he raised his head a little and sputtered a single word:

'Bullion!'

So shocked had I been by the wheel's sudden appearance that I had, up to that point, given no thought to the Simsby's bullion reserve, nor the solid steel monstrosity in which that reserve was secured. Now, however, I turned my head, very slowly, very carefully, and noticed with some alarm that the giant safe, which had previously stood flush against the wall, was now listing forward at an angle of some 20 degrees from the vertical. The floor beneath it appeared to have sagged rather and, even as I watched, there was a creaking, splitting sound and the safe dipped forward another couple of degrees. It was evidently only a matter of time before gravity got the better of it and it crashed downwards on to the head of Mr Popplethwaite beneath.

'Are you all right, Mr Phoenix?' came a voice from outside my office. 'We heard a crash.'

'Yes!' I replied, as quietly as possible. 'I'm perfectly OK. But don't come in. There's a big hole in the floor.'

'A hole in the floor!'

'Yes, yes. Just don't come in. And don't move. Stay where you are and don't clomp about.'

Very slowly, very delicately, hardly daring to breathe, I inched my way across the room until I was crouched beside the safe. There was

228

another groan and a creak and, with a horrible wrenching sound, one of the floorboards beneath the vault snapped in half and clattered down into the room below, narrowly missing Mr Popplethwaite's head. The safe trembled.

'Mr Popplethwaite,' I whispered, trying to keep my voice as low as possible, 'the bullion safe is in a rather precarious position. If you can, you must try to move.'

He stared up at me, uncomprehendingly, eyes blinking.

'Bullion!' he sputtered. 'Bullion. The very crux of banking!'

'Mr Popplethwaite, please! Your life is in danger. You must try to move.'

There was a deep groan, and beside me the safe listed forward at an even more precarious angle. The floor seemed to buckle before my very eyes, and splinters of wood rained down into the room beneath, piling up on Mr Popplethwaite's head and shoulders like pine needles. The least nudge would now have been enough to upset the safe and send it crashing downwards.

'For God's sake, move!' I snapped. 'Get out of the way, man. It's going to come straight down on top of you.'

For a moment it seemed as if my words had had some effect, for Mr Popplethwaite's feet, acting, it appeared, independently of the rest of his body, which remained slumped and motionless, began paddling up and down on the debris-strewn floor, each paddle moving his chair backward an inch or so away from the hole in his ceiling. After he had gone perhaps a foot, however, he came to a halt and moved no further.

'No!' he mumbled. 'No! Must stay with the bullion. We have our reputation to think of! Excellence and Security since 1781! Three lords, two admirals and 18 knights of the realm!'

Most people, I suspect, especially those actively involved in the world of finance, would have been deeply impressed by this show of selfless dedication to duty. This was a man who placed the wellbeing of a single, rather paltry, silver ingot above that of his own self. It is upon such heroes that the foundations of banking are built.

I, however, was not impressed. On the contrary, I was rather annoyed by his behaviour. Very annoyed by it. Here was I risking my life telling him to get out of the way, and all he could think about was the fucking bullion. His refusal to move struck me as a sort of personal insult; a spurning of the lifeline I was throwing him. I gave him one more chance – 'Move, damn it, you silly man!' – and, when he again insisted on staying where he was, hissed, 'Have it your own way then, you bloody prat!' and, leaning a little to my left, banged my elbow as hard as I could into the side of the teetering safe. The latter lurched drunkenly forward, stopped, teetered a little more and then, with an agonized screech of splintering wood and cracking joists, pitched forwards through the hole and landed with a loud thud straight on top of my portly superior. A thick plume of dust rose like ash from an erupting volcano, gradually clearing to reveal the safe lying on its front, with Mr Popplethwaite's plump hands sticking out on either side, as though actually a part of it.

'Mr Phoenix!' came the voice from the other side of the door. 'Mr Phoenix! What's going on?'

'Oh my God!' I cried. 'Oh my God. A terrible tragedy. Mr Popplethwaite's been squashed by the bullion safe. Help him! Help him, somebody!'

They were still trying to lever the safe off Mr Popplethwaite's pancaked body when I left the bank. No one noticed me go. Several female customers, I remarked, had passed out at the news of his demise, and were being revived by Mr Cree and Mr Blain, the twin heads of in-house security.

As always after a murder, I felt a need for fresh air and solitary reflection and, to this end, having purchased a bottle of lemonade and a packet of cigarettes, spent half an hour or so wandering through the streets of Liverpool trying to come to terms with what I'd just done, and wondering what I ought to do now that I'd done it.

'I can't very well carry on at Simsby's,' I thought. 'I've just murdered the manager, after all. Most inappropriate. I could go back to

London, I suppose. Or maybe I should just go down to the docks and get on the first ship I can find. Frankly, I don't know what I'm going to do. Except' – and here I delved into the inside pocket of my jacket and removed the call-up notice I had received only that morning – 'I'm not going to join the army. That much I do know. I might be a murderer, but there's nothing in the world that could persuade me to put on a uniform and fight. Nothing in the entire world!'

I became quite involved in this little soliloquy – stomping up the street, brandishing my enlistment card – and was so intent upon the idea of not joining the army that I quite failed to notice the woman walking towards me carrying a large pile of gift-wrapped boxes. Only when I slammed right into her, knocking her backwards and scattering her boxes about the pavement, did I emerge from my reverie and realize where I was.

'I'm most terribly sorry,' I said, falling to my knees and gathering up the spilled presents. 'I was miles away. I do hope I haven't caused any damage.'

'I'm sure you haven't,' said a familiar voice. 'They're just shoes.'

I looked up, amazed, for there before me, wrapped up in a thick coat against the cold, was none other than Emily. Dear Emily, her face as exquisite as ever, her hair just as golden.

'Emily!' I cried. 'Of all the amazing—'

I leapt to my feet and gave her a big hug.

'Raphael!' she gasped. 'You're crushing me!'

I released her and stepped backwards.

'You're all dusty,' she said. 'And you've got bits of plaster in your hair. You look like a bomb's dropped on you.'

'A wheel actually,' I said. 'I'll explain later. What on earth are you doing here?'

'I've been shopping. I've bought lots and lots of shoes. And where were you off to in such a hurry?'

I was about to say that I wasn't really off to anywhere in a hurry, and had just been wandering around aimlessly, when I suddenly re-called the enlistment notice still clutched in my right hand. Thirty seconds before, I'd been vowing that under no circumstances what-soever would I act upon it. Now, however, seeing an opportunity to impress Emily – and, let's face it, such opportunities don't come up that often – I flourished it theatrically and declared, in the most gung-ho sort of voice I could muster:

'I'm going to join the army, Emily! To fight for king and country. So help me God, I might not be a good man, but this is one fight I can't duck out of.'

If I had expected my companion to be impressed by this little speech, I was pleasantly surprised, for barely had I finished it than she cast aside the box she had just picked up, launched herself at me and planted a whopping kiss on my cheek.

'Oh Raphael!' she cried. 'You're so brave. I knew you'd do some-thing like this. You're my hero.'

'It's nothing,' I muttered modestly. 'Nothing at all. Every man should do his duty.'

'It's not nothing, Raphael. It's tremendously selfless and cour-ageous.'

'No, no.'

'Yes, yes. It's fantastic. You must let me see you off.'

'That really won't be necessary,' I said, feeling that perhaps things were getting a little out of hand. 'And, anyway, I haven't got to leave for a few days. Let's go and have a cup of tea somewhere. And then we could have lunch. And dinner as well.'

Before I could stop her, however, Emily had seized the enlistment notice and read it.

'It says you have to report today,' she said.

'Does it?' I laughed nervously. 'I must have got my dates mixed up.'

'Oh Raphael, I know you're just trying to be brave and spare my feelings, but there's no need. I've said I'll see you off, and see you off I will.'

With which, having gathered together her parcels, she bustled me up the street towards Lime Street Station, where, as Sod's Law would have it, there was a suitable train leaving in five minutes' time.

'I'll get a later one,' I said.

'There might not be a later one.'

'Then I'll go tomorrow.'

'You can't go tomorrow. It says you have to be there today. The army doesn't like people being late.'

'For God's sake, Emily, a day won't matter!'

'I won't be responsible for you being late for your first day in the army, Raphael. Look! There's a space in that carriage.'

And before I quite knew what was happening, she had shepherded me across the platform and into the train, where I found myself sharing a musty six-seater compartment with a nervous-looking ginger-haired young man with a very sweaty forehead. I turned and leant out of the window. Steam billowed all around.

'Emily, I've hardly had a chance to talk to you.'

'I know, I know. But that's war. It gets in the way of things. I'm so proud of you, Raphael.'

'You shouldn't be, Emily. I was lying when I said I was going to join the army.'

My words, however, were drowned out in a loud blast from the train's whistle. There was a clattering of closing doors, a hiss of steam from the engine, and we started to pull out. Emily dropped her boxes and, pulling a monogrammed white silk handkerchief from her pocket, hurried along beside the carriage, waving it above her head.

'For crying out loud, Emily,' I shouted, 'why does it always have to be so damned brief!'

'That's life,' she cried. 'Take care of yourself. Don't get killed!'

'What?'

'Don't get killed!'

'I doubt I'll have much choice in the matter. Think of me!'

'I will. I will. I always do!'

The train had by now reached the end of the platform, and she began to drop away behind me.

'You're a hero, Raphael!'

'I'm an idiot,' I muttered, clutching The Pill in my pocket and watching as she disappeared in a cloud of steam. 'A bloody idiot.'

'We're all going to die,' wailed the nervous-looking ginger-haired young man with the sweaty forehead. 'We're going to die! Die! Dieeeeeee!'

I shall end this particular room with an admission of ignorance, and a word of explanation.

The admission of ignorance is that, despite working for him for almost ten years, I never found out what the M. in Mr M. Popplethwaite stood for. I made extensive inquiries on the subject, but all to no avail, and he thus goes down as the only one of my victims for whom I'm unable to supply a Christian name. It rather niggles me. I feel it somehow leaves his murder incomplete.

The word of explanation, meanwhile, concerns the wheel. How, you may wonder, could I have known so much about it – about the low-level flying exercises, the jammed undercarriage, the radioing back to base. I was, after all, some 9,000 feet below at the time, and not privy to the inner secrets of His Majesty's Air Force.

Well, the strange thing was that a few years later, quite by chance, I happened to meet two of the men who'd actually been in the plane. They'd only recently joined the RAF, and described in excited tones how they'd had to make an emergency landing on just one wheel. They were an odd couple, brothers, twin brothers, and you can find more about them down in the cellar. Their names were Clive and Matthew Brain. Oh what a web of strange connections life is!

# Chapter Thirteen

Disaster has struck! Complete and utter bloody disaster. Not much over halfway through my note, with a good few murders yet to go and most of the castle's upper floor still gaping pristine white before me, and I've run out of felt-tips. Can you believe it! I'm living on borrowed time even now, writing with a pen that's liable to conk out any minute, as you can no doubt see by the faintness of the words it's forming.

To be fair, I haven't actually *run out* of pens. I still have 30 left, one entire box, half of what I started with. The problem is that those 30 have, in the 18 months since I bought them, all gone dry. Their ink has caked, like congealed blood, and their nibs shrivelled. I can't explain why this should have happened to one box and not the other – they both, after all, arrived at the castle on the same day, and have sat side by side ever since – but the fact remains that where I ought to have more than enough pens to carry me forward to my death, I now have none at all. Damn, damn, bloody damn and fuck.

And things were going so well too. After the horrors of the cellar, and the disturbances of yesterday evening, I'd been worried I might struggle to recover the momentum of the note. Last night, however, I wrote as speedily and contentedly as I've done at any time during the composing of my gargantuan epitaph. I didn't get started till almost

10 p.m., and yet, even taking into account several wine and cigarette breaks, I'd still murdered Mr Popplethwaite and set off to join the army by eight o'clock this morning.

What's more, the study, which I've just left, is the first place in which my note really achieves its full potential. You will remember that, downstairs, it never quite attained perfection. Mrs Bunshop filled two rooms; the eastern gallery contained two murders (albeit neatly arranged); and the kitchen threw up all sorts of problems with pipes and sideboards. As for the cellar, the less said about that the better.

In the study, however, note and castle embraced in consummate symbiosis. I started Mr Popplethwaite at the ceiling directly to the right of the door, and then wrote my way, cleanly and without obstacle, right around the room, my letters of a uniform size all the way (i.e. that of raisins), before concluding the whole episode at the skirting board directly to the left of the door. The result is profoundly stirring – neat, dramatic, contained, overwhelming – and is precisely what I dreamt of when I first came up with my one murder per room scheme.

'That,' I said to myself as I poked a final full stop at the inter-section of skirting board and doorframe, 'is a bloody masterpiece. It's almost worth delaying my death so I can have more time to admire it.'

And yet, within a couple of minutes, triumph had turned to despair when I discovered all my remaining pens were unusable.

I made the discovery on the landing, just as I emerged from Mr Popplethwaite's room. I had fetched the second box of felt-tips from my bedroom and, having selected one from the 30 contained therein, had mounted my ladder ready to start work near the landing ceiling. When I placed the nib against the wall, however, and tried to write, no words appeared, just a vague, ghostly smudge on the whitewashed plaster.

'Damn,' I muttered. 'Must be a dud.'

I threw the pen to the floor, climbed down the ladder and fetched another. Exactly the same thing happened with that, however, and the next one, and the next, and the next after that. Thirty times I climbed down and up that bloody ladder, each time with increasing desperation, until eventually there were no more pens left to fetch, every one of them having proved withered and hopeless.

'Bastards!' I wailed. 'This can't be! Please don't let it be! Aaaaaaargh!'

It is, I suppose, my own fault. I should have checked all the pens at the very beginning; given each a little scribble to make sure it was in good working order. That way I would have discovered the problem last Tuesday, giving me plenty of time to come up with an alternative plan. Now, however, I'm stranded high and dry, and there seems no immediate way out of my predicament. The above has been written with what little ink is left in the pens from the first box. It's taken me 20 of these to get this far, however – my writing faint to the point of illegibility – and the remaining ten will only last me another two or three paragraphs. I feel like a man who's slit his wrists and is helplessly watching his own life blood slowly drain away.

What to do now? Dr Bannen isn't coming till Friday, and even if he could get me some new pens I'd never have enough time to finish the note, due as I am to kill myself in the early hours of Saturday morning. Delaying my death is out of the question – when you set yourself a date to die you really have to stick to it – as is going down to the village in person. I simply couldn't cope with all those people. I could try carrying on in chalk, I suppose, or with my fountain pen, but what's the point? I only have a few sticks of the former, and a single ink cartridge for the latter. Neither would last anything like long enough to get the job done.

I might as well face up to it – the note's over. Finished. Caput. Terminito. After six days and God knows how many words, I can't go any further. I've reached an impasse. I am, as you can imagine, devastated. I'd say suicidal if I wasn't that already. All that work, all those memories – and all for nothing. I've juddered to a halt short of the mark. I am unable to complete myself. I want to cry. To scream. And my back's throbbing like buggery. And now that fucking knocking's . . . Oh Christ, come on you damned pen . . . that fucking knocking . . . oh bollocks, it's run out . . .

It's about midday on Wednesday, 29th December, two days after I wrote the above. As you can see, I'm writing again. And as you can also see, my words are strong and clear and vibrant and assured, quite different from the pale anaemia of the preceding few paragraphs. Yes, I've got new pens. And yes, I've been away from the castle to get them, although not quite as far away as I expected I'd have to go. I simply couldn't abandon the note. I had to keep on with my life. It's come to mean too much to me.

For two whole days after my felt-tips ran out I stayed up in the dome. I smoked, I drank, I fingered The Pill, I wallowed in self-pity.

'My note,' I mumbled to myself over and over. 'My beautiful note.'

On Monday someone knocked three times on the front door – once as my last pen conked out, once in the early afternoon, and once late at night. Boom, boom, boom. Each time I rushed to see who it was, but each time there was no one there. On Tuesday there was just a single, loud, solitary knock around midday, and then, late in the evening, someone threw an egg at the castle. It flew up over the battlements and landed with a splat on the side of the dome, leaving a trail of viscous goo running like a large yellow tear down the face of the metal plates.

'What sort of monster are you?' I screamed at my invisible tormentor. 'Why can't you leave me in peace?'

These assaults were the only fixed points in the otherwise all-consuming emptiness of those two terrible days. Between them I just sat, useless, wreathed in cigarette smoke, shackled to the void of my soon to be ended life, crumpled.

Only once I'd stopped writing it did I come to appreciate fully how important the note had been to me. How essential. How much colour it had imparted. Now it all seemed black and white. Not even black and white. Just grey. My life was a drab, grey, empty thing; a torn cobweb of a life. Without the note, I realized, I was nothing.

The note was me. I was the note. And when it ran out, puttered to a halt, faded, so too did I. Ending it was, in its own way, like ending my own life. I'd committed suicide without even knowing it.

'I might as well take The Pill now,' I thought late on Tuesday night. 'I'm as good as dead anyway. All I'll be doing is confirming the fact.'

But I did so want to get to my hundredth birthday. To complete a full century. And that, ultimately, is what persuaded me to swallow my fears and go out to find new pens. If I was to remain alive for the next four days, you see, I needed the note, because it is the note that brings me to life. I needed to keep it going. To carry on writing. To continue with my recollection of myself. Ludicrous, perhaps, like bringing someone back from the dead simply so as to be able to kill them again at a more appropriate moment. But that's just how it is. I can't finish my life until I've finished my note. I needed more pens. It was a matter of life and death.

Thus it was that early on Wednesday morning, this morning, after a hiatus of two days, I went into the bathroom and cleaned myself up (getting wax out of your hair is one hell of a bloody business). I put on some clothes, the very ones I had worn 15 years ago when I first arrived at the castle and which had lain untouched ever since in a heap beneath my bed, and took 20 pounds out of the biscuit tin in which I keep my paltry savings. I descended to the front door, opened it, passed through, closed and locked it behind me. And then, like an astronaut stepping out into a new and uncharted world, I started off down the track towards the village.

'Oh Jesus,' I muttered, terrified. 'Oh Jesus.'

Since I first arrived at the castle all those many years ago, I've never ventured more than 20 or so yards from its front door. I'm not an agoraphobic as such. I am not afraid of the sky, or the countryside, or the wide-open spaces. I don't have a problem with outside. I just don't like going away from my home. It holds me with a compelling gravity. It is there that I feel secure, content, calm. It is in the castle that I feel myself. Each step away from it is like a step away from my own sanity.

'Keep it together, Raphael,' I hissed to myself through clenched teeth. 'Stay in control.'

My plan, such as I had one, was to get down into the village, find the nearest suitable shop, buy my pens as quickly and with as little fuss as possible, and then get back to the castle pronto. To this end, clutching The Pill and The Photo for strength, teeth chattering, blood pounding in my temples, I made my way slowly step by step along the rutted track that loops and winds from the castle down into the valley below.

It was a crisp, clear day, the sky a pale, cloudless blue, the air sharp and clean. All around, the bracken-covered hills rolled sedately off towards the uneven line of horizon, whilst down in the valley, which because of the lay of the land you can't actually see from the castle, there were forests and fields and the white dots of distant houses, clinging to the hills like boats on a stormy sea of green. Had I not been so jittery, I might actually have quite enjoyed the view. As it was, it required my full concentration just to keep myself moving forward and down, and I remained largely oblivious to the splendour of the scenery.

'Easy does it, Raphael,' I muttered, taking deep breaths and trying to control the trembling of my hands. 'One step at a time, one foot in front of the other. It's going to be OK. It's all going to be OK.'

The track is about two miles long, eventually issuing on to a tarmacked road which in one direction, left, leads down to the village, and in the other, right, up and over the hills to the towns and cities and worlds beyond. More than once on my way down I had to stop, sweat pouring from my face, heart thumping, convinced I could go no further. I forced myself on, however, and eventually, after almost two hours of toil, reached the point where the track joins the road. Beyond that, however, I found I couldn't go.

I tried. I stepped out on to the tarmac and willed my legs to carry me left and down towards the village, but they simply wouldn't do it. They refused to work.

'Come on!' I shouted. 'Don't stop now! Come on!'

It was no good, however. I managed to totter a few yards, but then, like a fish on a line, found myself irresistibly reeled back. I put every ounce of strength I had into it, driving myself away from the track like a swimmer fighting against a strong current, powering my withered old limbs forward, straining, aching, but all to no avail. The castle's gravity was too fierce. There was a limit to how far it would let me go, and I'd reached that limit. I sunk down on a hummock at the foot of the track, put my head in my hands and wept.

I don't know how long I wept for, but I was still doing it, although less copiously, when the nurse pulled up in her car. She leaned across and wound down the window.

'Are you all right?' she said.

'Yes,' I snivelled, wiping my nose on my sleeve (something I hadn't done since my days with Walter). 'Fine. Just a bit of hayfever.'

She raised her eyebrows.

'At this time of year?'

'Yes, well, I'm very susceptible to it. Thank you.'

She was dark-skinned – Indian, perhaps – and was wearing one of those attractive blue uniforms with a little watch on the front. I couldn't help noticing, from the way she was leaning forward, that she had a marvellous pair of bosoms. Small but firm, like peaches, with slightly protuberant nipples. I hadn't seen bosoms for 15 years and tried hard not to stare. Despite my distressed state and extreme old age I felt a vague stirring in the depths of my trousers. I shifted my position slightly so she couldn't see it.

'Do you need a lift anywhere?' she asked.

'No, I'm all right, thank you.'

'Are you sure?'

'Yes, yes, quite sure.'

She stared at me for a moment and then, killing the engine, got out of the car and walked round to where I was sitting, squatting down on the grass in front of me. She was young, probably in her mid-twenties, and smelt faintly of perfume. The trouser-stirring intensified.

241

'Are you sure you're all right?' she asked, laying a hand on my arm.

'Yes,' I mumbled. 'Quite all right. It's just . . .'

'Yes?'

'I've run out of pens.'

'Pens?'

'Yes. Felt-tip pens. I'm doing some writing, you see, and all my pens have run out. I was just going to get some new ones.'

'Well, I could take you into the village if you like. I'm going that way.'

'You're very kind, but it's simply no good. I can't leave the castle.'

She narrowed her eyes, clearly unsure of my meaning. I noticed she had a small, crescent-shaped scar just below her left ear.

'I live in the castle up at the top of the track,' I explained. 'The old observatory. Do you know it?'

She shook her head.

'I've never been this far away from it before, you see. I know it sounds ridiculous, but if I go any further I think I'll have some sort of breakdown. You must think I'm mad.'

She gave my arm a reassuring squeeze.

'Not at all. It must be very hard if you don't feel comfortable being outside.'

'It's not the being outside that's difficult. It's just going away from the castle. I don't like to leave it. Which puts me in a bit of a fix, you see. I need these pens, but I can't actually get to the village to buy them. It's very frustrating.'

I bit my lip, trying hard not to start crying again. I hate crying in front of women. The nurse brushed a strand of dark hair out of her eye and looked hard at me.

'Would it be any good,' she asked after a long pause, 'if I drove down to the village for the pens and then brought them back to you here? Would that solve the problem?'

'Would you?' I cried. 'Would you do that?'

'Sure. It'll only take fifteen minutes, and I'm not in any hurry.'

'I've got the money,' I said excitedly. 'And I'll pay for your petrol.'

'It's fine. Don't worry about it.'

'I really don't know what to say,' I laughed, getting to my feet and pulling the cash from my pocket. 'This is wonderful. Marvellous. Quite unexpected. And I don't even know you. Thank you so much. Thank you. Thank you. I really thought the note was fucked. Oh I'm terribly sorry. Please excuse my language.'

'I'm a nurse,' she smiled. 'Unshockable.'

I handed her the money and issued precise instructions as to the type of pens I needed (black felt-tip) and how many (18). I then stood back and waved as she drove off with a toot and disappeared around the corner. Only after she'd gone did I notice the unsightly bulge in my trousers. I hoped she hadn't seen it and, rearranging myself, sat down again to await her return.

She had said she'd be back in 15 minutes, but it was closer to an hour before she reappeared.

'I was beginning to think you wouldn't come back,' I said as she pulled up beside me and wound down the window.

'Sorry. Flat tyre. I've got the pens.'

She indicated a brown paper bag on the passenger seat.

'Get in. I'll give you a lift home.'

'That's very kind, but I don't think your car would make it. The track's steep in places, and full of potholes. And, anyway, the walk will do me good. Going up should be a lot easier than coming down.'

'You're sure?'

'Absolutely.'

She shrugged and, leaning over, handed me my pens.

'You've got some change,' she said, fiddling with her purse.

'Keep it.'

'I couldn't.'

'Please. I don't need it. If you don't want it, give to charity or something.'

She smiled, and put her hand out of the window.

'Well, goodbye then.'

'Goodbye,' I said, taking the hand. 'I really don't know how to thank you. You've saved my life.'

'I wouldn't go that far.'

'Really, you have. I can't thank you enough. You've been a god-send. My name's Raphael, by the way. Raphael Phoenix.'

'That's a nice name,' she said. 'I'm Emily.'

She wound up her window, turned around and sped off back towards the village.

And now I should be getting on. It's mid-afternoon on Wednesday, 29th December and I've got a lot of catching up to do. It's going to be hard work, but I still think I can finish my note in time for my death. I can feel the energy flooding back through me. I'm raring to get murdering again.

The above has used up not only all the wall space between the study doorway and that of my bathroom, but also some of the bathroom wall too. I won't, it seems, be able to match my next victim to his room quite as precisely as I was able to match Mr Popplethwaite to his. It can't be helped, however. The events of the last 48 hours were important, and needed to be recounted in full. There's no point writing a suicide note if you can't be flexible.

The pens are all working perfectly – I've checked each and every one on a piece of paper, so as not to get any nasty surprises further down the line – although, as you will doubtless have noticed by now, they're not what I ordered. I told the nurse to get black felt-tips, since that's the colour in which the note has so far been written (and a very appropriate one too, given the subject matter). My new pens, however, are all sorts of different colours, each pack containing, in order of arrangement, starting from the left, a yellow, an orange, a pink, a red, a light green, a dark green, a blue that's neither strictly light nor dark, a purple, and a vile, disgusting-looking brown. I've already used the two yellows writing the above, and have just started on the first of the two oranges. Whether she simply forgot my instructions, or these were all the shop had, I can't say. From being a sombre, black and white affair, however, my note has suddenly taken on the appearance of a field of sunflowers. My demise, it seems, is fated to be a multicoloured one.

One final thing I should mention before my next murder is the face. As I trudged back up the track, pens in hand, whistling contentedly to myself, I heard a sudden rustle in the bracken away to my right. I looked over, and there, amongst the dense, curling fronds, I saw a face. A pale, rather beautiful face, surmounted by a heap of blonde hair. I only saw it for a moment before it shot back into the greenery, and by the time I'd waded through the bracken to the spot where it had been there was no sign of it. I might have imagined it. Or it could have been a rabbit or something. But I'm pretty sure it was a face. And a vaguely familiar one too. Very strange.

Enough rambling. Time to go to America. I can't stop thinking about that nurse's bosoms.

# Chapter Fourteen

WHEN I SET sail for America in the summer of 1919 I did so for one reason and one reason only – because Emily had said she'd be on the boat.

'I sail from Southampton today,' she had informed me the morning after the catapulting of Prince Gummy-Molars. 'Why don't you come too? I'm sure we'd have a lot of fun.'

And that was all the encouragement I needed.

'I'll meet you on board!' I cried, hurrying off into the dawn mist. 'If you get there first, order me a pink gin!'

Five hours later, feeling distinctly queasy, I was standing on the deck of the *Aquitania* as she nosed out into the choppy waters of the Solent, bound for New York via Cherbourg. I'd already been right round the ship once looking for Emily, and over the next seven days would do so at least another 50 times, covering every square inch of the vessel, even down into the engine room and stokers' quarters. All to no avail, however. Dear, darling Emily, my love, my life, was nowhere to be found.

'Don't worry, lad,' consoled Alf, a stoker who'd befriended me during my days of fruitless searching. 'It's a big ship. She'll turn up eventually.'

Which, as it happened, she did. That, however, was 12 years later, on a completely different boat going back the other way. For the present she had disappeared, and when the *Aquitania* finally slipped beneath the benevolent gaze of the Statue of Liberty and docked in New York I was not merely pale and drained and exhausted and limp after a week of uninterrupted vomiting and seasickness, but also very much alone. I had The Pill (in a small silver snuff-box in my pocket), The Photo, and some money which I'd stolen from my most recent victim. Aside from that, however, I was wholly at the mercy of fate. The Manhattan skyline reared over me like a petrified forest, and I remember feeling rather scared. It was the first time I'd ever been abroad.

Of my first eight years in the United States I shall say little. Not because they were uneventful. Quite the contrary. They were far *too* eventful. So much happened, so many acquaintances were made and things done and places visited that I would need at least four rooms to describe them, and even then would still have to reduce my writing to the size of a pin-head to get it all in.

America was, for me, a revelation. It was so vast and fast and loud and brazen. So extraordinarily open, as though the door of my life had hitherto been only slightly ajar, and I was now able to push it wide and charge through into the world beyond. Everything was so much bigger than in England – the people, the buildings, the streets, the food – and appeared to happen at twice the speed, and with twice the intensity. From the moment I arrived I was intoxicated by the place. Quite intoxicated.

I disembarked in New York with enough money to last me a month, at a pinch. As it was I took a room in rather a nice hotel fronting on to Central Park, ate out every night and was penniless within a week. Thereafter I was forced to work, something which, up to that point, I'd never actually done before.

My first job was as a waiter in Bisky's Kosher Salt-Beef Parlour on the Lower East Side. All day from morning to night I would charge to and fro through a fog of chicken-soup steam serving salt beef and latkas and chopped liver and gherkins to a predominantly immigrant clientele, my face drenched in a greasy sweat, my ears ringing to the cries of 'Chicken Kneidlach Double Sour Cream Bagel Table Four! Gefilte Fish Cream Soda Table Eight!' that emanated in a constant stream from the pungent inferno of the kitchens. The owner, Solly Bisky, pronounced my name 'Penix', and insisted I was by far the worst waiter he'd ever had the misfortune to employ, an appraisal that, given the number of plates I dropped and orders I mixed up, was probably not that far wide of the mark.

I remained at Bisky's for six months, renting a room in a tenement overlooking a clattering subway track, until Solly caught me humping his daughter behind a vat of gherkins in the restaurant storeroom, whereupon I was chased off the premises and found a new job selling refrigerators in Brooklyn. I was as bad at that as I had been at waitering, however, and soon gave it up in favour of a position in the bed department at Bloomingdale's. That didn't last long either – sacked for, quite literally, falling asleep on the job – after which I worked as an usher in a nickelodeon on Broadway, a bellhop at the Waldorf, a hotdog salesman in Central Park and a flower-delivery man in Manhattan, in the process enjoying intimate relations with most of the women to whom I was doing the delivering. Then I left New York altogether and went south to sunny Miami, where I got a job as a lifeguard. In six months of sitting in my swimsuit atop a rickety wooden tower, however, I was never once called upon to rescue anyone, which was fortunate, because I've never learned to swim.

From Miami I went west to New Orleans, where I found work as a croupier, and where news of my father's death finally caught up with me, almost a year after it had happened. Then it was north to Memphis to work as a car salesman; north again to Jersey City, where I enjoyed a brief career as a journalist (covering, incidentally, the legendary Dempsey–Carpentier world heavyweight title fight); and then over to Chicago for a spell of illegal liquor running.

From Chicago it was west to the Rocky Mountains for a fruitless season of gold prospecting; south to Denver, where I worked as a conman selling fake baronial titles to gullible millionaires; north, south, east and west as a travelling purveyor of Captain McCabe's Hair and Scalp Tonic; and then to Salt Lake City, then Seattle, then Portland, then San Francisco, then Phoenix (my name town!), then San Francisco again, and then lots of places I've forgotten, and so on, and so on, and so on, back and forth, and side to side, and up and down, and round and round. In those eight years I must have done every job, and visited every town, and stayed in every hotel that Twenties America had to offer.

So many names and faces drift back to me from those times. Wally Dingle, for instance, of Miami, a fellow lifeguard of such consummate ineptitude he generally ended up having to be rescued by the very swimmers he'd gone out to save. And Vince McLuskey, ace crime reporter on the *Jersey City Inquirer*, who smoked 300 cigarettes on a day ('I've cut right down') and was later arrested for committing most of the crimes he'd reported himself. And Reverend Parkes, a Chicago preacher who, when he wasn't campaigning for the National Temperance, ran a nice little side-line sneaking crates of illicit booze across the border from Canada. And, of course, dear old Mrs Clune, octogenarian multimillionaire widow from Baltimore who paid me 50 dollars a day to pose naked whilst her chauffeur, Perkins, took photographs of me.

I should like to devote more space to these people, and that period, for it was a triumphantly life-affirming time, and suicide notes should, in my opinion, be nothing if not life-affirming. Three days from my death, however, and with but a limited amount of wall space left before me, I have no choice but to turn my back on those years and instead, like a child playing leapfrog, hop over the first two thirds of my American life and land foursquare in early 1927, which is when I arrived at Union Station, Los Angeles, and when this murder really begins. Time to get into movies. Time to become a star!

*

I didn't actually go to Los Angeles to get involved in films. Far from it. I was at the time selling novelty lavatory chains – the novelty being that when you pulled them they played a tune – and was hoping that, Los Angeles apparently having more flush lavatories per square foot than almost any other town in America, I might be able to do some good business.

And as it turned out, I did. Some very good business. So good, in fact, that after a week, rather than heading south to San Diego as planned, I decided to extend my stay.

Everyone in Los Angeles, it seemed, wanted musical lavatory chains. I've never known such demand for a product. Captain McCabe's Hair and Scalp Tonic had been popular, but nothing like to the same degree as my novelty loo flushers. Barely had I placed an advert in the papers before Warner Brothers called and ordered 200 for the cast and crew of their recently completed musical *The Jazz Singer*. Thereafter, ablutions the length and breadth of town were enacted to the soothing strains of Al Jolson's 'Mammy!' whilst my newspaper advert received a dramatic strapline: 'Flush with the stars!'

I sold chains to some of the most famous names of the day. Boris Karloff bought 20 as gifts for his friends; newspaper tycoon William Randolph Hearst had three installed in his mansion up at San Simeon; whilst Greta Garbo invited me to her home to give a demonstration, although when I arrived she wasn't in. Even Charlie Chaplin purchased one, later, if industry rumours are to be believed, using it for a sequence in *Modern Times* (the latter, sadly, ending up on the cutting-room floor).

By the end of 1927 I was universally acknowledged as the loo-chain king of the western seaboard. I had orders coming out of my ears, and supply could barely keep up with demand. I didn't think things could get any better, and when I received a summons to present myself and my samples at the home of Luther J. Dextrus, in Beverly Hills, I knew I'd reached the pinnacle of my profession. An order from Mr Dextrus, after all, was the Hollywood equivalent of carrying a 'By Royal Appointment' sign outside your shop. There could be no greater affirmation of the desirability of one's wares.

Although nowadays less well remembered than the likes of, say, Sam Goldwyn and Louis B. Mayer, Luther Dextrus – real name Lemuel Drescovitz – was, in the Twenties, *the* movie mogul par excellence. His 1922 silent epic *America* was, until *Gone with the Wind*, the most successful movie of all time, whilst such was the popularity of his 1926 swashbuckler *The Rapier of Doom* that new cinemas actually had to be built to accommodate the huge crowds that flocked to see it. His five-reel feature *The Mississippi Swamp Monster*, meanwhile, was the first US movie ever to receive a release in Japan.

If his feature films were popular, however, Luther's real success lay with the weekly adventure serial. These would be screened in cinemas before the main film, and were churned out by his studio, Dextruscreen, with production-line regularity, and at an enormous profit. *The Fastest Gun in the West*, for instance, considered by many critics to be the first real Western series ever made, alone earned Luther more than the revenue of most other major producers put together. Also immensely remunerative were Dextruscreen's *The Little Detectives*, an adventure serial about a group of pre-pubescent private eyes who also happened to be orphans; *The Adventures of Aladdin*; and *Gangster Jo*, each episode of the latter ending with a shoot-out in which the entire cast would be shot dead, only to be resurrected the following week.

These serials were made not only extremely fast, but extremely cheaply. 'Don't pay for what you don't need,' was Luther's motto, and one he put into practice by using Aladdin's magic carpet as a rug for *The Fastest Gun in the West*'s horse, Winchester, whose stable in turn doubled as the orphanage dormitory in which the little detectives all slept. If there was a corner to be cut, or a dime to be saved, Luther would cut and save it. Not that it made any difference to his success. By the time I met him in 1927, his studio was grossing $10 million a year and he was the nineteenth richest man in America. No wonder

I was excited about going to see him. They didn't come any bigger than Luther J. Dextrus.

On the day and hour specified on his summons I duly presented myself at his sprawling Beverley Hills mansion, carrying a selection of my finest lavatory chains, one of which I'd programmed to play the score from his latest blockbuster, *Shoot-Out at Dodge City* (starring an as yet unknown Clark Gable). I was rather nervous. Dextrus, it was said, ate men like me for breakfast.

Those were the days before Hollywood became obsessed with its own security, and I was able to walk, unmolested, right up the lawn-flanked drive to the imposing front door. The latter – an exceedingly heavy wooden affair, with a discus-sized knocker and rows of metal studs across its face – looked distinctly familiar; and, indeed, after gazing at it for a moment I realized it was, in fact, modelled on the castle gateway of his 1919 epic *The Viking Beasts*. Beside it was a bell, which I pushed.

I had expected to be kept waiting for at least a couple of minutes – this was, after all, the town in which power was synonymous with bad timekeeping – and was surprised when the door opened almost immediately. I was even more surprised when I discovered it had been opened by a small, very ugly child wearing plus fours and holding what looked like a large brown baton in his hand.

'Yes!' said the ugly boy, his voice a high-pitched nasal squeak.

'I've come to see Mr Dextrus,' I replied, leaning down and patting him on the head. 'Could you go and fetch him, sonny.'

The child went very red, his ugly face scrunching up like a ball of scarlet paper.

'I am Luther Dextrus!' he bellowed, jabbing me in the stomach with his finger. 'Who the fuck are you?'

For a moment I was unable to answer, so amazed was I by the diminutive stature of the man before me. I had, of course, heard that he was small. I was, however, completely unprepared for something quite *this* small. The word, indeed, hardly did justice to the tininess of his physique. Even by child's standards he was minute. All he needed was a dress and a bonnet and he'd have looked exactly like a dolly, albeit an exceedingly unattractive one.

'I said, "Who the fuck are you!"' he repeated, shoving the brown baton in his mouth. Only then did I realize it was a cigar.

'I'm terribly sorry,' I stammered. 'A quite unforgivable mistake. I hadn't expected that you yourself would open . . . you know; I thought a butler or something.'

'What do I need a butler for?' he snapped. 'Waste of goddamn money! If I want servants I'll hire 'em by the day. Now, for the third and last time, who are you and what d'you want?'

'I'm Mr Phoenix,' I replied, handing him a card. 'I've come about the lavatory chains.'

'Lavatory chains?'

'Yes, the musical toilet flushers.'

'Is this some sort of half-assed joke? Because I'll tell you, mister, I don't like jokers.'

'Not at all,' I assured him. 'You wrote to me. We have an appointment.' I removed his letter from my jacket and showed it to him.

'Hunh!' he mumbled. 'OK, follow me. And keep your fucking hands off my head.'

'Yes, Mr Dextrus. I really am most terribly sorry about that.'

'You will be if you do it again,' he growled. 'I'll have your legs broken.'

He ushered me into the house, slammed the door behind me with a crash and headed off across a palatial marble hallway. Rooms opened off it in all directions, whilst I caught a glimpse of extensive landscaped gardens through windows at the back of the house. I thought I heard the dull thud of a tennis ball, and a shrill squeal of female laughter, but I couldn't be sure.

'A beautiful house you have, Mr Dextrus.'

'I deserve it,' he snarled.

We climbed a sweeping stairway, passed round a gallery on the first floor, through a bedroom, and so into what I presumed to be his private bathroom, the latter dominated by a bath the size of a small swimming pool. I later discovered it *was* a small swimming pool, and that when the weather outside was too cold to use the main pool, Dextrus would transfer his Lilo into the bathroom, where he would happily bob around for hours on end, scrutinizing screenplays and smoking one of his trademark cigars.

'Can's over there,' he said, jerking his thumb in the direction of a coral-pink lavatory set on a small dais against the far wall, beside which was a framed photograph of Dextrus shaking hands with Rudolph Valentino.

'You impressed?' he sneered, noticing me gawping at the picture.

'Yes, Mr Dextrus, I am. Very impressed.'

'Well, I ain't,' he growled. 'I ain't impressed by nobody. They're impressed by me. That's why I'm where I am today. Now show me what you've got, and make it quick. I ain't got all morning.'

'Might I inquire as to the sort of thing you're looking for?' I asked. 'We do have a very wide range. Handle-wise alone we offer over 45 separate designs.'

'Well, I don't fucking know,' he snapped. 'You're the salesman. Just show me a few examples.'

'Fine,' I said, setting my samples case down on the floor, clicking it open and removing the first chain that came to hand. 'Let's start with the Finnigan's Mark II Porcelain-Handled Musi-Flusher.'

I dangled the chain teasingly in front of his face, before stepping back and whirling it around in the air above my head. I like to think that, in my own way, I brought a little drama and excitement to the world of lavatory-chain selling.

'As you can see,' I continued, 'the Mark II has a hand-painted porcelain handle, with special indented design for ease of grip.'

I held out the handle to him, and he gripped it.

'Yeh, yeh,' he muttered. 'Great.'

'The chain itself is gold-plated and, of course, fully rust-resistant. Tests have shown that it can hold up to 400lbs dead weight, which is strong enough for even the largest of lavatory users.'

I whirled the chain around my head once more, and then leapt balletically on to the lavatory seat and attached it to the cistern.

'As you can see,' I explained, 'it's simple to install, and can be removed without difficulty should you wish to alter the tune, or increase or decrease the volume thereof. The actual mechanism is contained within this small and unobtrusive box' – I tapped the small, unobtrusive box – 'and operates on exactly the same principle as a pianola. If I might be permitted to demonstrate . . .'

I stepped down from the loo seat and, with a triumphant flourish, pulled the chain. There was a whoosh of water, accompanied by the theme tune from *Shoot-out in Dodge City*.

'You might,' I ventured with an obsequious smile, 'recognize the tune.'

He made no comment, however, just continued to stare at me with disconcerting intensity, and so I detached the Mark II and passed on to the Finnigan's Imperial, and then the Finnegan's Deluxe, and then the Mark III Pamper-Flush with optional detergent facility. I showed him chains with attached fragrance diffusers, glow-in-the-dark chains, easy-to-flush chains for the elderly and chains with tunes ranging from 'The Ride of the Valkyries' to 'It's a Long Way to Tipperary'. I demonstrated long chains, short chains, big chains, little chains, economy chains, wedding chains and even a chain for those in mourning, the latter providing a long, slow, lugubrious flush to the doleful strains of Chopin's 'Funeral March (in C Sharp Minor)'. I gave, though I say it myself, probably the most complete display of novelty lavatory flushing ever seen, and felt sure, by the end of my demonstration, that even one as hard-nosed as the legendary Luther J. Dextrus would be quite unable to resist the temptation of my wares.

'So,' I said, perched on top of his coral-pink lavatory as the final chords of Chopin died away in my ear, 'anything of interest?'

His reply, however, was not at all what I'd expected.

'You ever done any acting?' he inquired.

'Acting?'

'Yeh, acting.'

255

'Well,' I mused, 'I once had a small part in a school revue.'

He nodded slowly and rubbed his chin.

'You wanna be in movies?'

'I've never really thought about it,' I confessed. 'I wouldn't mind, I suppose.'

'OK,' he growled, 'here's the deal. I'm casting a new serial and I'm looking for a fresh face to play the lead. It's about knights and jousting and stuff and it's set in medieval England. We're doing it in sound, so I need someone with a British accent. It's the whirling that got me thinking.'

'The whirling?'

'Yeh. With the chains. They're like those weapon things knights used to have. What are they called?'

'Maces?'

'Yeh, that's it. Maces. The way you whirled the chain it was like a knight with a mace. I want you to do a screen test. If it's good we'll use you. If it's not you can go back to selling toilets or whatever the fuck it is you do. Be at the studio at seven o'clock tomorrow morning. I'll make the arrangements. Now clear up all this crap and get out.'

And with that he stomped out of the bathroom. I packed up my samples and hurried after him.

'But what about my novelty flushers?' I cried as he scampered down the stairs. 'What about the Finnegan's Mark III Pamper-Flush?'

'Screw the Pamper-Flush,' he shouted over his shoulder. 'I'm gonna make you a star!'

Some people get into movies through the front door, some through the back. So far as I know, however, I'm the only person to have ever got in through the lavatory.

The following day, as instructed, I presented myself at the Dextruscreen studios – still armed with my samples bag – where I was required to dress up as a medieval knight, read from a script, do profiles to camera, and then attack a chair with a large broadsword.

There were two other unknowns also up for the part – a tall, athletically built man named Cary Grant, and a quiet, softly spoken stage actor called Leslie Howard – but for some reason I was deemed the best and the role went to me. Later that same afternoon I signed my name to a seven-year contract and took delivery of the keys to my very own dressing room, to which I was instructed to report at 5.30 the following morning for costume fittings. Somewhere in all the rush and bustle I lost my lavatory chains, a fact which, curiously, left me more depressed than I was elated by my new-found fame and fortune.

The serial in which I was to appear was entitled *The White Knight of Bosworth*, and I had the dubious honour of playing the lead role. Dubious because, as I soon found out, although I was the hero of the show, and performed deeds of exceptional and highly improbable valour in every episode, I did so whilst encased in a cumbersome iron helmet. Aside from a pair of inadequate eyeholes, and a small slit through which I delivered my lines, the latter completely covered my face, and since I wore it throughout each episode I became, in the course of my four years as an actor, probably the least recognizable star Hollywood has ever known.

'He's a man of mystery,' Luther explained, puffing on his enormous cigar. 'He fights evil and saves broads from dragons but no one knows who the fuck he is. That's the appeal. He's the hero without a face.'

'So why did you need a new face to play him?' I inquired.

'Because new faces are cheap,' he replied, 'irrespective of whether you see them or not.' Which was a typical Luther reply. He was nothing if not frank.

*The White Knight of Bosworth* was, quality-wise, possibly one of the worst film series ever produced. It made *The Fastest Gun in the West*, which was dire, look positively accomplished. The acting, including my own, was abysmal; the sets cheap to the point of surrealism and the costumes so evidently made from cast-off curtains and re-stitched army-surplus stock that we would have attained greater historical accuracy had we performed the whole thing naked. If the censors had allowed it, we most likely *would* have performed the whole thing naked, since costumes cost money, and money, as Luther never failed to point out, 'is something I've got a lot of, and want to keep it that way'.

Any expense that could be spared was spared. My iron helmet was in fact a revamped janitor's bucket, whilst the budget never extended to more than one horse per episode, usually a mangy one, which made for some very curious jousting sequences.

To his credit, Luther did pay for the services of a professional scriptwriter to pen the first episode. That initial script, however, was thereafter used for every subsequent show, all 217 of them, the only difference being that the names were changed and each week there'd be a different bad guy. Sometimes it was a wicked baron, sometimes a sorcerer, sometimes a monster, and sometimes, if Luther was feeling extravagant, which he usually wasn't, all three at the same time. The Dragon of Death appeared in no fewer than 103 episodes, which was stretching credibility to breaking point, since he got killed at the end of every one of them.

Storylines were formulaic to the point of catatonia. A beautiful damsel, played by the same two women for the entire four years the show ran, each appearing on alternate weeks, in a different wig, would find herself harassed by one of the aforementioned bad guys. Cue the arrival of the White Knight of Bosworth to defend her honour and become the object of her unmitigated adoration. At the climax to each show the damsel would be kidnapped, tied up and threatened with death. At the last minute, however, I would arrive, kill the bad guy and save her. There would be a brief kissing sequence, me still in my iron helmet, before I rode off into the sunset, to the immortal voiceover: 'Where he came from, and where he went, no one knew. Once again, however, the White Knight done good.'

'It's drivel,' I remember saying to the director after we had attended a pilot screening of the first episode. 'I mean, who on earth is going to watch it? I don't think I've ever seen anything so bad.'

'Don't worry,' he replied, patting me on the back. 'Mr Dextrus knows what he's doing. You just watch. People'll love it.'

And, to my amazement, they did. Before it was ten episodes old *The White Knight of Bosworth* had surpassed even *The Fastest Gun in the West* in popularity. I can provide no explanation for its success, nor any excuse for it, but from the moment it arrived on the nation's – and later the world's – cinema screens, it was a monumental hit.

'Told you,' said the show's director jovially. 'Mr Dextrus knows exactly what he's doing. He has the Midas touch.'

As I result of the show's success I became, literally overnight, a very big star indeed, and was soon receiving more weekly fan letters than Gloria Swanson and Richard Barthelmess put together. I attended screenings and galas and star-studded charity events, was mobbed wherever I went, and even got to meet President Hoover, who told me, rather prosaically, that in a depressed world I was a great force for good.

My picture appeared on hoardings throughout the country, I fronted a National Healthy Teeth Campaign – 'The White Knight Says: Brush Before You Sleep!' – and contracted writer's elbow from signing so many autographs. In the words of *Variety* magazine, I was 'the most stirring character to have appeared on our screens since the heyday of Charlie's Little Tramp'.

There was but one slight drawback to all of this, and that was that, in accordance with a subclause in my contract, all public appearances had to be made in costume. The White Knight, as Luther never tired of telling me, was a man of mystery, and for mystery to be effective, 'it's got to damn well stay mysterious'.

Thus it was that my own name never appeared on the credits at the end of the show, I was only ever photographed wearing my helmet, and I was not permitted to reveal any details about my own personality to the press, who wouldn't have been remotely interested anyway. It was the White Knight they wanted; not a homicidal ex-lavatory-chain salesman.

'People don't give a shit about Raphael Phoenix,' explained Luther Dextrus, puffing acrid cigar fumes into my face. 'As a person, you're nobody. Nothing. Zilch. Zero. But as a knight, you're a fucking national icon. So let's keep it that way.'

The need to preserve my anonymity made for some very bizarre situations over the course of those four years. When I went to meet President Hoover, for instance, I did so on a (mange-free) battle-horse, accompanied by two squires and wielding an axe. The Dextruscreen publicity department went to great lengths to build me up as the long-lost son of Richard the Lionheart, and in interviews I found myself explaining, in all seriousness, that I had been born in Sherwood Forest and spent the early part of my life on crusades against the Saracens. I became so convincing at playing out this little charade that I almost came to believe the whole thing myself.

'I'm losing track of who I am,' I once moaned to Norman, the series make-up man. 'I don't have any personality of my own any more.'

'Of course you do, darling,' he chided, applying a dab of metal polish to the visor of my helmet. 'You just need to draw a clear line between your public and your private life.'

'But how can I do that,' I groaned, 'when most of my private life's made up? I mean, last week I spent the night with a woman who insisted I make love to her with my helmet on. It's ridiculous. People don't seem to realize the whole thing's fiction.'

'That's films for you, darling,' sighed Norman. 'They allow people to believe. Now sit back while I buff up your breastplate.'

If the truth be told, once the initial excitement had died down and I'd settled into my life as a film star, I found the whole thing rather irksome. It might have been different had I been working with a good script, or on a project that enthused me, but since with *The White Knight of Bosworth* neither situation held, disillusion set in almost immediately.

Every morning I would have to get up at four to be in the studio by five. I would then spend the next 12 to 14 hours performing extravagant deeds of derring-do encased in my converted bucket – absolute hell under the fierce glare of the studio lights – before grabbing a quick shower and then heading off in the evening, fully costumed again, for some glitzy premiere or swanky charity gala. I would rarely be home before midnight, usually much later, whereupon I would grab a couple of hours' sleep before getting up and starting the whole thing all over again. This I did six days a week, 52 weeks a year, for four years. I have no hesitation whatsoever in proclaiming film stardom to be the most exhausting job I've ever had.

That's not to say it didn't have its benefits. Although by the standards of the other major studios Dextruscreen paid peanuts, it was a fortune compared to what most people were getting in those days, and I was able to purchase my first car – a rather becoming 1926 Ford Model T in, appropriately enough, phoenix brown – and put a down payment on a house on Tropical Avenue. I also splashed out on a crassly ostentatious gold ring, the face of which could be unscrewed to reveal a secret compartment, wherein I stored The Pill. For the next few years, death was, quite literally, right at my fingertips.

I got to attend all the best parties – although I always had to do it in costume – and became close friends with, amongst others, Gary Cooper, Ronald Coleman and Mabel Normand. I had my own table at the Brown Derby Restaurant, played tennis with Charlie Chaplin and became a regular visitor to W. R. Hearst's sprawling neo-classical estate up at San Simeon. I even went skinny-dipping with Greta Garbo, who apologized for having stood me up the time I came round to demonstrate my musical lavatory chains.

Best of all, my sex life went into overdrive. I like to think that, even without a costume, I am a reasonably attractive man. Attired in a crusader cloak and fake chain-mail gauntlets, however, I became irresistible. Some of the most beautiful women of the day passed through the bedroom, and most other rooms, of my Tropical Avenue abode, and I only had to wave my broadsword to have girls falling at my feet. I shan't dwell on the matter for fear of seeming boastful, but I will say that Theda Bara had the most fantastic bosoms and Joan Crawford the most voluptuous mouth of any women I've ever known.

Yes, stardom had its fun side, its little perks and frivolities. In the main, however, I found it a hard, boring and burdensome affair; a relentless round of bad scripts, bad plots, bad publicity stunts and, for me at least, increasingly bad moods. I began drinking heavily – treble whiskeys at six in the morning – and became more and more reliant upon the dissolvable cocaine powder prescribed to me by the studio doctor. From being mildly irritated by the whole White Knight phenomenon I came to resent it, and then to hate it, and finally to detest it with every cell in my body, so that each morning I would get up and go into the studio with all the enthusiasm of a man about to face a firing squad. I detested my costume, I detested the ridiculous lines I had to say and I detested myself for carrying on with the whole charade. Most of all, however, I detested Luther Dextrus for making me play the part. Not a week went by without me going into his office and begging him to release me from my contract, and not a week went by without him refusing.

'You're making me big bucks, son,' he would say cheerfully, puffing on his Visible Inmensos. 'And big bucks is all I give a fuck about.'

'But Luther,' I would plead, 'I can't stand it any more. *I hate* the sodding *White Knight of Bosworth*. You can get someone else, for Christ's sake.'

'I don't want anyone else,' he would reply, patting me on the back. 'You *are* the White Knight. No one could be as good as you. You've made the part your own.'

'And what if I refuse to work?'

'I'll sue you.'

'I'll leave the country.'

'I'll send people after you. You've signed a contract, for Chrissakes.

Jeez, most people would be happy to be in your situation. Most people would be kissing my ass. Fucking ungrateful limeys! Now get back on set and do what I'm paying you for.'

By August 1931 I had reached the very end of my tether, and was, albeit in my drunker moments, seriously contemplating unscrewing the face of my gold ring and popping The Pill there and then, when I received an unexpected summons to Luther's office.

'Come in, come in!' he cried with unaccustomed joviality. 'Sit down. Have a cigar. Put your feet up. Relax.'

'What is it, Luther?' I said warily. 'What do you want now? If it's about doing another toothpaste campaign, I'm not interested.'

'It's nothing like that,' he laughed. 'I've got some good news!'

'Oh yes,' I said. 'What's that then? I'm getting a new helmet? We're getting an extra horse on the show?'

He chortled.

'English humour. Very funny. No, what I want to tell you is that I'm pulling *The White Knight of Bosworth*. I'm ending the series.'

'You're what?'

'It's over. Finito. The White Knight is no more. Quit while you're ahead, that's what I say.'

'Oh Luther!' I cried, literally falling at his feet. 'That's the best news I've ever heard! Thank you! Thank you!'

'It gets better,' he squeaked. 'I'm putting together a new show and you're gonna be the star!'

I stopped fawning and looked up at him – or rather across at him, for kneeling down I came to about the same height.

'Oh yes.'

'It's set in ancient Rome,' he enthused. 'With chariots and slaves and vestal virgins and all that shit. It's gonna be huge.'

My heart sank.

'What's it called, Luther?' I groaned.

'You're gonna love this,' he chuckled. 'It's called *The Masked Gladiator*. And guess who gets to play the gladiator?'

*

263

Two weeks later a press conference was held to launch the new serial.

Luther's press conferences were legendary. Had he expended a fraction of the effort, thought, time and money on his productions as he did on publicizing them, he would doubtless have been hailed as the most extravagantly imaginative producer Hollywood had ever known.

'It's not the product,' he explained, 'but the way you sell it. People'll eat turd if you dress it up enough.'

A truism proved over and over again by the success of his productions. Each episode of *The White Knight*, for instance, cost somewhere in the region of $2,500 to make. Ten times that amount, however, would regularly be spent on advertisements and publicity stunts to help promote the programme and attract viewers. He once paid Los Angeles Municipal Council $60,000 to close off Sunset Strip for a day so he could hold a promotional jousting tournament thereon. The ruse worked. Viewing figures went up by almost 17 per cent and he recouped his money in a matter of days.

For Luther Dextrus, publicity was all, and he never stinted in his efforts to obtain it. No string remained unpulled, no cliché unexploited in the struggle to promote his studio's output. The launch of *The Little Detectives* was celebrated by the sending of a chocolate bar to every single orphan in America, irrespective of whether they wanted one or not, whilst those attending the premiere of his 1922 epic *America* each received a miniature, gold-plated Statue of Liberty, with bubble-bath inside. *The White Knight* opened with a medieval pageant that made the average Cecil B. de Mille production look positively pedestrian.

For his *Masked Gladiator* press conference, however, Luther had excelled himself even by his standards. A large area of the Dextru-screen back lot had been cordoned off and upon it built nothing less than a life-sized segment of Rome's Coliseum. From the rear this just looked like a lot of wooden panels supported by scaffolding. Walk round the other side, however, and the effect was startlingly realistic, with banks of seats, a satin-draped imperial box and, to either side of the latter, two dark tunnels through which the gladiators could emerge. The whole thing would, of course, later be used in the filming of the series itself, but the wealth of detail that had been lavished upon it and the sturdiness of its construction were entirely down to the fact that Luther wanted to hold his conference in it.

He himself was to speak from the imperial box. This sat bang in the middle of the structure, some ten feet above the arena floor, with a purple canopy over it and a battery of microphones arranged along its railed front edge. To left and right were seated over 500 costumed extras – specially employed at a dollar a day to roar and shout and conjure up the ambience of ancient Rome – whilst on either side of the podium, at ground level, issued the tunnels from which, at the climax to the conference, myself and another gladiator would emerge to enact a carefully choreographed swordfight for the benefit of the press. The latter were seated on the arena floor, looking up at Luther and some 50 feet back from him.

The most striking feature of the whole affair, however, came in the form of a large enclosure that had been installed at the foot of the imperial box, between the entrances to the two tunnels. This somewhat anomalous addition to the proceedings had a small pond at its centre and was surrounded by a 5-foot-high chain-link fence, a necessary precaution, since the enclosure was full of live alligators. The idea was that, as we fought, my fellow gladiator and I would crash against the fence, hence agitating the reptiles and heightening the drama of our conflict.

'I wanted to have lions as well,' declared Luther with a frustrated chomp on his cigar, 'but apparently the 'gators would have eaten them. Lions would really have made it.'

'I think the alligators are fine on their own,' I assured him.

'They fucking well better be,' he snapped, 'after the money I paid to bring 'em over from Florida. You know how much a train ticket costs for a 'gator?'

Precisely why Luther had chosen alligators for his press conference was uncertain. Their effectiveness, however, could not be denied.

They swished around and snapped their jaws and peered menacingly at anyone who cared to look at them, and when the assembled journalists threw them the steaks with which they'd been issued on arrival at the studio, the reptiles went obligingly berserk.

Such was the outlandish scene in which I found myself that stiflingly hot morning in the summer of 1931. With my fellow gladiator I was stationed in a sort of makeshift room beneath the imperial box, each of us ready to charge out of our respective tunnels and do battle for the benefit of the press. Directly above our heads stood Luther Dextrus, his check-suited form easily visible through gaps in the planked floor. The extras were roaring, and nearby could be heard the plop and slither of the alligators, the latter clearly upset by all the noise and attention.

'Ladies and gentlemen,' squeaked Luther from above, 'or should I say ladies, gentlemen and citizens of Rome!'

A huge, well-rehearsed roar from the extras.

'How long before we're on?' asked my companion.

'About ten minutes,' I replied.

'OK,' he said, laying aside the net and trident with which he was armed. 'I'm gonna take a leak.' Whereupon he exited through a door at the back of our lair, leaving me alone.

I was not, to put it mildly, in the best of moods. Quite aside from the fact that I wanted nothing whatsoever to do with *The Masked Gladiator*, I was, as the show's eponymous hero, required to sport singularly the most uncomfortable item of headgear ever devised. A cross between a fencing mask and a giant clam, this encased my cranium like a large tin mouth and was done up with so many straps and fittings that it took upwards of 15 minutes to get it either on or off. Not only was it shoulder-bendingly heavy, it was also extremely hot, particularly in the 100 degree heat of summer. Rivers of sweat snaked across my naked torso before losing themselves in the folds of my skimpy loincloth.

'Bugger you, Luther Dextrus!' I muttered to myself, pacing back and forth beneath him. 'Bugger, bugger, bugger!'

'With films such as *America*,' came his voice from above, 'incidentally the highest grossing movie of all time, and series like *The Fastest Gun in the West*, *The Little Detectives* and *The White Knight of Bosworth*, Dextruscreen has become one of, if not *the*, most successful film studios ever.' Another roar of approval from the crowd. A popping of flashbulbs. A swish and snap from the 'gator enclosure.

'Today I am pleased to announce our newest and most ambitious project to date.'

Roar, pop, swish, snap.

I looked up. Luther was almost directly above me, the soles of his patent-leather shoes some four feet from the top of my head. An occasional fine rain of cigar ash descended through gaps between the planks on which he was standing. One of these gaps, I noticed, was rather wider than the others. Luther was positioned right over it, affording me a perfect view of the crotch of his check trousers.

'*The Masked Gladiator* will be an epic adventure serial,' he was saying, 'set in ancient Rome. There'll be excitement and thrills and spills like you've never seen before . . .'

For no other reason than to pass the time, I picked up my companion's discarded trident – a seven-foot-long wooden pole surmounted by three rubber-tipped metal prongs – and raised it towards the gap. The latter was just wide enough for the trident to fit through. I prodded Luther's left foot.

'We're gonna have chariot races, and hand-to-hand combat with wild animals, and stunts like you wouldn't believe . . .' he enthused to the assembled ranks of the press.

I poked his foot again. He lifted it a little, shook it, and then put it down. Again I poked, and again he shook it, this time replacing it slightly to the left of where it had been before, affording me an even clearer view of the area between his legs.

'*The Masked Gladiator* will be the story of one man's fight against the forces of evil!'

I pushed the trident right up through the gap towards his crotch.

No one could have seen it because the flimsy wooden rail behind which Luther was standing was draped with a silk hanging, making everything from his waist down invisible. I touched one of the trident prongs lightly against his buttock.

'The greatest fighter Rome has ever known, the masked gladiator' – he stopped mid-sentence and swished his hand at the trident – 'Sorry, folks. Damned flies. As I was saying, the masked gladiator is the greatest fighter . . .'

I prodded his buttock a little harder, and his hand swished downwards angrily.

'. . . Rome has ever known. And although he's a slave . . .'

Another prod, another swish.

'. . . he nonetheless becomes a symbol of freedom for the poor and downtrodden.'

And then, I just did it. I hadn't planned it. I hadn't thought about it. It was completely unpremeditated. All the anger and frustration of the last couple of years simply came rushing to the surface. I bent my knees, I took a deep breath, and with every ounce of strength I had I jammed the trident upwards into Luther's crotch. The force of the blow lifted his diminutive frame up into the air and threw it forwards on to the microphones, which let out a squeal of static in protest. I heard him cry, 'Some fucker bit me!' and then there was a loud splitting sound as the flimsy rail at the front of the podium gave way, pitching the screaming midget face forwards into the alligator pond beneath. There was a gasp from the crowd, a loud splash, and a swishing of alligator tails.

'Help me!' wailed Luther. 'For Christ's sake, somebody help me!'

Casting the trident aside, I pressed my eye to a crack in the front wall of the podium. The 'gator enclosure was directly in front of me, with a bedraggled Luther crouching on the far side of the pond, up to his waist in water. Alligators were creeping up on him from all directions, their massive jaws chomping lasciviously.

'Please,' squealed the beleaguered dwarf. 'Get me out of here. Someone get me out of here.'

No one moved, however. Ninety reporters and 500 extras stood rooted to the spot as the 'gators closed in. Luther stared at the reptiles in horror and then, with a desperate lunge, pulled himself out of the pond and made a rush for the side of the enclosure. The 'gators were too quick, however. They charged at him and, to a chorus of spine-tingling screams from their victim, literally tore him to pieces. Fragments of check cloth flew about like confetti, and the water of the pond turned a sickly shade of red. One burly male reporter fainted as a severed foot flew through the air and landed on his lap.

'Oh my God,' whimpered one woman. 'They're eating Luther Dextrus.'

Even as the alligators snapped at the tattered remains of my diminutive employer I had but one thought in my head, and that was to get out of my costume, out of the movies, out of America and back to England (four thoughts, actually).

'Home,' I sighed to myself. 'That's where I want to be. Back in good old England. I've been away too long.'

Whilst a pair of studio hands tried to fish bits of Luther out of the 'gator enclosure, therefore, and the assembled crowd argued as to just how he'd fallen into the enclosure in the first place – 'Tripped on microphone cables,' suggested one man. 'No, no, he got stung by a wasp or something,' said another – I slipped quietly back to my changing room, where I unbuckled my helmet and changed into my normal clothes. Half an hour later, The Pill on my finger and The Photo in my pocket, I was in a taxi heading to Union Station; an hour later I was on the *Santa Fe Chief* roaring eastwards; and three days later was settling into a second-class cabin on board the *Scythia*, bound for Liverpool, one way. What happened to my house, my car, my bank account and my studio contract I have no idea, for such had been my hurry to get away that I left my American affairs quite unsettled. For all I know they might all still be waiting for me. At the time I didn't really care. I was just glad to be going home.

'To Luther!' I said, raising a glass of champagne to my lips as we slipped away from the Manhattan dockside. 'May his digestion be long and peaceful.'

It was an eight-day journey back to Britain, and I spent the first three of them fast asleep in my cabin. It was, I believe, the first proper rest I had had for four years. Thereafter, free, thank God, of the seasickness that had marred my outward journey, I ventured forth about the ship, eating in the restaurant, promenading around the deck, drinking a lot of whisky and indulging in the odd game of quoits with fellow travellers.

It was during one such game, on the penultimate afternoon of our voyage, that something quite extraordinary happened. I was supposed to be playing doubles with a Mr and Mrs Flumstein, an elderly couple from Wisconsin, but my partner had failed to appear and I was therefore casting around for someone else to make up the foursome. Sitting on a deckchair at the far end of the deck was a woman with extremely shiny red shoes, her face hidden behind a magazine. I walked over and inquired whether she might like to play.

'Love to,' she replied, lowering the paper. It was Emily.

'Emily! My God! How long have you been on board?'

'Since we left America, of course. I didn't just drop out of the sky.'

'Well, I haven't seen you. Where have you been hiding?'

'I haven't been hiding. We must have simply missed each other.'

'It's a miracle, Emily! A miracle. Come on, I'll buy you a drink.'

'I thought we were going to play quoits.'

'Quoits!' I cried. 'Bugger quoits!'

I turned to the elderly couple from Wisconsin.

'Bugger quoits!'

'Don't be so rude, Raphael,' she sniggered, slapping my hand. 'Anyway, I want to play. Come on.'

She stood up and skipped across to our opponents, explaining, with an innocent smile, that I had in fact said, 'Rubber quoits,' these being the type we were used to playing with in England, as opposed to the rope ones on board the *Scythia*. The Flumsteins apparently found all this perfectly reasonable, and we duly spent the next hour launching our hoops up and down the deck as the ship pitched and rolled its way back across the Atlantic.

'What happened to you on the *Aquitania*?' I asked, bending my knees and spinning my quoit towards the peg, which I missed by a foot. 'When we last met you said you were going to be on it.'

'I *was* on it,' she replied. 'You weren't, though. I looked all over.'

'So did I, and you definitely weren't there.'

'Yes I was! I had a lovely cabin. They put fresh flowers in it every day. It was a fun crossing, wasn't it?'

'No, it damned well wasn't. I was seasick all the way. Oh bad luck, Mrs Flumstein! Very close!'

'Poor Raphael!'

'I would never have gone on the damned thing if you hadn't said you were going to be on it. But I couldn't find you anywhere. You're never where you say you're going to be when you say you're going to be there. It's damned annoying. Go on, it's your go.'

My partner leaned back, her blonde hair whipping in the breeze, and launched her hoop, which landed square on its target.

'Good shot,' I mumbled grudgingly.

'This is fun!' cried Emily.

'Your turn, Mr Flumstein. So what have you been doing for the last . . . how long is it?'

'Twelve years?'

'Twelve years! Christ, time flies. It's hard to keep up with ourselves. Take as long as you need, Mr Flumstein. No hurry. So come on. What have you been doing?'

'Oh, not much really,' she sighed. 'Mother died.'

'I'm very sorry. My father too.'

'I'm sorry.'

'He liked you, you know.'

'I liked him. He was a very interesting man.'

'I suppose he was. I never really thought about it. That's the way of these things. You only really fully appreciate people when they're dead. Life clouds your judgement. Very near, Mr Flumstein! Very near indeed!'

And so we played our quoits, and having resoundingly beaten the Flumsteins – mainly because Mrs Flumstein kept throwing her hoops overboard by accident – retired to the bar, where, more than a decade after I said I would, I finally got to drink my pink gin.

'Better late than never,' I sighed. 'Cheers!'

'Cheers!' said Emily. 'Isn't this exciting?'

We spent the rest of the day together, wandering arm in arm around the promenade deck, playing table tennis (Emily giving me a thorough drubbing – her serve was quite unplayable) and even eating at the captain's table, to which Emily secured an invitation by flashing one of her most winning smiles at the ship's purser. After dinner we danced until the early hours and then, when the band were too tired to play any more, went outside and gazed up at the starry sky.

'Aren't the stars pretty?' sighed Emily.

'They are. It's been a wonderful night. I wish it would go on for ever.'

She slipped her arm through mine.

'What time do we dock in Liverpool?' she asked.

'Early, I think. About eight in the morning.'

'And what are you going to do once you're back in England?'

'No idea, really. Go back to London, I suppose.'

'Raphael, you're absolutely hopeless. I've never known anyone so disorganized. You really should take charge of your life.'

I must have looked rather crestfallen, for she squeezed my hand and kissed my cheek.

'I'll tell you what. I'm going to have packing to do in the morn-ing, and it's going to be an almighty crush getting off the boat, but why don't we meet on the dock front? Then we can have breakfast together and, in the meantime, I'll make a plan.'

'Thanks, Emily,' I said, putting my arm around her and hugging her to me. 'I couldn't get on without you.'

As it turned out, however, I had to; because, as I've already described, we missed each other on the docks at Liverpool and Emily disappeared for another nine years. What her plan was I never discovered. Instead I found myself coerced into the world of high-street banking, where I might have had a bright future had I not taken it upon myself to kill my employer. How many bright futures have I scuppered by murdering people? Then again, how many bright futures have I opened up by doing exactly the same thing?

I have about a foot of wall space left in this room and will fill it with an account of an extraordinary coincidence. You may remember, some six rooms back, whilst describing the ignition of Mrs Bunshop in her room at Nannybrook House, I mentioned her television set was on. Moreover, I also mentioned it was showing an old black-and-white silent film. At the time, however, I didn't give the name of the film, even though I recognized it immediately. I shall now rectify that omission. It was called *America*, and was produced by one Luther J. Dextrus. My murders, it seems, call to each other across the years, like dogs barking in a wilderness.

# Chapter Fifteen

The note's starting to look like a herbaceous border. What began as a dignified procession of mournful black letters now looks like something out of the Chelsea Flower Show. Luther dies in a splurge of garish oranges and pinks, the grotesqueness of his murder undermined by the prettiness of the colours in which it's described. I feel a little guilty that his decease should unfold in such cheerful, heart-warming hues – it seems somehow disrespectful – but at this stage there's not much I can do about it. And it doesn't actually look that bad, in a sort of child's drawing-book kind of way.

It's now about seven o'clock on Thursday morning, and I'm back out on the first-floor landing, about three quarters of the way between the bathroom door and that of the upstairs gallery. My writing is still pink, and although I've been up all night I'm not feeling too tired, which is lucky because I haven't got time to sleep even if I wanted to.

It's been hard work writing about Luther Dextrus, and I've had one hell of a job trying to keep him in the bathroom. He might have been the smallest of my victims, but his story just went on and on. Things weren't helped by the fact that I'd already used some of the bathroom's wall space to describe the extraordinary events of yesterday, whilst much of what space was left was rendered unusable by the presence of a large iron bathtub, a sink, a lavatory, a copper immersion heater and, a most anomalous addition to the castle's otherwise spartan utilities, a bidet.

The upshot of all of this was that even after reducing my writing to the size of lentils and pushing it into nooks and corners that I might otherwise have ignored – i.e. right behind the loo and underneath the sink – the story still filled the entire room and, like champagne bursting from a bottle, fizzed out all over the wall of the landing. I was a little disappointed about this, particularly after fitting Mr Popplethwaite so perfectly into *his* room, but not overly so. I do think I've been getting just a touch too literal about my one murder per room scheme. So long as the *bulk* of the murder fits, that's the main thing.

I didn't get going on Luther until past two o'clock yesterday afternoon, and have, aside from one extended cigarette break in the dome, been at the task solidly ever since. That's 17 hours, just a few short of the number it took me to describe the albino twins down in the cellar. The note, after a brief spurt in the study, appears to be slowing down again.

There's no obvious practical reason for this. The bathroom walls, after all, are neither bumpy nor damp like those of the cellar, nor did I have to waste time moving bric-a-brac around as I did downstairs. I *was* obliged to keep my writing small, of course, and that always slows things down a bit, whilst in places, such as behind the immersion heater and down the side of the bidet, the whole thing got very fiddly. Taken as a whole, however, the bathroom offers no more challenging a literary environment than the downstairs kitchen, and yet I wrote my way around that in under 13 hours. So why the big delay?

Two factors, mainly. The first was my back. The strange tingling sensation that I've been experiencing for the last few days has now intensified to the point where it's become a serious distraction. Initially it felt like ants scurrying around beneath my skin. Then it became amplified to one of scampering rodents. Since yesterday afternoon it's felt as though there was a little goblin in there, several little goblins in fact, all hammering on the inside of my back, as though knocking on a door demanding to be let out. If I close my eyes and concentrate I can even imagine their voices:

'Hey, you! Open up! Let us out! It's dark in here. We can't breathe!'

It's not actually causing me any pain. Quite the contrary; it's a vaguely pleasant sensation, like being given an extremely vigorous massage, save that the massaging's being done from the inside out. It has, however, been wreaking havoc with my concentration, particularly since, rather than being a constant irritation, it comes and goes at random. One moment I'll be writing away calm as you like, and the next Crash! Bang! Wallop! there it is again.

It could just be a muscle spasm, or a nervous tic, or a hangover from the fall I had last Saturday. What I suspect, however, is that it's something to do with my wings. Ironic, really. Ninety-nine years I've been waiting for them to unfold, and now that it feels like they're doing just that I don't want them to. Not if they're going to cause me this much grief I don't. Crash! Bang! Wallop! I wish I'd never been born with the damned things.

That's one reason the killing of Luther has taken so long. The other, which in a sense mirrors the disturbance in my back, has been the knocking on the front door. This has now reached epidemic proportions, to the extent that I've stopped even bothering trying to keep count of the number of times it's happened. All yesterday afternoon it went on, and yesterday evening, and through the night – boom, boom, boom, the whole building trembling under the onslaught, distracting me from my work, shredding my concentration, flaying me. The force of the blows has left deep indentations in my front door, and chipped all the paint away beneath the knocker so the bare wood is now showing. If I wasn't going to die so soon I'd contact the police about it. I feel like I'm besieged in my own home.

I've tried to catch the culprit, but they're proving frustratingly elusive. Several times now I've positioned myself in the downstairs foyer directly behind the front door and then thrown it open as soon as the knocking starts, but there never seems to be anyone there. On one occasion late yesterday evening I did see what looked like a small figure disappearing into the bracken, but I'm yet to come close to laying my hands on them. If I did I'd rip them to pieces.

There hasn't been any knocking for a couple of hours now, but I'm still on tenterhooks. It's too much to hope that it's stopped for good. I've considered sneaking out and hiding in the bracken myself, lying in wait for my tormentor and then ambushing them as soon as they approach the front door, but I somehow don't think it would work. They're too sly to fall for something like that. Instead I've left a letter on the doorstep pleading with them to leave me alone, and included with it a crisp 20-pound note which I've told them they can keep if only they'll go away and stop torturing me. So far it seems to have worked but, like I say, I'm not hopeful. I think someone's out to destroy me.

I need to make the most of the silence, however, even if it is only temporary, and push on with my work. Dawn's breaking, and through the window of the gallery a grey-green stain is spreading slowly across the eastern horizon. I've brought the note round the landing wall and am now writing down the left-hand side of the gallery door, across whose threshold I shall soon be passing. Other than a brief glass of wine and perhaps a quick stretch on the roof, I've no time for a break. I'm still behind, and every minute is precious.

I must, however, just make one final point before I move on, and that concerns doorways. Or, more precisely, the space above doorways. To date, I have been leaving this area empty, a rectangular oasis of whiteness amidst the lettering all around. The bathroom doorway, for instance, as you look at it from the landing, has a wall of writing to the left of it, and a wall of writing to the right, but nothing whatsoever directly above.

There's a practical reason for this. If I were to write above each doorway as well as to either side of it, then it would be by no means clear that the note actually passes *through* the doorway. It would seem to continue along a single plain. By leaving a space it becomes

277

evident that the column to the doorway's left, written before the note passes through, has nothing to do with the column to its right, written after it emerges again. Potential confusion is thus avoided.

Now, however, suddenly and for no obvious reason, I have become dissatisfied with these white spaces. It hit me late last night, as I closed the front door after yet another abortive attempt to catch the elusive knocker. As I walked back across the foyer I flicked on the light for a quick peek at my handiwork, and was immediately struck by how odd it looked to have those thick blocks of emptiness hovering in the midst of my narrative. I don't know whether it was the effect of the cheap 40 watt bulb – in daylight I hadn't noticed any problem – or whether my judgement had been affected by the trauma of the banging, but I wasn't at all happy with it, and remain unhappy now, as I write. It looks incomplete and unprofessional, and I shall have to do something about it. Precisely what, however, I don't know. I'll keep you informed.

Now, I really must be getting on. My pink felt-tip is all but exhausted, and at the end of this paragraph I shall be dispensing with it altogether and taking up the first of my two red pens. The red should look extremely effective, especially against the white of the castle walls.

Onwards, onwards.

# CHAPTER SIXTEEN

Prince Oduduwa Iwe Ogunmola, known to his Cambridge colleagues as Prince Gummy-Molars, both as a pun upon his last name and for the exceptional brilliance of his teeth, is unique amongst my victims for a number of reasons. He was, for starters, the only royal person I've ever killed. Also the only black one. Most significantly, his murder is the only one in which I had associates. Usually I do my killing alone. In this case, however, it was a group effort. Not that that diminishes my culpability in the whole affair. It was, after all, me who actually sprung the catapult.

Emily, bless her heart, got me into Cambridge, albeit indirectly. Prior to her departure for America, you see, I had never been much good academically. It wasn't that I was stupid, just that I was far too busy thinking about my golden-haired playmate to bother much with anything as trivial as schoolwork. 'Slothful and distracted,' my termly reports would declare bleakly. 'Lives in a fantasy world.' 'Bottom of the class again.' 'A dreamer.'

Then, however, Emily disappeared and I suddenly began applying myself. Not because I felt I had something to prove, you understand, but simply because I had nothing else to do. In Latin and maths and Greek and history I sought refuge from the enormity of my alone-ness. She turned me into a swot. Or rather, her absence turned me into a swot. That's the extraordinary thing about Emily. She's even more influential when she's not there than she is when she is, if you get my meaning.

With my darling off the scene I gained a place at a good public school in Sussex, where I toiled diligently for five years until the summer of 1917 when, following an excellent showing in my Higher Certificate exams, I landed an open scholarship in classics to St John's College, Cambridge. Emily, of course, knew nothing of this, although if she had I think she would have been quite proud of me.

I went up to St John's in the October of that year, and was sent down 20 months later. If I got into Cambridge because of Emily, I got out purely on my own demerits. I am not, after all, *totally* reliant upon her.

St John's is, in my humble opinion, the most profoundly beautiful of all Cambridge colleges. Obviously, I'm biased, since I was, albeit briefly, a student there. Even without my partisan ties, however, I would still come to the same conclusion. From its magnificent arched sixteenth-century gateway a succession of red-bricked quadrangles march back towards the Cam, across whose lugubrious green-brown flow a Bridge of Sighs leaps effortlessly into New Court beyond. Gardens and lawns sweep away to the north of the college, whilst about the whole there rests an air of tranquillity and repose quite at odds with the fact that it was home to over 200 undergraduates and nearly as many dons and college servants. My abiding impression of the place is of its extreme, one might even say deathly, silence, which given the state of world affairs at the time, is perhaps not entirely surprising.

My first year in college was an uneventful one. I was assigned rooms in Third Court, on the ground floor, backing directly on to the Cam, and from the word go immersed myself in my studies. Each morning I would attend lectures and tutorials, whilst each afternoon would be spent in private study in the college library. I joined the Cambridge antiquarian and classical societies, won prizes for my Greek verse composition, and was widely praised for my translation of Ovid's 'On Facial Treatments for Ladies' (if there are any ladies reading, by the way, try smothering your cheeks in Libyan barley and raw eggs – guaranteed to smooth away those niggling morning wrinkles). I even stayed in college throughout the long vac of 1918 researching a brief paper entitled 'Aristophanes: The Comedy of Life', a copy of which is, so far as I'm aware, still available from the college library.

Studying consumed most of my energies during that first year, and I left myself time for few other activities. I dined each night in hall and played a little lawn tennis, but with the exception of attending meetings of the antiquarian and classical societies I had no social life to speak of. There was certainly nothing in my early university career to hint at the debauchery to follow.

Work and society meetings aside, the only other interesting thing that happened at that time – or rather didn't happen – was that I wasn't sent to France to fight in the First World War. The latter had, of course, been raging since 1914, and I should, by rights, have been called up to serve as soon as I reached my 18th birthday. Early in January 1918 I did indeed receive a summons to attend an army medical board. On the designated morning, however, I woke to discover my entire body was, quite inexplicably, covered from head to foot in a livid, crumbling rash of eczema. The medical officer took one look at me and pronounced me wholly unfit for service, either abroad or at home. Whilst my fellow countrymen were getting their heads blown off in the trenches of Flanders, therefore, I was safely ensconced in St John's College library, my nose thrust into a copy of Quintilian's *Institutio Oratoria*. The inexplicable eczema disappeared as suddenly as it had come, and has never afflicted me since. I shall always be grateful to it, however. Murderer I might be, but I've never had the least desire to fight in a war.

Thus my first year at Cambridge passed; quietly, studiously, introvertedly. The Pill I kept in a small silver snuff-box which Mrs Eggs, our housekeeper, had given me by way of congratulations on achieving my open scholarship, whilst The Photo I always carried in the breast pocket of my jacket.

By the time I embarked upon my second year – in the October of 1918 – I was regarded as one of the college's most promising undergraduates and was being widely tipped for a position as a future fellow. Then, however, I met Meaty, and things went badly off the rails.

Maximilian Heaty, only son of minor Tory politician Earl Heaty of Gosport, was a renowned college rogue. Avoiding conscription on account of his flat feet, he waged his own war in Cambridge against the restrictions of college life. Meaty's instincts gravitated towards misbehaviour as surely as a plant's leaves turn towards light, and so frequent were his visits to Reverend Creed, the dean, that he eventually took up rooms directly above the latter's office so as to save himself a journey whenever he was summoned thereto, which he was on a weekly basis. Had his family not been fabulously wealthy he would have been sent down long since. As it was, they *were* fabulously wealthy, so that rather than punishing Meaty for his misdemeanours the college instead sent his father lists of rare volumes that were wanted for its book collection. By dint of having the worst behaved pupil in Cambridge, St John's also boasted the city's finest library.

I had seen Meaty on numerous occasions during my first year – usually face down in the middle of a quadrangle – but had never actually spoken to him. All that changed, however, on the night of Monday, 11th November 1918, the night the First World War ended, the night I was kidnapped.

I had spent the evening by the fireside perusing my Plato – in the original Greek, naturally – and had retired to bed early, lulled to sleep by the distant sounds of Armistice-night revelry. How Meaty and his friend Pepper got into my room, I've no idea, but I suddenly woke to discover them standing beside my bed, one wearing a pirate hat, the other cricket whites and a fez. They were both drunk, and smelt strongly of cigars.

'What is this!' I cried, sitting up. 'Who are you?'

'Wepwesentatives of His Majesty's Government,' said the one in the pirate hat, lisping his 'r's outrageously. In the pale moonlight I could see it was Meaty. 'Department of Jolly Japes. We've been sent to wescue you. Top Secwet. Don't make a sound.'

Whereupon the two of them stepped forward and, before I had time to protest, thrust a large sack over my head.

'Get off me!' I cried. 'Let me alone, I say!'

'Now, now, dear boy!' admonished Meaty. 'Don't be so obstweperous. It's all for your own good. Give me a hand here, Pepper.'

'What a wheeze!' cried Pepper, his voice high-pitched and querulous. 'I feel like the Scarlet Pimpernel!'

I was bundled out of bed and across the room – struggling violently all the way – and then, to my horror, was lifted bodily from the floor and thrust out of the window. For a moment I thought they were intent on drowning me, for the window gave directly on to the river Cam. As I was pushed out, however, I felt myself grasped by other, gentler hands and, after much pulling and wriggling, tumbled forwards into the bottom of a punt, the latter rocking violently with all the commotion. Meaty and Pepper clambered out after me and, once I had been manoeuvred into a seat, the sack still over my head, we pushed off upstream.

'I can see his dickie,' giggled a woman's voice.

I was, as you can imagine, none too pleased at such rough handling, and made my displeasure known in no uncertain terms. My threats to report them all to the dean, however, were greeted with cheers and laughter, whilst my demands to be put ashore elicited nothing but a loud raspberry from Pepper. Eventually I lapsed into a sultry silence, huddling in my seat with arms around my legs whilst my kidnappers chattered and laughed all around me. The sporadic pop of champagne corks suggested they were making quite a party of it. Someone kept stroking my knee.

We'd been on the water for some ten minutes when a voice I'd not yet heard – a deep, booming, cavernous voice, like the rumble of a distant explosion – suddenly declared:

'Unsack the prisoner! Show me his face!'

Whereupon, with a cry of 'The Gummy has spoken! Let all who hear obey!', the sack was whisked from my head and my surroundings revealed.

We were by that point on the stretch of river that flows behind King's College, the shadowy mass of whose chapel loomed against the night sky away to my left. Facing me, his arm draped around the shoulder of a buxom, red-haired woman, and still wearing his pirate hat, lounged Meaty, whilst behind me stood Pepper, who was doing the punting. Beside me sat a rather attractive blonde-haired woman, her hand resting on my knee.

The person who really caught my attention, however, and who was clearly the possessor of the deep, booming voice, reclined on a leopard-skin rug at the prow-end of the punt, a fluted champagne glass in one hand and a fly-whisk in the other. From the floor at his feet a shuttered hurricane lamp cast a ghostly beam of light in which his prodigiously lipped black face glowed like a large tropical fruit. He had jug-ears and exceedingly white teeth.

'What do you weckon, Gummy,' cried Meaty. 'A marvellous specimen of Homo Pyjamaclad, eh, what!'

Prince Gummy-Molars, for he it was, said nothing, merely downed his champagne and swished his fly-whisk nonchalantly back and forth. The blonde-haired woman whispered: 'His dickie's huge!' before collapsing in giggles.

'Now look here,' I snapped, crossing my legs, 'what is all this? What do you chaps want with me?'

'I've alweady told you, dear boy,' chided Meaty. 'We've been sent to wescue you.'

'Wescue . . . Rescue me from what?'

'Fwom what?' lisped my abductor, all wide eyes and mock-amazement. 'From borwingness, of course. From howwible, fwightful, dweadful, terminal borwingness. Across the land men and women are celebwating the utter destwuction of the Hun, and there are you, lonely as a dodo, all tucked up in bed, borwing as borwing can be. It's simply not to be countenanced!'

'What I do in the privacy of my own bedroom is my business and nobody else's,' I responded angrily. 'And if I want to sleep, that's what I'll jolly well do.'

'Of course it is!' cried Meaty. 'I'm not saying *don't* sleep. I'm just saying all things in modewation. There are times to sleep, to whit duwing lectures and sermons, and times to wassail, to whit now. And we'd better jolly well get on with it. We've a dozen bottles to get through yet.'

He pulled a magnum of champagne from a large ice-bucket, popped the cork and poured a glass, handing it across to me.

'Have some bubbles, old boy. Take the chill off the night.'

'I don't want anything to drink,' I said. 'I want to be put ashore.'

Meaty shook his head and tutted.

'I'm lost for words! Such ingwatitude. And after we wisked life and limb to bwing you here as well. What should we do with him, Pwince Gummy?'

The prince leaned forward and prodded my crotch with his whisk.

'Off with his testicles!' he boomed.

I downed the glass in one.

'That's the spiwit!' laughed Meaty. 'I say, Gummy, you weally are the life and soul of the party.'

He refilled my glass and clinked his own against it.

'May the blessings of Bacchus be upon you!' he cried.

I downed this second glass, and a third, and a fourth, and several more after that, on each occasion urged on by a booming 'Off with his testicles!' from Gummy, so that by the time we slipped out of Cambridge into the silent water meadows beyond I was feeling distinctly light-headed and, despite my best efforts not to, beginning to have rather a good time. It got even better when the blonde-haired woman clambered on to my lap. I'd never had a woman on my lap before, and tried not to move lest she decided to get off again.

'Are you really a prince?' I asked Gummy-Molars as the lights of town dropped away behind us.

'Of course he is!' cried Meaty, who'd taken over the punting duties from Pepper. 'He's Pwince of the Kikiwe, aren't you, Gummy?'

By way of an answer Gummy raised his left buttock slightly and farted.

'Good God, what a frightful stench,' trilled Pepper. 'Too many mangoes, old boy.'

'Daddy's one of the wichest men in Afwica, isn't he?' continued Meaty. 'More gold than he knows what to do with.'

'My lineage is mighty,' admitted Gummy, before noticing my glass was empty and roaring, 'Off with the testicles!'

'And will you be king one day?' inquired the buxom red-haired woman. 'Will all that gold be yours?'

'I am the eldest,' said Gummy. 'It is my destiny.'

The redhead leaned forward and whispered something in the blonde girl's ear, the two of them bursting into giggles.

'I suppose you'll be wanting a wife when you're king, won't you?' cooed the redhead, resuming her seat and batting her eyelids at Gummy. 'Someone to spend all that lovely gold on.'

Gummy shrugged and worked his finger around the inside of his right nostril, withdrawing it for closer examination under the light of the hurricane lamp.

'I shall take many wives,' he said, turning his glistening finger backwards and forwards. 'Perhaps 20. Perhaps more.'

'I don't know where you get the energy,' cackled the blonde girl.

'They've got potions!' yelped Pepper. 'Jungle fuck potions. Isn't that right, Gummy? Keep you going all night.'

'I say!' cried Meaty. 'I could do with a bit of that!'

'You certainly could,' said the redhead.

Meaty and Pepper exchanged punting duties again, Meaty sinking on to the seat beside me and, rather to my disappointment, yanking the blonde-haired girl on to his own lap. I downed another couple of glasses of champagne and accepted a cigarette from Gummy, the first time I'd ever smoked. It made me cough.

'When you're king, Gummy, old fwuit, you've got to pwomise to make me your pwime minister,' said Meaty.

'Top hole,' laughed Pepper. 'And I shall be captain of the guard!'

'And I'll be court jester!' I cried, getting into the spirit of things.

Gummy began delving into his nose again, the left nostril this time, working his finger in almost up to the knuckle. The blonde girl began tickling my ribs with her foot. I mustered as much courage as I could, and winked at her. She dissolved into giggles.

'When I am king,' said Gummy, 'I shall . . .'

He paused, thinking.

'Yes?' said Pepper.

'. . . be a great king.'

We all applauded.

'So you shall, Gummy, old boy,' said Meaty. 'You shall be a vewitable Afwican potentate.'

'I shall have 200 motor cars,' continued Gummy, removing his glistening finger and wagging it at us, 'and many aeroplanes. And battleships!'

'Those are no good,' said Pepper. 'Your country's landlocked.'

'Battleships!' roared Gummy. 'Hundreds of them. And I shall have more gold than my father. More gold than any ruler in Africa. Than any ruler in the world. Mountains of gold!'

'Sounds all right to me!' bawled the red-haired woman. 'Are you sure you're not looking for a wife?'

'When I am king,' cried Gummy, warming to his subject, 'I shall have my own motor-racing track, and a palace with toilets you can sit on, and many servants to do my bidding, and beautiful wives! Dozens of beautiful wives!'

Waving his fly-whisk above his head, he struggled to his feet, setting the punt rocking violently.

'When I am king of the Kikiwe I shall build golf courses,' he boomed, 'and restaurants, and ice-skating rinks, and caviar!'

'How do you build caviar?' whispered the blonde girl.

'I shall crush my enemies,' he yelled, stamping on the bottom of the punt, 'and rip out their eyes with my fingers, and bite off their ears. And I shall hunt lions and elephants and tigers and buffalo, and kill them with my bare hands!'

He was now bouncing up and down.

'I shall be the greatest ruler in Africa! The name Ogunmola shall be spoken with awe. People shall bow down and kiss my knees! I shall be great. I shall be supreme. I shall be . . . I shall be . . . I shall be king!'

Whereupon he raised his fly-whisk high into the air and duly tumbled backwards into the river, surfacing a moment later with a large wig of foul-smelling weed clamped to his skull.

'Bugger,' he sputtered. 'I'm sopping wet!'

Of the subsequent events of that most eventful of evenings I recall little, my memory from that point onwards becoming rather confused. I know for sure we made a campfire on the bank and sat beside it singing 'We won the war' over and over again. And I'm also pretty certain I drank a lot more champagne, smoked more cigarettes, and went swimming in the freezing river. Whether or not Meaty fell face-first into a cowpat whilst chasing the red-haired woman around a field, however, I cannot be certain. I seem to remember it, but then again it might have been a memory transplanted from some totally different night. Likewise Meaty trying to pole-vault over the river using a punt pole, and Gummy singing 'Roll out the Barrel' whilst eating a champagne glass, and my vomiting copiously from the side of the punt as we slipped back into Cambridge with the dawn. Things only came back into focus when, somewhat to my amazement, I found myself in bed with the pretty blonde-haired girl, my pyjama trousers around my ankles, making love for the first time in my life. I would like to say it went on for hours, but in truth I think lasted 30 seconds, if indeed that. Crisp November sunlight was pouring through the window, and birds were twittering in the trees.

'I think I love you,' I whispered to the girl beneath me.

'That'll be 20 shillings,' she said coldly. 'And you can't stay over.'

From that point forward things went rapidly downhill. Meaty was an appalling influence, and I fell under his spell entirely. As speedily as I had converted from school dunce to school swot after the departure of Emily, I now reverted to my former state, adding to my old vices of laziness and murder new ones of drunkenness, loutishness, promiscuousness and a 50-a-day cigarette habit.

Meaty was the self-proclaimed president of The Invincibles, a motley collection of university ne'er-do-wells including Pepper and Gummy from Magdalen, Topper Harris and Jonty Johanssen from Christ, Bunty Grosvenor from Jesus and Lord Charlie Gore Evans from Pembroke.

'It's a strictly British cabala,' admitted Meaty, 'although Gummy's an exception. When you buy as much champagne as he does, nationality ceases to count.'

Two weeks after first meeting Meaty I was admitted to The Invincibles as a junior member, undergoing a rather unpleasant initiation in which I had to drink a pint of brandy down in one, push a walnut up my bottom and jump naked off every bridge from Magdalen down to Queens'.

'Bwavo!' lisped my patron as I clambered ashore after the last of these initiatory immersions. 'An Invincible is born. Let the glad tidings wing out. Now you've got to buy us all a dwink.'

As a junior Invincible I seemed to be expected to buy rather a lot of drinks, a fact which, taken with my perpetual and not inconsiderable losses at cards and billiards, soon exhausted the small allowance granted me by my father. I wrote to him requesting more money, saying it was for books, and he sent some, but that particular ruse could only be used on a limited number of occasions, and eventually I was forced to take out a large loan at an extortionate rate of interest with a local moneylender. Even that wasn't enough, however, and in desperation I began pilfering volumes from the college library and selling them to a shady second-hand-book dealer in Huntingdon. Where once I had enthusiastically read these works, I now, with equal enthusiasm, purloined them, walking from the library with an innocent smile on my face and half-a-dozen volumes concealed beneath my gown. How the librarian failed to notice my activities I shall never know, particularly when I removed an entire set of Gibbons' *Decline and Fall of the Roman Empire*. Somehow, however, I got away with it, and by the time I left John's in the summer of 1919 its book stacks were looking noticeably sparser than when I had arrived 18 months previously.

Involvement with The Invincibles was wholly incompatible with any form of scholastic endeavour, and the achievements of my first year were quite forgotten in a welter of missed lectures, bunked tutorials, never-completed essays and half-hearted, mistake-strewn translations. Whereas previously I had risen at seven and spent the morning in lectures, I now rose at four of an afternoon and spent the rest of the day getting drunk with Meaty and my new-found friends. Plato and Aristophanes, Ovid and Horace, Virgil and Quintilian were all forgotten.

If one area of study was dropped, however, another was taken up and pursued with equal gusto, namely the Science of Vice. I learned all there was to be learned about wine, and cards, and billiards and gambling. I was initiated into the subtle and inestimably valuable mysteries of playing one debtor off against another. I discovered how to take care of myself in a street brawl, how to drive a car and the best way to mix a Harvey Wallbanger ('Dweadful American habit, cocktails,' sighed Meaty, 'but quite iwwesistible!'). After its rather precipitous 30-second start, meanwhile, my sex life went into top gear, one of my many willing partners being none other than the dean's secretary, the latter taking particular delight in bonking me immediately after I'd been given a good dressing-down in her employer's study.

The Invincibles were inveterate pranksters, and no evening was complete without Meaty crying at the top of his voice, 'To work, dear boys!' Whereupon we would troop off like a platoon of soldiers,

Gummy blowing strident blasts on an old hunting bugle, in order to wreak havoc the length and breadth of Cambridge.

The ambitiousness of Meaty's pranks increased in direct proportion to the amount of alcohol we'd consumed beforehand. A reasonably sober evening might culminate in the unleashing of a dozen or so helium-filled contraceptives into the College Chapel, or the lashing of Reverend Creed's bicycle to the weathervane on the roof of the library. More inebriated occasions, on the other hand, would generally result in various (live) farmyard animals being released into the bedrooms of unwitting undergraduates, or the careful sprinkling of mustard seeds on the college lawns, said seeds spelling out the words 'Bugger the Bursar!' once they'd grown.

Our truly legendary pranks, however – the ones that made the front pages of local newspapers and led to police investigations, and are, so far as I know, still talked about even today – were the ones performed at a level of intoxication so great that any fears as to the possible consequences were dulled to the point of non-existence. Many of these pranks have now attained the status of urban myth, with successive generations of undergraduates claiming them as their own. It is therefore as much to set the record straight as to advance this, my life story, that I confess it was we, The Invincibles, who first stole a car, rolled it on to a pair of punts, took it downstream to the Bridge of Sighs and suspended it therefrom, leaving the unfortunate vehicle swinging a couple of feet above the Cam whilst we punted off into the night. It was we who removed an amputated forearm from Addenbrooke's Hospital and posted it to a local vicar who'd advertised for 'willing hands to help decorate our church for harvest festival'; and we who dumped two barrels' worth of potassium permanganate crystals in a local reservoir, thereby turning the town's water supply bright purple. Most famous – infamous – of all, it was we, The Invincibles, who distributed letters to all St John's College first-year students instructing them, as a matter of national security, to post a stool sample to No. 10 Downing Street, something which, amazingly, 96 of them did. That little escapade resulted not merely in a police but a full government investigation, in the light of which we decided to curtail our activities somewhat.

Although we all enjoyed our pranks, none of us did so more than Prince Gummy. His enjoyment was such, indeed, that his involvement in our escapades could often prove something of a liability, his booming laugh and cries of encouragement more often than not alerting the authorities to our activities long before those activities had come to a proper fruition. I remember several occasions on which I was caught weathervaning Reverend Creed's bicycle because Gummy's shouts of 'Higher! Higher!' were heard by the college porters, whilst he had to be forcibly bundled ashore the night we punted our stolen car towards the Bridge of Sighs because his giggles threatened to upset the entire convoy.

'Pity the poor buggers who end up with him as their wuler,' sighed Meaty. 'The man's a wewitable fwuit-cake.'

The more I associated with Meaty, Gummy, Pepper et al, the more degenerate I became. I smoked opium – supplied by Gummy, who kept a large hookah pipe in his rooms and was, I suspect, addicted to the drug – and augmented my local romantic dalliances with regular trips to a brothel in London. I ran up monumental debts; became incapable of coherent conversation unless I had at least half a bottle of Cognac inside me; and lied, cheated, stole and swindled as though these traits were second nature to me.

In the eight months from November 1918 to June 1919 I plummeted into the abyss as precipitously as Icarus plummeted into the turquoise waters of the Aegean. So daring did our escapades become, and so universal our debauched reputation, that we began to believe our own myth and suspect that we were, indeed, invincible. For Meaty and Gummy and the others, this may well have been the case, for they were all fabulously wealthy and the university could ill afford to lose them. For me, however, such considerations did not apply. The debtor son of a failed inventor, my presence was by no means integral to the continued prosperity of the college. To their credit, they gave me every opportunity to

mend my ways. When I failed my end-of-year exams, however –
with the lowest marks ever recorded in Part I of the Classical Tripos
– they finally decided they could muddle along without me. I was
summoned to the office of Reverend Creed, the dean, and duly sent
down. To add insult to injury, his secretary refused to have sex with
me afterwards, explaining that, as an ex-student, I was no longer
worthy of her affections.

'Don't worry, old boy,' Meaty consoled. 'Come down to Hampshire for the weekend. Mumsy and Pa are away and I'm having a
house party. You must dwink yourself cheerful again!'

Which is precisely what I did. The fact that I also murdered
Gummy merely added to the fun.

On the way down to Lord Heaty's Hampshire estate, I stopped off in
London to visit my father.

Although I'd written regularly, usually when I needed money,
I hadn't actually seen Father since the spring of the previous year,
the intervening holidays having all been spent up at Cambridge. I
was neither dreading nor especially looking forward to the meeting.
Engaged as he habitually was with his inventions, he'd never taken
much interest in my affairs. Nor I, for my part, in his. We lived in
very different worlds.

I reached White Lodge, our crumbling, whitewashed abode in
Regent's Park, late in the morning, and was let in by Mrs Eggs, the
housekeeper. She looked the same as ever, with her bright piggy eyes
and enormous bosom squashed beneath an overly tight white apron,
and clapped me in a lung-bursting hug.

'Master Raphael!' she cried, delighted. 'Oh, you naughty boy, surprising me like that! You always were a naughty boy, and you haven't
changed a bit. My, how you've grown.'

'I do believe I'm the same size as when you last saw me, Mrs Eggs.'

'Stuff and nonsense. You're at least a foot bigger, and so handsome. I could marry you myself.'

She planted a rubbery kiss on my cheek.

'Will you be staying?' she inquired, indicating the suitcase in my hand.

'Not this time, Mrs Eggs. I'm on my way to Hampshire. I just thought I'd pop by to see Father.'

'Well, he'll be very grateful, I'm sure,' she said, bustling me into the house and closing the door behind me. 'And how's our young professor? Still top of the class, eh?'

Mrs Eggs had always been far more excited by my academic achievements than my father – she wept for three days when I announced I'd won a scholarship to Cambridge – and I had not the heart to confess that those achievements now lay in ruins. I therefore answered her question with a wan smile and, tickling her beneath the chin, left my suitcase in the front hall and set off in search of Father.

Lawrence Boethius Phoenix, for such was my father's name, was an inventor. A spectacularly unsuccessful inventor, I might add, for in a lifetime of determined appliance-making he'd never once produced anything the general public considered worth spending their money on. He had, I believe, sold three of his steam-driven bottle openers in the early 1900s, and his plans for a cream-whipper powered by mice had caused quite a stir at the Royal Society. Those exceptions aside, however, the remainder of his life's work had crashed headlong into a wall of universal indifference. Nobody wanted ice skates that, with a subtle modification, could be turned into tap shoes; nor were they interested in wind-powered gramophones, or croquet mallets that played 'Rule, Britannia!' whenever they hit a ball. His motorized tennis racquet attracted nothing but derision, as did his proposal for a cavalry division mounted on pogo sticks and, had he not been left a sizeable inheritance by an elderly dowager aunt, he, and me too, would long since have tumbled into abject penury.

His workshop was at the back of the house, overlooking the gardens: a large, chaotic room smelling strongly of chemicals, its floor knee-deep in tools and gadgets, its shelves piled high with back copies of the various obscure publications to which he subscribed

(*Patents Magazine, Inventors' Review*, etc.). It was here that he spent most of his time, and it was here that I found him that day, standing at the far end of the room wearing what looked like a large colander on his head, the latter sending forth a tangled spaghetti of wires into a metal cabinet with flashing lights on the front.

'Hello, Father,' I said, crossing the room.

'Ah,' he mumbled, turning towards me, seeming, as he usually did, rather embarrassed by my presence. 'Um . . . yes! Very good.'

He was by that point close on 75 years of age, having been well into his fifties when I was conceived, and, although much the same height as me, was now rather stooped. Since our last encounter the skin of his face had yellowed somewhat, and his beard seemed a little threadbare. There were heavy bags under his eyes.

'You look well,' I said.

'Yes, yes,' he replied. 'Trundling along.' And then, almost as an afterthought: 'You?'

'Fine, thank you. I'm afraid I've been sent down from Cambridge.'

'Oh well.' He shrugged, displaying, as I knew he would, not the slightest interest in my news. 'Can't be helped. Look at this.'

He stood aside and indicated the metal cabinet with the flashing lights on the front, patting it with his hand.

'This is it,' he announced excitedly. 'This is the one. They won't be able to ignore me after this!'

I said nothing, knowing he would, without prompting, explain what the cabinet was all about.

'It's an echo-box,' he continued. 'A gateway to the past. With this machine we can listen to the voices of our own history. It'll cause a revolution. They won't be able to ignore me now!'

He adjusted the colander on his head, and fiddled with some dials.

'What I've discovered, you see, is that sounds don't actually disappear. They simply get absorbed into their surroundings, like water into a sponge. As I'm speaking now, my words are sinking into the walls and the floor and the ceiling and the furniture. They're sinking in all around us. And so have voices throughout history.

They've been absorbed and locked in. And now with this' – he tapped the cabinet – 'we can release them. Listen once again. Five years it's taken me. But it was worth it. It'll cause a revolution, by God!'

He removed the colander from his head and placed it on mine before picking up what looked like a large stethoscope and applying it to the forehead of a small Egyptian bust sitting on the floor.

'Listen,' he said. 'Listen to the past.'

He bent down and fiddled with some knobs. A faint buzzing sound echoed in my ears, as of a distant swarm of bees.

'Hear anything?' he asked.

'A sort of buzzing.'

'Any voices?'

'Not really.'

He played with the dials some more, and flicked a couple of switches.

'Now?'

'No. Just a buzzing, with an occasional crackle.'

He looked disappointed, and checked over the wires on my helmet.

'You should be hearing voices. I spent the whole of yesterday listening to the High Priest of Amun. Clear as anything. Ah, there's a loose connection. Just tighten it up a bit. Now it should be working.'

He seemed so expectant, so needful of my acknowledgement, that I couldn't bring myself to tell him that even the buzzing had now ceased.

'Yes!' I cried, with as much conviction as I could muster. 'Yes, I can hear it. Voices! Egyptian voices!'

'By God, I knew it worked!' he cried. 'I knew I wasn't mad! Old Eggs said I was, but I knew better. Oh, I'm so happy! They won't be able to ignore me now!'

He capered around the room – cutting a rather ridiculous figure in his sky-blue velvet smoking jacket and embroidered slippers – before collapsing into an old armchair from which a cloud of dust flew up all around him. I removed the colander from my head and went to his side. He was breathing heavily.

'Congratulations, Father,' I said.

He removed a handkerchief and blew his nose.

'Actually,' he snuffled, 'I was rather hoping to hear your mother's voice again. It's been such a long time.'

He scratched his beard and lapsed into a silent reverie, his lips moving slightly as though he were talking to someone.

'She was very beautiful, you know,' he said after a while. 'Some said she was the most beautiful woman in London. What a waste.'

He leaned forward and, picking up the colander from the sideboard where I'd deposited it, began fiddling with the protruding wires.

'Just a few minor modifications and then I can sit and listen to her all day. I've got her old jewellery box, you know. There should be lots of sounds in that.'

He removed a small screwdriver from his top pocket and set to work on the underside of the colander. I watched him for a while, and then, when it became evident he had no more to say to me, stood and told him I had a train to catch.

'Yes, yes,' he replied. 'Don't let me keep you. Come by again soon. Your input has been invaluable.'

We shook hands rather awkwardly, and I made my way back across the cluttered workshop.

'School all right?' he called after me.

'Fine,' I replied. 'Just fine.'

At the door I turned and waved a final farewell.

'You look just like her,' he said softly. 'The spitting image. Sometimes, when you were young, I would see you out of the corner of my eye and think maybe . . .'

I never saw him again. The next day, at almost precisely the same moment as I was sending him a telegram from Southampton announcing my departure to America, a freak electrical surge sent 15,000 volts flying into his colander and thence directly through his head, killing him instantly. His death was, of course, a complete accident. I might be many things, but a patricide is not one of them.

*

By the time I arrived at Meaty's family home, an ornate, neo-classical mansion 15 miles north of Southampton, it was 8 p.m. and they'd started dinner without me. I changed quickly into my evening dress and, having joined the group, was made to down a pint of claret as punishment for being so late.

'We're all pissed as twoopers already,' exclaimed Meaty triumphantly. 'Been at it pwetty much since lunchtime. More wine here, Fwiggs! More wine, I say!'

Friggs, the aged butler, shuffled forwards and refilled my glass.

'Down the pwoverbial!' cried Meaty. 'Or is it up the pwoverbial? God, I weally am in a lather!'

As well as myself and Meaty, the party included Pepper, Charlie, Topper, Bunty, Bongo McCabe and, seated at the head of the table and resplendent in black tie and a necklace of translucent white shells, Prince Gummy-Molars himself.

'What's the necklace for?' I asked.

'A charm!' he boomed. 'Those who wear it can never become drunk.'

'Obviously not working in your case,' chipped in Bongo, 'because you're pickled as Somerset chutney, old boy!'

'I am not!' roared the prince, banging his fist upon the table. 'I'm sober. Sober, I say! Sober! Sober! Sober!'

Whereupon he struggled to his feet, lurched across the room and was violently sick in the fireplace.

'Bwavo, Gummy!' called Meaty. 'I say, Fwiggs, scoop that up and take it through to Mrs Lockhart in the kitchen. She might be able to make a soup of it. And get some more wine while you're there, will you!'

'Yes, m'lud,' sighed the long-suffering Friggs, shuffling dejectedly from the room. Gummy rejoined the table and tucked contentedly into a large plate of quail's eggs.

'You see,' he chortled. 'Very sober.'

We remained at dinner for the next three hours, polishing off at least half Lord Heaty's famously well-stocked wine cellar and driving poor Friggs to distraction by constantly sending him away for more alcohol and then throwing food at him whenever he returned. By the time we'd finished port and cigars and retired from the table the poor man looked like he'd had a dustbin emptied over his head, whilst we were, to a man, incoherent with drink. We played a couple of games of billiards, and then, with Gummy fast asleep in an armchair – his broad nostrils flaring prodigiously as he snored, his lips wobbling like a pair of jellies – the rest of us trooped on to the terrace for a breath of fresh air. Which is where we saw the giant catapult.

'I say,' cried Bunty, 'what an absolutely spiffing toy.'

It was a huge machine, some ten feet high, supported on four wooden wheels, with a long arm with a dish at one end, into which, presumably, was put whatever object was due to be catapulted.

'What is it?' asked Charlie.

'A catapult,' replied Meaty.

'I can see that. But what's it doing here?'

'Father had it built,' explained Meaty. 'For the five-hundwedth anniversary of Agincourt. We had a pageant here on the lawn. It's been here ever since.'

'It looks like a spoon,' opined Bongo. 'A huge great medicine spoon, like the one matron used at school. I wouldn't fancy one of those full of cod liver oil!'

We walked around the catapult a couple of times, and then climbed on to it, clambering around like children on a climbing frame. Pepper ensconced himself in the concave wooden dish at the end of the catapult arm, reclining with his hands behind his head as though he were on a sofa.

'Very comfortable,' he proclaimed querulously. 'Very damned comfortable.'

'Does it still work?' inquired Topper, swigging from a bottle of vintage port.

'No idea, old boy,' replied Meaty. 'It did at one time, but that was four years ago.'

'I say,' cried Bunty excitedly, 'shall we have a go? I bet it's got a hell of a shot.'

'It'll probably fall to bits as soon as we crank it up,' opined Bongo. 'I'm for another game of Bulldogs.'

'Don't be such a misewable defeatist, Bong-Bong,' said Meaty. 'I think Bunty's quite wight. It's our duty as Englishmen and Invincibles to get this catapult working. We shall be like knights of the Round Table! Come on down, Pepper, you slouch, and lend a hand.'

We gathered at the rear end of the catapult and, with Meaty shouting instructions, pushed it slowly into the middle of the terrace, its giant wheels crunching on the gravel. Some lamps were brought out – it was by now well into the early hours, although still perfectly warm – and by their flickering light we set about preparing the contraption to fire.

This was by no means an easy task, since none of us had the least idea how it worked. Topper got a nasty crack on the head when the catapult arm smashed down on top of it, and Bongo somehow contrived to get his finger stuck in the ratchet mechanism. After much pulling of ropes and cranking of levers, however, we finally had it ready for action. Meaty placed a decanter of Armagnac in the firing cradle and, with a cry of 'Tally-ho!' sprung the catapult. There was a loud whoosh, a snap of wood, and the bottle disappeared into the night. We were speechless.

'Crikey,' exclaimed Charlie eventually. 'Did you see it fly!'

'It must have gone half a mile!' whooped Bunty.

'I didn't hear it smash,' said Meaty. 'It must have gone wight over the woods and into the lake. What a wheeze!'

We let out a loud cheer and charged back into the house in search of other objects to catapult, returning with cushions, books, bottles, an umbrella stand and an old gramophone, all of which we duly dispatched over the garden and into the woods beyond. Some, such as the gramophone, we heard crash into the trees; others just disappeared gracefully into the night, never to be seen or heard of again.

'What we need,' opined Pepper drunkenly after an hour of un-interrupted catapulting, 'is something really heavy, like a large rock.'

'Pepper's wight,' said Meaty. 'We need something that will test our machine's capabilities to the full.'

Bunty scratched his head.

'An armchair?' he suggested.

'Too cumbersome,' said Meaty.

'A suit of armour,' offered Topper.

'No, no, no. Father would be absolutely fuwious. He's very par-ticular about his armour.'

'A big cooking pot?' wondered Charlie.

'Hmm, possibly,' mused Meaty. 'Not very inspiwing, though.'

We fell silent, each of us racking our brains to come up with a pro-jectile worthy of such an enormous catapult. From the living room came the gurgling rasp of Gummy's snoring.

I don't think anyone specifically suggested using the prince as a missile. Not in the sense of actually vocalizing the idea. I think rather that it sprung up in all our brains simultaneously, prompted by the monstrous cacophony issuing from his giant rubbery nostrils. We stood around uncertainly, eyes flicking from one face to the next, each person wondering if anyone else was thinking the same thing, and then suddenly, decisively, without a word being spoken or an objection raised, we trooped back into the living room, lifted Gummy from his armchair and brought him outside. Pepper and Meaty held on to his somnolent form whilst the rest of us cranked the apparatus into preparedness, and we then hoisted him into the firing cradle.

'I am your master,' he muttered in his sleep. 'Bring me sweet-meats!'

'Off we go then,' cried Meaty. 'Gummy away!'

I was nearest the firing lever and, with a yank, pulled it back. There was a crack and a whoosh, and Oduduwa Ifa Ogunmola, Prince of the Kikiwe, was launched skywards to tumultuous applause from his inebriated friends. Up and up and up he went, cartwheeling across the face of the moon and looking for a moment as if he might be on his way out of the earth's atmosphere altogether. Eventually, however, he attained optimum height and, after hanging in the air for a seemingly impossible length of time, began his descent. Much to our surprise, he woke up on the way down, shouting, 'My head's spinning!' before plummeting headlong into the trees at the end of the garden. There was a crashing of branches, followed almost instantaneously by a resounding thud. A hundred birds rose up into the air screaming, and then everything fell quiet.

'What a marvellous show!' said Meaty. 'Gummy weally is the life and soul.'

Soon after that everyone went to bed. Topper expressed vague reservations as to the legality of the night's proceedings, but that was the closest any of us got to remorse for our activities. The truth was that catapulting Gummy had been extremely good fun, and had there been anyone else suitable to hand we would doubtless have catapulted them too. Bongo suggested going and getting Friggs, but was outvoted, and everyone duly trudged off upstairs.

Everyone, that is, except me; for although feeling drunk I wasn't yet tired, and with a quick squeeze of The Pill in its silver snuffbox, and pat of The Photo in my jacket pocket, I therefore wandered off across the lawn and into the woods at the bottom of the garden. Dawn was breaking, and the ground was covered in dew. My dinner suit was rather crumpled.

I had gone about 50 yards into the trees, and had already stumbled across the shattered remains of the catapulted gramophone, when I found Prince Gummy-Molars hanging upside down from a large oak tree, his foot caught in the crook of a branch. His head was some 15 feet off the forest floor and appeared to have split clean in half, spilling brains and all sorts of gunge across the trunk and lower branches. His eyes were wide open; or at least one of them was, the other having apparently popped right out of its socket, whilst his lips hung pendulously downwards as though he were blowing me a kiss.

He cut a most unappealing figure, and after gazing for a moment in horrified fascination I turned to my left and hurried off into the trees. I returned a moment later, however, and picked up his wallet from the forest floor. It appeared to have quite a lot of money in it.

'I'm sure he would have wanted me to have it,' I thought.

I wandered on for 20 minutes or so, feeling increasingly tired and heavy-headed, and finally, emerging from the trees into a misty glade, decided to sit down and take 40 winks. I duly slumped at the foot of mossy silver birch and, face to the rising sun, closed my eyes, drifting into a sleep almost immediately. When her voice came, I presumed I was just dreaming.

'You're sitting on the mushrooms!'

'Hmmm,' I mumbled.

'You're sitting on the mushrooms, Raphael.'

'Yes, Emily, I know. I'll eat them later.'

'Raphael, do stop talking gibberish. I can't pick mushrooms if you're sitting on them.'

'Of course not, Emily. Emily. Emily!'

My eyes jerked open and I sprang to my feet.

'Emily! Is it you?'

Indeed it was, standing right in front of me, calm as you like, framed in a halo of dawn sunlight. I'm always startled by Emily's sudden appearances, but on this occasion I was particularly so, for after her departure in 1910 I'd genuinely thought I'd never see her again. Now, however, she was back, unexpectedly, miraculously, as though from the dead. Aside from being a little taller, and possessed of certain womanly convexities that hadn't been apparent when we'd last been together, she looked exactly the same as when we'd parted.

'Emily, my darling! This is impossible. I never thought we'd see each other again.'

She stooped to pick an enormous, umbrella-sized mushroom.

'Well, it all happened rather suddenly,' she said, dropping the mushroom in her basket. 'I thought maybe you wouldn't want to hear from me.'

'Wouldn't want to hear from you!'

'I thought you might be cross and upset. About my disappearing like that.'

'Of course I was cross and upset. But that just made me want to hear from you more. God, Emily, you amaze me sometimes. You really do amaze me!'

She shrugged, and indicated that I should hold out the basket so she could drop some mushrooms into it.

For the next half-hour or so we zigzagged to and fro across the misty glade, and I filled Emily in on what I'd been doing for the last eight years – omitting to mention I'd been sent down from Cambridge and had just killed someone with a giant catapult. By the time the basket was full the sun was up and peeping over the tops of the trees.

'So how long are you here for?' I asked.

'Not long,' she replied. 'I sail to America this afternoon, from Southampton. On the *Aquitania*.'

She must have noticed the spasm of disappointment that crossed my face, for she added:

'Why don't you come too? It's a super ship. I'm sure we'd have a lot of fun.'

'What, to America? Do you really mean it?'

'Of course I mean it.'

'But Emily, this is wonderful! Wonderful! It's more than I could ever have hoped for!'

I leapt forward and embraced her and then, taking a last long look at her beautiful pale face, set off immediately into the swirling dawn mist. 'I'll meet you on board!' I cried over my shoulder. 'If you get there first, order me a pink gin!'

But of course she couldn't order me a pink gin because she never actually boarded the ship (although she always swears she did). And so I rolled and puked my way over to America alone, and didn't see my angel for another 12 long years, about which you can read more back in the bathroom. God, how I missed her.

304

And that's really everything there is to say about Gummy, although I ought, before finishing, to tie off a few loose ends.

Gummy's body was discovered two days after we killed him. It caused quite a stir, and Meaty and his friends were brought in for questioning by the local police. Since Lord Gosport had that very year donated £5,000 to the Police Benevolent Fund, however, the questioning was neither intense nor protracted, and no charges were brought. A coroner's inquiry later concluded Gummy had slipped whilst tree-climbing.

Dayo Obafemi, Gummy's younger brother, subsequently ascended to the throneship of the Kikiwe and proved, by all accounts, an excellent ruler. Far better, I suspect, than poor old Gummy would ever have been.

My father's corpse, the colander still smouldering on his head, was discovered by Mrs Eggs, who wrote immediately to inform me of what had occurred. Her letter, however, only caught up with me eight months later, in New Orleans, by which point White Lodge and everything in it had been sold to pay off my father's mountainous debts, and our former housekeeper had moved to Eastbourne to live with her sister. I neither saw nor spoke to her ever again.

Of my fellow Invincibles – of Bunty, and Bongo, and Jonty, and Topper, and Pepper, and Charlie – I can tell you little, although I did hear a rumour that Jonty had married into the Norwegian royal family, and Pepper became something big in the Tory Party.

The blonde-haired girl to whom I lost my virginity died in the Spanish influenza epidemic of 1919.

And finally, Meaty. For 40 years I heard nothing either of or about him until, quite by chance, our paths happened to cross, in the early Sixties. I was, at the time, in the service of Lord Slaggsby, and, as you may remember from my account of that period, there was an evening when His lordship, quite contrary to his usual practice, had a guest to dinner. That guest was none other than Maximilian Heaty, now Lord Heaty, 4th Earl of Gosport. Fat, gouty and riddled with the cancer that was soon to kill him, he quite failed to recognize me and spent the entire evening complaining about coloured immigrants.

'Not that I'm a wacialist, of course,' he lisped. 'Quite the contwary. Used to have a vewy good black chum myself. Spiffing fellow. Called him Gummy-Molars. Life and soul of the party, he was. Absolute life and soul.'

# Chapter Seventeen

At last, it's all coming together! After all the traumas and upsets and fuck-ups of the early part of the week my death is finally getting back up to speed. I'm feeling good. Really good. Better than I've felt for years. As Keith would have put it: 'We're rocking, man! Like, really rocking!'

Whoopee!

Part of the reason for my improved spirits is that that damned knocking finally seems to have stopped. It had been getting louder and more intense and more frequent all week, until by Wednesday night it had become so furious I genuinely thought whoever was doing it was going to smash their way right through the castle's front door.

I tried to catch the culprit, but to no avail, and eventually, beside myself, left a pleading letter on the doorstep begging them to go away, accompanied by a 20-pound bribe. It was a desperate act, and I held out little hope that it would work. Rather to my surprise, however, it has. Or, so far, at least. Early on Thursday morning, that being yesterday, the knocking stopped, and there hasn't been a peep since. You could hear a pin drop in the castle. Yesterday evening I sneaked down and eased the front door open a few inches and saw that the letter and money had gone. If I'd known they just wanted cash I could have solved the problem days ago. That knocking really has been screwing me up.

I do feel a bit cheapened that I've had to buy my peace and quiet. Such things are, I feel, a man's by right (and a woman's too). With less than a day left to live, however, I'm not overly bothered about the expenditure. If it gives me the space and security to get my note done then it was a price worth paying. I just hope I haven't set some sort of precedent. I haven't got much money left, and need to keep some back to pay Dr Bannen when he comes later this afternoon.

Curiously, the thumping inside my back, around the area of my wings, also seems to have quietened down. It's still there, thud thud thud, but softer and, more importantly, it seems to have settled down into a regular pattern, like a pulse, or a heartbeat. What I found so distracting about it before was that it would come and go, never giving me the chance to get used to it, to assimilate the sensation. One minute it was there, the next it wasn't, and then it was again, jerking me in and out of my concentration like a marionette on a string.

Now, however, it has evened out into a consistent, soft, metronomic pounding, and although I'd rather it wasn't there at all I have at least been able to adjust myself to the rhythm of its hammering. It's no longer disturbing my work. It has become a part of my bodily process. If it would just stay like this for the next 20 hours or so I'll be a happy man. Down, wings! Down!

So, I'm feeling happy because the knocking on the front door has stopped, and because the knocking in my back has eased off, and because I'm rather pleased with my description of the whole Prince Gummy episode. Above all, however, I'm happy because I've come up with a solution to the vexed question of what to do above my doorframes. And a bloody marvellous solution it is too!

You may remember that on Wednesday night I suddenly decided I didn't like leaving the space above each doorframe empty. Since then I've been racking my brains as to what to do with those frustrating rectangles of hovering whiteness. Amongst other options I've considered:

1) Painting them in (there are a couple of tins of black matt down in the basement).
2) Putting a big thick cross through each one, as though they were boxes on some gigantic questionnaire.
3) Drawing pictures in them.
4) Filling them with abstract loops and spirals, like the designs on the pages of an illuminated manuscript.
5) Collecting some bracken and grasses and doing a sort of flower arrangement in them.

Then, however, at about six o'clock last night, as the first stars twinkled coldly through the smudged windows of the upstairs gallery, the answer suddenly burst upon me.

'Of course!' I cried. 'It's so obvious. I'll fill the space with names! Each doorway leads to a murder, so above each doorway should be the name of the victim. Like a sort of chapter heading.'

It was indeed the obvious solution, and I felt a trifle foolish not to have thought of it before.

'Flower arranging indeed!' I chided myself. 'You're a fool, Raphael. Always have been, always will be. A bloody fool!'

I was delighted with my new idea, and got to work immediately, abandoning Gummy-Molars mid-flow and transporting my ladder downstairs to the foyer, where I set it up before the doorway to the first of the ground-floor rooms. I then climbed up and, in large purple letters – good colour, purple; very eye-catching – wrote *Mrs Ethel Bunshop* above the doorframe, underlining the name and surrounding it with a garland of curlicues and squiggles. I climbed down to admire my handiwork and then, on a whim, remounted and drew a picture of a matchstick figure with its hair on fire in the top-right-hand corner of the panel.

The effect of these minor additions was startling. I had thought the note looked good before, but now, by dint of a single purple-lettered name and a rather childish drawing, it seemed to come alive before my eyes. Where previously it had all appeared rather uniform and two-dimensional, it now leapt right off the walls at me, demanding to be read. It felt richer and more satisfying, just as a seascape is more satisfying when there's a sail or an island to break the ceaseless, distended monotony of the water.

'It works!' I cried excitedly, standing on the far side of the dim foyer and gazing across my work like an artist gazing at a newly painted portrait. 'By God, it works! Just look how much perspective it's added. How much depth!'

I stared proudly at my masterpiece for several minutes, moving about the foyer so as to view it from different angles – it looked particularly good from the castle's south-eastern corner, near the entrance to the kitchen – and then set about filling in the names of all my other victims. Above the next doorway I wrote *Mrs Bunshop (cont.)* – if you remember, she filled two rooms – accompanying her moniker with another matchstick person, this one engulfed in flames from head to foot. I then moved on to the doorway to the downstairs gallery, over which I wrote *Walter X. & Keith Cream* (with, respectively, drawings of a hot-air balloon and a pumpkin); then the kitchen (*Lord Slaggsby* and a cream cake); the cellar (*The Albino Twins* and two teddy bears); the study (*Mr Popplethwaite* and a large safe); the bathroom (*Luther Dextrus* and an alligator) and, finally, the upstairs gallery (*Prince Gummy-Molars & Miss Dorothy Wasply*, with a catapult and an exploding bath). I haven't yet decided what to put over the door to my bedroom, but since I won't get there till late this afternoon there's no real hurry. I've got plenty of time to think about it.

(I should perhaps remark that whilst I filled in the spaces above the *outside* of each door, I left those above the *inside* empty. Aside from wishing to save time, I'm also much less concerned about these interior blanks, since you can't actually see them unless you physically enter the room. Out of sight, as they say, out of mind.)

It took me almost five hours to complete all the doorways in the castle – I'm a slow artist – and I then wasted another 30 minutes wandering around marvelling at my efforts, so that it wasn't until almost midnight that I finally returned to the note proper. Thereafter things progressed steadily enough, and by 3.30 a.m., the very last 3.30 a.m. of my life, I finally brought Gummy to a close. He occupies the northern half of the upstairs gallery, starting to the right of the door and ending to the left of the windows, and, as with Walter below, I've cordoned him off by scraping a deep and rather unsightly groove across the dusty wooden floor. His death unfolds in two colours, red and a sort of algae-coloured light green, and in letters of about average height. Perhaps very slightly smaller than average.

I am currently writing between the two east-facing gallery windows, closer to the right-hand one than to the left, and, aside from the persistent drum-roll in my back, am feeling fit and confident. My eyes in particular appear to be sharper and more focused than they've been at any time in my life, as though death were a sort of grindstone, honing the blade of my vision to a perfect edge. Yesterday afternoon I noticed for the first time that one of the eastward islands has a small house on its leeward side. I had no idea people lived out there.

I should now by rights be getting on with my next murder. It's been a good night, but time is still of the essence. I'm reticent to start, however, until I've passed the right-hand gallery window – that way I can fit Miss Wasply precisely into the space between the window and the door. That leaves me about two and a half columns' worth of wall space to fill. I haven't got much else to say about the note, or my health, or my splendid door-headings, and so I've decided to increase the size of my writing a little, each letter swelling to the size of a nice fat gooseberry, and tell you about the time as a child when I went on a picnic to Greenwich with Father, Emily and Mrs Eggs.

Mrs Eggs was always taking me and Emily on picnics. We had picnics in Regent's Park, picnics in Hyde Park, picnics in Richmond

Park, picnics in the garden and even picnics upstairs in the nursery when the weather was bad and it was too wet to go outside.

Father, however, never came on these excursions. He was far too busy with his inventing.

'Please, Father,' I'd implore. 'We've got fairy cakes and jam sandwiches and lemonade. And Emily's coming too. It's going to be the best fun in the world.'

'Oh, if only I could,' he'd sigh. 'If only I could. But my experiments are at a critical stage, don't you see? I simply can't leave them. You run along and have a good time and I'll see you when you come home. Off you go!'

And so we'd troop off to Regent's Park, or Hyde Park, or Richmond Park, or into the garden, or upstairs to the nursery, with our fairy cakes and jam sandwiches and lemonade, and always without Father.

Until one day, to everyone's consternation, including, I suspect, his own, he announced that, for once, his experiments weren't at a critical stage and he was coming too.

'Your father's coming on the picnic!' screamed Mrs Eggs, getting quite hysterical at the thought. 'It'll have to be cucumber sandwiches! Only cucumber sandwiches will do. But where am I going to get a cucumber at this short notice! I'm going to have a heart attack!'

Eventually, after much to-do, she managed to track down a cumbumber (that's what Emily always called them) without suffering a coronary, and, the sandwiches made and packed in a large basket, we all set out on the train to Greenwich, Emily and I peering out of the window, Father smoking his pipe and Mrs Eggs fretting that she hadn't made enough food, something she always did, despite having invariably packed enough to feed a small army.

It was a fine, warm summer's day, and in Greenwich we marched up through the park and laid out a blanket on the grass beside the Royal Observatory.

'Well, this is nice,' said Father, gazing out across the Thames and puffing on his pipe. 'I really should do this more often.'

'You can come whenever you want,' I said.

'I'm sure I haven't made enough,' moaned Mrs Eggs, fiddling around in the picnic basket, which was so heavy it had taken two of us to lug it up the hill. 'We're all going to starve!'

We didn't, however, and after we'd devoured a mountain of sandwiches and cakes and biscuits and sweets and drunk a lake's worth of lemonade, Emily and I ran off to play hide-and-seek amongst the trees whilst Mrs Eggs passed out in an exhausted slumber and Father sat reading that month's issue of the *Inventors' Review*. Every now and then I would look back at him, a halo of pipe smoke hovering above his head, a faint smile on his face, just to make sure he was still there and that his presence on our picnic wasn't simply a daydream. He *was* still there, however, and I remember feeling happier than I had ever felt before.

'Race you to that tree over there!' cried Emily.

'OK,' I said. 'Last one's a sissy. Wait a minute! I haven't said "Go" yet!'

Later Father joined us for another round of hide-and-seek, and gave us each a piggy-back, and played some I Spy, although we soon got bored of the latter because all the things Father spied were so impossible to guess.

'No,' he'd say after we'd spent half an hour trying to work out what the particular something beginning with 'a' was, 'it's not an apple, or an ant, it's that amputee sitting down there on the bench. Can you see, children, he's only got one arm.'

Later still, Mrs Eggs told us a story about a prince who was turned into a toad. Father supplied the toad sound effects and Emily and I rolled about laughing.

We stayed in the park until the sun started to drop westwards beyond the river and then packed up our things and wandered slowly back down the hill. Father bought us all iced-creams, and we stopped for a while to throw sticks in the river. On the train home I started to cry.

'Why can't you come on every picnic, Father,' I snivelled. 'It's been such a good day.'

'From now on, I will,' he declared, patting my head. 'Every single one.'

He never did, however. The cumbumber sandwich picnic in Greenwich Park was the only one he ever came on. That's probably why I remember it so fondly. Why it occupies such a special place in the museum of my memories. Why, even now, over 90 years later, I still break into a huge smile whenever I think about it. Cumbumber sandwiches and lemonade and hide-and-seek – it really was the best fun in the world.

All of which brings me very nicely down to the skirting board directly to the left of the second gallery window. My writing is now back to its normal size (i.e. that of raisins) and I'm still using that algae-coloured light-green pen. It's almost five o'clock on the morning of Friday, 31st December 1999, the last day of the millennium, the last full day of my life, and Dr Bannen's coming in ten hours' time. I know I can kill Ms Wasply by then. I know I can. I just need . . . What the fuck! Someone's just blown a raspberry through my letterbox! A bloody great loud rippling raspberry! And now – oh no, no, no! – that bloody knocking's started again! Boom, boom, fucking boom! I AM GOING TO RIP SOMEONE'S FUCKING HAND OFF!

Twenty minutes later. Didn't catch them, of course, the knocker, the raspberry blower, the shit. They obviously want more cash, but they're not going to get it. I've had enough. Standing on the doorstep, I screamed at the very top of my voice: *Fuck off, you cunt! You're not getting any more money out of me!* So now they know.

The stress has set my back off again. Thud thud thud. Hammering inside. Knocking outside. It's a wonder I'm managing to keep my sanity. And I've now gone past the second of the two gallery windows. Bollocks!

Come on, Raphael!

# Chapter Eighteen

Although in terms of strict chronology Dorothy Wasply was the second person I killed, she was actually my first proper victim in the sense that her death was deliberately planned and executed. The more generous amongst you might even consider her my *only* proper victim – in no other instance have I murdered with quite the same degree of premeditation as I did in the case of Emily's dragon-faced governess. Her removal – oh, sweet explosion! – is inextricably bound up with my childhood and early days with Emily, and it is somehow fitting that now at the very end of my life the time has come to transport myself, and you too, almost right the way back to its very beginning.

Time and wall space being pressing – I still have to tell you what happened with Emily the other night – I shan't waste too much of either with an excessively detailed account of my very earliest years.

I was born not long after midnight in the cold, dark, early hours of 1st January 1900, and was, if the photos are anything to go by, a marvellously healthy baby, with a huge toothless smile and a full head of shimmering blond hair. When he beheld me for the first time, apparently, my father wept.

I stepped off into the world at White Lodge, our crumbling, whitewashed home in Regent's Park, and it was here, as well as committing my first murder, that I spent the early part of my life.

Mother wasn't around, of course, and Father spent most of his time secreted in his workshop, emerging only to confront his more voluble creditors and when accidents with chemicals necessitated the evacuation of the room on safety grounds. Aside from that, however, and the fact that people were forever commenting on my unnaturally large blue eyes, my existence was a consummately normal one.

I played with my toy soldiers, built camps in the attic, surveyed the world through a miniature telescope my aunt had bought me and went on long walks in the park with dear old Mrs Eggs, always taking a bag of breadcrumbs with us so we could feed the ducks around the lake. I drank copious amounts of milk, detested semolina (still do) and developed, about the age of three, a taste for woodlice, which I would pluck from beneath stones and eat raw. My knees, I seem to recall, were permanently grazed, and my favourite books were an illustrated volume of *Grimms' Fairy Tales*, and *The Magic Castle*, by someone whose name I can't remember.

At the age of three or thereabouts I started at a small nursery school near our home, where I made a number of friends, including a pasty-faced child called Ginger. For a year Ginger and I were inseparable, until he stole my W. G. Grace cigarette card, whereupon I punched him on the nose and we never spoke again.

Other memories of those early years include a week's holiday in Margate, where I rode on a donkey and was violently ill after eating five sticks of rock; a severe bout of measles from which it was touch and go whether or not I'd recover; a stern dressing-down from a policeman after I'd fired my catapult at a passing hansom cab, causing the horses to rear; and a Christmas carol concert where a large candle fell out of its holder and set light to baby Jesus in his manger beneath. These and various other minor occurrences aside, however, nothing of any great note happened to me until the afternoon of my sixth birthday, that being 1st January 1906. Then, however, something of very great note happened. I met Emily. And with her my life really begins.

I heard her before I saw her, and saw her before she saw me. It was a cold, clear afternoon, and I was playing in the garden when, from beyond the wall surrounding our house, I heard the most enchanting sound.

'Go on, Miss Wasply! Throw it high up.'

There followed a considerably less enchanting sound – 'I will not throw it high up, young lady! Particularly when you address me in that disgraceful tone of voice!' – before the first voice, more insistent this time, was heard again:

'You will throw it high up, Miss Wasply! You will, I say.'

Casting aside the toy sword with which I had up to that point been amusing myself, I hurried over to the garden wall and, clambering up an old plum tree – *the* old plum tree, the one from whose branches Father used to pluck coins – gazed over into the park beyond. Ten yards away, her arms outspread ready to catch, was a young girl with blonde hair and extremely green eyes. She was wearing a thick blue coat and was standing opposite a tall, stern-looking woman who, with her flared nostrils, bulging eyes and enormous chin, bore, a striking resemblance to a dragon.

'Come on, Miss Wasply,' cried the girl, her eyes flashing in the pale winter sunlight. 'Throw it to me!'

'Not until I hear the word!' responded the woman. 'The most important word in the dictionary.'

The girl sighed and raised her eyebrows in exasperation. This was clearly a situation she'd been in before.

'Come on, young lady. Out with it! The word God loves to hear all children use. Out with it, or we're going straight home for two hours of mathematics.'

'Please,' mumbled the girl grudgingly. 'Please hurry up and throw the ball, Miss Wasply. Please, please, please, please, please.'

'One please will do,' said Miss Wasply. 'And kindly remember to use it in the future. Because, as we know, those who *don't* get polio and have to spend the rest of their lives in a wheelchair.'

Whereupon, with a rustle of grey skirts and a bending of what I imagined to be extremely knobbly knees, she threw a large red ball up into the air, whence it described a graceful parabola into the arms of the young girl. The latter screamed in delight and, flinging both arms behind her head, launched the ball back at her huge-chinned governess.

'Catch it, Miss Wasply!'

Ms Wasply, however – for whom, in the matter of seconds I'd known her, I'd already developed a disregard bordering on the malevolent – quite failed to do so, standing stock still as the ball landed some two feet to her right.

'You didn't catch it, Miss Wasply!'

'That is correct. And I shall continue to not catch it until you learn to throw it in a civilized manner. Flinging your arms about like some sort of monkey!'

She stepped stiffly to her right, retrieved the ball and, clucking her tongue as if to say, 'The things I put myself through to earn a wage!' threw it once again to the girl, the latter clasping it with both hands and hugging it to her bosom.

'If you won't catch it, Miss Wasply, I won't throw it any more.'

'In which case, young lady, we shall return home, where you will spend the rest of the afternoon reciting your times tables.'

The girl screwed up her face in annoyance, clearly feeling she'd been outwitted, and with a petulant stamp swung both arms to her right and flung the ball at her governess as hard as she could. It sailed right over Miss Wasply's head, however, and, clearing the top of our wall, landed in our garden, where it bounced along the lawn and splashed into our ornamental pond.

'Ooops!' giggled the girl. 'Sorry, Miss Wasply.'

Miss Wasply clasped her hands behind her back, her knuckles white with displeasure.

'We could go round and ask for it,' suggested the girl.

'Certainly not!' snapped her governess, nostrils flaring. 'Knocking on strangers' doors, indeed!'

318

'Then I'll climb over and get it. It's not that high and I can climb up that ivy. It's like a ladder.'

'Never!' cried Miss Wasply, aghast. 'Your clothes will be ruined! I'm shocked you should even think of such a thing.'

The girl fell silent and stared at her feet. I thought for a moment she was about to burst into tears, and was as surprised as Miss Wasply when, without a word of warning, she suddenly charged at the wall, swerving around her companion and launching herself at the thick tendrils of ivy that hung downwards across the bulging brickwork. For a moment she struggled to find her grip, but, once she'd got it, swarmed upwards like a sailor through rigging, leaving her governess open-mouthed below.

'See, Miss Wasply,' she cried, reaching the top and swinging herself astride the summit as though it were the saddle of a horse. 'It's easy!'

'Come down! Come down, I say! Oh just look at your dress!'

'I can see for miles up here, Miss Wasply. I can see the zoo.'

'Come down, or I won't be responsible for the consequences!'

'You don't have to be!' laughed the girl precociously. 'I can answer for myself, thank you very much! Oh!'

This 'Oh' was an exclamation of surprise, prompted by the fact that, perched in my plum tree some three feet to her right and hitherto unnoticed, I had suddenly sneezed very loudly.

'Oh!' she repeated.

I said nothing, just wiped my nose on the sleeve of my coat and stared at her, mesmerized. Her eyes were even greener up close than they had been from a distance. I decided she must be a princess, or an angel.

'Hello,' she said.

'Hello,' I replied. And then, after a moment, 'It's my birthday today.'

'Is it?' she said. 'How old are you?'

'Six.'

'I'm six too, although my birthday's in July, so I'm older than you by half a year.'

I fell silent, digesting this information, wondering how it affected the dynamic of our 20-second-old relationship.

'What's going on up there?' bellowed her governess. 'Who are you talking to?'

'There's a boy up here, Miss Wasply. It's his birthday today. We're exactly the same age.'

'That's no concern of yours! Come down this instant!'

'That's Waspy Wasply,' whispered the girl. 'She's my governess.'

'She looks like a dragon,' I said. 'A nasty old dragon.'

The girl burst into giggles.

'Miss Wasply, the boy says you look like a dragon.'

Miss Wasply stepped backwards and, raising the pince-nez that hung about her neck, glared at me fiercely through its lenses.

'If some mothers raise their children as savages,' she intoned drily, 'that is their prerogative. We are under no obligation to mix with them, however, and should indeed avoid doing so lest their vile behaviour rub off on us.'

Under normal circumstances I would have been cowed by such a speech, particularly when accompanied by as vicious a look as Miss Wasply was currently throwing in my direction. Up in my plum tree, however, and with the beautiful girl beside me, I felt uncharacteristically strong-willed, and rather than crumbling beneath the woman's gaze I instead stuck my tongue out at her and re-addressed myself to my new acquaintance.

'Your ball's in our garden,' I said.

'I know. I threw it over by accident.'

'I didn't think girls could throw a ball that high.'

She smiled, flattered by the compliment.

'Shall I get it for you?' I asked.

'Yes, please. If you wouldn't mind.'

I turned back to Miss Wasply and crossed my eyes, something Mrs Eggs had told me was very impolite, and then without further ado shinned down the plum tree and ran across to the ball.

'Watch this!' I shouted boastfully, pulling it dripping from of the pond and kicking it as hard as I could towards the wall. Rather than flying over into the park as I had intended, however, the ball hit the brickwork full on and rebounded spectacularly straight into my face, knocking me to the ground, where I curled up and promptly burst into tears.

'Miss Wasply!' cried the girl, concerned. 'The boy's hurt himself!'

'I'm not surprised,' answered her governess, an unmistakeable note of satisfaction in her voice. 'Bad things invariably come to bad people. Now I shan't ask you again, young lady. Come down from that wall.'

'But I can't leave him, Miss Wasply! He was helping get my ball.'

'And we're very grateful, I'm sure. His distress, however, is none of our concern. Now kindly stop being so disobedient and *get off that wall!*'

There was a moment of silence, and then the sound of snapping ivy twigs and rustling leaves as the girl clambered from her perch. I presumed she was leaving me to my tears, which redoubled as a result, and was thus surprised – and delighted – when I heard a thud on *my* side of the wall, followed by the patter of approaching feet. Miss Wasply screamed and began tugging at the ivy tendrils, threatening the most dire recriminations for the girl's behaviour, but the object of her threats took no notice of them whatsoever.

'Don't worry about Waspy Wasply,' she said, coming up beside me. 'She's an old humbug. Are you hurt?'

'My head!' I wailed. 'My head hurts.'

I felt her kneeling down and heard a crumpling of paper.

'Would you like a chocolate?' asked the girl. 'They're very tasty.'

I raised my head, the shock of my accident momentarily forgotten.

'And look,' she continued, 'they're shaped like animals. There's an elephant, a snake, a monkey, a penguin and something that I don't know what it is. I've eaten all the tigers.'

I selected a penguin, which was, in fact, a parrot, and popped it in my mouth.

'Nice,' I said.

'Belgian,' explained the girl.

I ate three parrots, and a couple of the things that Emily didn't know what they were (bears, I think), after which I felt a lot less tearful and a lot more talkative.

'My name's Raphael Ignatius Phoenix,' I said. 'And I live in that house with Father and Mrs Eggs. What's your name?'

'Emily,' replied the girl, nibbling a chocolate elephant. 'Emily Emilie.'

'Emily Emily?'

'No, Emily Emilieeee. One's got a Y on the end, and the other's IE.'

I must have looked baffled, for she went on:

'My first name's the same as my last name, you see. Except they're spelt differently. It's easy to remember.'

'Emily Emilie!' I cried, laughing. 'Emily Emilie! That's funny!'

'Is it?' she said, furrowing her brow. 'Why?'

'Because your name goes round in a circle, of course. Round and round and round, like a dog chasing its tail. Emily Emilie! Woof woof! Emily Emilie!'

I struggled to my feet and began prancing around the garden, shouting 'Emily Emilie!' at the top of my voice. The girl stared at me for a moment, and then, laughing, stood up, stuffed the bag of chocolates back in her pocket and began skipping back and forth too, crying 'Phoenix the bird! Phoenix the bird!' as loud as she could. We became quite engrossed in our shouting, enchanted by the power of our voices, and it was only when, like a cat amongst doves, a third voice cried: 'There he is! That's the kidnapper!' that we fell silent. Coming towards us across the lawn, having issued unnoticed from the back of the house, were Mrs Eggs, my father, a policeman and Miss Wasply, the latter pointing at me accusingly with her long, thin skewer of a finger.

'That's the kidnapper!' she repeated. 'Arrest him immediately. I insist he be charged!'

There ensued a considerable to-do as Emily's governess rushed to her side and began shouting at me, Mrs Eggs rushed to my side

322

and began shouting at Emily's governess, the policeman shouted at both of them and my father – clearly itching to get back to his wind-powered gramophone or whatever it was he was inventing at the time – sat down on an upturned wheelbarrow and mumbled, 'Please, ladies! Please!' whilst dabbing at his brow with a large green handkerchief. The fracas continued for some time and only abated after I had apologized for calling Miss Wasply a dragon and Emily had said sorry for entering our garden uninvited, whereupon the constable declared the matter closed and escorted Emily and her governess back through the house and out of our front door. In the confusion they almost forgot their red ball, but I fetched it and chased after them.

'Your ball!' I cried as they hurried down the street, Emily's hand clutched firmly in that of her governess. 'Your ball!'

'Shoo!' cried Miss Wasply. 'Shoo, you dirty boy!'

'Keep it for me,' called Emily over her shoulder, almost tripping as she strained to see me. 'I'll come back for it. I'll see you again. I promise. Nothing can keep us apart!'

At the time I don't think even Emily realized just how true those words would prove.

I loved her from the word go. Literally, since 'Go' was the first word I ever heard her speak. Loved her, wanted her, needed her, fell completely under her spell. I can't properly explain why, any more than I can properly explain why I kill people. It was just one of those instantaneous, spur-of-the-moment things. One of those divine mysteries. One of those joys.

She was beautiful, of course, and fun, and, a definite recommendation, had a large bag of tasty Belgian chocolates. We were also the same age, which at the time struck me as a coincidence of positively mystical proportions. From the outset I imagined us to be fatally connected.

It runs deeper than that, however. There was something about her – the way her voice echoed from the far side of the wall as though from another world; the way her face shone so perfectly in the winter sunlight; the flashing angelic brilliance of her eyes – that swept me up, like a butterfly in a collector's net. Swept me up and locked me for ever in the cabinet of her perfection. From the outset I knew we'd always be together, clutched in one another's arms, never letting go, indissoluble, connected. We were meant for each other. I knew it from the start. From the first second. But I can't explain. Words would simply cheapen it. Silence is better. The ceaseless eternal hum of silence: that's where my love for Emily sings. Oh my dear, darling Emily. My life, my life.

When she promised we'd see each other again I didn't for one moment doubt her word, a faith that was vindicated three days after our first fateful meeting, when I received an invitation to Sunday tea at her house.

This had not, I later discovered, been issued without some considerable soul-searching on the part of Emily's parents. Miss Wasply had been strongly against the idea, and the fact that I had called her a dragon and shown her my tongue did not stand well in my favour. Emily, however, had been most insistent, dissolving into fits of tears at the least suggestion that I wouldn't be welcome in their house and threatening to drown herself unless I was summoned forthwith for scones and cake. Even that, however, might have been insufficient to secure my invitation had it not been for a most curious chance. Of the three steam-powered bottle openers my father had sold in the early years of the century, one had been purchased by none other than Emily's father. He considered it a splendid appliance and, on the assumption that the son of the inventor of such an exhilarating gadget could not be all bad, the invitation was duly dispatched.

The Emilies lived in Baker Street, in a three-storey house whose upper levels were given over to private use and whose ground floor was taken up by Mr Emilie's pharmacy ('Emilie's of Baker Street, Druggists by Appointment'). To one side of the building – oh how well I remember it! – was a florist's shop, to the other a narrow, sooty alleyway that no one ever used.

My invitation to tea was for 3.30 p.m., at which hour I was duly delivered to the Emilies' front door by Mrs Eggs, who'd spent most of the day scrubbing my face and polishing my shoes in preparation for the outing. I was met by Edie the maid, who escorted me upstairs, Mrs Eggs promising to return at 5.30 to bring me home.

'Raphael!' cried Emily as I was shown into the drawing room. 'This is him, Mama! The boy who got my ball.'

Mr and Mrs Emilie, neither of whom looked remotely like their daughter, Mrs Emilie being short and dumpy, her spouse even shorter and bald, were seated side by side on a yellow chaise longue, with Miss Wasply hovering menacingly behind them. She looked even more like a dragon than I'd remembered, and fixed me with a look of quite murderous distaste. I shuffled my feet nervously.

'I do hope your head is better,' said Mrs Emilie.

'Yes, thank you, ma'am,' I replied.

'Bell's Fairy Cure,' announced her husband. 'That's what you need for a sore head. Never fails.'

'Yes, dear,' said Mrs Emilie, laying her hand on his.

'I am very honoured to be here, ma'am,' I said, repeating a phrase Mrs Eggs had been drumming into my head for the past two days. 'Thank you for having me.'

'Why, Miss Wasply!' cried Mrs Emilie. 'The boy is charming. Positively charming.'

Miss Wasply grimaced.

'Interested in medicinals?' asked Mr Emilie. 'Compounds, purgatives, proprietaries and such like?'

'Yes, sir,' I lied. 'Very interested.'

'Hah!' snorted the pharmacist in evident satisfaction. 'I said he'd be OK. Father's a damn clever man. Would you like to see the shop?'

'I'd be delighted, sir!'

'Now, now dear,' chided his wife. 'The boy's only just arrived. At least let him have his tea. Miss Wasply, kindly take the children upstairs to the nursery. Raphael, we're most pleased to have you here.'

She held out her hand, which, for want of anything better to do, I stepped forward and kissed.

'But how delightful,' laughed Mrs Emilie. 'How utterly charming.'

'I told you you'd like him,' said Emily. 'Didn't I tell you?'

'Yes, you did, dear. Now hurry along with Miss Wasply. And don't eat too much or you'll get indigestion.'

'Mother Seigel's Curative Syrup,' said Mr Emilie as we left the room. 'That's what you need for indigestion. Mother Seigel's Curative Syrup, and if symptoms persist a good dose of Dinneford's Magnesia.'

Tea was held upstairs in Emily's nursery. Miss Wasply sat between us, dispensing fish-paste sandwiches with a look of utmost sourness on her face, constantly interrupting my and Emily's chatter with exhortations to wipe our mouths, not eat so quickly, sit still, cease slurping, not be greedy and, in short, stop doing anything that might reasonably be expected to enhance our enjoyment of the afternoon. When she accidentally spilled scalding tea on my hand I caught a look in her eyes that suggested perhaps the accident wasn't so accidental after all.

'I do so apologize,' she purred. 'I hope it doesn't smart too much!'

'No,' I said, clenching my teeth. 'I can't feel it at all.'

After tea, and much to my relief, Miss Wasply went to her bedroom to write letters to her sisters (of whom she had eight, all married off to clergymen the length and breadth of England) and Emily and I were left to our own devices. She introduced me to her dolls – each, for some reason, named after a month of the year – and took me into her parents' bedroom to show me their giant four-poster bed, which I thought looked like a ship. We did some drawing, spent a while trying to catch a bluebottle that had buzzed in through the window, and then set to work making potions. This was a messy business, involving salt, paint, sugar, talcum powder and several cups of water, and when Miss Wasply eventually returned it was to discover two exceedingly grubby children and a badly stained nursery floor.

'I said you should never have been invited,' she hissed, grabbing me by the ear. 'Just look at all this mess, you filthy boy! Mr Emilie will have something to say about this!'

Which, as it happened, he did, although not at all what Miss Wasply wanted him to say. Far from being upset by our potion making he was, on the contrary, rather pleased with it, patting us both on the head and calling us his 'young apothecaries' before suggesting a guided tour around his chemist's shop.

'But the nursery,' objected Miss Wasply. 'Just look at the state of the nursery!'

'Yes, yes, well, we can sort that our later,' huffed Mr Emilie. 'This is pharmaceuticals, dear lady. And pharmaceuticals must always take precedence.'

And so, to Miss Wasply's evident torment, and our evident delight, Emily and I spent the rest of the day downstairs in her father's pharmacy, standing hand in hand whilst he discoursed at great length on the miraculous laxative effect of Dr Brookes' Cod-Liver Oil, and the extraordinary benefits of Russell's Anti-Corpulent preparation.

'The fat just drops off you,' he trilled. 'Drops off like a skin.'

He allowed us to pry into some of the rosewood drawers lining the wall behind the counter, to reach the highest of which we had to climb a rickety old ladder, and then took us into his workshop, where he brought out, and enthused over, a Boggett's Patent Gas Spatula, whatever the hell that might have been. Then it was back out into the shop proper for a look at his set of graduated glass dispensing measures.

'And this,' he said at the very end of the tour, leading us to a small, glass-fronted cabinet standing at the far end of the counter, 'is the poisons cabinet, where all the dangerous things are kept locked up. Do you see how the bottles have special ridged glass? That's to show their contents might be harmful.'

I pressed my face up against the cabinet, standing on tiptoe to reach it.

'What's that?' I asked, pointing to something on the middle shelf, between a bottle of chloric ether and one of nitric acid. 'That pill.'

'Ah!' said Mr Emilie, smiling. 'That, young man, is a very dangerous poison pill.'

There was nothing inherently attractive about the pill – The Pill – in the way that there was, say, about the tall glass carboys in the shop window, or the display of shiny silver hairbrushes beneath the glass counter. It was just a small, round, white pill, with a slight nick on its edge and no other defining features. I nonetheless felt myself irresistibly drawn to it.

'Yes, indeed, very dangerous,' continued Mr Emilie. 'Made it myself. One and a half grains of strychnine, one and a half grains of arsenic, half a grain of, um, yes, that's right, salt of hydrocyanic acid, and half a grain of crushed ipecacuanha root. Know what a grain is? It's a unit of measurement, about one five-thousandth of a pound. Mix it all together with some syrup of liquid glucose, mould it into shape, and hey presto! Very dangerous. Kill you in seconds, that will!'

I listened intently to this speech, and then turned back to The Pill nestling on its glass dish in the middle of the display cabinet. It seemed to throb somewhat as I looked at it and, although I was probably just imagining things, to emit a very faint humming sound. It really was the most alluring thing I'd ever seen in my life. Apart from Emily, of course.

'I like that,' I said.

'Well, well,' laughed Mr Emilie, putting his arms around our shoulders. 'What a pair of young apothecaries you are!'

Later, as I walked home through the park with Mrs Eggs, I recited The Pill's formula over and over again to myself. By the time we reached White Lodge I had it by heart, and have never forgotten it since.

From that day onwards Emily and I were inseparable. Each morning I would be delivered to Baker Street by Mrs Eggs, or Emily to White

Lodge by Miss Wasply, who steadfastly refused to come beyond our front gate as though to do so would be to expose herself to some hopelessly incurable contagion, and the hours would then be whiled away engaged in the sort of pursuits that to adults appear inconsequential but are to children of the very greatest significance.

Encampments would be built out of cushions and old sheets and then defended against hordes of imaginary invaders. Expeditions would be launched to the farthest reaches of our not very big garden, and plays written and then performed in front of Emily's doll collection, who always gave us a standing ovation for our efforts. We did paintings, and made potions, and rang Emily's next-door neighbour's bell before running off to hide in the alley that separated their houses. Sometimes we would watch Mr Emilie in his pharmacy, or my father in his workshop. Always, when the opportunity arose, I would gaze longingly at The Pill.

We were taken to museums, and galleries, and parks, and, once, to St Paul's Cathedral, where we climbed right up into the vast dome and made our voices echo back and forth inside it. We went to Madame Tussauds, and for picnics in Kew Gardens, and to the Hippodrome to watch the Australian Tree Fellers, who could cut their way through a tree-trunk in under three minutes. And, our favourite trip of all, across Regent's Park to London Zoo, where we would each pay our 6d entrance fee and spend the day peering at the giraffes, and the reptiles, and the lions, and pleading with Miss Wasply to let us have a go on the giant wrinkly elephant that gave rides to the public.

'Absolutely not,' she would snap. 'Now come away or it'll tread on you.'

'I wish it'd tread on you,' I'd mutter.

'What was that? What did you say, you frightful boy?'

'Nothing, Miss Wasply. Just talking to myself!'

'Huh! Dreadful child!'

In the September of 1906 I was, despite the most violent and lachrymose protests on my part, sent away to continue my education at a

329

small boarding school in Kent. Far from diminishing the intensity of my relationship with Emily, however, this enforced separation only served to augment it, just as some plants, when shut away from the light, will sprout to a far greater height than those left in it. Deprived of each other's physical presence, we merely resorted to other means of communication, writing to each other at least four times daily, and composing long, ill-rhyming poetic eulogies to friendship, chocolate, Australian tree fellers and other subjects of mutual concern. Where I should have been learning my Latin subjunctives, and times tables, and important dates in British history, my mental energies were instead focused exclusively upon Emily, which largely explains my abysmal school record of the period.

And then in the holidays I'd come home and we'd pick up precisely where we'd left off, as though our days apart had not been real days at all but rather dream ones, from which we awoke to find ourselves once again in each other's company. The thought has sometimes struck me, indeed, that perhaps my entire life has just been a dream, punctuated by occasional moments of waking when Emily appears to pull me back to the reality of myself.

Thus our friendship – what a risibly small word for such an im-measurably vast experience – grew and developed as the years went by. In 1907 I was taken with the Emilies for a summer holiday in Scotland, exacerbating still further my unpopularity with Miss Wasply by putting a crab in her bed, and in 1909 Emily came down with Mrs Eggs to watch me take part in the school sports day (I was in four races and came last in all of them). We still made camps and performed plays, although less often as we grew older, and went through a long phase of nurses and patients, in which I would spend entire days mummified in bandages whilst Emily clucked about and tended to my every need. On Sunday, 1st January 1910, the afternoon of my tenth birthday, we stole The Pill. And with that my world was complete.

And then, suddenly, unexpectedly, insanely, after four years of unmitigated bliss, the most wonderful four years of my life, the four years upon which, in a sense, all my other years have been built, my darling Emily was taken from me. And I lay the blame entirely at the feet of that purse-lipped, bug-eyed killjoy of a governess.

But I had, of course, decided to kill Miss Wasply some time before Emily's departure. It was the start of the Christmas holidays, 1909, and I had gone to bed as usual the night before, tucked up and given a big slobbery kiss by Mrs Eggs, then woken up with the dawn, intent on murder.

'I'm going to kill her,' I thought to myself as a robin redbreast chirruped on my windowsill. 'It's time to slay the dragon.'

I had always hated Miss Wasply. Had hated her from the moment I first set eyes on her. I hated her giant shovel of a chin, and I hated the way she reprimanded Emily, and I hated the way she took every possible opportunity to demean and hurt and humiliate and undermine me. I hated everything about the woman, to the extent that I even harboured a vague dislike for the chairs she sat on and the cutlery she used and the clothes she wore (which were always grey, and shiny, and very tight-fitting, like a sort of chain-mail).

I hated Miss Wasply, and Miss Wasply, in turn, hated me. I don't believe I've ever met anyone either before or since who disliked me with quite the same degree of intensity and spleen that old Waspy Wasply brought to the task. Her eyes smouldered venomously whenever I was nearby, and her body went rigid, and her chest heaved as though she were about to gag. She chided and rebuked and insulted and snapped at me as though my very existence was some sort of personal insult, and although it's really no excuse for what I did to her, I nonetheless sincerely believe that had I not acted first it could well have been Emily's governess who murdered me rather than the other way around, such was the depth of her animosity.

'Vile boy!' she would hiss at the very least provocation. 'You'll come to no good, mark my words! It'll be a bad end for you.'

And, to be fair, she wasn't that far wrong.

I toyed with a variety of scenarios to bump her off, such as shooting her, or poisoning her, or stabbing her, or bludgeoning her to death with the giant bible she kept beside her bed, or even kidnapping her, drugging her, stripping her naked, covering her in honey and dumping her on top of a large beehive, the occupants of which would then, if all went according to plan, swarm all over her and sting her to death.

Then, however, I remembered there was a small barrel of gunpowder in the cellar, and decided to do it with that instead.

The gunpowder had been made up by Father some months previously for use in a series of experiments he was conducting about the effects on mice of being sent to the moon attached to large home-made rockets. The resultant ear-shattering bangs and whooshes and terrified mousey squeaks hadn't been at all to the liking of our neighbours, however, and after an avalanche of complaints the experiments had eventually been abandoned, the few surviving rodents being released into the park, and the half-empty barrel of gunpowder consigned to a lonely corner of the basement. I went down to see if it was still there, which it was, and to check the powder hadn't got damp, which it hadn't.

'Perfect!' I chuckled to myself, stirring my finger around inside the barrel. 'Absolutely damned perfect!'

I started that same day by smuggling two small, gunpowder-filled paper bags into Emily's house, sneaking upstairs late in the afternoon during a game of hide-and-seek and hiding them in the shadows beneath Miss Wasply's bath (she had her own private bathroom, next door to her bedroom, right at the very top of the house and overlooking the sooty alleyway beneath).

I did the same the following day, and the day after, and for the three days after that, at which point Emily was starting to wonder where this sudden fixation for hide-and-seek had come from. I, meanwhile, had slipped into a sort of homicidal trance. As others around me gorged themselves on Christmas treats, my energies were focused on the exploding of Miss Wasply. It was like being caught up in a carefully choreographed dance, one step leading inexorably onwards to the next, and then the next, and then the next, and so on, and so on. I lost myself in the rhythm of murder. I danced the gunpowder tango. It was all so very obvious and easy. All so engrossing. And all the while, an unsuspecting Miss Wasply was nightly soaping her armpits atop a small but growing mound of high explosive.

After days of feverish preparation I crept up to the bathroom for the last time. Crouching under the bathtub, I pushed one end of a makeshift fuse (string soaked in methylated spirits) into the match-box, and ran the other up behind a pipe, through a vent in the wall and so downwards into the alley below. Things very nearly fell apart at this final stage, when my intended victim came back upstairs unexpectedly. Fortunately, however, she was so intent on twisting my ear and informing me what a vile, thieving little sneak I was for invading the sanctuary of her private bathroom that she quite failed to notice the thin thread of fuse emerging from the air vent high up in the wall.

'Gross little boy,' she spat, dragging me back down the stairs. 'If you belonged to me I'd give you a jolly good spanking!'

'Sorry, Miss Wasply,' I said humbly. 'I promise I won't do it again. Really I do.'

I now had a quite brilliant means of disposing of the old boot, yet I held back from lighting the fuse at my first available opportunity. I hadn't yet told Emily of my murderous intentions, and had a nagging feeling that she wouldn't approve.

It wasn't until a week or so later, as the Christmas holidays drew to a close, that I felt I was ready to bring my plans to fruition.

On the night in question I clambered into bed fully clothed, pulling the sheets up to my neck so Mrs Eggs wouldn't notice I was still dressed when she came to give me my good-night kiss. I pretended to go to sleep. I got up again, crept downstairs, sneaked out of the house and hurried over to Baker Street. I looked left and right and then slipped into the sooty alleyway that ran down the side of Emily's home. I located my hanging fuse. I pulled out a box of matches. I took a deep breath. Finally, I looked up at the bathroom, where, as I knew she would be, Miss Wasply was splashing around in her bath, just as she did every night at this hour, regular as clockwork.

Steam billowed from the window, and I could hear a faint sound of singing.

> Onward, Christian soldiers,
> Marching as to war,
> With the cross of Jesus
> Going on before.

It crossed my mind that I hadn't used enough gunpowder – or perhaps too much – but there was no turning back now. Without further ado, like the climax to a particularly vigorous polka, I struck a match and held it to the fuse, standing on tiptoes because its end was swaying two feet above my head. A thin tongue of orange-blue flame swept upwards into the night, hissed through the air vent and disappeared into the bathroom.

> Christ, the royal master,
> Leads against the foe,
> Forward into battle
> See his banners—

The last word was drowned out in an ear-splitting boom. The alleyway lit up momentarily in infernal shades of red, a fist of smoke and debris punched out of the bathroom window and, at the same instant, like a cork out of a champagne bottle, Miss Dorothy Wasply's large iron bathtub, with her still in it, blasted straight through the roof of the house and up into the night sky, rising to a height of some 20 feet above the chimney-pots before coming down with a crash on to the roof of a neighbouring residence.

Such was my short-sightedness then – and, indeed, throughout my life – it never occurred to me to think beyond the thrilling act of murdering Emily's governess. I thought that life could go on as before, that my friendship with Emily would somehow continue unchecked or, at the very least, Emily would write to me. Which of course she didn't. Every day I expected a letter, but none ever came, and eventually I stopped expecting altogether. In the absence of anything else to take my mind off the pain, I started working very hard at school.

'Remarkable improvements,' said my report at the end of the first term after Emily's departure. 'Young Phoenix really has become a completely different person.'

There are about 30 inches left at the bottom of this wall, and I shall fill them – scrunching my letters up a little so as to fit them all in – not so much with an anecdote as a brief snapshot of a moment of my past.

The time is June 1919 – 13th June, to be precise. I have just seen my father for the last time, and have left him sitting in his workshop with a colander on his head. I am due to catch a train down to Hampshire, for dinner with Meaty, but have a half-hour or so to kill before I need to be at the station, and therefore decide to take a brief turn around the garden at White Lodge. Somewhere deep within me I suspect it will be the last time I will see it, and I wish to store up some memories to fuel me through my life.

I run my hand along the garden wall – its brickwork buckled and bulging; its beard of ivy now, for the most part, dead – and for old times' sake climb the plum tree. I poke into the shrubbery where Emily and I used to build camps, and throw stones into the algaed pond. I breathe the air, and kneel down to sniff the grass, and remember all the happy days I've spent there.

I do all this, and then turn to go back into the house. As I do so, however, something catches my eye, at the very far end of the garden, half hidden in the long grass that tufts about the foot of the wall. I cross to it, and pull it out. It is an old punctured red ball, with which, evidently, no one has played for a good ten years. I turn it over in my hands a couple of times, and then, calmly, collectedly, without fuss, drop kick it over the wall and into the park beyond. I smile, and then set off to murder Prince Gummy-Molars.

# CHAPTER NINETEEN

I'VE HAD THE most unfortunate experience with Dr Bannen. So engrossed was I in writing the above that I didn't hear his Land Rover when it pulled up outside at 3 p.m. And then when he knocked at the door I assumed it was the phantom knocker again, and I rushed up to the roof and leant over the battlements and shouted: 'Fuck off, you horrible little shit! Fuck off and leave me alone!' And poor old Dr Bannen thought I was talking to him and had the most appalling wheezing fit, huffing and puffing, and practically coughing himself right off the edge of the cliff.

'I'm so sorry, Dr Bannen,' I cried, hurrying downstairs and out of the front door. 'What a terrible mistake. I thought you were somebody else. A blond child.'

This seemed to upset him even more, his face turning so purple it was practically black, as though he'd been down a coal mine.

'What can I do, Dr Bannen?' I asked, concerned. 'Should I slap you on the back?'

He waved his arms frantically, indicating that that was the last thing on God's earth I should do.

'Wa . . . huh huh huh . . . wa . . . huh huh huh . . . water.'

'Yes, yes, of course, I'll fetch you some right away.'

I slipped back into the castle and returned with a large glass of tap water with an apologetic slice of lemon in it.

'Here you are, Dr Bannen.'

He shook his head despairingly.

'Allergic to citrus fruits,' he wheezed.

I threw the water away and fetched another glass, which he downed in one gulp. His breathing eased up a little, and his face inched its way slowly back through the colour spectrum from purple to pink.

'I really can't say how sorry I am, Dr Bannen,' I apologized again. 'A terrible misunderstanding. It's just that someone's been banging on my castle door all week, and making rude noises through the letterbox, and I'm at the end of my tether. I feel like a prisoner in my own home.'

I explained about the knocking, and the raspberries, and the stone throwing, and the face in the bracken and all the other strange things that had gone on since I last saw him.

'I don't know who's doing it, but it's driving me mad. To start with, it was innocuous enough, but now it's happening on an hourly basis. A half-hourly basis. It's like I'm under siege. Someone seems to want to drive me insane.'

Dr Bannen, now all but recovered from his convulsions, tutted and shook his head.

'I can understand your frustration, Mr Phoenix,' he wheezed. 'You gave me a bit of a shock there, but having heard your story I can see why you were so upset. A face in the bracken, you say?'

'That's right. A pale face, with blond hair. I thought it might have been a rabbit or something. And they threw an egg too. It landed on the dome.'

'Extraordinary,' he said, scratching his head. 'Extraordinary.'

'I've tried to catch them, but they're always too quick. Even when I stand right behind the door I still can't get it open in time to see who it is. I've even tried giving them money to go away, but it hasn't done any good. I'm at my wits' end.'

'Have you contacted the police?'

'I don't see what they could do. And I don't want to make a big fuss. I just want to be left alone and in peace. I don't want people blowing raspberries through my letterbox.'

He agreed that it was indeed a most unacceptable state of affairs, and promised to ask around in the village for anyone matching the description of my tormentor, although I doubt he will. Despite his professions of support, I don't think he actually believed a word I'd said and was simply humouring me, like a psychiatrist humours a particularly truculent patient. I could see it in his eyes. He thought I'd made the whole thing up. That I'd gone gaga.

'Anyway, it doesn't matter,' I said, sighing. 'Your arrival seems to have frightened him off, whoever he is, and hopefully he won't come back again. Come on, let's unload the car. And I really am very sorry about swearing at you like that.'

'Not at all,' he coughed. 'All in the line of duty.'

We went to and fro in silence, removing the boxes of provisions and placing them on the doorstep. (I had, of course, kept the front door well closed – couldn't have Dr Bannen seeing my suicide note. His lungs wouldn't have coped.) I thought about mentioning the hammering in my back, which was by now so intense it at times threatened to knock me right off my feet, but decided against it. If he had trouble believing there was someone knocking on my door, I couldn't see the erstwhile doctor having much idea what to do about a pair of delinquent wings. So I kept quiet on the matter.

'I heard you went down to the village the other day,' he said after a while, trying to sound casual but clearly itching to hear about my little foray into the outside world. 'I met Nurse Patel in the post office and she told me.'

'You know her?'

'By sight. Nice woman. Indian. She said you needed some pens.'

I heaved the last box out of the Land Rover and trudged towards the front door.

'She was very kind. I was rather tired after the walk down the track and so she went into the village for me. It was a great help.'

'You should have asked me. I would have got them for you.'

'It was something of an emergency,' I explained. 'I needed them immediately and couldn't wait till today.'

He shrugged.

'She said her name was Emily.'

'Who?'

'The nurse.'

'Did she? I don't know. Doesn't sound very Indian, does it? Here, let me help you with that.'

He relieved me of the last box, plonked it on the doorstep and then counted out my pension money. For the following week we left it that he'd simply bring the same again. I naturally made no mention of the fact that the following week I'd be dead.

'Perhaps I misheard,' I said as he handed me my cash.

'Misheard?' He repeated as I handed him back most of the money to pay for my supplies.

'Nurse Patel's first name. Perhaps she didn't say Emily at all. It's just that I once knew someone called Emily. Maybe she's called something completely different.'

He clearly didn't have the least idea what I was going on about, and, as he always did when I was confusing him, took refuge in his notebook, carefully folding away the notes I had just given him and ticking off the provisions he'd just unloaded as though the familiarity of the goods on his list offered some sort of shield against my ramblings. He remained in the book until I'd fallen silent, whereupon he judged it safe to emerge once again.

'Now,' he huffed, going round to the far side of his Land Rover, opening the door and removing a plastic bag with 'Gordon's Grapes' stencilled on the side from the passenger seat. 'I've got that wine you ordered. The special wine. I'm afraid they didn't have any of the ones you asked for, so I got this. I hope it's OK. The man in the shop recommended it. Said for the price it was very reasonable. You get a free poster of the wine-growing regions of France as well.'

He came back round and gave me the bag. I pulled out a slightly dusty bottle with a frayed label.

'A Domaine de Chevalier 1982,' I said, delighted. 'Excellent. Absolutely excellent. I couldn't have chosen better myself.'

'It was £32.50. You did say it had to be over £30.'

'I did indeed,' I replied. 'Your man was right. For the price it's very reasonable.'

I disappeared into the castle and returned with the money to pay him, my meagre savings now utterly exhausted.

'Seeing the year out in style, are we?' he rasped.

'Absolutely. It's not every day you get to stand on the threshold of a new millennium. This should ease things along very nicely.'

I examined the bottle for a moment in the watery afternoon light, and then returned it to its bag.

'They've got a big firework display down in the village tonight,' said Dr Bannen. 'You should have a good view from up here. Apparently it's going to be a corker, although I'll have to watch it from indoors. The smoke gets right down my windpipe.'

He removed a large check handkerchief from his pocket and blew his nose into it, and then made for the front of his car.

'Anyway, I'd better be off, Mr Phoenix. Elsie doesn't like to be left alone in the surgery for too long. Gives her the jitters.'

I smiled at his traditional parting line, feeling, as I did so, a twinge of sadness that this was the last time I'd ever see him. He might have thought I was a fruitcake, but he's always been civil to me, and I took a step forward, intending to shake hands with him. As I did so, however, he turned towards me and the handshake somehow transmuted into a full-scale hug.

'Goodbye, dear Dr Bannen,' I said, patting the back of his tweed jacket. 'You've been so good to me.'

He didn't actually push me off, he was far too polite for that, but he stiffened noticeably, and his breath, still wheezy after his earlier coughing fit, began to scrape and scratch like sandpaper rubbed across a brick. I was tempted to exacerbate his discomfort by planting a kiss on his cheek, but, realizing that such a gesture might well cause his ailing respiratory system to pack in altogether, settled instead for giving him a good hard squeeze, before letting him go.

'I just wanted you to know how much I appreciate your coming all the way up here with my shopping,' I went on, backing away slightly. 'I know you think I'm a bit strange, but you've always been very kind to me and I don't think I've ever thanked you properly for that.'

'Don't mention it,' he gasped painfully, moving a little to his left so as to bring the Land Rover's open front door between us. 'Please don't mention it. Ever again. It's really not necessary. All part of the job.'

'Well, just so long as you know I'm grateful.'

'I do!' he wheezed. 'I do!'

He pulled the door protectively around him as though it were some sort of bathrobe, and stared at me nervously. He was clearly terrified I might try to embrace him a second time, and to put him at his ease I backed away several more feet.

'Anyway,' I said, 'you've been my lifeline. A Happy New Year, Dr Bannen. A Happy New Thousand Years. And the same to Mrs Bannen.'

He remained motionless for a moment, his cheek twitching slightly, his chest heaving in and out like a pair of blacksmith's bellows, and then, apparently convinced the danger was over, relaxed somewhat.

'Thank you, Mr Phoenix,' he said. 'Thank you. And the same to you.'

He edged out from behind his door and, rather to my surprise, extended his hand.

'Happy New Year.'

It was a touching gesture, especially considering how scared of me he clearly was, and, stepping forward, I shook. It's strange how even the most insubstantial of people assume an overwhelming significance when you know you'll never see them again. I held his palm, his rather sweaty palm, for a moment, and then we each backed

341

away, me to the castle doorstep, he into the driver's seat of his Land Rover.

'I didn't even ask you if you had a good Christmas,' I said.

'Very nice,' he replied, slamming the Land Rover door and starting the engine. 'Although Elsie's mother had a bit of a turn during *The Towering Inferno*. Seemed to think the whole thing had been sparked off by her electric blanket. Got very upset. What about yourself?'

'Very peaceful,' I said. 'By the way, I've still got Mrs Bannen's pudding bowl.'

'Give it to me next week,' he said, swinging the Land Rover around and pointing it down towards the village. 'Hope you enjoyed it.'

'It was the most wonderful pudding I've ever tasted.'

'I'll let Elsie know,' he shouted. 'She'll be ever so pleased. Good-bye, Mr Phoenix. See you next week!'

And with a beep of his horn he lurched off downhill. He stopped after 50 yards, however, and reversed back up to the castle.

'I'll forget my own head one of these days,' he said. 'This came for you.'

He handed a large white envelope out of the window before driving off again with a toot and a cough. I watched him as he wound his way down towards the village, and then, when he was out of sight, ripped open the letter, the first I had ever received at the castle – and probably the last too. This is what it said inside.

'I am delighted to send you my warm congratulations on your hundredth birthday, together with my best wishes for an enjoyable celebration. Elizabeth R.'

Would you believe it! A telegram from the Queen. I wonder what she'd say if she knew what sort of celebration I'd got planned to-night. Silly old moo.

It's 7 p.m. and in just six hours I'll be dead. There's still a lot to do, and not much time to do it in. I need to keep pushing on. No rest for the suicidal.

I hadn't finished describing Miss Wasply's murder when Dr

Bannen arrived at 3 p.m. – so much for my boast that I could get it done in under ten hours – and it was only two hours after he'd left that I finally brought the whole episode to a close. It spilled out of the upstairs gallery by a few lines, but only a few. Aside from Mr Popplethwaite. it's by far the best-fitting of all my murders.

I've now written my way across and around the landing wall from the door of the gallery to that of my bedroom, through which I will be passing in just a couple of paragraphs' time. My bedroom, of course, is the last room of my life. A quarter of the way around it is the door to the roof stairs, which is where my note will end, and with it me too. I need to increase the size of my writing somewhat, so as to hit the mark perfectly. I don't have much more to say now.

I'm using the second of my two purple pens (the first, remember, was used up filling in the space above each doorway). If I write sparingly it should last me right the way through to the end. I'm glad. It's so much nicer than that horrible shit-brown of the last pen in each pack. Purple is a good colour to die in.

The knocking's started up again, and the raspberries – they stopped briefly after Dr Bannen's visit – but I'm just ignoring them. And my back too. I'm closing myself off. Barricading myself in the mansions of my memory. Fuck them. Fuck the world. They – it – can't hurt me now. Nothing and no one can hurt me now. Except me, of course.

Now, however, I must do my last murder. Or my first murder, depending on which way you look at these things. It's a quick one, and I reckon I can probably fit it into a single column. Let's see.

# CHAPTER TWENTY

I DON'T REALLY remember much about my very first murder, committed in the early hours of Monday, 1st January 1900. In fact, I don't remember anything about it at all, and am therefore wholly reliant upon second-hand accounts for what follows.

It was my mother that I killed, and I did it with my head, which had, apparently, assumed a most unnatural position relative to the entrance to her womb. The more she tried to force me from her, the more damage I caused, ripping her poor delicate insides to shreds. I was eventually delivered by Caesarean section, but by then she was gone. Father, I am told, wept for an entire week.

Notices of her death appeared in *The Times*, the *Inventors' Review* and on page nine of the February issue of *Patents Magazine*, alongside an article on Mr Hardcastle's Patent Pneumatic Boot-Trees. I used to possess copies of all of these, but they have, over the years, been lost or destroyed.

I do, however, still have a photo of her – a dog-eared, fading, crumpled old thing that I carry with me wherever I go. The Photo. She is wearing a high-necked white dress and is smiling wanly into camera. Father was right. She *was* beautiful. Aside from Emily, she's the only person I've ever really loved, even though I never actually knew her.

She's buried in a desolate corner of Highgate Cemetery, in a grave with a large stone angel in place of a headstone. I used to visit it a lot as a child, but haven't been for years now. The last I saw of it the angel was wrapped in a thick muffler of ivy, and one of its outspread wings had dropped off.

And that's all I can really tell you. I wasn't even a minute old when I started murdering. Like I said way back at the beginning of this note, I'm a natural-born killer. Always have been, always will be. There's no escaping destiny.

# Chapter Twenty-One

And that completes my tally. Ten decades, ten murders (eleven, if you count the albino twins as two). And now the story's all but finished. And so, too, my life. I must give the castle a quick tidy, spruce myself up a bit, maybe make myself one final meal (curried mackerel fillets with melted cheese on top . . . Yummmmm!). And then it's up to the dome to die. I'd like to see the fireworks before I go. I've always enjoyed fireworks. They're like dreams in the sky.

Before any of that, however, I must tell you what happened the other night with Emily. The night before I started the note. The night *why* I started the note. It is, you see, the key to the whole thing. Had Emily not done what she did, none of this would be going on. I'd still be wanting to live. The Pill would have stayed in my pocket. As with so many things in my life, with *all* things in my life, it all leads back to Emily.

Eleven nights ago, that being the night of Monday, 20th December, I was sitting up in my dome gazing out into the darkness, as I had done every night, without exception, since I first arrived in the castle 15 years previously. The air was cold, with a slight hint of frost, and I had wrapped a thick blanket around my shoulders, like a shawl.

The sky was clear, and full of stars. I was on my thirtieth or fortieth cigarette of the day.

I didn't notice the knocking at first, for I was lost in a twilight world of empty thoughts and barren recollections. Gradually, however, over a period of minutes, I became aware of a hammering on the front door. It took a further few moments for awareness to translate itself into action, whereupon I rose stiffly to my feet and shuffled across the roof to the western battlements (how much older I was just a week ago!).

'Yes,' I croaked into the darkness beneath. 'Who's there?'

'Raphael?' came a familiar voice. 'Raphael, are you up there?'

'Emily? Is that you?'

'Of course it's me. Come on down and let me in. It's cold out here.'

I leaned over the battlements to try to get a glimpse of her, but aside from a hint of golden hair I could make out nothing in the gloom. My old heart thudding with excitement, I therefore fumbled my way downstairs, switched on the hall light and heaved open the castle's front door. She was standing on the doorstep, swamped inside a large duffel coat with a newspaper sticking out of one pocket, as beautiful and youthful as ever. Her nose, I noticed, was red with the cold, and I ushered her in immediately.

'What a wonderful surprise,' I said, leading her into the kitchen. 'What brings you to this neck of the woods?'

'Oh, I was just passing.'

'No one just passes here, Emily. There's nowhere to pass to. It's the middle of nowhere.'

'Well, I thought it would be nice to see you. It's been a long time.'

'It has indeed,' I said, pouring her out a glass of red wine. 'It's always a long time. Here, this should take the edge off the chill.'

'I'd prefer a cup of tea if you've got one,' she said.

'Of course, of course. I'll boil some water.' I took back the glass and downed it myself, moving across the room and switching on the electric kettle.

'You look well,' I remarked, searching in the cupboard for tea bags.

'Just like you always do. It never fails to amaze me. Most people, if you didn't see them for 15 years, would have changed at least a bit in the interim. But you look just the same. Always have looked just the same. You never change. It's extraordinary. Is it some sort of cream you use?'

She laughed.

'Not that I'm aware of. I guess life's been kind to me. You look well too, Raphael.'

'Don't patronize me, Emily,' I said, still searching for my tea bags. 'I neither look nor feel well, and you damned well know it. I've grown old these last few years. Very old. My joints ache, my eyesight's going and it's as much as I can do to get out of bed in the morning. Look at all these frightful wrinkles. It's like I'm cracking up. Now what on earth have I done with the tea bags? I'm sure they were in here somewhere.'

She stepped forward and, reaching over my shoulder, removed a box of Earl Grey from the shelf directly in front of me.

'See what I mean,' I sighed. 'I'm going senile.'

'Shall I make the tea?' she asked, laying a hand on my arm.

'I think it might be best. Milk's in the fridge. Don't worry about me. I'll stick with the wine. God, it's good to see you. I've missed you terribly. I only really feel alive when I'm with you.'

She gave me a kiss on the cheek, and then made her drink. It was chilly in the kitchen, so we trooped upstairs to my bedroom, where we switched on my old bar heater and sat down in front of it, side by side on the edge of the bed. I sipped at my wine, and lit a cigarette. Emily took off her duffel coat with the newspaper in the pocket, as she did so removing a gift-wrapped parcel with a ribbon tied round it from an inner recess of the coat.

'I almost forgot,' she said. 'I brought you a present. Christmas and birthday combined. I hope you like it.'

I laid aside my glass and, with unsteady hands, removed the wrapping paper. Inside was a purple silk shirt, its fabric shimmering in the crimson light of the heater.

'A purple shirt,' I said. 'Thank you. Just what I've always wanted.'

'Aren't you going to try it on?'

'Not just now,' I coughed, folding the gift and putting it on my pillow. 'I can't be bothered to change. Maybe later.'

She took my withered old hand in hers, and stared into my eyes.

'Are you OK here in the castle, Raphael?' she asked. 'Perhaps it wasn't such a good idea you coming here. It seems to have worn you down.'

'It's not the castle,' I sighed. 'And by the way, thank you for letting me stay here. No, it's me, Emily. Like I told you, I'm getting old. It's all catching up with me. It had to happen eventually. If it hadn't been here it would have been somewhere else. You can't go on for ever. I think I'm coming to the end.'

She was silent for a moment, and then said:

'Well, at least your face is better. Last time I saw you it was all covered in bandages.'

'Yes,' I admitted, 'at least my face is better.'

We supped our respective drinks, and warmed our feet at the fire, and, after some further small talk, began, as we always do when we're together, to mull over the old days. My present with Emily has always, in a sense, been a step backwards into the past, and tonight was no exception. We recalled old dragon Wasply, and the garden at White Lodge, and our time together on the *Scythia* ('What were that old American couple called?' she asked. 'The ones we played quoits with?' 'The Flumsteins,' I replied), and a host of other shared memories, drifting back through time whilst around us time itself moved forwards to the faint tick-tick of my watch. I chain-smoked, and soon the atmosphere was thick and hazy.

I don't know how long we'd been talking for, although it must have been a while, because I was nearing the end of my second bottle of wine, when Emily suddenly asked, a propos of nothing:

'Do you remember that old pill, Raphael? The poison pill, the one we switched with the mint?'

She couldn't have surprised me more if she'd ripped off her

clothes and done a handstand right there in front of me (now there's a thought!). Since the day we'd stolen it all those many years before there'd been no mention whatsoever of The Pill between us. Not even a flicker of a mention. So silent had Emily been on the subject, indeed, that I'd convinced myself it was somehow taboo, and had avoided ever bringing it up. That she should ask about it now, so suddenly, and after so long, really took me aback. And delighted me too. It was, after all, a part of our shared experience.

'Do you?' she asked again. 'Do you remember it?'

'Of course I do,' I said. 'In fact, I've still got it. Look.'

I dipped my fingers into my pyjama pocket and removed The Pill, holding it out on the flat of my palm. It looked to all intents and purposes exactly as it had that day I first saw it in the poisons cabinet of Mr Emilie's pharmacy, way back at the start of the century. As it did then, it seemed to exude a faint hum. It was almost as if it was pleased to see Emily.

'What on earth makes you mention it now?' I asked. 'After all these years?'

'I was just curious,' she smiled. 'Fancy you keeping it all this time. Can I hold it?'

'Of course you can.' I dropped The Pill into her outstretched hand. 'I thought you'd completely forgotten about it. Or didn't want to talk about it. I thought perhaps you felt guilty that we'd stolen it. It's one of the few things I've kept from those days, you know. I never let it out of my sight.'

Emily weighed The Pill in her palm. It was, I noticed, almost the same colour as her skin, so that it seemed to be a part of her, like a small white pimple.

'Isn't it funny?' she said. 'Here we are talking about the past, and then an actual piece of it suddenly appears. A tiny blob of our youth. Why have you kept it all this time?'

'It's hard to explain,' I sighed, lighting another cigarette and blowing a halo of smoke over my companion's golden head. 'I don't really understand it myself. It just makes me feel . . . secure. It's something to cling to. To hold.'

'How very eccentric you are, Raphael,' she laughed, standing up. 'You and your little ways. You're a law unto yourself.'

She was still for a moment, examining The Pill, and then, suddenly, shaking her hair and giggling, she cried: 'Catch me if you can!' and disappeared out of the bedroom on to the landing.

'What are you doing, Emily?' I called after her. 'Where are you going?'

There was no reply, however, just a loud 'Oooooooo!' such as ghosts make, followed by a faint patter of feet on the stairs.

'Emily, stop this!' I shouted. 'I'm an old man! I want my pill.'

I struggled to my feet and went out on to the landing. The castle was very dark and silent.

'Emily? Emily?'

No reply.

I crossed to the top of the stairs.

'Emily?'

'Ooooooooo!' came a ghostly wail from below. 'Ooooooo!'

I was annoyed at her for teasing me like this – I was nearly a hundred years old, for God's sake! – and yet at the same time couldn't help smiling to myself. The challenge, the receding patter of feet, the silly noises, the hunt – it took me back to the days of my youth, when Emily and I would chase each other for hours around the dark, dusty recesses of White Lodge. I felt, for a moment, like a child again. I felt the excitement of the game.

'I'm going to get you!' I cooed softly. 'Fee fi fo fum!'

I crept down the stairs and into the front hall, moving from room to room, hunting my quarry.

'Come out, come out wherever you are!' I sang. 'I'm going to find you!'

I heard a faint footfall in the kitchen and rushed in, but she somehow managed to slip out behind me and scurried up the stairs again.

'Too slow,' she called, laughing. 'Too slow, old man!'

I followed her upstairs again, and then down, and then up, and then down, and all round the castle. She always managed to keep one step ahead, however, laughing and goading me and then slipping away into the darkness, and eventually I gave up chasing altogether and instead crouched down in the shadows at the foot of the roof stairs, remaining there in total silence until, uncertain where I'd gone, she crept cautiously back into my bedroom again, whereupon I leapt out with a roar of triumph, seized her and threw her on to the bed, collapsing beside her, both of us laughing till we were red in the face.

'I got you!' I cried. 'I got you!'

'That wasn't fair!'

'Why wasn't it fair?'

'You laid a trap, you sneak!'

'Traps are fair! There's no rule that says I have to chase you all the time.'

'You're a cheat,' she said, pinching my arm.

'And you're a bad loser,' I replied, pinching hers. 'Where's my pill?'

'I think I dropped it downstairs somewhere.'

'Emily!'

She laughed, and opened her hand. There it was in her palm.

'Do be careful with it, won't you, Raphael?' she said, handing it back to me. 'Remember what father said about it being so dangerous?'

'One and a half grains of strychnine, one and a half grains of arsenic, half a grain of salt of hydrocyanic acid and half a grain of crushed ipecacuanha root,' I smiled, returning The Pill to my pyjama pocket. 'How could I ever forget?'

'Oh Raphael, you are silly.'

We fell silent. I can't recall her ever looking quite as beautiful as she did at that particular moment. She's always been beautiful, of course, but there, then, in the rich glow of my old bar heater, her pale face slightly flushed with laughter, her perfection reached its peak. (Question: Can perfection reach a peak, or is it by definition already there?) I reached out my withered old hand and stroked her golden hair, and tickled her downy earlobe and then, leaning forward, went to kiss her on the lips. As I did so, however, she raised a finger and touched it to my chin.

'It's over, Raphael,' she said gently.

I moved back a little.

'What's over?'

'It's time to go.'

I sat up and, fumbling for my cigarettes, lit one.

'When will I see you again?'

She came up beside me.

'I don't think you will see me again.'

'Look, I'm sorry if I've upset you, Emily. I didn't mean to. Really, I didn't. I shouldn't have tried to kiss you, I know I shouldn't. I just couldn't help it. I love you so much.'

She took my withered hand in hers. Cupped between her two perfect white hands, it looked, I thought, like a piece of stale luncheon meat.

'It's not because of the kiss, you silly billy,' she said. 'It's just time. It was time long ago. Time to let go.'

'What are you saying, Emily?' I said, my voice rising slightly. 'I don't understand you.'

'Don't you, Raphael?'

'No, I don't. I damn well don't.'

'Sure?'

'Yes, sure. Why do you always have to be so damn . . . so damn . . . cryptic, Emily? What do you mean, it's time to let go? It's you who always comes looking for me, remember. I never come looking for you. I never know where the fuck you are. How can I let go of something I never manage to hold on to in the first place, eh? Tell me that!'

She stroked my head, and smiled.

'Poor Raphael.'

'Don't "Poor Raphael" me. I want to know what you're talking about. Why won't I ever see you again?'

She shook her head.

'Look in the paper, Raphael. It explains it all in the paper.'

For a moment I didn't know what she was talking about. Then, however, I remembered the newspaper in the pocket of her duffel coat. I leaned over and pulled it out. It was *The Times*.

'So what's this supposed to tell me?' I said, flicking through the pages. 'There's been a train crash in Scotland. Unrest in Russia. Riots in Delhi. I can't see the relevance.'

She said nothing, just raised her eyebrows slightly and tilted her head, as if to say, 'Keep looking.'

I went through the whole paper from front to back before I found it, although I think deep down I maybe knew where it was all along and was just trying to put off the moment when I had to confront it, just as at school mealtimes I always used to leave to last the thing on my plate I liked the least. It was only a couple of lines long, if that, and was tucked away amongst a long list of names in a column headed *Deaths*, wedged between Colgate (Priscilla) of Sheffield Park, Sussex, and Honey (Edward) of Bristol. It read as follows:

> **Emilie** – On 6th January, at Baker Street, London, of a fever, Emily, beloved only daughter of Thomas and Sophia Emilie. No flowers by request.

The paper was dated 8th January 1910.

I sat staring at these words for a long time, my cigarette burning itself out in my hand. When I eventually turned back towards her, she'd already started to fade.

'Oh Emily,' I said through the tears. 'Oh Emily.'

It took about an hour for her to go completely, her skin becoming ever more translucent, her hair ever paler, her eyes ever dimmer, until all that was left was just the very faintest shadow of a person. Not even a shadow. Just a rumour of a person. A faint disturbance of the air. A feeling. I held her hand until the end, and whispered her name, and told her how very much I loved her, and how much better my life had been because of her. I told her she was my angel, over and over. And then, finally, with a whispered 'Goodbye, dear Raphael,' she disappeared completely, leaving me alone. So very alone. I've always been so very alone.

I fell asleep quite soon after that. When I woke the following morning I knew for sure it was time to die.

And so now it's the end. Having increased the size of my writing slightly (each letter now about the size of a small toy soldier), I have at last brought the note, after so many rooms, so many pens, so much whiteness, all those hundreds of feet of wall, flush up against the doorway to the roof stairs. Not only that, but I've managed to do it in purple felt-tip too, although, as you can no doubt see from the faintness of my writing, it was a damn close-run thing. The fact that the note has ended precisely where it was supposed to end, and in precisely the right colour, would seem to confirm the correctness of my decision to go ahead with killing myself. A sign! A sign!

It took longer than I expected to write the above. Much longer. I found myself lingering over Emily, drawing out each word, holding back from the moment when I finally had to let her go, so that it is now close on midnight and I have no time left to tidy the castle or make my curried mackerel fillets with melted cheese on top. To be honest, I don't really care. All I want to do now is die.

The fireworks have started down in the village, so it must have gone twelve. A new century has begun. A new millennium. A new life. A time has been ushered in to which I no longer belong. My world now lies firmly in the past. I need to be going.

The hammering on the door is more furious and sustained than ever; likewise the hammering in my back. Boom. Boom. Boom. My whole being is reverberating to the thuds. A few minutes ago I heard one of the downstairs windows shattering. I'm beyond caring.

In a moment I shall pull on a pair of clean trousers and my new purple shirt – might as well keep this purple thing going right to the end – and head up to the dome to take my pill. Before I do, however, I should tell you what I've written above my bedroom doorway.

Over every door in the castle, you will remember, there is now a heading. Above that to the kitchen, for instance, you will find inscribed the words *Lord Slaggsby*, with a drawing of a cream cake; above that to the bathroom, *Luther Dextrus* and a crocodile, and so on, and so on. I have yet to tell you, however, what I've written over the entrance to the final room of my note.

It was a difficult decision, and one with which I've been wrestling for some time now. I very nearly titled it '*First Murder, Last Day, New Millennium*', but in the end settled for something just a little less verbose. You'll see it if you step out on to the landing. No drawing for this last room; just two simple words: 'The End.' Which, as my pen goes dry and I run out of space, it now most assuredly is. Ta-ra.

# AFTERWARDS

THINK OF THE biggest shock you've ever had in your entire life, multiply it by 10 million, then square it, then cube it, then multiply it by another 10 million, and another, and another, and you're still not halfway to understanding how I feel at this present moment.

It didn't work. The Pill didn't work. I popped it, I swallowed it, I sat back – and lived. That was over seven hours ago, and I still haven't come to terms with the whole thing. I doubt I ever will come to terms with the whole thing. The Pill didn't work. It didn't work. It didn't fucking work. Bollocks.

I don't know what to say. Words are wholly inadequate to describe just how betrayed I feel. Ninety fucking years I've carried that Pill around with me; pampering it, caring for it, protecting it, loving it; and the one time I really need the damn thing, it sodding well lets me down. So much for friendship.

And it was all going so perfectly too. I'd finished the note precisely where I'd wanted to finish it, and in precisely the right colour. I'd opened and tasted my bottle of Domaine de Chevalier 1982 and found it to be absolutely delicious (yes, yes, I know, I should have let it breathe, but time was pressing). I'd watched the most glorious firework display down below in the village, the millennial sky graffitied with spatters of red and white and green and blue. Even the knocking on the front door had suddenly ceased, and with it the thudding in my back. Everything seemed so right. So ready. So focused.

'This is it,' I said to myself. 'This is the moment to die. This is the time.'

And so, with the fireworks still popping down below, I crossed to the dome and winched it right the way open so I could see the stars overhead, and sat myself down inside, and smoked a last cigarette, and propped The Photo on my knee. And then I poured myself a glass of claret and, at about half-past midnight, to the sound of an immense bang from the last firework of the night, and without further ado, I placed The Pill on my outstretched tongue and washed it down with a long gulp of wine, settling back in my red wickerwork chair and waiting for the poisons – the strychnine and the arsenic and the salt of hydrocyanic acid – to take effect. I felt neither happy nor sad, nor anything very much at all, except empty. Very, very empty.

But of course they didn't take effect, the strychnine and the arsenic and the salt of sodding hydrocyanic acid. Five seconds passed, then another five, then ten, and before long it was a whole minute since I'd taken The Pill and still nothing had happened.

'Perhaps it has a delayed reaction,' I thought to myself. 'Perhaps it'll hit me any moment.'

The minutes slipped by, however, and any moment never came.

Around the ten-minute mark the thought suddenly struck me that perhaps I *had* died and simply pitched up in an afterlife that was similar in all respects to the one I'd just left. For a moment I felt a surge of relief, but it soon wore off, and by the time 15 minutes had elapsed, at which point I was feeling as fit and healthy as I'd ever felt in my life, I was left with no option but to face up to the truth. The Pill had failed me. I was alive. My suicide was a non-event.

'It didn't work,' I mumbled over and over. 'It didn't fucking work.'

I remained sitting thus, numb, shell-shocked, dazed, right the way through the night, perched on the ruins of my expectations as though on the rubble of a bombed-out city. I didn't move when the great racks of cloud came rolling westwards across the sky like curtains. And I didn't move when the first faint froth of snow began to fall, nor when the fall became heavier and the flakes started to settle on my head and legs and feet, and all around me, colonizing the world with glistening multitudes of whiteness. My wine glass filled with snow, tinged pink by the dregs of my suicidal claret, and snow piled up on top of my head like a hat, and on my hands, and the tip of my nose, and The Photo disappeared beneath a shroud of snow.

'It didn't work,' I mumbled over and over. 'It didn't fucking work.'

And still it snowed and snowed and snowed, so that everything started merging into everything else, and it all became a huge blank.

Only when the clouds eventually began to break like ice-floes, fragmenting and drifting off towards the west, and a thin white streak of dawn began to show over the sea, and the last snow flurries ceased, and the world was wholly silent, did I at last heave myself to my icy feet and slope dejectedly back to my bedroom, the bedroom I thought I'd never see again. Since both my purple felt-tips were empty, I had to use one of those disgusting shit-brown ones; and since there was no space left on the wall before the roof stairs, I was left with no choice but to start again on the other side, to the right of the doorway. Not only, therefore, has my suicide gone for a ball of shit, but my note too. After ending so perfectly, and with such precision, it's now dribbling on like a splatter of watery diarrhoea. The knocking's started again downstairs, and my wings are raging.

I can provide no satisfactory explanation as to why The Pill didn't work. It may be that it had simply faded with age – humans do, after all, so why not pharmaceuticals? – or been affected by the cold weather of the last few days. Possibly the five years it spent Sellotaped beneath my armpit damaged it, or the 24 years in the tight, clammy pocket of my butler's livery, or the five years in the cold, damp atmosphere of Offlag 18B. Maybe Mr Emilie got the formula wrong. Maybe he just made the whole thing up for a bit of fun. Maybe I possess some freak genetic immunity to that particular combination of poisons. Maybe. Maybe. Maybe. There are so many possibilities.

The one idea that I can't seem get out of my head, however – and feel free to laugh if you want to – is that The Pill was somehow *dependent* upon Emily. That her power was its power, and that when she faded, so too, in a sense, did it. I can't really explain what I mean here, because I don't really understand what I mean myself. It's more of a feeling than a theory. No doubt it's complete rubbish, and the real culprit is, after all, age, or the weather, or some inherent flaw in The Pill's constitution. Deep down, however, something within me insists that Emily *was* responsible. She gave me The Pill. And in the end she took it away too. Her departure has thus ruined the death I was about to embrace for no other reason than her departure. What a complete and utter fucking mess.

Anyway, there's no point going on about it. The Pill is gone. Emily is gone. The night is gone. And, in a moment, I will be too. Oh yes, I'm not finished yet. Not by a long shot. I've no intention whatsoever of not dying. Quite the contrary. The failure of my suicide has rendered me more determinedly suicidal than ever, and I fully intend to try again. The Pill, after all, wasn't the only means available to me. Don't forget that I live perched on a cliff, 300 feet above jagged incisors of razor-toothed rock. What pharmacology can't achieve, gravity certainly will. It's now a matter of principle. I'm going up and over, and that'll be the end of it. I refuse to give in and live.

It's almost eight o'clock on the first morning of the third millennium, and the light of dawn is spreading in the eastern sky. The attack on my castle appears to have reached its climax. Downstairs I can hear windows breaking and a splintering of wood as the front door finally succumbs to the fury of the knocking upon it. My sanctuary has been breached and it's time to evacuate. My back, too, feels as though it's about to split open. No more. I must go and kill myself a second time. I urgently need to die.

# MORE AFTERWARDS

Jesus Christ, I'm flying! Flying through the air like a bird! Whoosh! Swoop! Weeeeeeee! Ha-ha! I'm going up and up and up, and now dowwwwwwwn! Weh-heh! Tra-la-la! This is fantastic. I feel so happy! I feel so free!

You've got to hear what's happened. It's incredible! (Watch this, I'm going to do a loop-the-loop – Wo-oh-oh-oh-oh-oh-oh!)

I went up to the roof to jump off the battlements, just as I said I would. And behind me, in the depths of the castle, I could hear the smashing of wood as the front door was broken down, and the shattering of windows, and the crash and roar of collapsing masonry. But I ignored it all and rushed across the roof, damn nearly breaking my neck when I slipped over on the snow, and got to the battlements, and clambered up, and shouted: 'Fuck the world!' at the top of my voice and then without a backward look threw myself headlong into the void. Geronimo!

Well, I fell and fell and fell. And the cliff was rushing by on my right-hand side, and the sky on my left, and everything was very blurred, and the wind was screaming in my ears, and my back was going boom, boom, boom, harder than it had ever done before. And there was this loud splitting sound that I couldn't account for.

Anyway, I fell and fell and fell. And fell and fell and fell. And fell and fell and fell. And fell and fell and fell and fell and fell. And then, after a while, I thought, 'This is strange, I should have hit the rocks by now. The castle's not that high up.' So I had a look around, and what do you know but I'm not falling at all. I'm just sort of bobbing gently up and down.

'Very damned strange,' I thought. 'Either I've died, or got caught in a freak thermal, or else—'

And I craned my neck around, and there they were! Right behind me. Wings! Huge, white, flapping, feathery wings, with bloodstains on them, presumably where they'd burst out of my back. (That explains the ripping sound.)

Well, to start with, I wasn't at all happy.

'You bastards!' I screamed. 'You total tossers! You've had all these fucking years to come out, and you have to do it now, just when I want to die. Leave me alone! Stop flapping. I want to die, I say. I have to die!'

The wings didn't do anything, however, just continued to beat, slowly, rhythmically, calmly, as though they weren't a part of me at all, keeping me exactly where I was in the middle of the sky. I reached my hands round and tried to grab them, but, as anyone who's got wings will know, that's not very easy, and apart from pulling out a couple of feathers – very damned painful – I didn't have much success.

So I shouted and screamed for a bit, and kicked my feet, and said all sorts of rude and unmentionable things. And the wings just flapped and flapped, ever so gently, keeping me right where I was, suspended in mid-air.

And after a while I had to admit, despite myself, that it felt rather good to be floating thus. Very good, in fact. One of the best thing I'd ever felt in my life.

So, anyway, I was still pissed off, but I thought, 'Well, now I'm here I might as well have a go,' so I sort of clenched my buttocks, and moved my shoulders around, and arched my back, and basically tried to control the flapping. And, much to my surprise, it worked!

I could use my wings! It wasn't easy, rather like someone who's been limbless from birth suddenly sprouting a pair of new legs, but after a bit of practice I gradually got the hang of it, and before long I was going up and down and round and round as though I'd been doing it for the whole of my life. It was much less tiring than walking. And much more invigorating. The only thing I had some problems with was gliding. Very difficult, gliding. Takes a lot of skill. And confidence too.

So, anyway, I flew around for a while, acclimatizing to my new situation, and then I suddenly remembered the castle, and the note, and I looked down and what do you think I saw? Rubble. A vast mound of smouldering rubble, with here and there amongst the chaos a fragment of white wall with indecipherable words upon it. I swooped a little lower – swooping really is an orgasmic sensation – and there on the western edge of the rubble, tiny against the mound of ruins in front of them, hand in hand in the snow, stood two children, a boy and a girl, both with beautiful blond hair, both laughing.

'So you're the ones who've been hammering on my door, are you?' I thought to myself. 'You're the tormentors!'

I was having such a good time in the air, however, and feeling so light-hearted, that I just couldn't feel angry at them for knocking my castle down, and so instead swooped a little lower and shouted to them, and when they looked up – the boy with glittering blue eyes, the girl burning green – I waved at them, and they waved back at me, and then we played for a while, me dive-bombing from above, they rushing to and fro through the snowy bracken, screaming in delight. And then I left them and flew out to sea a way, looping and rolling in the icy dawn air.

I think I shall stay alive for a little longer. I don't know how much longer, but the way I'm feeling at the moment, it could be centuries.

I'm also thinking that perhaps I could rewrite my note. I'm sad that it's all crumbled to ruins after so much hard work, but not overly so. It will be fun to do it again. To recreate myself once more.

Obviously, I can't do it in the castle, but there are plenty of other places. The snow-covered hills, I can't help noticing, look like a large, undulating sheet of paper.

I do feel bad about cancelling my suicide, but what can I do? I took The Pill and it didn't work. I jumped off a cliff and I grew wings. It obviously wasn't meant to happen. Not yet, at least. Maybe at a later date. I should still like to top myself, if only to prove that it can be done. For the moment, however, I think I shall err on the side of life.

It is the most glorious morning, a truly fitting start to the new millennium. The clouds have now all disappeared westwards, and on the other side of the sky dawn is blooming in pinks and greens and swirling trumpets of delicate blue. The air is cool and fresh, the sea as calm and still as a millpond. In a moment I think I might come down for a quick snooze, although how on earth I'm supposed to land is anybody's guess. First, however, I want to fly out and have a look at those islands. One of the more noticeable by-products of *not* killing yourself is a quite extraordinary surfeit of energy. Not to put too fine a point on it, I feel absolutely fucking fantastic.

# ACKNOWLEDGEMENTS

When Paul wrote the acknowledgements for his books he always took great care to thank everybody who had played a part in bringing them to fruition. As I was not involved in the editorial of this book until recently, it's impossible to know exactly whom to thank for what.

I do believe, however, that Paul has left some clues. In all of his books he would name characters and places after people that he knew. This was his way of acknowledging many of his friends and influences, and this first novel is no exception. I hope that those who have been acknowledged in this way will take pleasure in finding themselves in these pages.

For my part, I would like to thank Paul's agent, Laura Susijn, who first suggested the possibility of publishing this book, and his editor, Simon Taylor, for his advice, encouragement and insightful editorial notes. I am hugely grateful to have been able to edit the book with the help of those who knew and loved Paul and who shared the same determination to stay true to his unique spirit.

I'd also like to thank Paul's parents, Stanley and Sue, for their support and love.